Saving Us

Wendy Million

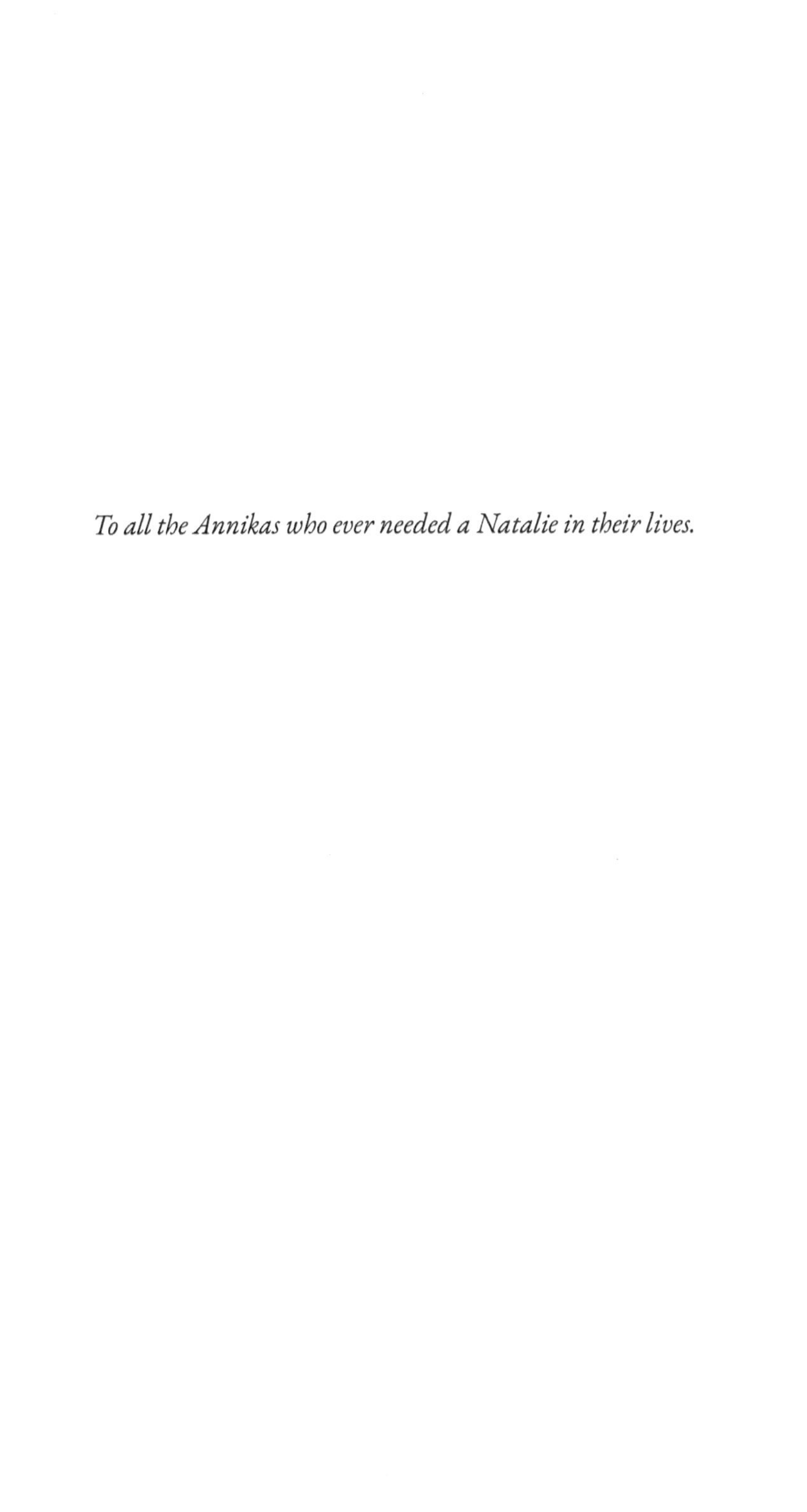

To all the Annikas who ever needed a Natalie in their lives.

Chapter One

♥

The football players' tangy sweat mingled with the crisp fall air at just the right balance. If our seats were any closer to the athletes' bench, the stench might have been overwhelming.

The teams ran around the field, but I couldn't absorb any of the action. Or maybe I didn't want to. Football was a foreign language.

"First down! Yes!" Annika screamed and clutched my arm, her brown face and flushed cheeks, joyous.

I jumped up and down with her, feigning enthusiasm. Her midnight hair bounced on her shoulders with the perfect amount of curl. Far more admirable than what was happening on the field.

"Isn't this great, Natalie?" She was glued to the action.

Annika's father was a high school football coach, and my theory was that, somehow, the sport had worked its way into her blood. If there was a game on television or if she could access it on the internet, she was watching it. An Exercise and Sports Science student, she intended to become a football coach herself.

Last year, our dorm room at Northern University was a haven for football fans, and now our off-campus house was headquarters for every fan within a five-mile radius. When I first met Annika, I tried for a few months to exhibit an appropriate level of enthusiasm (Go Northern University Ravens!), but I couldn't do it. There was something about grown men running full tilt into each other that didn't appeal to me. Some players enjoyed the violence more than the win.

Annika worshipped the quarterback of our college football team, so here we were at yet another game.

"Yeah, this is an amazing game!" Which one of them would look best without his padding? Not that their appearance mattered. The idea of hooking up with any player made me gagtastic. What would we discuss? I supposed that was the point—no talking. Still, the risk of an STD would be sky high and not worth the two minutes of moderate entertainment they'd provide. Most people didn't share my opinion. The guys on the team were popular with everyone at our college.

Annika glanced at me, her dark eyes sparkling, before turning back to the field. "Yeah, your enthusiasm is overwhelming."

"Hey, I came." I rubbed my pale hands together. The crisp September air wasn't good for my circulation. My toes were growing numb. Some nights were still relatively warm. Tonight was not one of them. "I also agreed to go to the after-party at the frat house, which I never do."

"Yeah, you and Clay breaking up was the best thing to ever happen to my social life." Annika puffed her warm breath into her palms.

At the mention of Clay, my heart sank. He was still calling me, even though we'd broken up at the start of the summer. We'd been together since freshman year, but when he started dropping hints about engagements and kids, I bolted.

"So, how long is this game? Is it three periods or something?" My dark red nails had a few chips. I should have painted them again today.

"Oh, my God." Annika huffed. "Seriously, Natalie, it's not that hard to figure out the basics. I get that you might not know what a two-point conversion is or what the kicker does." When I interjected, she held up her hand, partially covered by the sleeve of her sweater. "Yeah, that one *is* easy. A football game is four quarters. It's the coin version of a dollar bill."

She'd used that analogy before, and it never stuck. "So, which quarter are we in?" We had the intermission, didn't we?

"Fourth quarter. Soon enough, we'll be headed to the frat house to get drunk." Annika let out a loud whoop.

"If we're going, you've gotta find the nerve to speak to Johnny. You're not going to just gaze at him from afar, right?" One player running by drew my attention. "Who's that?" The words left my mouth without me realizing.

She grinned. "Potential? Am I hearing potential interest? In a football player?"

"No, idle curiosity. You've dragged me to enough games now that his face looks weird to me." Weird was the wrong word. *Familiar.* He reminded me of someone.

While I did not enjoy the sport in real life, I loved the TV show *Friday Night Lights. Clear eyes, full hearts, can't lose.* It was the one program Annika and I could agree on when we were hung over. The guy on the field resembled Vince or, as I later found out by looking him up on IMDb, Michael B. Jordan. My favorite character was Tim Riggins, but Vince was a close, close second. Fictional bad boys with a heart of gold? Sign me up.

"So, are you going to tell me or make me wait for the frat party?" The way he moved was stealing my focus. A shot of annoyance ran through me. Football players were not a dating option.

She laughed and nudged me with her shoulder. "I'm going to make you wait. I'm curious to see if you'll actually try at this party instead of being a stick in the mud."

"I always make an effort." I went to flick my long dark brown hair off my shoulders, but then I remembered I didn't have it anymore. Another breakup casualty. My long hair. Tucking my chin-length hair behind my ears didn't have the same sass.

The hotter than normal teammate was making me reconsider my stance on dressing up for the frat party. Developing a crush on a real-life player might make these nights a little easier to stomach. Only if I didn't like him *too* much. That was unlikely, so there was no harm in looking.

Once I had someone interesting on the field, the time passed much faster than it ever had before. Maybe this crush was a winner? Time with my best friend and man candy. Best of both worlds.

The buzzer and whistle sounded to signal the end of the game, and we piled out of the stadium with the rest of the crowd, heading to Annika's car. We could walk to the frat house from our place, and it would give us a chance to change out of our warm, comfy clothes into something with a bit less fabric.

***

"Promise me you're going to talk to him," I said.

The evening was brisk, but tolerable if we kept moving. The last vestiges of summer were turning into fall. I rubbed my arms to keep the goose bumps away.

"Yes!" Annoyance tinged her voice. "We have a bet. I won't lose it."

"For one week, I get your car for my classes and anything else, and you take public transit." I removed my flask from my purse and swigged.

Usually, frat parties didn't interest me. I didn't trust their alcohol and often refused to go. My freedom present to myself after I broke up with Clay was the flask I was carrying. Boyfriend gone, alcohol consumption up.

We heard the house before we saw it. The music reverberated along the street, and as we got closer, the vibrations went through my feet and invaded the rest of my body. A shiver pierced me, and I stared up at the dark, almost starless sky. Unease blanketed me, and I took another swig from my flask before dropping it into my purse.

"You're sure about this?" I eyed the line to get in and took money out of my wallet for the cover charge for charity.

When I turned my head, expecting an answer, she was enraptured by something. At the door was Johnny McDade. He was whispering something into his friend's ear. His sandy hair was damp from his shower, and his chiseled features were impressive even from a distance.

"Let's go." Annika took long strides toward the door.

We joined the line, and I took in every other girl dressed in skimpy, sparkly clothes. The guys were in jeans and T-shirts. Criminal that girls got so done up while guys plucked whatever they found off the floor, smelled it, and threw it on, wrinkles and all.

Not that I was any different tonight from the other women. When I pulled my best ensemble out of the back of the closet, a deep purple minidress, Annika gave me a look I knew well. While she might put on this outfit without a second thought, I was a jean and T-shirt girl.

At the top of the stairs, Johnny's shoulders lifted, and his gaze focused somewhere behind us. He waved to someone with a hint of impatience. "Seb!" he shouted. He made a reeling motion with his hand.

I turned around, annoyed someone so far back was getting the VIP treatment. This dress wasn't meant for cold weather.

The fabric was stitched for the crush of bodies in a hot, sweaty frat house.

It took a moment for me to see who he signaled, but it shouldn't have. He was tall, broad, and unmistakably the beautiful man I'd spotted on the field. Annika leaned into me and whispered in my ear, "Sebastian Swan. Running back. Junior. Not that you care about the football part."

While he walked past us, my gaze traveled along his fit frame. If he was running, I'd let him catch me.

Oh, God. Did I really just think that? Judging by the other girls whose heads whipped in his direction, competition for his attention was a certainty.

Chapter Two

♥

Annika nudged me, and I gave her a wry smile. "Thanks, but I think that's a lost cause. We'll see if I can put this dress to good use on someone else." I did a little shimmy.

She laughed and the sound, always contagious, drifted up the stairs to Johnny and Sebastian. Just before Johnny disappeared in the door, he hesitated and turned back, watching Annika with her head tipped back in a laugh. Her dark hair cascaded down her spine, and I knew how pretty she was normally, but when she laughed, few could compare. From where I stood, his gaze appeared calculated, assessing. He returned to the guy at the door to whisper something in his ear before heading into the house.

The frat brother left behind scanned the crowd, bewildered for a moment, and then he pinpointed us. "Ladies! Purple dress and immigrant girl. Come here." He motioned for us to move through the crowd.

My back stiffened. *Immigrant girl?* Annika seemed too focused on getting to the front of the line to notice. Later, after a few drinks, she'd likely replay his words. I could never let mean or racist comments slide.

When we got to him, I burst out, "Immigrant girl? What kind of racist bullshit is that? She grew up in this country. Her parents are American."

He rolled his eyes. "Whatever." He focused on Annika. "If I offended you, I'm sorry. Johnny singled you out, but he didn't know your name." He shrugged. "Meet him in the kitchen. Fundraiser charge is waved." He motioned for us to go in.

Had the immigrant comment come out of Johnny's mouth and been repeated by the douche on the door? Better not be the case. I'd be punching the quarterback in the face the first time I met him. My kickboxing classes might be beneficial after all.

"Isn't this amazing?" Annika's voice trembled. For her, meeting him was coming face-to-face with a celebrity. We'd talked about him a million times, and he was more myth than man.

As we pushed through the crowd, I grabbed her arm. "Annika?" She half-turned, moving through and around more people. "Be you, okay?"

She laughed, and heads tilted in our direction. "Who else would I be? Nat, seriously, sometimes you can be so dramatic." She took my hand and led us around people toward the kitchen.

We were both above average height, and in heels we were even taller. The path to the kitchen was clear over many of the shorter girls and some guys. One thing I liked about Clay was his height. I wasn't a tall girl who could date a short guy and not mind the height difference. The few times I'd tried it, I'd ended up feeling giant. Tall guys—the taller the better—were my kryptonite.

Finally, we were standing in the kitchen's doorway. Annika was in front of me, her hand clutching mine, and there was Johnny, leaning against the counter by the sink, a beer in his hand, chatting with his friends. His broad shoulders tapered into narrow hips, and even a blind person could map his features and find them attractive.

I wasn't blind.

He zeroed in on Annika and pushed off the counter, sauntering over. With his hand thrust out, he grinned. God, he even had dimples. *Swoon.*

"Johnny." He was so focused on Annika it was like I didn't exist.

"Annika." A blush rose to her cheeks.

"I've seen you around." Johnny sipped his beer. "You come watch our practices sometimes, right?"

The pink in her cheeks deepened. "I do," she admitted. "My dad coaches high school football, and I'm taking Exercise and Sports Science."

"Me too. What year?"

I removed my flask from my purse and took a swig. Great, I was a third wheel. Now what?

As though he could read my mind, Johnny broke eye contact with Annika to glance at me. "Johnny." His voice was flat with disinterest.

I shook his hand and smiled. "Natalie." Distanced politeness I could do. Annika wanted him, and I couldn't care less if he found me attractive.

"You know, we have alcohol here, Natalie." He gestured toward my flask. "It is a keg party."

"Yeah, but this is rum swizzle. Do you have that?"

A deep laugh sounded over my shoulder, and I turned to look.

"That's rum swizzle?" Sebastian came to stand at my shoulder. Where had he come from? I would have noticed if he'd been among Johnny's crew when we entered the kitchen.

"It is," I confirmed. "Has anyone ever told you—"

"Yes." He grinned. "I look like that guy from *Friday Night Lights.* I've taken pictures with fans, signed autographs, and once, I was chased by the paparazzi."

I laughed. "Really?" I took another drink from my flask.

"I swear on the team." He made a cross on his chest.

"Hey now, you just joined the team. You can't swear on us yet." Johnny slapped him on the shoulder.

Sebastian's laugh was deep and full. In answer, a smile spread across my face. He took my flask from my hand and tipped it back. He made a satisfied sound and grinned at me with even straight teeth. His hazel eyes glittered with amusement in his Black face. "Man, that reminds me of home."

"Home?" He couldn't mean what I thought he meant. I learned to mix that drink on my last family vacation.

"I grew up in Bermuda—origin of the best rum swizzle—until I decided I'd rather play football with my hands than my feet. Then we relocated from the ocean to dryer land." He took another swig from my flask before handing it back.

"And now you're here, playing college ball."

He nodded. "Gunning for the pros. Keep my head down and get it done."

Something foreign and welcome moved through my body at the curiosity lighting his gaze. He was bad news for me, for sure. My libido was getting the wrong memo.

"What about you?" He sipped his beer and grimaced. Shitty keg beer had nothing on my rum swizzle.

"I don't play football," I said, deliberately misunderstanding him.

He chuckled and the flame in my stomach grew. I wasn't seeing the guy from *Friday Night Lights* anymore, I was seeing him.

"What brought you here?" he asked.

To my right, Annika was deep in discussion with Johnny. A beer was in her hand, and she looked lit up from the inside.

"I came for Exercise and Sports Science like Annika, but I switched out. Apparently, I'm not a person who enjoys the science behind exercise."

His lips twitched in amusement, and he took another drink of his beer. "You were at the game tonight?"

"Under protest. I don't enjoy football—I should get that out of the way—my roommate loves it. I love her."

"Sebastian!" A voice bellowed from deeper in the house.

Our gazes connected. "One for the road?" He held out his hand for my flask, and I passed it to him.

He tipped it up enough to wet his lips. When he returned it to me, our fingers brushed, and heat crept into my cheeks. I cursed my fair coloring. I had been doing so well. When I glanced up, he was grinning.

"I think we should hang out sometime." He glanced over his shoulder as the voice hollered his name again.

I shook my head. "That's probably—I'm not sure—I think it's not—I just got out of a—" Did I want to hang out with him? A crush on a football player from afar was acceptable, but it was quite another to get *involved* with one.

He shrugged, and there was an emotion in his hazel depths that I couldn't decipher. Disappointment?

"Maybe I'll see you around, Nattie." He backed up and disappeared through the doorway. Once he was swallowed by the crowd, he yelled a response to the obnoxious voices floating down the stairs inside the house. A twinge of regret landed in the middle of my chest.

Hours later, when my flask was empty and we were leaving, Sebastian was seated on the couch, a brunette beauty perched in his lap. Johnny eventually extricated himself from Annika, but I'd caught him staring at her a few times throughout the night. As we reached the doorway to leave, he appeared.

"Phone?" He held out his hand.

Annika took her phone out of her purse and handed it to him. He passed her his, and they both typed away for a minute while I waited. When he glanced up at her to return it, the connection between them was clear. A small frisson of unease snaked along my spine. There was something about him I couldn't connect with, but I wasn't sure what.

We slipped out the door, and she clutched my arm. "That was the best night of my life, I swear."

Chapter Three

T he knock on my bedroom door the next afternoon brought on my groan. Rum swizzle hangovers, unlike the drink, were the worst. I was also hoping to sleep long enough to forget that I'd met Michael B. Jordan's doppelganger and told him I couldn't possibly hang out with him. I was such an idiot.

"What do you want?" I asked from under my pillow.

Sunlight was death. Maybe I should check myself for bite marks? If I'd become a vampire, at least I might be able to avoid Sebastian for eternity. Vampires are only sexy in fiction.

"Ah, Johnny and some of his friends are going to be here in an hour to watch the game with us," Annika called from behind the bedroom door.

I groaned again and rolled over. "Okay!" I stared at the ceiling. "You want me to stick around?"

"Uh..." Annika trailed off.

"You can come in." I bunched the surrounding covers, and she opened the door. Raising myself onto my elbows, I scooted over so she could sit at the foot of my bed. "What's wrong?"

Annika took a deep breath. "We need to clean the house, get snacks, get booze, get ready and"—she checked her watch, panic clear on her face—"we only have an hour." She collapsed back onto my bed.

I flopped back and enjoyed the moment of peace. Any second, she was going to erupt into a volcano of action. Annika had two speeds: do everything all the time or impersonate a sloth. There was no in-between.

"Okay!" She jumped up and clapped her hands. "You clean because you enjoy that more. I'll go out and get alcohol, snacks, and then get ready."

I nodded but made no motion to get up. "You know this isn't the Super Bowl game, right?" Or maybe it was? There was a lot of pre-planning for that game last year, so it was unlikely she was starting preparations this late.

She paused in the doorway, thrust out her hip, and attached her hand to it. "Nat."

Her warning tone and stance were familiar. "Right." I threw back the covers.

"It's just..." She clutched her hands together in prayer. "I've spent a year hoping he'd notice me, and he has. He wants to spend time with me and I..." She faltered, her dark eyes pleading.

I sighed. "Honestly, I get it." I shoved my feet into my slippers and stood up. "I'm sorry. I'm hung over, and I feel like an ass about Sebastian. Sorry."

She grinned. "He's coming today. I didn't want to say anything until I knew whether you were going to be weird about it."

"He'll bore me to death—that's what'll happen. There's no way we have anything even remotely in common." I shuffled around my room. My hand strayed to my hair. I'd kill for a ponytail. At this rate, I would never cut my hair again. What had I been thinking?

On the dresser, my phone buzzed, and my heart kicked at the name.

Heard you were at the frat party last night. Just texting to make sure you got home okay.

I flipped the screen facedown and followed Annika out of my room. Not in the mood for that bullshit this morning. When I'd called off our relationship, I'd told Clay I wanted to stay friends, but his version of that and mine were different. Sometimes his texts were possessive instead of friendly.

"Clay?" Annika eyed my empty hand. She teased me that my phone was a third appendage.

"Yep." I grabbed the cleaning supplies from under the sink. I surveyed the living room and kitchen. We weren't super clean, but we were tidy. Maybe I could get this done quickly? "We're doing a round clean, right?"

"Yeah, of course. Go around everything. Guys don't care if you move stuff and clean under it." She grabbed her keys, a shopping list, and disappeared out the door.

As I squirted cleaners and wiped down surfaces, I wondered if I'd get a chance to change my mind about Sebastian. Did I even want to make a different choice? He was so freaking hot, but it was clear from watching him last night that he had no trouble attracting female company. Why would he try with me again? One rejection was probably more than enough for his ego.

Annika was back before I realized, and we flew around the house in a blur of showers, blow-dryers, and subtly applied makeup. Scratch that—Annika's makeup wasn't subtle. The annoying part was that she needed little makeup. She went from pretty to stop in your tracks gorgeous with a few swishes from a mascara brush. Her typical jeans and jersey completed her outfit.

"Do you have another jersey?" I asked on impulse.

"What?" She flicked her loose waves over her shoulder and turned to me. "Did you just ask to borrow a football jersey?"

I shrugged. "We've never had actual football players in the house before, just a bunch of wannabes. Maybe I need a jersey?"

She raised her eyebrows, opened a drawer, and threw a jersey at me. "It's outdated, but you'll look retro. He was a good player once." She winked and then picked up the mascara brush for one last swish.

I tugged it on over my T-shirt and admired myself in the mirror beside her. A knock sounded at the door. Our eyes met in the mirror, and she didn't have to ask. I turned on my heel and headed to answer, not checking to see who was there first.

I swung the door open and immediately regretted not peeking.

"Clay," I said in a flat voice. "What are you doing here?"

He scanned me from head to toe and raised his eyebrows. "It worried me when you didn't text back. I wanted to make sure you were okay."

Voices drifted on the wind, coming up the street behind him, and I hoped it wasn't the football guys.

I threw my hands out and gave him a tight smile. "Nope, I'm totally fine."

"You're wearing a football jersey?" He cocked his head to the side.

"Yep." The loud voices were football players, for sure. This was going to get super weird in a minute.

The worst part of having him turn up unexpectedly was that he made my heart hurt. I thought we'd broken up on good terms, but here he was on my doorstep, wearing his good jeans and one of his best plaid shirts. Not an outfit to check up on someone.

"Was there something else you were wondering about?" Behind him, Johnny turned up the pathway to our townhouse flanked by five or six other guys. No Sebastian. My shoulders slumped.

"Are you okay?" Clay glanced over his shoulder. When he focused on me again, his eyes were wide. "Is that Johnny Mc-Dade?"

I shrugged. "Yes?"

They swarmed Clay from behind. Johnny checked him over and smiled, but the warmth didn't reach his eyes. "You here for the game?" Johnny asked. "Annika said there was sometimes a crowd."

Clay was starstruck, and I was about to answer for him when he said, "Yeah, I am. My name's Clay. It's so great to meet you. I'm a big fan." He thrust out his hand, and I cringed.

Great. Just great.

Chapter Four

♥

They moved past me into the house, and Johnny scooped Annika into a hug. I pictured her heart beating a million miles a minute. *Please let him be a good guy.* I turned away from the door to ease it closed, and then I felt resistance. Frowning, I re-opened it and peeked around the edge.

"Oh, hey, Nattie. I got left behind." Sebastian grinned, a case of beer in his arms. He took me in from head to toe, but unlike when Clay did it, this perusal sent my heart into overdrive. "Not a football fan, but you own an ancient jersey?" He made a *tsking* noise as he angled past me.

I jerked my thumb over my shoulder toward Annika. "Super fan over there has like one thousand jerseys. She gave me one she didn't care about anymore."

He chuckled, and the sound moved like a wave across my body. Having him around was something I could get used to. "Oh, I doubt she doesn't care anymore. That guy's going into the hall of fame this year. I bet *that* jersey is worth serious coin."

I examined my shirt with new appreciation. "So, what you're saying is that spilling salsa and nacho cheese dip on it would be a bad thing?"

Annika swung her arm around my shoulders. "It means, roomie, that I trust you to take good care of my things." She grinned at Sebastian. "You can put the beer in the fridge."

When he angled past us, Annika dragged my head to her ear. "Why is Clayton here sitting on our couch, mooning over Johnny? That's my job. My job is mooning over Johnny."

"He invited himself before I could make it clear and not super awkward that he *wasn't* invited."

"He's drinking our beer. You broke up with him months ago." She took a swig from her own bottle and released my head.

"And he's wearing his best outfit." His dark hair was visible over the back of the couch. "He said he came to check up on me because I didn't text him, but I'm not sure."

"Nat, he wanted to *marry* you. He wanted you to bear his babies. He's not hanging around because he wants to be your friend. You need to cut him off at the knees."

Johnny half-turned on the couch, and he caught Annika's attention. He patted the seat beside him. She gave me a triumphant smile and flounced over to sit next to him.

In the kitchen, Sebastian and one of the other guys were talking, leaning against the counter. When I bent over to get a beer from the fridge, Sebastian's gaze burned into me. The other guy was definitely checking out my ass too, and I didn't even know his name. Grabbing the beer, I closed the fridge with a bump from my hip. Taking the bottle opener off the counter, I popped the top and took a swig.

"I'm Natalie," I said, holding out my hand. "I'm the person attached to the ass you were just admiring." With a sassy grin, I raised my bottle to my lips.

Sebastian choked on his beer and started coughing. The other guy, who I'd nicknamed Steroids in my head, grinned.

"I'm Troy." He laughed and shook my hand. "A fine ass has to be admired. Not my fault." He held up his hands, a beer still clutched in one of them. He clapped Sebastian on the shoulder. "Nice jersey," he said to me before going to the living room.

His comment was probably meant to be a peace offering, but it only annoyed me more. "Troy's the kind of guy who grabs a girl's ass in a bar and then gets offended when the girl gets angry." Troy wasn't who I was upset with; it was Clay. His voice kept drifting into the kitchen, and I wished he wasn't here.

Sebastian eyed me. "I could be wrong, we only met last night, but you don't seem like yourself today."

I drained my beer and put the empty in the sink, leaning down for another. When I glanced over my shoulder, Sebastian's gaze was averted. He wasn't risking another peek with my mood.

"My ex-boyfriend is here." The bottle top popped, and I tossed it toward the garbage. It hit the rim and tipped in.

"Ah," he said. We drank in silence for a beat. "So, he broke up with you but still comes around to hang out with Annika and watch football?" He squinted as though this was the only logical explanation his brain could formulate.

I laughed, and the tension eased out of me. "No, sort of the opposite. I broke up with him, and he showed up today, dressed in his Sunday best. I'm not sure what's going on." I leaned my hip against the kitchen counter but faced Sebastian. If a man could be described as beautiful, this guy nailed it.

He put his bottle to his lips and grinned. "You want me to explain it to you?"

"I don't know. Are you going to do it with a football analogy?" I raised my eyebrows and took a sip of my beer.

He chuckled and shook his head. "He wants you back."

"I was hoping you'd go with the football analogy so I could pretend I didn't know what you were talking about." I pressed my lower back into the counter.

"What are you going to do about it?"

When I glanced at Sebastian, the urge to touch him was almost overwhelming. Letting Clay catch me making out with a football player in the kitchen would pound the final nail into our relationship coffin. A cruel thing to do, even if it was efficient.

"Annika thinks I should cut him loose." I rubbed my finger along the edge of the counter instead of reaching for him. We were close enough that the faint whiff of his cologne caressed my senses whenever he shifted his feet. A guy who understood the right amount of cologne to put on? Priceless.

We drank our beers in companionable silence before I asked, "If you were him, would you want to be cut loose?"

One side of Sebastian's mouth quirked up, and I was mesmerized. *Not good, Nat. Not good.* A crush was fine, but full on *I want to have your babies* was not cool. I'd have to join a line. Women probably lined up to be with him.

He glanced over, and the air between us electrified. "You mean if I was chasing a girl who wasn't interested? Would I want to be cut loose?"

"Yes," I whispered. Were we still talking about Clay and me?

He faced me with an intense gaze. "I enjoy the thrill of the chase. I'm not sure I could be easily deterred if I wanted someone."

He was a hair's breadth from me now. The tart bitterness of the beer he'd chosen from the fridge mingled in the air with his cologne. I glanced at him under my lashes, almost willing him to kiss me.

"Oh, ah, I was just—I'm just grabbing a beer." Clay stood at the side of the kitchen closest to the living room. I jumped back from Sebastian as though Clay dumped cold water on us. I could only imagine how Sebastian and I looked right now, standing so close, electricity sparking between us. Clay's interruption was both wonderful and awful. I didn't want to start something with Sebastian. The *worst* idea.

I pushed off the counter without a word and wandered into the living room. Avoiding Sebastian for the next little while was the best plan. Instead, I studied Annika and Johnny bonding over plays and strategy as the game progressed. She'd told me she'd dated football guys before, but Johnny was different. He was eligible for the draft at the end of this school year. Annika was sure someone would pick him up; he was *that* good.

"So, you and the football guy? That transferred junior superstar?" Clay sidled up beside me, his annoyance on full display.

"Me and Sebastian what?" I refused to look at him. Letting him believe what he already thought was an exit strategy. Most of the time, I was a horrible liar. In the year we'd been together, I'd never told more than the tiniest white lie and that had been about my weight, which had almost felt truthful. Who tells their boyfriend how much they weigh, anyway?

"Is he why you're wearing a football jersey and out of your room during one of Annika's football parties?" Apparently, he wouldn't assume. He wanted me to say it.

"There's nothing going on between me and Sebastian." But I couldn't help glancing in Sebastian's direction when I said it. "I just met him last night." There was a smattering of freckles across Clay's cheeks, and I focused on those instead of making eye contact. In a minute, I'd see his one crooked tooth when he spoke. I forced myself to meet his gaze. "There's nothing there." I hesitated. "You know there's nothing *here* anymore either, right?" I tried to keep my voice quiet and gentle.

Clay let out a strangled laugh. "Yeah, you've been pretty clear. I told you I was worried. If I'm not allowed to be worried, maybe we shouldn't be friends." His voice was tinged with bitterness.

His tone made pieces of me curl up in shame and then unfurl in rage. "If you don't want to be friends with me, that's your choice. But if I go to a frat party or out with Annika somewhere, it's not your job to make sure I get home safe."

He chugged the rest of his beer, his Adam's apple working as he tipped the last bit back. His eyes blazed when they met mine. "Noted." He headed into the kitchen with purpose.

Please tell me he didn't drive here. I didn't want his hungover, sorry ass coming tomorrow to get his keys and car.

"That looked smooth." Sebastian took Clay's spot beside me.

"Like glass." I nodded at the TV. "You don't seem to be watching the game as intensely as other people."

"Not my team." He angled his head at Annika and Johnny. "Speaking of intense."

"Every team is Annika's team, I think." I shrugged. "I have heard more times than I can count that there is always something to learn whenever I criticize her for watching yet another game."

A hint of a grin peeked out around the rim of his beer bottle. That was starting to be one of my favorite things about him—his concealed amusement. "Annika seems intense."

"Two speeds." I held up two fingers. "Everything always and nothing ever."

"I saw that," Annika called over the back of the couch. She laughed, and the sound floated around the room. "You're giving your Annika speech again."

"You couldn't have seen that," I said.

"Reflection in the TV. Today is an everything always day." She grinned at me in the reflection as the commercial played.

I rolled my eyes. "Whatever. It's true. You're the tortoise *and* the hare."

Sebastian chuckled at our easy banter, but then his smile faded. "You didn't drop the hammer hard enough on your ex. He's still staring us down."

"He didn't believe me when I said nothing was going on between us." I gave Sebastian a sideways glance.

The same amused look crossed his face. He shook his head once and took a drink. "Strange."

Our eyes connected for a beat too long. "I know, right? I just met you." I didn't sound convincing, even to myself.

The game ended and people milled around us, gathering up empties, putting away food, but we were still standing next to each other. Finally, Sebastian leaned over and said, "If you were still his girlfriend, he'd be right to be worried." He kissed my cheek and finished his beer as he sauntered into the kitchen.

My brain shouted *yes, yes, yes* and *oh shit, oh shit, oh shit* like dueling personalities, and my fingers skimmed the place on my cheek his lips had just been.

Everyone started to pile out of the house, but Clay hung around until the bitter end to deliver a parting shot. "Nothing going on, huh? Whatever, Natalie. I thought you'd at least be honest with me."

As he walked down the path, Annika put her arm around my waist and pulled me close. "Out with the old and in with the new."

Chapter Five

A few days later, Annika was packing for classes in the living room while I ate my breakfast. I hadn't run into Sebastian, and my heart rate was finally returning to normal. Clay had gotten the message and was staying away.

"I'm going to watch the football practice tonight. Did you want to come?" Annika shoved the last book in her bag.

With a raised eyebrow, I took another bite of my toast. "Is that a trick question?" I sipped my coffee.

She grinned. "Maybe? Come on. He's clearly interested."

"Can't be too interested. Unlike Mr. Quarterback, I haven't been exchanging frantic text messages with Sebastian."

Annika sighed and sat on the edge of the couch, her rush out the door forgotten. "I like him, Nat. Like, really like him. He doesn't talk down to me about football, and he hasn't said even once that it's dumb or impossible that I want to coach football someday."

"Good. You deserve a guy who believes in you." I threw the last bite of toast in my mouth. "You guys going to do anything other than text each other back and forth?"

"Friday night out to a club?" She gave me a hopeful look.

"You want me to go too?" I swallowed my sigh.

With my plate in the sink, I grabbed my mug off the table before sitting on the couch beside her. "Aren't you going to be late?" I glanced at the clock above the TV.

"Gah!" Annika jumped up. "Friday, please?" She slung her bag over her shoulder.

"You know I will." I took a long drink. "I'd never make you go alone. Should I call everyone from our dorm last year?"

"Yes—yes—do that!" Annika grabbed her keys and threw open the door.

As soon as Annika was gone, I picked up my phone and started texting people. I'd no sooner hit send on a text to Kristy, one of the girls who was also into football, when I got a reply.

I heard Annika has been hanging out with Johnny McDade.

The level of envy Kristy must be experiencing was probably out of control. She and Annika had spent hours talking about football and the shape of Johnny's ass in his uniform. After I confirmed, I waited for her reply. When it didn't come immediately, I decided to shower.

Once I was done with the bare-bones beauty routine I kept, I checked my phone and saw several excited responses about the night out. But it was Kristy's reply that kicked my heart into gear.

Tell Annika to be careful. I've heard a few rumors. Nothing for sure.

My fingers flew across my screen. She couldn't say that and have me leave it alone. When he'd come to the house for the game, he'd been cool with me but the right temperature with her. He'd been charming and interested in what she was talking about. Since the football party here, Annika had been glued to her phone, texting him constantly, and he always responded.

We'll talk Friday. Like I said, rumors. Maybe it's nothing.

If the rumor was serious, she'd tell me now, right? Maybe he sleeps around. Wouldn't surprise me with his looks and status on campus. Were he and Annika even a couple at this point? They spent a lot of time texting and talking, and they'd hung out a few more times. But had they labeled it?

Kristy planted the seed of uncertainty, and I had a hard time not cultivating it.

When I got back from class later that day, Annika was home texting Johnny while streaming game tape on her laptop.

"Whatcha doing?" I peered over her shoulder.

"Johnny sent me his footage and we're talking about their away game." Annika paused the video and typed to him in a chat window.

"So, what's going on between you two?" I asked. "I know you like him, but has he made a move on you, or does he just enjoy talking about football with hot girls?"

She stopped typing to him mid-stroke and turned to me. "We kissed the other night under the bleachers after his game."

"So, are you two..." I trailed off, not sure what I should say. "Exclusive?"

Annika rolled her eyes. "He's the quarterback of the college football team. A Division I school. I'm not even sure the word 'exclusive' is in his vocabulary."

"Are you okay with that?" Kristy's earlier text messages were at the forefront of my mind.

"For now, yeah. It's fun. He's fun. When it's not fun anymore, I guess I'll decide what to do then. Do I push for exclusive? Do I accept that he might never be a one-woman man?"

I shuddered. "You'd accept that?" My mind drifted to Sebastian. No matter how hot he was, no matter what kind of attraction I felt, I couldn't do that. One thing I'd always known about Clay, without ever having to question it or think about it, was that he was faithful.

Annika closed the chat window and lowered her laptop lid. "One hundred percent he'll be turning pro when he's done with college. The only way that doesn't happen is if he suffers some sort of catastrophic injury. How many professional athletes are faithful? Like one hundred percent faithful? I bet it's a painfully small number. Think about the girls throwing themselves at them here, then magnify that across a country. If it comes to it, I have to decide if he's worth it. If being with him is worth knowing I'm probably not the only one." Annika shrugged her shoulders. "Where do you think the term side-chick comes from? Male-dominated professional sports."

"You've considered this." It was sort of stunning.

"Yep." She drew out the word. "Far, far too much. My high school fantasy was marrying a pro football player."

When I started to interject at her mention of marriage when they'd only kissed, she laughed, and the sound bounced around the room, causing me to grin involuntarily.

"Don't worry. I'm not thinking about marrying Johnny after one kiss and knowing him for a week. What I'm saying is that this guy, this moment, it's not the first time these things have crossed my mind. It's been years of obsessing." She let out a sigh. "Years."

"I don't want you to get hurt." A beat stretched between us. Kristy's ominous text gnawed at my mind.

"He's intense," Annika agreed. "It's kinda one of the things I appreciate about him. He's me on an everything always day except he's that every day."

"Balance is good, right?" I flicked on the coffee maker.

"He's balanced."

I was on the cusp of offending her. "Cup of coffee?" I held up a mug and effectively shut down the conversation. She nodded but said nothing else. For a few minutes, I listened to the coffee percolate. "What time is practice?"

She checked the clock above the TV. "It'll be starting now. Are you coming?"

"Can I drop you off and take your car to the bookstore? I'll swing back and pick you up after?" I got out a couple of to-go cups.

"Sure." She walked down the hall to her room. "Just grabbing a sweater!"

We drove to the field, mostly in silence. Her rationalization replayed in my head. Being with a football player, professional or not, couldn't be worth such a massive moral compromise.

"How good is Sebastian?" I asked Annika before she got out of the car.

She glanced over her shoulder and slumped down in the seat instead of exiting the vehicle. "Don't overthink it," she said. "I'm not overthinking it with Johnny, I'm going with the flow for now. It can be fun. It doesn't have to be forever."

Sebastian's half smile when he was amused, his hazel eyes, the depth of his laugh, all surfaced in my mind. "It's so risky." A pit formed in my stomach.

She sighed. "Then I guess you deserve to know the risk. He's good. The reason he came to our college was to have a year playing with Johnny, and the second-string QB is also very good when Johnny leaves. Sebastian could go pro if he stays healthy. College ball is a long program, though, and a lot happens." Annika hiked her bag up on her shoulder and pushed the door wider. "Be back in an hour and a half?"

"Sooner, if I can."

At the bookstore, my focus was on everything but buying books. Annika's words kept floating around in my head. I couldn't get involved with Sebastian if there was a chance he was one of those guys. It didn't matter how hot he was or how charming he seemed.

I drove into the parking lot at the field just as practice ended. Getting out of the car, I leaned against the passenger door. I'd have to have to figure out a way to avoid Sebastian on Friday night if we were going out together. This attraction wouldn't gain traction in me.

As Annika made her way to the car, Johnny had his arm slung across her shoulders and she clutched his waist. Involuntarily, I scanned the mix of guys and groupies, looking for Sebastian. When I spotted him, my heart sank. There was a dark-skinned, dark-haired girl clinging on to him as he tried to walk. He was laughing, and the sound drifted in my direction. I turned away; it didn't matter.

When I focused on Annika again, she was watching Sebastian, annoyance clear in her features, but he didn't seem to notice either of us.

At the car, Johnny kissed Annika on the forehead and smoothed her hair behind her ears. The tenderness made me wonder if Annika would be different from the other girls. They did have a lot in common.

"Nat." Johnny acknowledged me before squeezing Annika one last time and disappearing into the locker rooms.

Annika slid into the passenger seat and sighed. I looked over, but I said nothing. She probably needed to sort out her stance on cheating sooner rather than later. It seemed like she was slipping deeper and deeper into something with him.

I knew where I stood, and it was nowhere near that relationship quicksand.

Chapter Six

♥

The doorbell rang, and I ran to get it. Annika was applying one last coat of foundation on her face. She'd had a minor breakout and was stressing about how stress had caused her face to combust. The smallest pimple I'd ever seen in my life, but she was convinced the redness stood out more on her brown skin than it would on my pale skin. I didn't know how to argue that, so I didn't bother. Instead, I got the door and regretted it.

Johnny, Sebastian, Troy, and what felt like a boatload of other football players were standing on the threshold. Many of them were armed with cases of beer.

"Nattie!" Sebastian exclaimed and enveloped me in a hug. Apparently, he wasn't carrying the beer today; he drank it before he came. His enthusiasm for me could only be alcohol inspired.

"Where's Annika?" Johnny zoned in on the one person who seemed to hold his interest. Should I be offended he couldn't even manage a hello?

"She's getting ready," I said over Sebastian's shoulder while he hugged me a little too long. His muscles fit against my body, but that didn't matter because my emotions were rock solid under control. As soon as my heart rate got the memo, I'd be golden. Why did he have to smell so *good*?

"You smell amazing," he whispered into my hair before drawing back.

"Soap." Not true. My scent had layers. Body wash, lotion, some sort of spray Annika had insisted on using, and then my normal perfume spritz into my crown. Something delicious that had just finished baking had nothing on me.

Not that it mattered if he thought I smelled nice. Nope. I had other fish to fry tonight. I was most definitely not going to be frying his fish.

Annika emerged out of the hall, and Johnny's gaze raked over her. My heart rate sped up, but not in a good way. That possessive glint was back. Annika flushed and let him drag her into a kiss in front of everyone.

Looked pretty official to me. The other guys continued talking as though Johnny devouring someone was normal. Maybe it was.

The location of our house straddled the best of both worlds. We could walk to campus if we wanted, and we were also close enough to the downtown core to walk there too. We joked we'd be party central. Neither of us could have predicted these party guests when we got this place.

The other girls showed up not long after the football guys cracked a beer. Pre-drinking commenced, and I did a surprisingly good job of avoiding Sebastian. The fact he was doing a remarkably good job of introducing himself to my girlfriends was also not lost on me.

So great for him and the girls fawning over him. I did not care who he talked to or what he did. That's right, not a care in the world about him.

Annika eyed me as she grabbed two beers out of the fridge in the kitchen. "Why are you hanging out in here? Sebastian's out there flirting with everyone else." She flipped off the tops of the bottles with the opener and held them between her fingers.

"Exactly." I took another drink of my beer.

"Oh, come on. You have to be in it to win it." She gave an exaggerated wink.

"I don't want to be in it. Our talk the other night put this crush in perspective. Maybe you can watch Johnny flirt with other girls and maybe you can think about him sleeping around, but that's not me. There's a reason I've avoided sporty would-be-famous guys."

"Any guy can cheat, Nat." She peeked around the corner of the kitchen. Johnny was chatting with a few other girls. "If it's fun, just let it be fun." She leaned against the counter, her focus divided between me and Johnny. The norm lately—only having half her attention.

"Are you actually happy?" I asked.

Annika shrugged. "Yeah, I am. We have so much in common, and he treats me with respect. Isn't that what your dad is always going on about? Find a guy who treats you right and hang on tight?" She laughed. A few people in the living room turned and grinned at the sound.

Kristy wandered over, a drink poised between her fingers. "What's so funny over here?" She sipped her drink.

Annika patted my shoulder and nodded toward Johnny. "I'm going back. Don't hang out here permanently, okay?"

I took a sip of my drink. "What's up, Kristy?" She slid into position beside me.

"They're dating, huh?" She watched Annika with a mix of envy and another emotion I couldn't place. Her dark hair cascaded off her shoulders.

"They are, I think," I said. "Annika seems to be trying to keep it low key. But I'm sure you understand how excited she is that he's interested."

"Mmm hmm." Kristy took another sip.

We both stood watching them for a minute before I decided to ask what had been on my mind since we made our night-out plan. "What was with those cryptic text messages?"

Her blue eyes darkened, and she shook her head. "I've just heard something about him. Bit of 'roid rage."

"What?" I asked in disbelief. "Like he has a temper because he uses steroids, or he hits girls?" My dad was a police officer in my hometown, and I'd heard heartbreaking stories at the dinner table for much of my childhood.

Kristy frowned, and her petite features clouded as she focused on me. "I don't know. I asked around when someone said Annika needed to be careful, but as soon as I started asking questions, people clammed up." Her crop top lifted and lowered with the tiniest shrug. "He'll be drafted at the end of this year. First round, probably. No one wants to say anything that'll get him in trouble if there isn't any proof."

I looked at Johnny with fresh eyes. "How certain are you that this has happened before?"

Her dark hair swirled around her shoulders when she followed my gaze to Johnny. "Not at all certain. It was one comment by one girl in my class because she realized I was friends with Annika. Maybe she's jealous? When I pressed her, she wouldn't tell me anything else. Everyone always just says he's 'intense.'"

Intense. I wasn't about to disagree with that assessment. His laser focus on Annika was either flattering or disturbing. I hadn't decided which yet.

"Has Annika—I mean—have they been alone together?" Kristy's eyes were glued to the couple in question, her lips pursed over her straw.

"Not much, I don't think. I'll talk to her." Would she hear this bit of gossip? More than once she'd gushed about how well he treated her. There was no proof that he'd ever do otherwise. One unsupported rumor.

"You ladies ready to go?" Sebastian entered the kitchen, an empty bottle in his hand. "You avoiding me, Nat?" He slipped past me and planted himself on my other side. Across my body, he thrust out his hand to Kristy. "I'm not sure we've met. I'm Sebastian."

Kristy giggled and took his hand in a limp shake. I liked her, but sometimes she was so lame. He was just a boy. A good-looking one. By all accounts talented on the field. But just a guy.

"I'm Kristy," she said. "I lived with Annika and Natalie last year."

He grinned and placed his beer to his lips. "I can't believe the college put all the hot girls on one floor."

She giggled again. Ugh. Part of me wanted her to drift off somewhere else. Unkind? Sure. The giggle-flirt was my least favorite to watch. Annika, always with eyes in the back of her head, called to Kristy.

"Come meet Johnny." Annika waved Kristy over.

As soon as she was gone, Sebastian bumped my shoulder and leaned in, so his breath stirred my hair. "So, are you avoiding me, Nattie?"

The scent of beer mixed with the faint whiff of his cologne. A combination I never realized I loved. I turned my head toward him, and our faces were inches apart. A slight shift on either of our parts would connect our lips. My breath hitched.

"Why would I avoid you?" My voice was barely more than a whisper.

"I saw you picking up Annika the other night. You didn't even say hi." His shifted closer to me.

"You looked busy."

He grinned; the straight whiteness of his teeth surprising when it shouldn't be. When I flicked my gaze to his, the deep hazel of his eyes and the thick lashes that framed them caught my attention. Pretty, almost. The man was built to seduce women.

"I'm never too busy for you." He slid his hand along the counter behind my back and leaned closer.

"Yo, Seb!" Troy called.

After a beat, he tore his gaze from mine and jerked his chin in Troy's direction. A silent answer.

"We're heading out, bro. Are you and Nat staying here or coming with us?"

Sebastian turned to me with an amused expression and took a sip of his beer, leaving me to answer.

"We're coming." I laughed. "We're definitely *not* staying here."

With a chuckle, he looped his arm around my waist and leaned in to whisper in my ear, "Someday, you'll be begging me to stay in with you instead of going out." He didn't wait for my response. Instead, he dragged his hand across my midriff, and he walked over to his friends.

I chugged the rest of my beer, grabbed my keys, and followed him. Resisting him was becoming more and more impossible.

Chapter Seven

♥

The club was packed, and it didn't take long for people to disperse. A few were at the bar, some were on the dance floor, and a group of us had to use the bathroom.

Standing in line for a stall, I half listened to the surrounding chatter until Sebastian's name pierced my consciousness. "Sebastian Swan?" I asked, unable to help myself.

Julia, one of my least favorite people from our dorm, laughed. "Yeah. Have you hooked up with him too? By the time he hits senior year, he'll only have freshmen left. He's such a flirt, but when he follows through?" She fanned herself. "Amazing."

My stomach clenched, and I fought to keep the smile on my face. Any questions I had about whether I could see myself with Sebastian were answered. There was no way—no way. If Julia was his type, I was not.

"No," I said. "I have no intention of hooking up with him."

"Well." She fluffed her hair. "You're missing out."

Sebastian with Julia was enough to make my stomach curdle like sour milk. We'd known each other for a couple weeks. He flirted with me. I had no claim on him. In fact, I turned him down. Being upset about him having sex with Julia was the height of ridiculousness.

I glanced in the mirror across from us and hollow brown eyes stared back at me. I mentally shook myself. There were lots of guys at the college, and I didn't even *enjoy* football. Much better if I didn't want Sebastian either.

When I exited the bathroom, Johnny had Annika pressed against one of the walls, kissing her neck and speaking against her ear. I hovered for a minute, indecisive. Kristy said he had a temper. Was it true? Annika seemed happy.

"Annika, I'm going to the bar. Do you want a drink?"

Johnny raised his head out of her neck and glanced at me moodily before whispering in Annika's ear. She stared at him for a beat, and then shifted toward me. A lamp of happiness lived in her, and he'd turned the setting to full blast. She glowed. "I have a drink." She lifted her far hand that I couldn't see around Johnny's back. A plastic cup dangled from her fingers.

"You're okay?" Something about his dismissive attitude made me hesitate. Would it kill him to acknowledge I exist?

Annika grinned and moved so his head came out of her neck. He stared at her as if he could consume her and another frisson of uncertainty sparked in me. Was it normal for a guy to look at a girl like that?

"I'm good," Annika said.

"Just good?" Johnny murmured.

"Excellent, then." Annika's carefree laugh floated in the air, circling them.

"I'll be back," I said.

"No rush." Johnny tore his gaze from Annika to pierce me with his intensity.

Annika hit him in the chest playfully. "Be nice. She's one of my best friends." She turned to me. "He's teasing." Rising, she kissed him on the cheek.

I smiled, but it was tight on my face. "I'll see you in a little while." I headed for the bar.

The club was a huge warehouse that probably seemed less impressive in the daytime. With the flashing lights, dim lighting, and high ceilings, the place was a whole mood.

At the sweeping bar on the far side of the building, I sidled up to Troy. I leaned on the smooth surface, holding out my money, and tried to catch any bartender's attention.

A hand brushed against my ass, and I swiveled to pinpoint the culprit. "Did you grab my ass?" I asked Troy. My instincts about him had been right.

He held up both hands. "Nope. Not me. I'm a looker. I also know better after the attitude you gave me the other night."

I glanced in the other direction and was met with another football player I vaguely recognized. "So, you're the one who grabbed my ass?"

He grinned, expecting me to go along with it. "I needed to see if your ass was fresh enough for me."

I rolled my eyes. "If my ass was fresh enough? You know what—" Anger spiked in me, but I was thrown off my rant when a hand appeared on my elbow.

"Nattie, I've been looking all over for you." Sebastian led me away from the bar and from his teammate. "Jeff—hands off—all right?" Sebastian called over his shoulder.

Over my shoulder, Jeff presented his raised palms. "I didn't realize she was yours, man."

Literal smoke had to be pouring out of my ears. "*Yours?* I'm some kind of plaything? Please. I'm not anyone's possession, and I certainly don't need *you* standing up for me." I yanked my elbow away from him. The thumping music gave me a good excuse to yell. "I could have handled him."

Sebastian stood in the middle of the bar area and tipped his beer to his lips. People were milling around us, but he said nothing.

"You're just going to stand there, drinking your beer and watching me?"

Amusement poured out of him, and he half smiled against his bottle as he took another drink. "I'm going to wait this out."

I huffed. "That's insulting, you understand that, right?"

He shrugged but remained silent. I tried to step around him, but he stepped with me.

I threw up my hands. "I need a drink."

He passed me his beer, and I chugged the rest of it.

"Will you stay here, and I'll get us more?" He eyed me.

"I'm not going over to ream Jeff out if that's what you're asking. He's not worth my time." I searched the crowd for Annika. "Have you seen Annika?"

"Annika and Johnny are glued together. I'm sure she's fine." He stepped toward the bar. "Wait here."

He was back quicker than I expected and handed me a drink.

"Thanks." I accepted the beer.

"Jeff bought them as an apology for groping my girl." When I turned to give him another earful, he laughed.

"You're trying to wind me up." I sighed.

"Why does it bother you so much?"

"Which part?" Whenever I let myself focus on him, my heart rate jumped into overdrive. Men like him shouldn't be allowed to exist. They were a danger to a woman's sanity.

"The ass grab."

"One of your signature moves?" I examined his dark hands as though they might be coated with the asses they'd touched.

He laughed. "Nope, not my thing."

I contemplated how much I wanted to tell him. "My dad's a cop. He worked in sex crimes for a while. I heard a lot growing up, and he spent time talking to me and my friends about consent. For me, the ass grab is an indication of a person's character.

If a guy in a bar thinks it's okay to grab my ass, what else will he think it's okay to do without my consent?"

He studied me, and there wasn't a trace of his usual amusement. It was the first time I was sure he was seeing me. "I never thought about it like that."

I shrugged. "Why would you? You're a guy. You probably don't have random girls grabbing your ass."

He laughed. The humor had returned. "Oh, you might be surprised about that."

I raised my eyebrows. "Really? There are a lot of girls that randomly grab your ass?"

"It's not usually my ass they reach for." He chuckled. Then he took another drink of his beer before continuing, "You have a point, though. Weird to admit this, but if I don't know the girl, it does feel...invasive? Presumptuous? I don't know. Definitely not one hundred percent comfortable."

"But you still go home with them, don't you?" I gave him a wry smile and tried not to show my disappointment.

He suppressed a grin. "I need another drink." He held up his empty bottle. "You?"

I nodded, and he disappeared again for a fraction of a second.

"How do you get them so fast?" My solo trip to the bar hadn't produced even one drink.

"Troy's girlfriend is bartending. She's very attentive."

We drank in silence for a minute before I leaned toward him and said, "What's your major, anyway? I don't think we've had a single normal conversation."

We were close together now, and when he turned to look at me, I could smell his cologne again. *Bad idea, Natalie, bad idea.*

"Do you want the pick-up line or the truth?" The cocky half grin I was beginning to enjoy a little too much bloomed on his face.

"Pick-up line, followed by the truth."

"I'm studying to be a gynecologist. Want me to take a look?" He waggled his eyebrows.

My answering laugh burst out. "Oh, my God. Does that actually work?" I was glad I hadn't taken a drink before he dropped that one in my lap or I'd have spewed beer everywhere.

"More often than you'd think."

"Truth?"

"Business degree. Not nearly as exciting." He tilted his beer at me. "You?"

"Political science with a minor in business. Then, law school."

"Following in Daddy's lawman footsteps?" He leaned closer when he spoke, so he didn't have to yell.

"He's an influence on me for sure." Sebastian's allure was sucking me in again. "Righting the world's wrongs." I smiled at him. His tall, bulky stature made me feel smaller than normal and protected. The thought annoyed me. I was neither tiny, nor did I need protection.

"Do you want to get out of here?" He held his empty bottle in his fist.

I didn't answer right away, nursing my beer. Did I? Yes. Leaving with him would make me about a thousand things I didn't want to be. "Where did you want to go?" Curiosity got the best of me.

"Anywhere—as long as I don't have to keep shouting at you or hunching my back to talk in your ear." He took my empty beer bottle to the bar before returning. "Yes?"

"I have to check in with Annika first. Roommate rules." There was also the niggling doubt Kristy had planted. Was Johnny a danger to Annika?

He held out his hand and left it midair for me to grasp. I scanned his face, my heart beating a heavy staccato. With a small nod, I took it and followed behind him through the crowd as we searched for Annika and Johnny.

When we got to the dance floor, shouting could be heard over the loud music. I dragged Sebastian toward the commotion as people started to back up, forming a circle. There, in the middle, was Johnny, red with rage. Annika was behind him, her worried eyes visible at his shoulder, while he spewed a torrent of verbal attacks on a guy and his friends. The guy's hands were held up, a bewildered expression on his face. The other football players circled Johnny in solidarity. Sebastian tensed beside me, but made no motion to dive in.

"Johnny won't fight," he muttered close to my ear.

"Are you sure?" I called over the increasing noise. "He looks angry."

"None of us on the starting line can risk an injury. His hands are money. Coach would literally kill us."

"You understand what literally means, right?"

Sebastian looked grim. "Oh, I know. He'd rather see one of us dead than lose a game."

I frowned, but then he drew me closer to where the other football players were standing, and he released me to wade into the fray. Sebastian's voice boomed out Johnny's name, and he did what no teammate had done. He approached Johnny and gripped his shoulder. At first, Johnny shrugged him off and glared at him. Then, Sebastian leaned in and spoke in Johnny's ear, and while the tension didn't leave him, whatever was said seemed to calm him.

Was he reminding him about the coach? They exchanged a few terse words before Johnny snaked out a hand and grasped Annika's wrist, tugging her through the crowd to the door. It didn't take long for me to lose sight of them.

Weaving around the spectators, Sebastian found me. "I don't understand that whole possessive, jealous thing. It's not my bag."

"That's what it was about?"

"Apparently. Guy was hitting on Annika. They're going to your house to watch football. Annika's suggestion. Calm Johnny the hell down."

"Should we go too?" I tucked my hair behind my ears, wishing I could gather it into a ponytail.

He raised his eyebrows and frowned. "You want to go back to your house and talk about football?" He placed the back of his hand on my forehead. "Doesn't feel like a fever..."

I swatted him away and laughed. "No, that—seemed intense, didn't it?"

He searched my face. "We can go there if you want. I just want to get to know you."

"I hear you enjoy getting acquainted with lots of girls."

He chuckled. "I'm the new guy. I gotta make friends. Are you throwing shade at me for associating with my fellow college students?"

"Associating? You mean in the carnal sense? You've been all over campus making yourself welcome."

He grinned, but this time it didn't quite meet his eyes. "I have standards."

"Must be low if you slept with *Julia*." The words tumbled out of my mouth before I could consider how they'd sound. Jealous. I sounded jealous. God, I was such an idiot.

His gaze zeroed in on me. "You been asking around about me?"

I shook my head and avoided eye contact. "No. Bathroom gossip. Girls were in there talking about you."

He held out his hand toward me. "Let's go talk football." He waited for me to meet him halfway.

"Anything is better than this conversation?" I teased.

His customary half grin appeared and he gave me a side-eye. "Pretty much." With our linked hands, he gathered me to his side.

Chapter Eight

♥

We walked in silence back to my house. What was he thinking about? I couldn't stop wondering whether encouraging the curiosity we seemed to have about each other was a good idea. He didn't once let go of my hand on the walk and every once in a while, when I looked over at him, he was looking at me, too.

At my townhouse, Sebastian knocked before we unlocked it. "Just in case."

Smart. I probably would have burst in and ended up yelling, "My eyes" as they tried to cover up.

When we opened the door and stepped into the open living room, Johnny and Annika were sitting on the couch, watching one of the football games Annika had on the DVR from that week. I stood there stunned by the scene. Them actually watching football hadn't occurred to me. I expected them to be arguing or making out. Could the intensity I saw on the dance floor be lessened by taped games?

"Seb." Johnny glanced over the back of the couch. The change in him was incredible—so calm and collected now.

"You're re-watching the Bucs game?" Excitement tinged Sebastian's voice.

"Yeah, man. It was a good game. Tom Brady is a god." Johnny raised his beer in a toast.

"You want a beer?" Sebastian headed to the kitchen.

"Sure." I hovered behind the sectional couch before sitting down as far away from Annika and Johnny as I could get. There was still something about what happened at the bar eating at my gut. He'd been so full of rage over such a small thing.

When Sebastian came back, he passed me the beer and then sat so close to me our thighs brushed. When I cocked an eyebrow at him, he grinned. If I shifted away, I'd fall off the couch. I shoved him a little with my shoulder, and when I looked up, Annika was examining us with a smile on her face.

"Looks cozy," she said.

Johnny's hand rested on Annika's leg, and they were touching from the waist down.

"Right back at ya." I avoided Sebastian's smug gaze.

Names, positions, plays, strategy, and scoring flew around my head while they viewed the game. None of it registered. Everything in me was fine-tuned to Sebastian's leg brushing against mine each time he moved. Or the way his hand would rest on my leg, as though it was the most natural thing in the world to touch me. Was it possible to overheat from suppressed lust while dying of boredom from a football game? When I couldn't take my skyrocketing libido anymore, I stood and went to the kitchen for more drinks.

I pressed my hands into the counter, lost in the stupidity of developing a crush on a womanizing football player. He was the opposite of anyone I would have ever wanted. Footsteps sounded from the living room, and I opened the fridge.

Sebastian slid behind me, and my entire body vibrated on a frequency meant just for him. Unfair. Completely and utterly unfair to want someone so wrong for me. I stifled a groan.

"No beer left?"

Several bottles of beer were right in front of me, and he'd be able to see them from where he was standing. I grabbed the pineapple and orange juice from the fridge and gathered the ingredients for a rum swizzle as though that had been my intent all along.

"You have enough for everyone?" Sebastian tipped his head in Annika and Johnny's direction.

I nodded, still not trusting myself to speak just yet.

"You guys want a swizzle?" Sebastian raised his voice over the noise of the game.

"Is that the girly drink you like?" Johnny called back, at ease with Sebastian in a way he wasn't with me. Maybe Johnny just didn't like me.

Sebastian laughed. "It's de drink of de rock!" Sebastian adopted the Bermudian accent I'd heard so much while on vacation.

"Mmm...beer!" Johnny responded. "Make sure you get something a man would pick." Annika's voice wasn't quite audible, but her admonishing tone was clear. "Okay, fine. The drink of real football fans!"

Sebastian chuckled and shook his head. I passed him the first rum swizzle while I mixed my own.

"Mmm...it's liquid Bermy. How'd you learn to mix this?"

I half smiled while I shook the next one in the canister. "Truth?"

"Always." He took another long gulp.

"The bartender at the Hamilton Princess had a thing for me, and I had a thing for learning how to mix this drink. I spent time with him after hours."

Sebastian raised his eyebrows. "Is that code for something else?"

"Yes." I grinned. "And I still learned how to make a mean cocktail." I poured the now frothy concoction into another glass.

He gave me an appraising look across the rim. "So, not a fan of *me* sleeping around, but you don't have a problem with casual sex." He sniffed and scanned the kitchen. "What's that I smell? Oh, yes! It would be a double standard."

"'Cause that's never existed in the history of *man*. You're just not used to being on the other side of it." I lifted my chin in challenge, my own glass poised between my fingers.

He laughed, and an amused smile elevated the edges of his mouth. "You may be right."

"So, can you turn your accent off and on?"

"At this point, yeah, I can. It's a carefully acquired skill." His smile faded. "If football doesn't work out, I need the lingo for a career in business on de rock. But, if I go pro, I want people to be able to understand me."

"I understood everyone when I was on the island."

"All the time?"

I considered the question, my mind drawn back to my vacation. "Okay, maybe not *all* the time."

"Imagine being interviewed and being asked to repeat yourself over and over. I've been there. No one wants that."

From the living room, Johnny and Annika's excited voices drifted into the kitchen.

"You came here to play with Johnny?" I put the ingredients together for another swizzle.

"I did." He drained the last of his and set his glass on the counter with a soft thud.

"What's he like?"

"Johnny?" His expression turned to one of surprise. He examined me for a minute, trying to assess why I'd asked. "You're wondering about Annika?"

I shrugged and shook the mixture in the container. "She's my friend. I just want to know if I should be worried."

He crossed his arms and focused on the fridge. "I'm not sure how to answer that." He frowned. "He's my ace boy. He's a good guy." He gave me a wry smile. "Sometimes women define *good* differently."

"You mean he sleeps with a lot of women or he's mean to them? One's kind of gross, but the other...?"

He turned so one hand was leaning on the counter, his shoulder almost brushing mine as he took his next drink. He looked into my eyes. "Yeah, he sleeps with a lot of women. But in the last week or two, it's been less. Does that help?"

I wasn't sure if he was avoiding the comment about Johnny being mean to girls or he assumed I was concerned with Johnny's sex life. My heart beat so loudly I feared he'd hear it as I tried to read him. When he came closer and ducked his head as though he might kiss me, I turned to mix another swizzle.

"I'm going to win you over." Sebastian shifted and leaned back against the counter.

I grinned while shaking the container. "Unlikely."

"Give me one good reason why you can't be with me."

"You only want one?"

"I already know you're fine with casual sex." He took a big gulp.

"When I'm on vacation and it's not my real life, sure. This"—I gestured around the house—"is my everyday life." I sighed in frustration, but I wasn't sure if I was upset with myself or him. The thought of sleeping with him sent heat rushing to places I didn't want to get heated. "I don't even like football. You can find lots of girls who enjoy football and don't mind casual sex. From what I've heard, you already have. You don't need to get me just to prove you can."

Sebastian drank in silence while I poured mine into a cup. I'd mixed it too much, and the ice was melted. Part of me wanted to grab Sebastian's shirt and drag him to my room, but the other part of me, the more rational part, wanted to go to my bedroom alone, lock the door, and never come out. How could I get off this slippery slope with him?

"I'll be your wing-woman." The words tumbled out. Oh, God. Where did that suggestion come from? *Insane.* His proximity had turned my brain to mush. *Wing-woman?*

He gave me a half-appraising, amused look. "I'm not sure that'll work."

"Sebastian!" Johnny said from the living room. "We have practice at stupid o'clock in the morning. We gotta get out of here or we'll be dragging our asses."

Sebastian fished out his phone and checked the time. He grimaced. "There in a sec." He opened his contacts, typed something into it, and passed it to me.

Nattie—Wing-woman. There was an emoji of a girl with short, dark hair in a cape. I glanced up at him, and my heart pitter-pattered in my chest. The sincerity mixed with humor I always found in his eyes would undo me. I wasn't there yet, and if I was smart, maybe I could sidestep whatever this was.

"If you're my wing-woman, I'm going to need a number. I may have to send out the bat signal when I can't get a girl to sleep with me."

I laughed in spite of myself and typed in my number, shaking my head. I passed it to him, grinning.

Before I realized what he was doing, he leaned forward and kissed my temple.

"You know what my coaches say is my best quality?" His hand lingered on my waist.

Reluctantly, I lifted my gaze from his broad chest to look into his eyes one last time. "No idea."

"Perseverance. I'm going to persevere the hell out of you, Nattie." He took a step back from me and wiggled his cell. "I have your number now."

"My superpower is blocking your calls." I stifled a laugh.

"You wouldn't dare. I'd have to send out a real bat signal then. Nobody wants that." Sebastian chuckled and headed for the door, slapping Johnny on the shoulder as they both slipped into the night.

I followed behind him to stand with Annika. At the exact same time, we both sighed.

She turned to examine me. "You're in deep."

"Don't I know it." Sebastian's wide back disappeared around the corner. "You seem happy."

She nodded. "I am. He's perfect for me. I can't believe how lucky I am." A wistful smile was on her face. I stared into the dark night and wondered how many other girls he'd be perfect for this week.

Chapter Nine

A few days later, I was glued to my phone as one more text message rolled in from Sebastian. Another random photo of a pretty girl in a superhero costume. A burst of laughter escaped me.

If you're going to resist me, you're going to need a hot superhero outfit. As my wing-woman, costumes are essential.

"Sebastian?" Annika asked from behind her laptop.

I wiped the grin off my face and nodded. "Yeah. Another stupid picture." My tone was carefree, like I didn't find the whole thing amusing.

Annika typed more and then rubbed her wrist again.

"Is your wrist sore?" I'd noticed her babying it a few times over the last couple of days, but I hadn't remembered to ask until just now.

She frowned. "It's a bit sore." She shrugged as though it was no big deal.

I rose from my part of the sectional and went to sit beside her. I took her arm and examined her wrist. Yellow and blue bloomed on her brown skin. A fading bruise. "How'd that happen? Was it while you were coaching? Those little kids too rough on you?"

"Um." She flicked her dark hair over her shoulder. "We left the bar because Johnny almost got in a fight with a guy who started grinding on me on the dance floor."

My frown deepened. "Okay." I took a beat to try to connect the dots. "What's that have to do with your wrist being bruised?"

"Sebastian talked Johnny into walking away from the fight," Annika said, as though that explained the mark.

"And..." I cocked my head.

"I'm sure he didn't mean to, but he grabbed my wrist a little hard when we walked out of the club. He let me go as soon as I said he was hurting me, and he apologized a lot."

I collapsed onto the couch beside her, and my brain ticked away in silence. She said I overreacted about things because of my dad's job, so I took an extra beat. The whole episode with Johnny had gotten lost in a flurry of text messages between me and Sebastian this week. Now, remembering his face, his rage had been frightening. "That's a pretty substantial bruise for him just leading you out of the club."

"You're reading into this and there's nothing to see. I knew you'd do this, which is why I didn't tell you." Annika snapped her laptop shut and faced me. "It was an accident. The guy was being rude to me, and then he was *really* terrible to Johnny once he realized who he was. Johnny was so wound up. He didn't mean to hurt me. He'd never hurt me."

I was quiet for a moment, weighing the best way forward. I had to say something. "Kristy has heard rumors about his temper."

"Kristy is a gossip. She'd believe there were leprechauns at the bottom of every rainbow if someone whispered it to her in a conspiratorial voice."

"So, you haven't seen his temper?" His face, contorted in rage, was burned into my brain.

Annika sighed, and her shoulders slumped. "The thing at the bar was nothing. He got carried away, heat of the moment, and he apologized. If something happens a second time, I'll break it off." She stared at her wrist. "Can you get me ice?"

"You'd tell me, right? If something else happened?"

"It's not going to happen again," Annika said as I rose to grab the ice.

My phone pinged while I was retrieving the ice from the freezer.

Accidents happened. He was a strong guy, and maybe he didn't realize his strength. Even as I tried to talk myself around, I wasn't convinced. I wanted to go in there and tell Annika to break it off, that no one was worth that risk.

Instead, I took the ice pack to her but said nothing more about Johnny. My phone lit up with another text from Sebastian. The giddy feeling I'd had a few minutes ago was gone.

What was I doing? I wasn't going to become one of his conquests, and he wasn't boyfriend material.

Switching it off, I grabbed my textbook from the kitchen table and headed for my room at the end of the hall. I left the door open in case Annika wanted to talk. With my laptop on the bed, I started making course notes while I went through the week's readings. Sebastian and Johnny were pushed out of my mind as I got lost in political science jargon.

There was a soft knock on my doorframe.

Annika smiled, back to her bubbling and confident self. "I'm going to practice. Do you want to come?" She twirled her necklace.

"No, I have a lot of reading this week. Have fun." I flipped a page in my textbook. "Take lots of careful notes about the shape of his ass." An afterthought, a peace offering.

"Johnny said a few of them might go to a pub for drinks after. Did you want to come?" Annika cocked her head.

"Are you going?" Given Johnny's rage, unsupervised drinking time with him might be a bad idea, at least until I was sure the other night was a fluke. Sebastian would likely be there, so I had to weight his presence too.

"Yeah, it's just a couple drinks. They have practice again tomorrow morning..." Annika trailed off, but she wasn't giving me the usual pleading look. She was comfortable enough around Johnny and the other football players, and she didn't need me to go anymore.

"Text me where you are, and I'll show up."

She nodded and disappeared down the hall. The front door closed, and I stared off into the distance for a minute, unsure whether the unease in my stomach was about Johnny or Sebastian or both.

A couple hours later, I turned my phone back on and saw I'd missed five text messages from Sebastian, full of outrageous outfits, superhero memes, and fifteen minutes ago, a video of the bat signal.

Ridiculous. I wasn't sure if I was referring to my giddy smile or the messages. Ugh. Why did he have to be so annoyingly charming?

I changed out of my sweats and searched for clothing that walked the line between trying too hard and looking good. No one needed to think I'd made an effort, and yet I was going to make an effort. If Annika was here right now, she'd laugh at me.

Jeans and a fitted T-shirt would fit the bill just fine. I grabbed my keys and headed to the pub that wasn't far from our house.

The Irish pub had cozy booths and dark wood. The dim, intimate lighting made the place one of my favorites for a chat while drinking. Perfect for deep conversations over a pint or two. Annika and I had spent many nights there since we started college together last year.

Opening the heavy wooden door, I stood at the entry for a moment, scanning the booths and listening for familiar voices. When my phone pinged, Sebastian's name appeared.

At the back.

I didn't bother to respond to any of his messages, so how did he know I arrived? Wasn't I supposed to be the one with superpowers?

I slid my phone into my pocket and wandered deeper into the pub. Annika's laughter floated over, and my uncertainty vanished. Sebastian spotted me first, and a grin broke out across his face, lighting up the room.

There were five football players, including Sebastian and Troy, spread out around the booth. Annika was the lone girl, and she was tucked up against Johnny on the far side. He was watching her talk, and as she made a gesture with her hands, he leaned over and kissed her temple. She turned to him and rested her head on his shoulder, a silly sweet grin on her face.

Her hand cradled her pint glass, and now that I realized the bruise was there, it was all I could see.

Sebastian shifted and patted the seat beside him. "Wing-woman! I've been waiting for you."

Annika glanced at me. "Wing-woman?" Confusion settled over her face.

"She volunteered to help me find women willing to sleep with me." He took a drink from his pint. "She thinks my taste is questionable."

Halfway through sipping her beer, she sputtered. "She what now?"

God, what must she be thinking? When our gazes connected, I hoped she could read my helpless expression.

"Sebastian doesn't need to convince girls to have sex with him. They show up ready and willing all hours of the night." Johnny's voice was bored. He took another long pull from his drink and glanced at Sebastian. "What was the name of the girl last night? Did you get it?"

Sympathy coated Annika's expression, and I refused to make eye contact with either Sebastian or Johnny, but then Sebastian let out a laugh tinged with annoyance.

"What are you playing at? Don't be a dick, Johnny. There was no girl last night."

I snuck a glance out of the corner of my eye. Was he being serious or was he hoping Johnny would play along?

"My mistake. Must have been the night before. There are so many, it's hard to keep track." Johnny drank his beer while scanning the bar.

Annika snatched her purse off the seat and stood up, pushing at Johnny's knees. "Let me out."

"Where are you going?" He made no effort to move.

"I'm not sitting here while you make my friend feel uncomfortable." Annika gestured toward me.

When the two of them started arguing, Sebastian leaned over and whispered in my ear, "He's in a shitty mood. There was no woman last night or the night before. Honest."

I faced him, searching for sincerity. Not that it mattered. Sebastian and I weren't together, and if I had my way, we'd never go beyond whatever we were right now. The speculation going on—did he or did he not sleep with girls the last two nights—would ruin me.

Annika pushed at Johnny's legs, the two of them bickering in hushed tones.

"It's okay, Annika." I broke eye contact with Sebastian. "Seems like Johnny's having trouble controlling himself again tonight." I stared at Annika's wrist, and he flushed.

He avoided meeting my gaze and took another gulp of his beer. After a beat, he offered her a pleading expression. "Please, just stay. Natalie said she's okay. I'll tone it down. Practice was awful, and I'm not handling it well. Just stay."

Annika's shoulders slumped, and she slid into the seat beside him. "You did fine at practice." She took out her phone. "Here, let's look at it. You were better than you think."

They huddled together over her phone, re-watching sections of the practice.

I sighed and stood. Sebastian followed me, and his hazel eyes were full of questions.

"I'm getting a drink. Do you want one?"

"I'll come with you."

Chapter Ten

♥

While we made our way to the bar, I asked, "Is Johnny always like that?"

Sebastian raised his eyebrows and glanced back at the table. "Moody?"

"I was going to say assholeish, but I guess moody works too."

Sebastian laughed. "When something rattles him, he has a difficult time letting it go. Then, he gets moody."

"He has a temper too, right?" I slid onto a stool at the bar to wait for the bartender, but Sebastian stayed standing beside me.

"He does, yeah. We all do."

"I'm sure not all of you grab a girl's wrist hard enough to bruise it." I gave Sebastian a pointed look.

He frowned. "You were there. You saw what happened. He felt bad. Said he couldn't understand how he left a mark on her."

The bartender came over, and we ordered our drinks. Sebastian's words floated through my head while we waited. "You think it was an accident?" I drew my pint toward me when it arrived. Surprise coated Sebastian's face when I glanced over my shoulder.

"Yeah, it was an accident. Johnny's not that kind of guy." He grabbed his glass off the bar. "Even if he was, and he's not, but even if he was, he'd be a fool to lay a hand on any woman this year with the draft so close. You can't play if you're in prison." He stared at me for a long moment. "He's not dumb."

Johnny's level of intelligence wasn't my concern. "Annika likes him, and I don't want to see her get hurt." All the ways I was worried Johnny could injure her hung between us.

"If it makes you feel any better, this is the most time I've seen him spend with anyone since I got here three months ago. The guys were giving him a hard time in the locker room the other day, and he took it." He slid into the seat beside me.

Apparently, we were both getting comfortable here. I understood why I didn't want to go back. With raised eyebrows, I took a drink, my question implied.

"I don't wanna go back over there," he said. "We should hang out, the two of us, for a bit." Over the rim of his beer, he sized me up. "What's your last name, Natalie?"

"Chapman." I shifted on my stool to face him. "I already know yours."

"The myth, the legend." He grinned.

"The bird!" I concluded with a laugh. "You know, like Superman?"

Sebastian laughed and shook his head, taking a drink of his beer. "That was rough."

I relaxed into our easy banter. "How old were you when you moved stateside?" I leaned one arm on the smooth wood surface in front of us and the other ran across the high-backed stool.

"Thirteen. My mom's American." Sebastian smiled. "My dad's Bermudian."

"They're still together?" He'd called Bermuda home.

"No. They divorced when I was thirteen, which was part of the reason for the move. My mom wanted to come back, and I was into American football. It's not big on de rock, so it made sense for me to move with her. I go back to Bermuda to visit my dad pretty often."

"Why'd they split?"

He grimaced. "Monogamy is hard?"

"Is that your motto or theirs?"

He slung his arm over his chair, mirroring my posture. "I've never tried it, so I wouldn't know."

"Never?" My stomach dropped at the confession.

He pursed his lips. "Never."

I swiveled away from him and took a bigger drink of my beer. "I guess that makes my wing-woman job easier. No need to worry about complications from past girlfriends." My tone was light, but his admission was crushing. Whatever was building between us had zero chance of becoming anything more than this. Flirtation. Casual sex if I was willing.

"No girlfriends." He shifted forward too. "But lots of—"

"Girls?" Our elbows were so close they were almost touching. "Don't worry." I leaned toward him, mocking a whisper. "I won't tell anyone your secret."

He grinned and closed the distance a little more. "What's that?"

"You're afraid of commitment." I put the space back between us and took another drink.

An air of confidence wafted off him, and he straightened in his chair. "I'm not afraid of commitment, Nattie. It's a subtle difference for an over-committer like you, but I haven't found anyone *worth* committing to."

I scoffed. "An over-committer? Is that even a word?"

He held the beer on the edge of his lips, and the hint of a smile I loved so much played at the corners of his mouth. "It's you. You didn't bother to deny it; you just didn't like my word choice."

"Because it's not a word." He might be right. I did enjoy commitment in my relationships. Clay had been too much, but I'd have the opposite problem with Sebastian. There'd never be enough with him. I'd probably always want more than he could give. This conversation was a good reminder of that truth.

Could I slip out my phone and record him to play to myself in my moments of weakness? That'd be normal, right?

"So." I sat back and searched the pub. "Any prospects?"

"Nah, we can't start tonight. You don't have your outfit yet." His eyes danced as he gave me the once-over. "Do I get to pick what you wear as my wing-woman or...?" He raised his eyebrows.

I almost spit out my beer. "No, you don't get to pick what I wear. *Please.* The day I let a guy do that is the day pigs sprout wings and fly."

"So, what I'm hearing here is that if I can somehow find pigs, give them wings, and make them fly, I get to pick what you wear?"

I shook my head and laughed. "This is not some sort of challenge for you to find a way to make it happen."

"That's what I'm hearing, Nattie. Pigs flying equals Natalie Chapman wearing whatever I want."

I cocked my head. "What would you even dress me in? Come on."

He pursed his lips and stared at me for a beat too long. With a sigh, he took his phone out of his pocket. He scrolled through his photos before passing me his device. "That." A cocky grin replaced his easygoing expression.

Red leather, tight fitting, and skimpy as hell with a tiny cape. "You can't be serious." Disbelief oozed out of my voice. "I'd look terrible in that."

"You'd look *hot* in that. I'd be beating guys off my wing-woman." He cocked his elbows as though he was fending off a crowd.

"You're ridiculous."

"This is true. You don't want to know how much time I've spent considering this. I normally only think about football this much." He lowered his elbows.

I went to scroll to the next photo, and he snatched his phone back. "Whoa, whoa, whoa. You do *not* have scrolling privileges." He clicked it closed and winked. "I'll save the other pictures for later. That was the best one, anyway."

"I thought you texted me the best ones."

"No way." Sebastian chuckled. "I sent you the ones that wouldn't scare you off seeing me again."

"How many photos of half-naked girls in capes do you have on your phone?" I pretended to try to steal it back.

"No comment." He blocked my hand, and once again the glass was poised at his lips and that smile touched them before he took another drink. "Seriously, Nattie, if you're going to be my wing-woman, you need an outfit. I insist."

"Maybe I don't want to be your wing-woman anymore."

He cocked his head to the side and looked at me. "That works better for me, anyway."

"What? You're firing me?" I feigned incredulity.

"You quit, actually. Shame. I had big plans for you, Nattie. You were going places."

"Nah, I was just supposed to convince other girls to go to those places." I grinned.

He choked on his beer and started laughing. Once he got himself together, he stared at me for a moment while I drank my beer in silence. "I've never had to work this hard for a girl before."

"How's it feel?"

"Strange, but I'm getting used to it." His gaze raked over me. "I kinda like having you around, and I can't believe I'm saying this, but I'm glad you turned me down."

"You're giving up?" I held out my hand to shake on it. My heart rate spiked. Blood rushed to my head. "Just friends?"

He chuckled and held his hands up to avoid my offer. "Not a chance. I'm basking in the chase." He relaxed into his stool, elbow on the bar.

Troy approached us from behind. "Seb, we're heading out. You coming, man?"

"Where are we going?" Sebastian leaned over the back of the chair to give Troy his undivided attention.

"Home, dude. We have practice in the morning and Johnny's on a mission after he and Annika dissected tonight's practice about five times. That girl, man. He's so whipped."

Sebastian grinned and glanced at me as if to say he'd told me so.

"All right, I'm coming. I'm going to finish my beer." Sebastian raised his almost empty pint and took the last of the beer in big gulps. He slid his glass along the polished wood. "Until we meet again, Nattie."

He trailed Troy out of the bar. Annika came up behind me, keys in hand.

"Ready to go?" Her gaze tracked Johnny's as he left, a frown creasing her brow.

"You okay?"

"Yeah, Johnny's so hard on himself all the time. It can't be good for him." She gave her head a shake.

Johnny and his happiness weren't her responsibility. We were back on even ground, so I held my tongue. Other than Johnny's shitty attitude toward me and Sebastian, he'd been attentive to Annika, affectionate. Maybe the other night had been a fluke, a mistake.

I slung my arm around her shoulders and said, "Let's go home."

Chapter Eleven

♥

A few weeks later, I came out of my bedroom and found a half-naked Johnny making eggs. Dressed in his boxer briefs, he whizzed around the kitchen as though he was born to cook. I froze. Where was our dorm room sock on the door code? I wasn't wearing pajamas for the quarterback of the college football team to see. Slowly, I turned to head to my room, but he caught sight of me.

"I'm making Annika breakfast. Do you want any?" His disinterested gaze swept over me before turning to the eggs in the pan.

"Ah, that's okay." I crossed my arms over my braless chest. "I didn't realize you were here." My tank top and shorts didn't leave a lot to the imagination, but now that I was caught, I shouldn't be rude.

"Anni told me about the spare key. I used it when we got home from our away game. Some of the guys were going out. She wasn't in the mood." He took a plate out of the cupboard and slid the eggs onto it.

The toast popped, and he buttered the slices before stacking them on the side. He grabbed a knife from the drawer, the ketchup and jam from the fridge, and balanced everything as he sauntered back to Annika's room. In another life, he must have been a skilled waiter.

Grabbing a bowl of cereal, I headed to my room to eat it. I wasn't in the mood to talk to Johnny again when both of us were half dressed. When I checked my phone, there was a text from Sebastian at four in the morning.

I need a Nattie fix. I'm going through withdrawal.

My heart thumped. I stared at the text. How did I respond to that? Should I? Finally, I closed my phone and got ready for my class, deciding he'd probably been drunk. Maybe didn't even remember sending it.

I threw on jeans and a sweater, packed my bag, and dumped my dishes in the sink. Here's hoping Johnny did cleanup as well as cooking.

Before I got to my class, I spotted Sebastian at a distance. I grinned and opened my mouth to call to him when a girl approached him. She was tall, blonde, and model thin. She threw her arms around his neck and pressed her body close. My grin faded, and I shook my head, focusing on the building in front of me.

Those hand slaps when I was on the cusp of opening the cookie jar were a good reminder. Someone fell into step beside me, and I looked over in surprise.

"It's been a while." Clay smiled. "How ya been?"

I returned his smile, pleased to run into him. "Really good. How about you? Where are you headed?"

"204. You're in 200, right?"

"You always knew my schedule better than me," I teased.

When we reached the threshold of my classroom, Clay said, "Are you going to the football party tomorrow night?"

I frowned and shrugged. "Maybe? I don't know. Since Annika and Johnny have gotten so tight, she doesn't make me tag along anymore."

"Well, I'm going. Maybe I'll see you there. It'd be nice to catch up." Clay rubbed my shoulder and then he continued along the hall.

As I walked in and took a seat, I realized I couldn't go to the football party if Clay wanted to *catch up*. Now, if I did turn up, he might take it as a sign I was interested again.

While I took notes, mentally bemoaning Clay's inability to let go, my phone buzzed. I glanced down, trying to make it less obvious. The professor had a no phones policy, but I had an addiction problem.

On campus. If you want a ride home, meet me at the field.

Annika. I could walk, but the weather had turned cooler, and a ride was a much better idea. There was a chance I might be able to convince her to spend a girly afternoon getting manicures and pedicures.

As soon as the professor dismissed the class, I hustled to the football stadium. Would Annika give up any details about her night with Johnny? Did I want to know? Something about the guy rubbed me the wrong way. Was it that he didn't like me?

Outside the main entrance to the playing field, Annika chatted to Johnny and a couple other football players. When I approached, Johnny plucked Annika's phone out of her hand, typed in her password, and started scrolling.

Weird. When had Annika given him the code? And why? My life was in my phone. I couldn't imagine giving the password to a guy I'd been dating for a month.

"Who's Brian?" Johnny frowned.

Annika peered over the edge, a matching frown on her face. "A guy I went on a date with ages ago. It didn't go well. I should delete his contact."

Even from where I stood, Johnny's thumb hitting the trash-can icon was crystal clear.

"Anyone else you want to get rid of on here?" He scrolled through her contacts.

She snatched her phone back. "Maybe just you." Her tone was teasing.

He looped his arm around her waist and yanked her to him. "You wouldn't dare," he growled and then leaned down to kiss her neck while the rest of us looked on.

Annika giggled and pushed at his shoulders. "Stop!" She turned her head away. "Seriously, Johnny! I don't want a hickey. They're gross. Stop sucking on my neck!" Annika shoved on his shoulders again, and I stepped forward, uneasy.

Johnny raised his head and gave Annika a quick kiss on the forehead. "Don't worry, Natalie." He didn't bother to look at me. "We have practice, so you can have her back now." His hands lingered on Annika's waist. "I'll see you later?" He studied Annika.

She nodded and grabbed him around the neck to give him another quick kiss before looping her arm with mine and walking to her car.

"He knows your phone password?" I asked as we slid into the vehicle.

Annika sighed. "I guess? I told it to him weeks ago when he wanted to watch one of the videos I had on my phone. He has a crazy memory though, so I'm not surprised he remembered."

"It's kind of weird he deleted Brad's information, isn't it?" I tried to keep my voice light and casual.

"Nat." Annika's tone was full of warning. "It was Brian, not Brad, and it's not *that* weird. He's good. We're good." She rubbed her hands together. "I'm happy. I'm really, freaking happy."

With a deep breath, I said, "I was surprised to see him this morning when I came out of my room in the tiniest pajamas I own."

Annika gave me a half grin and shook her head. "Sorry. It just kinda happened."

"And it was good?" That was the only detail I wanted.

Annika tugged her sleeves over her hands and started the car. "So good. If you'd said any of this would happen last year, I'd have laughed in your face. But he told me last night that he doesn't want to be with any other girls anymore. Just me." She gave me a triumphant grin. "So, if he wants to check my phone and delete guys, I couldn't care less."

With pursed lips, I contemplated my next comment. "You know his password?"

"Nope. Doesn't matter. I trust him. We spend all our time together. When's he going to be with anyone else?"

A valid point. I hardly saw her anymore without Johnny attached. Impossible he could be doing anything with anyone else who wasn't her or a member of the football team, right? Still, doubt ate at my gut.

She took her phone out and changed her password in front of me. "Happy?" That lamp shone out of her eyes again. It was the same way I pictured an addict looking—enthralled.

I held up my hands. "It's your phone. It would have bothered me to have a guy do that to my phone." The Annika I'd known before Johnny would have been bothered by it too.

She shifted the car into gear, and we drove toward the exit. When I looked over my shoulder, Johnny stood inside the main doors, watching us leave.

"Have you heard from Sebastian? It's been a couple days. He must be going through withdrawals." Annika signaled out of the parking lot.

"Funny you should say that. I got a text from him at four in the morning saying pretty much that."

"Are you coming to the football party tomorrow?"

I shook my head. "Nope. I ran into Clay today and he said he was going and it would be good to 'catch up,' so I can't go now."

"God, Clay. Always ruining everything."

"That's a bit of an exaggeration." I opened my phone to read Sebastian's text again.

"Did you text him back?"

"No."

"Why not?"

"Texting him is an admission of something, sort of. He thinks about me when I'm not around. He notices when I'm not around. But today on the way to class, this tall blonde girl was clinging to him as though he was the second coming of Christ." I sighed. "I can't sleep with him. Maybe the first night I could have. But I like him too much now, and liking him this much won't go anywhere. He's never been in a monogamous relationship."

"Never?"

"He says never. So, all he must want from me is sex, right?" I shrugged. "I'm not sure I can do just sex. Not with him. But, God. He's so *freaking* hot." My hands covered my face before I brushed my hair off my cheeks in frustration. I missed ponytails.

"Maybe he does want more? I mean, look at me and Johnny." Annika turned into our parking lot. "You never know."

"Even if he did want more—and I don't think he does—but if he did, I'm not sure I could handle it. That girl was draped over him today. We're not dating and seeing it deflated me. How would I feel if I had a reason to be upset? Ten times worse. Maybe a hundred times, depending on what the girl was trying to do to him."

"Well, the last few weeks with Johnny have been the best of my life. Maybe Sebastian would be worth the heartbreak too?" She faced me with her hand poised on the car door handle.

"I'll think about it."

The truth was, lately, he dominated my thoughts without me having a say.

Chapter Twelve

♥

My Spidey sense kicked into overdrive whenever Sebastian was within one hundred yards. In the crowded room, I could pinpoint where he was. My ears were tuned to the deep timbre of his voice, the pitch of his laugh, even over the din of other voices, other laughs, and louder conversations.

I wasn't going to glance at him, though. There would be no looking in his direction for the duration of the football party.

I threw my head back and laughed, probably louder than Troy's girlfriend, Gabriella's, joke warranted. He hadn't spoken to me since I arrived. I wouldn't break first and seek him out. Every bone in my body ached with awareness, with the desire to move toward the sound of his voice, to breathe in the familiar scent of beer mixed with the right amount of tangy cologne. I was dying a slow death, in equal parts from his absence and his presence. How was that possible? No idea. Didn't make it less true.

"You're winning." Gabriella put a hand on her curvy hip.

"Winning?"

"Sebastian can't keep his eyes off you. He's tracking you the same as he tracks a football on the field. I heard you two were hanging out, but I noticed neither of you has said one word to the other tonight. What's up with that?" Gabriella drank from her red cup and grimaced. "They need to buy better beer."

When I'd shown up an hour ago, the party had been in full swing. As soon as I'd walked in the door to the enormous living room of the frat house, my gaze had zeroed in on Sebastian like the last drop of water in a desert. He'd taken me in from head to toe, grinned, and turned back to the girl he was talking to.

"There's nothing going on between us," I said to Gabriella. "Annika and Johnny are attached at the hip lately, so I've been spending time with lots of the football players." I sipped my beer. "I even accused your boyfriend of checking out my ass at a party."

Gabriella chuckled good-naturedly. "He's an ass man—or just an ass—I'm never completely sure which." Her lips twitched in amusement. Her olive skin and hazel eyes were expertly made up. Her long dark hair could have been in a shampoo commercial. Pretty, funny, and with an ass that looked amazing in the jeans she was wearing tonight, she was fun company.

I'd met Gabriella a handful of times, and she and Troy were solid. Apart from checking out a few girls' asses, they appeared happy together.

"You never worry about Troy?" I tried to keep my voice light, even if my question was serious.

She mulled over my question. "I wouldn't say I never worry, or I don't get jealous, or I don't sometimes wonder, 'why me', but for the most part, no." She tipped her head from side to side as she seemed to consider her words. "We have a 'hands off' policy we agreed on one time after we got into a huge fight over basically nothing. Neither of us lets anyone touch us. We can flirt, we can check out other people, but it's 'hands off' otherwise." She nodded to where Troy was towering over a gaggle of petite girls.

"It works for you?"

Gabriella shrugged. "We work at it. Sometimes we work hard at it. But if he decides we're not worth that anymore, there's not much I can do." She gave me a half smile. "But I'll tell you what. What we've had so far? He's worth the heartbreak. The highs pay for any lows in the future."

Over the crowd, Johnny's voice boomed, indignant, furious. "You changed your password?"

Across the room, he had Annika's phone clenched in his hand. I'd come to the party alone because Johnny insisted Annika had to arrive before everyone else. He wanted "quality time." I turned to Gabriella with an excuse to go to my friend ready on my lips.

"Johnny can be such a dick sometimes." Gabriella frowned. "He's probably my least favorite player from a basic human being standpoint."

I needed to be beside Annika in case this got ugly, but I filed her comment away for a future drunken conversation. "I'm going to head over there in case he flies into a rage."

While I weaved through the thick crowd, Johnny's voice became louder, accusing Annika of hiding something or someone from him.

"What, are you screwing other guys behind my back?"

A small group encircled Annika and Johnny. With some effort, I bulldozed my way into the ring. Annika was close to Johnny with her arms crossed and her face flushed, not even attempting to retrieve her phone.

"You don't need to have my password. It's called trust. Like how I trust you're not sleeping with every girl at this party behind my back." The words came out through clenched teeth. "You want to exchange passcodes? We can do that. Otherwise, back off."

Pride coursed through me at how well she was standing her ground. This was the Annika I knew—confident, smart, in control. She searched the crowd, and when she found me, her shoulders slumped.

"You can keep it for all I care. I'm leaving. No one, superstar quarterback or not, implies I'm a slut." She turned on her heel.

Johnny snaked out a hand and grabbed her elbow. I stepped forward, remembering the bruise she had the last time he tried to steer her in the direction he wanted.

Before any words left my mouth, Sebastian called from the other side of the crowd, "Johnny, bruh, give her phone back. She's not fucking around on you, man. Don't be an ass."

At his words, Johnny's rage snapped, and he released Annika's elbow as though she'd scorched him. He opened his palm, revealing her cracked device.

She plucked it out of his hand and then walked over to me. "I wanna leave." Her voice was monotone.

"Anni," Johnny called from behind her. "Don't go. I'm sorry. Don't go."

She didn't acknowledge him. Instead, she pushed through people to get us to the door. When I looked over my shoulder, it was Sebastian I sought. He held my gaze for a beat, but I couldn't figure out what his expression revealed.

Annika and I walked home in silence. What could I say? Once we got to our place, she dropped her phone, keys, and purse on the table by the door, flipped off her shoes, and headed for her bedroom without a word.

"Did you want to talk about it?"

"No. I want to sleep." She kept her back to me, but she didn't go into her room. "I want to sleep and sleep and sleep. Maybe when I wake up tomorrow, I'll understand what the hell I'm supposed to do about what happened tonight. Right now? Just the thought is exhausting."

There was a soft knock on the door, and I turned, uncertain. "What if it's him?" I asked in a low voice.

"Tell him to leave. I'm going to bed." Any trace of the giddy girl or the confident woman was gone.

I waited until she was out of sight before checking the peephole. I sighed. Clay was on the threshold. Reluctantly, I opened the door.

"Hey. Sorry. I followed you guys from the party. I saw what happened with Johnny. Is Annika okay?" He glanced around my shoulder into the house.

I stepped into the front path and drew the door closed behind me. He wasn't getting an invitation. "She's rattled, and I doubt she'll want a reminder about the public spectacle." I crossed my arms. A chilly breeze swept across the lawn, and I hadn't worn a coat.

"I was hoping we could catch up," Clay said when it was clear I wasn't going to invite him in.

"Didn't we do that the other day on the way to class?" I cocked my head.

"I was hoping we could grab a coffee or something. Chat?" He ignored my rudeness.

I was about to reply when the breeze kicked up a notch, and a faint whiff of a familiar scent floated to me. Over Clay's shoulder, I searched him out, hungry for a glimpse. Unless I was going crazy, Sebastian was somewhere close by. Like the cavalry cresting the hill, Sebastian appeared at the bend in the path.

His confident stride faltered when he saw Clay, but the minute he registered who was standing with me, his face broke into a wide smile. Damn him and his contagious grin.

I shifted my attention back to Clay, trying not to give the wrong impression to either of them. "Sorry. I don't think I should leave Annika alone tonight."

"We can stay here—" He trailed off when Sebastian's hand landed on his shoulder. He turned and flushed when their gazes connected.

Sebastian side-stepped him and looped an arm around my waist, drawing me close to kiss my temple. "Sorry, Nattie. I got held up saying goodbye to people. Annika okay?" His gaze bored into me as though we were the only ones on the path.

The adoring expression, the hand at my waist, my irregular heartbeat, and the heat rushing to new places made me unsteady on my feet. I wanted to sink into him, into this feeling.

He scanned me, and amusement entered his eyes. He turned to Clay and thrust out his free hand. "Have we met? I'm Sebastian."

"Clay." He was clearly at a loss for what to think, but he shook Sebastian's hand then shot me a flustered look. "I didn't realize you two were..."

"Together?" Sebastian finished for him, and then he leaned over and kissed my temple again. "How do you two know each other? Are you a friend of Annika's? You look familiar." Sebastian was playing this exchange for all it was worth.

Part of me was anxious about the expression on Clay's face. He didn't seem to know what to do with himself. Sweet of him to come check on Annika, if that had been his intention.

Trapped out here with the two men, I made a gut decision. I tugged Sebastian close and said, "You can go in, if you want. I'll be a minute."

He squeezed my waist and said to Clay, "It was nice meeting you."

Once the door clicked closed behind me, I focused on Clay, expecting him to tuck his tail and go.

His cheeks were a ruddy red, and I didn't think it was from the cold. "I know what this looks like, but I didn't come here to get you back or whatever. I wanted to talk to you about

Annika." He shifted his feet and glanced at the door behind me. "Maybe about you too. I don't know. I didn't realize you and Sebastian were a thing. Heard he didn't do repeats."

Humiliation tinged with jealousy bloomed in my chest. I hated that his comment got to me. "What did you want to tell me?" I aimed for a patient voice when I wanted to scream. What would I scream? No idea.

"I was at a party a couple weekends ago and a couple of the girls were drunk," Clay started to say.

I half-turned to go into the house. His drunken conquests were none of my business. Not even a twinge of jealousy stirred in my gut.

"No, wait—it's—the girls. They said Johnny can get rough. That he's rough with g-girls," Clay stuttered. He took a deep breath. "I don't know if it's just Johnny or what. But be careful, okay? I always liked Annika, and what I saw tonight? Didn't seem like a normal reaction to a changed phone password."

"Who were the girls?"

Clay sighed and shoved his hands into his pockets. "I didn't get their names."

I leaned against the door. "I've already tried to talk to Annika about him. This isn't the first time I've heard he's *rough* or *intense* or whatever label you want to put on it."

Admitting this to Clay made me a traitor to Annika, but I dated Clay for a year, and I needed to talk to someone about this. My dad would drive here in a heartbeat if I even hinted Annika was in too deep with a bad guy, so I couldn't count on someone objective there. Sebastian waited inside. I couldn't talk to him either. Johnny was his ace boy, whatever that meant. A rumor was just a rumor.

"Have you talked to your dad?" Clay shifted his weight from one foot to the other.

"Yeah, no. My dad would move in here and start an intervention program. I'm hoping tonight was the end. Annika seemed to feel what you and I saw."

Clay nodded and was quiet for a beat. "I probably shouldn't say this, but if you ever need me—call. If anything happens and you need me, no matter what time it is or no matter what's happened, please call."

I gave him a soft smile. "Thanks, Clay. I hope I never need to."

"Me too." He tipped his chin toward the door. "I won't hold you up anymore."

"Sorry about Sebastian." I placed my hand on the doorknob.

"I get it. Me being here probably looked bad." Clay shrugged. "I hope it works out for you, if that's what you want."

I turned to look at him one last time before opening the door. "The jury's still out. I'll see you around."

Chapter Thirteen

♥

Sebastian glanced over the rear of the couch. He'd gotten us both a beer and was watching Annika's old game tape from the DVR. "That took longer than I expected. Am I losing my touch?" His grin was playful.

An answering smile blossomed against my will. Worry burrowed deeper into my stomach. Tonight would be enough. Annika would let Johnny go.

"What are you even doing here?" I took a seat beside him on the couch.

"Truth?" Sebastian's smile disappeared.

"Always." My heart kicked up a notch.

"Johnny asked me to come check on Annika." Seeing my confused expression, he continued, "I was going to come anyway, maybe not quite as quickly as I did."

Johnny asked him to come check on Annika? Bile rose into my throat. "He was out of line."

"He wouldn't have hurt her." He passed me my beer.

"How do you know that?" I mirrored him on the couch.

"How do you know he would have?" He fired in response. "Which of us has spent more time with him?" The challenge in his voice was clear.

The problem with his rationale was that once I was sure Johnny was a bad guy, Annika might already be hurt. Correction. She'd already *been* hurt.

"He had that reaction tonight over a changed phone password. Seemed a bit over the top to me. What happens next time? Or the next? Or the next? Reactions like his don't deescalate."

"Annika's fine. Johnny's sorry. He's got a jealous streak a mile long. I told him they needed to slow things down if he was going to lose his mind over stupid things." He eyed me. "Are you reading more into their fight because of your dad?"

I gave him a wry look. "Sure—always. But that doesn't mean it's not happening. If I sit back and Annika gets hurt again, I'm not sure I'll be able to forgive myself. If the signs are there and I say nothing, I'm an accomplice. I let it happen."

Sebastian took a drink. "You can't put that on yourself."

"But I do. That's like telling someone not to be afraid of something or not to worry. Just because you say I *can't* feel that way doesn't mean I don't."

When I glanced at Sebastian, he'd settled into the couch, a pensive expression on his face. He toyed with his beer bottle and then drained it in silence.

"You want another?" He checked my almost full beer.

"No, I'm okay," I said as he rose and disappeared into the kitchen. When he returned, he had a glass of water. "Are you okay?"

He nodded and then looked at me. "The whole 'you can't tell people how to feel' thing hit me a little hard."

"How so?" I prodded.

He stared at his hands clutching the cup. "How come you never texted me back?"

"You mean your four a.m. text?" I frowned.

"Yeah."

"I figured it was a drunk text. I didn't realize it needed a response." Not entirely truthful. I didn't understand why I hadn't texted him, but responding was dangerous, slippery. As though I'd be admitting something too.

We said nothing for a few minutes, examining each other. I'd done something wrong because the flirtatious vibe between us was gone. Was his mood about the text or was it my mistrust of Johnny?

"Do you think Annika's okay?" Sebastian asked, breaking the silence.

"She's rattled." Rehashing the same argument seemed fruitless. He didn't believe Johnny would ever hurt Annika, and the opposite was becoming more plausible.

"Are you coming to our next home game?" He leaned into the couch and watched me.

"I guess that depends on what happens with Annika and Johnny. If they cool off, probably not. I'm not into football, you know that." Was that the question he wanted to ask?

"What if I wanted you to come?" He peered into his half-full glass.

I smiled, trying to work out his meaning. "You want me to come watch your game, even if Annika doesn't come?"

"Yeah." He scooted closer on the couch. "I like knowing you're in the stands, even if you have no idea what's going on."

I chuckled, but the seriousness of his face dried up the sound. "No promises. Annika is one of my best friends and going to the game if Johnny is out of the picture doesn't feel right."

Sebastian grabbed my hand, lacing our fingers together. "So, if they are done, *this* is done too?" He didn't quite meet my gaze.

My heart dropped into my toes. A coherent response eluded me. There was no *this*, was there? We hung out sometimes. Texted each other. "I don't understand what *this* is—our friendship?"

"I don't wanna be your friend, Nattie." He glanced at me under his lashes.

Heat surged through my body, and a tingling erupted deep in my stomach. The temptation to tug him closer, to give in to whatever had been swirling around us for weeks, now rose to the surface. I wouldn't be able to handle the fallout from grabbing what I wanted in *this* moment. Every time I saw him with other girls, I'd wonder if he was sleeping with them. Every time he didn't text me right away, I'd wonder who he was with. No, I couldn't go there.

"I can't give you what you want, Sebastian. I'm not built that way," I said. "We can be friends—hang out, chat about whatever as long as it's not football."

"You don't feel it?" He sank deeper into the couch and observed me out of the corner of his eye.

"If Annika and Johnny are done, we'll hardly see each other anymore anyway," I reminded him. "You'll forget about me under the crush of other girls."

His expression was serious when he sat forward again. "Nattie—"

Annika's door down the hall opened, and I scooted away from Sebastian, aware of how close we were to each other. After what happened tonight, was it a betrayal to be sitting here flirting with Sebastian?

She wandered into the living room and stopped short when her gaze landed on Sebastian. "Oh, sorry. I'm having trouble sleeping. I was going to watch some TV." She crossed her arms over her chest.

Sebastian gave me one last loaded look before standing and draining his water. "I'll get out of your way." Once he was around the couch, he stood in front of Annika. "Johnny wanted me to tell you—"

She held up a hand. "Save it. Please. If Johnny isn't man enough to apologize in person, then I don't want to hear it. You can quote me on that when you scurry back to talk to him."

Sebastian reeled as though she'd hit him. He shoved his hands into the pockets of his jeans, and his shoulders lifted. "I'll tell him." We made eye contact over the rear of the couch. He stepped past Annika and unlocked the door. Just before he disappeared, he said, "I'll text you later, Nattie."

Annika crossed to the door, flipped the lock, and then came around the couch to collapse beside me. "Sorry. I was rude to him."

I shrugged. "He can take it. Johnny's an ass for sending him."

"Johnny knew I wouldn't see him." She reached over the couch to grab her phone off the little table by the door. Her home screen was littered with multiple missed calls and text messages.

"What are you going to do?"

She shook her head. "I realize what you want me to say, Nat. But the truth is, I don't know. When it's the two of us, he's amazing. So amazing. We get along so well. There's so much potential in us. We could go the distance. But then he does something like tonight, and I wonder what the hell I'm doing."

I nodded, not saying anything else. "I guess we'll see what tomorrow brings?" I handed her the TV remote.

She stared at her phone and then turned it off. She ran her finger over the crack in the screen.

"It wasn't cracked before, was it?" I kept my voice quiet.

She shook her head. "He did it. With his hand."

The amount of force needed to do that to her screen was terrifying. Discretely, I glanced at the bruise on her wrist, a faint yellow still visible.

"I'm worried about you, Annika."

She smiled. "You saw how quickly he let me go. He wouldn't hurt me on purpose. I know he wouldn't. He doesn't have it in him."

"He has a temper." I tried to keep my voice even and without accusation.

"Who doesn't?" She turned off the DVR game and switched to an old episode of *The Big Bang Theory*. "He wouldn't have hurt me." She sank deeper into the couch with her damaged phone still clutched to her chest.

"Clay stopped by."

Annika rolled her eyes. "I used to feel sorry for him, but lately he's annoying."

"He came to check on you."

She laughed. "Sure he did. Come on, Nat!"

I smiled. "Okay, maybe he didn't come *just* to check on you. That's what he said, anyway. He also said he'd been at a party where girls were talking about Johnny."

She tensed beside me. "Girls talk about Johnny all the time. He's hot. He's an amazing football player. One day he'll be rich and famous."

In that moment, I realized she'd heard something too. She knew what was coming. "He heard Johnny can get rough with girls."

Annika shook her head. "I know you're a 'believe a girl when she cries wolf' person, but I'm not. People are always looking for a way to get a piece of the pie."

"How would accusing him of being rough give them that?" Her attitude about other women drove me nuts. Why did we leap to a man's defense?

"Everyone loves gossip. A piece of gossip about the star quarterback? The golden nugget of gossip currency. Why not spread it?" Annika glanced at me. "Who were these girls? Any names?"

She was challenging me for evidence I didn't have. She wouldn't listen to me if I couldn't provide proof. "I don't have any," I admitted.

"What did Sebastian say when he was here? Did he think Johnny would hurt me? You two looked pretty cozy." Her temper flared.

I hesitated. Sebastian's comment justified her beliefs about Johnny. He'd known Johnny a few months in a very specific setting. Did he know him that well? Even though I wanted her to see Johnny from another angle, I couldn't lie.

"He didn't think Johnny would have hurt you."

"See?" Annika threw up her hands. "Johnny and Sebastian spend a lot of time together. If he doesn't think Johnny has it in him and I don't think he does either, you need to let it go."

I slumped into the couch. Was I overreacting? Despite his closeness with Annika, I had only spent a few minutes here and there talking to him. He'd always been cool to me, sometimes outright cold. Maybe we rubbed each other the wrong way? Doubt seeped in. Without proof, neither of us could be sure who was right.

Chapter Fourteen

♥

When the doorbell rang at an ungodly hour, there was only one person it could be. *Johnny*. I pried open an eye and checked my bedside clock. They had early morning practice today.

I groaned. Their schedule now lived in my brain, taking up vital space. What was happening to me?

I stumbled around my room, throwing on a bathrobe and trudging to the door, but Annika was already there. In the hall, out of sight, I froze.

Johnny's charm was turned to full blast. His dimples popped, and he stared at Annika as though she was a piece of candy he'd love to swallow whole. In one hand, he held a large bouquet of red roses, and in the other, a card or envelope.

Annika was framed in the doorway, still in her pajamas, arms crossed, not meeting his gaze. Reluctantly, she took the flowers.

"I wrote you this last night." Johnny thrust the envelope toward her. "I'm not good at saying the right words, but everything's in this letter. I poured my heart out. I mean it, Anni. Every word is true." With his hands empty, he shoved them into his pockets and gave her a hopeful look. "I want to see you at practice later."

Annika kept her gaze averted, but she'd accepted both of his peace offerings. "Is that all?" Her voice remained cool.

"I hope not." Johnny backed up. "I want to see you later tonight."

When Annika closed the door and flipped the lock, I tiptoed to my room, letting out my breath.

On the nightstand, my phone was lit up with notifications. Sebastian had sent me another text after he left. Did he return to the party? Did he find someone else to amuse him? Those questions were exactly why I couldn't let him get any closer.

Remembering the slivers of hurt in his hazel eyes the night before, I fired off a quick reply. Deliberately hurting his feelings wasn't in me. As soon as the text said delivered, it was read, and three dots appeared.

Breakfast, sleepyhead?

I grinned. *Your early morning practices are insanity. I don't understand how you survive on so little sleep.*

Is that a yes to food?

I cradled my phone. No need to overthink it. Breakfast was a meal. That was it. Taking a deep breath, I replied. *Ready in 30.*

I tossed my phone onto my unmade bed, and I headed for the shower. Annika's door was open, and I peeked in. She wasn't there. I checked the living room and then the kitchen. On the table, strewn across it, was Johnny's letter.

I stared at the pages from a distance.

Whatever Johnny had decided to tell Annika, it was long. I moved closer, keeping my hands gripped together to avoid picking up the papers. If Annika left them here, she must have known I'd see them.

It was wrong to read them. Maybe skimming them would make me understand his raging temper.

I leaned over the table, speed-reading. Comments Annika had made the night before jumped out at me—*go the distance, so much potential, never felt this way before.* Everything Annika had been dying to hear was mirrored in the letter. His sentiment should be a comfort, a positive sign. The words *mine* and *no one will ever love you like I do* also sprung off the page.

I considered gathering the pages into a neat stack and putting them in her room. But then she'd realize I saw them, read them.

Turning on my heel, I went to the bathroom to shower. Reading her letter was wrong, and I used more soap than normal trying to scrub the icky off. Even if I suspected Johnny wasn't good for her, I shouldn't have so much as peeked at her personal note.

In the mirror, my brown eyes were tired in my pale face, but at least my jeans and sweatshirt were clean. Grabbing mascara and lip gloss out of my makeup bag, I tried to conceal my fatigue. Would Sebastian even notice?

At the knock on the door, I grabbed my keys and purse from the hall table. Sebastian was dressed in jeans and a hoodie. The weather was getting increasingly cooler, and the leaves on the trees outside our townhouse were beginning to turn color.

"Where are we going?" I asked, stepping out.

"Diner down the street." He threw a thumb over his shoulder. "My treat."

"I can pay my own way."

"Sure, but I asked you. When you ask me, you can pay." He smirked as though he assumed an invitation from me would never happen.

"Sounds like a challenge."

"However you want to take that, that's up to you." He grinned.

"I don't normally do mornings. You're lucky I'm awake, so I doubt I'll ever invite you to breakfast." I tugged my sleeves over my hands to combat the chill, and a leaf twirled to the ground in front of me onto the sidewalk.

"You disappoint me, Nattie. I thought you'd rise to the challenge."

"There are lots of things I'll rise for. Breakfast, out of the house, isn't generally one of them." I gave him a sideways glance.

"Johnny came over? That's why you're gracing me with your presence? I saw him hot footing it after practice. Figured he was headed to your place." He stuffed his hands in his pockets. "They in there making up?"

"Not at my house. You and Annika must have been two ships passing in the early morning light."

"A long, leisurely breakfast it is, then. I would hate to interrupt them at our house. Never much privacy there." He held open the door to the '50s-inspired diner.

"What made you decide to live there when you transferred?" I asked while the waitress got our table ready.

Sebastian shrugged. "All the guys there are on the team. Frat house. Parties. Win-win-win?"

We followed the waitress to our booth near the window. The napkin holder was in the shape of an old jukebox. The atmosphere was rundown and vintage. The vinyl seats had rips patched with duct tape. Like always, it was busy, though. Decent, cheap food was a college staple. There was a nice buzz circling us as people sobered up or fueled up for the day ahead.

"What about you? Why Annika out of the others on your floor?" He perused the menu.

The waitress reappeared, and we ordered while I mulled over his question. "Annika and I get each other, accept each other for who we are. We don't share a love of football, but we enjoy and appreciate each other. We're both passionate, opinionated people. I thought we saw the world the same way, for the most part." I stirred cream into my coffee.

"But you don't anymore?" He sipped his black coffee.

I froze, realizing what I'd said. He was the same as Annika and didn't see the potential menace in her relationship with Johnny. "Forget I said that. It's probably not what I meant."

He gave me a wry grin, "You mean, Johnny, right?"

I sighed. "Yeah, I do. I don't want to talk about him anymore. You and Annika think he walks on water, I suspect he's standing at the gates of hell. The conversation will go in circles until either something happens or it doesn't, you know?"

"The gates of hell are a little overboard." Sebastian frowned.

A slow smile spread across my face. "So is the walking on water part, but you didn't dispute that."

He chuckled. "You're quick, Natalie Chapman. You'll make a hell of a lawyer one day. You going to climb onto your soapbox as a public defender?" The tension eased out his shoulders, and we were on playful banter ground.

"I'm not sure. My dad doesn't want me to go that route. No money in it." I stacked the creamers into a tower. "I can't imagine being a criminal lawyer defending the assholes my dad has uncovered over the years. Wouldn't be right. Corporate law would bore me."

"Sounds as though your dad brought his work home with him. What was that like?"

"Hard. Annoying. Eye-opening. Everything you'd expect it to be. He was pretty strict when I was growing up, set in his ways. He still is, but now that I'm a bit older, he at least listens to my opinion from time to time."

"My parents were liberal when I was a kid. They could have been hippies in a commune." He shrugged. "Very civil about the divorce. Neither believed monogamy was best for them in the end. No hard feelings."

"Either of them ever remarry? Do you have any siblings?"

"No, neither remarried. Surprise, surprise." He smiled. "I have an older sister."

"Are you two close?" My heart squeezed in my chest at the tenderness on his face while he talked about his family. Their situation might be unusual, but it was clear they were much loved.

"Yeah." He nodded. "She chose to stay in Bermy with my dad when my parents split. So, I don't see her as often. She flies in for big games with my dad, which is nice." He eyed me for a minute and then tipped his chin. "What about you? Siblings? Your mother? I haven't heard you say anything about her yet."

My stomach dropped out in that familiar way it always did whenever the subject of my mother was raised. I carefully crafted my words to leave her out, which had been the hardest piece to get used to when she died. An erasure. Years later, her death still felt wrong, not final, as though she'd turn up knocking on my door.

"She died a few years ago. Cancer," I said. "I have a younger sister."

"I'm sorry to hear about your mom," he said. "I can't even imagine. I'm tight with my mom. It would crush me if anything happened to her."

Tears pricked at my eyes, and I willed them to stay in. *Crushed* was the perfect word. I wasn't going to cry about my mother in a '50s diner with a guy I barely knew. "Yeah," I agreed. "Impossible for anyone to imagine until it happens. Even then, sometimes it doesn't feel real, and other times it's breathtakingly permanent." My voice caught on the last word, thickening with tears. "It's not a club you want to be part of."

He reached across the table and intertwined his fingers with mine. When I looked up, he drew my hand to his lips and kissed my palm. He sandwiched my palm between his and stared at me. The air grew thick and heavy, and the things we weren't saying to each other stretched, another layer laid over top.

The waitress appeared with our food, and Sebastian eased his grip out of mine. We spent a few minutes in a deep companionable silence, adding ketchup, salt, and pepper to our breakfast plates.

"Have you been here before?" Sebastian took his first bite.

"Truth?"

"Always." His lips twitched. "What, did you bring a one-night-stand here? Is this place your unnamed walk of shame?"

"If I sleep with any guy, there's no walk of shame or else I shouldn't have done it in the first place." I squeezed more ketchup onto my plate. "Clay and I came here a few times at the start of the semester."

He took a bite of his toast and examined me. "So you were sending mixed signals to the poor guy? Here I was thinking he was kinda pathetic for not understanding the two of you were done, and now you tell me you were still hanging out when I first met you?"

I flushed. "I wanted to stay friends. He said he wanted to be friends too. You can't say that and then avoid each other."

"He was in love with you?"

I shifted uncomfortably in my seat. I wasn't sure I liked where this was going. "He was."

"Why'd you break up?"

Picking up my coffee, I took a long sip. The liquid burned, but I needed a minute to formulate a response. "He wanted things from our relationship that I didn't. Maybe if I'd met Clay ten years from now, our outcome would have been different."

Sebastian frowned. "I doubt it."

I gaped at the iron certainty in his voice. "You've never even been in a monogamous relationship. Ever. How would you know?"

"If the word 'maybe' enters a sentence about getting married and having kids with someone then the answer might as well be no, 'cause it sure as hell ain't yes." Sebastian threw his last piece of toast in his mouth, and his expression oozed self-satisfaction as he chewed.

"You think you're some sort of love expert?" I arched my eyebrows.

"No, Nattie. I am a decision-making expert. With something that important, you go all in, balls to the wall, and you dig in, burrow deep."

"I sense a football analogy coming," I teased.

He laughed. "Nah, I wouldn't do that to you. I'd lose you the minute I started. I enjoy amusing you, not boring you."

"And yet, you still want me attending your games."

"You don't enjoy watching me prance around the field in my tight pants?"

Heat rose to my cheeks, but I managed a laugh. "Prance is an excellent word. I approve." His tight pants were a reason I didn't mind going to the games lately.

"We should do this more often."

"Go out for breakfast after you've been prancing around the field?" I slopped up the last of my egg with my toast.

"No, hang out. Just the two of us."

I glanced up and then hesitated. "I'm not sure. People might get the wrong idea."

"Not if you wear this." He slid his phone across the table.

A woman who resembled me was wearing a tight white T-shirt with the words wing-woman emblazoned across it. I burst out laughing. "What in the world?" I wiped my mouth with my napkin and leaned closer to the image.

"You can touch the phone; it won't bite. You didn't go for my other suggestion."

"I'm worried it'll suck me in, and I'll emerge wearing that shirt. She looks like me." I turned my attention to him, and he smirked.

"Photoshop." He shifted in his seat. "I was bored?"

I slid the phone back to him. "That's weird. I'm not wearing that."

"Too soon for the white T-shirt. Got it." He nodded as though our exchange made complete sense. "But you'll still hang out with me again?"

"You *are* persistent." The last sip of my coffee slid along my throat.

He slotted his phone into his pocket. Then he sat, drinking his coffee, watching me. Silence stretched between us. He planned to wait me out.

"Okay." I relented. "Fine. We can hang out more if you want." I rolled my eyes, but inside my stomach fluttered. I couldn't let these feelings for him get out of control. "People will talk, though. You know that, right? Wing-woman or not, I'll be a cock-blocker."

He choked on his coffee, stifling a laugh. "How did wing-woman and cock-blocker end up in the same sentence? That was amazing."

I shrugged. "That's because I'm amazing."

His grin widened, and his hazel eyes, so different from my darker brown, twinkled. "That you are," he said. "That you are."

My stomach dropped to my feet at the naked admiration. I was already in way too deep.

Chapter Fifteen

♥

Two weeks later, Annika still hadn't been home. I'd spoken to her on the phone, so I knew she was fine or, as she put it, "excellent," camping out in Johnny's room. Was she going to her classes? Sebastian said Johnny hadn't missed any football practices, which also wasn't surprising.

Not having Annika around was weird and lonely. We'd spent the last year telling each other everything, whether we wanted to hear it or not. Right now, I needed to dissect what was happening between me and Sebastian. By my logic, spending more time with him should have dulled the tension between us. We should be falling into an easy friendship.

Instead, we were tightrope walking across Niagara Falls without a net. I kept waiting for the rushing water to sweep me over the edge.

We were together almost every day. He'd started parking at my place a few days ago and walking to school with me. He claimed it was good cardio for him, but the walk was short and there weren't any hills. I wasn't sure exercise was the real reason, but I didn't press him. My house was probably an equal distance to campus as the frat house. Coming to my house made no sense.

"You saw Annika this morning?" I asked as we walked.

"Yeah, she was running late, as always," Sebastian said. "For an organized girl, she can't ever seem to get anywhere on time. If she wants to be a coach for real, she'll have to sort that out. If the coach is late, why can't the players be late too?"

I gave him a sideways look. "That logic never flew with my dad."

"All right, all right. I see your point. However high Annika's aiming to climb on the coaching ladder, at some point her lateness *will* hold her back."

I shrugged. "If there's something I'm sure of about Annika, beyond a shadow of a doubt, when she's backed into a corner, she'll come out swinging. She'll either find a way to make her lateness work for her, or she'll fix it."

"You're having lunch with her today, aren't you?" Sebastian asked.

"Yes! I can't wait. We've never gone this long without seeing each other. So weird. I never would have expected her to become that girl." I sunk my hands deeper into my coat pockets.

"That girl?" Sebastian's brow furrowed.

"The one who gets so wrapped up in a boy they throw away their friendships. She used to make fun of how much time I spent with Clay, and it wasn't anywhere close to this." I turned onto the campus.

"Are you jealous of Johnny?" Sebastian asked.

"Kind of? I'm happy for her if she's happy, but she's been hunkered down with him for two weeks. She's only come home to get a few odds and ends. Johnny waited in the car, so she didn't stay long." My classroom building loomed ahead. "What class did you say you had?" He wasn't wearing his usual back-pack.

"No class. I have a meeting with Coach about the game this weekend, then I'm hitting the gym." Sebastian nodded in the direction of the stadium.

I frowned. "Don't you usually work out in the mornings when you don't have practice?"

His grin split his face. "Nat, are you keeping tabs on me?"

I groaned. "I'm starting to know things I never wanted to have in my brain."

"Next up, watching game tape and doing the running commentary."

"Oh, God. No. No." I laughed. "But seriously, I thought you always worked out in the morning? Something about stimulating the muscles or something..." I trailed off at the growing amusement on his face. "What? I listen—sometimes."

"Johnny's been hitting the gym with Annika the last week or so. Means I'm free to go whenever the mood strikes." He shrugged.

We stopped outside my building and his claim niggled. "Annika's been going to the gym with Johnny?" Did I hear that right?

"Yeah, why? Your girl not normally a gym rat?"

"She runs, takes fitness classes, recreational team sports, but going to a gym to lift weights? She'd rather be caught dead."

"Well, look at the two of you. You're keeping track of a football player's schedule, and she's lifting weights in the gym. Times are a'changin'." He walked backward toward the stadium. "I'll text you later. Gotta get my car."

I stood at the entrance to my building for a minute longer. He hunched his shoulders, shoved his hands deeper into his pockets, and picked up the pace in the chilly weather. I opened the door and took the stairs to my classroom. A seat near the window with a clear view toward the stadium called my name. I slid into it and stared out.

In the distance, Sebastian was side tackled by a brunette girl I didn't recognize. He threw his arm around her and put his lips close to her ear. She threw back her head, laughing. I faced the front, wishing I hadn't picked a window seat.

Annika poked at her salad.

"Do you want half my burger?" I lifted my knife, prepared to cut.

"No, no. I can't cheat. Johnny and I agreed we would be super strict. This is the same diet Gisele and Tom are on." She glanced up at me from her plate. "I want to be supportive."

To my eyes, she looked tired, thin, and moved like she was a hundred years old. Whatever she and Johnny were doing in the house, she wasn't getting much benefit.

"So, this whole gym thing. What's that about?" I tried to keep my voice light and curious.

"If I want to coach, I should get practical experience, right? Johnny offered to take me through their weight programs. Show me how to do everything. It's a great opportunity." She smiled, but it didn't reach her eyes.

"When are you coming home? I miss you. I can't believe you enjoy living in a frat house."

She took a long drink of her water and met my eyes. "Johnny asked me to move in with him. Get a place for the two of us."

I sat up straighter. "What? You've only been dating a few months. The football season is longer than you two have been dating."

She raised her eyebrows, amusement sparkling in their dark depths. "You remember how long a football season is?"

"Okay, I have no idea. But football is still happening, and it started before you and Johnny hooked up, so by default the season is longer, right?"

She pursed her lips. "Yeah, it seems quick, maybe. But we're happy. Why not seize the day?"

"You're planning that far ahead? Our lease isn't up until May." I took a bite of my burger. Finding another roommate would be a gigantic task. I'd miss her. Up until the last little while, we were tight.

"Uh, Johnny was hoping we'd move in together after Christmas."

"Oh." I set down my burger with a thud.

It was already November. That didn't give me a lot of time to find a roommate, and I couldn't afford to keep our place by myself.

"I told him I wouldn't leave you unless you had someone to take my place. It's an expensive house for one person."

An *impossible* house for one person. An unfamiliar ache flickered in my chest. This felt like a friendship breakup. "Does this have anything to do with me? With the doubts I've had about Johnny?"

Something was off in her request, but I wasn't sure if it was the suddenness, Annika's overall appearance, or my increasing dislike of Johnny. Sebastian was right. I was jealous, but it wasn't *just* that, was it?

"No, no. I never told Johnny you thought he'd hurt me on purpose or how judgmental you were about the phone."

Tears pricked at the back of my eyes. She was mad. At me. "Annika—"

"It's okay, Nat. You've been trying to watch out for me," Annika said. "But if I'm moving ahead with Johnny, I need you to be on board with us. We're together. We're happy."

"If he's good to you and good for you, I'm happy for you. Maybe I overreacted before. I'm sorry. I certainly didn't mean for my hesitation to hurt our friendship. You've been so distant the last couple of weeks. You were caught up in Johnny, but it wasn't only that, was it?"

Annika frowned and toyed with her salad. "I wanted you to be happy for me, and from the minute Johnny and I got together you've been everything but happy."

Her words were stones in my gut. I could defend myself or I could save our friendship. "You're right," I said. "I'm sorry. I really am." With another bite of my burger in my mouth, I chewed while examining her hopeful expression. "I'll put up a post for a roommate. If this is what you want, I'll do my best to make sure you can move in with Johnny in January."

She came around the table to hug me. "Thank you. Thank you. I want everyone to be happy, you know? Everyone can be happy."

She returned to her seat with her old spark. Johnny hadn't been the problem; it had been me.

"Want to get ready for the game together this weekend? You're coming, aren't you? Sebastian said he asked you, and you said you'd come."

I gave her a half smile. "He said that, did he?"

"What's going on with you two, anyway?" Annika dug into her salad with a renewed effort.

"Oh, God. I wish I knew. Not a clue. He's always around. He's even fixing things at our house—those little things we couldn't be bothered to tell the landlord about."

Annika grinned. "That's a nice perk."

"It is. When we're alone together, I could—I want to..." I trailed off. "Around campus with other girls he's a massive flirt, and I crash into reality. I can't do it. I'm not built like you. Insecurity would destroy me."

"Have you said any of this to him?" Annika dipped her lettuce into her salad dressing.

"No. No way." I shook my head.

"So, you'll let this pass you by? You'll let another girl sweep him off his feet?"

I popped a French fry into my mouth. "She'll be built of better stuff than me," I said. "Look, Sebastian hasn't declared anything other than his undying lust. He wants to sleep with me. I'm in too deep to have sex with him and have it mean nothing. Possibly the first night I met him I could have done it, but now? I like him. Once I sleep with him, the chase is over, and he'll move on."

"You should tell him how you feel. You could be surprised. Maybe he isn't in it for one night. At the start of the semester, I never suspected I'd be where I am now. We're exclusive. We're moving in together. He's even talking about where he might get drafted, what it'll mean for us."

I raised my eyebrows and then worried I appeared too shocked. "That's amazing, Annika. Really. That's so great."

She rolled her eyes. "I want you to be happy for me, not un-Natalie-like."

"Too much?"

"Just a bit." She measured on her fingers. "But I appreciate the effort. I do."

"I'll try harder to be in your corner. You're one of my best friends, and I don't want to lose our friendship because of any guy."

Chapter Sixteen

♥

"**W**hat are you doing?" Sebastian asked from the sectional.

The more time Annika spent at the frat house, the more time he spent here. He came to get his car and never left. Today was the only day during the week when they didn't have practice, and he'd put himself to work for me. *Again.* So far, he'd fixed the running toilet and unclogged the drain in the shower.

"I'm trying to figure out how to access the student housing website to make a post," I said from the kitchen table.

"You moving?"

"I hope not. Annika and Johnny are moving in together in January. I need a new roommate."

Sebastian took a drink of the fruit punch I'd made and then said, "Yeah, Johnny mentioned he was hoping you'd agree."

"Why'd they tell you before me?" A flare of annoyance ignited.

"Uh, probably because you called Annika's boyfriend an abusive asshole who was standing at the gates of hell." Sebastian chuckled.

"Hey now—*most* of those words never crossed my lips." I held up a finger while I sent an email to student housing. Every single one had crossed my mind. I had to try harder to keep an open mind. "Johnny must think I'm a real bitch."

"No comment." He sipped his drink.

"He said that? He actually said that?" I asked in disbelief. Annika would defend me, wouldn't she?

"No, he didn't *say* it. He wouldn't say it to her or to me. She'd whip him with her words, and I'd whip him with my fists." He glanced at me over the couch. "But it's pretty clear the dislike is mutual."

"You'd beat him up for me?" The wrong piece to get stuck on since violence shouldn't be appealing in any form. The sense of protectiveness warmed my chest against my will.

He held my gaze for a beat. "You're my wing-woman and cock-blocker. I couldn't function without you."

I laughed and left the laptop on the kitchen table to sit beside him on the couch. He put his hand on my leg, and I gazed at his familiar face, enjoying him, here.

With a sigh, I said, "I don't want a random for a roommate. But I smiled and pretended to be happy for Annika because *apparently* I've been the world's worst friend the last few months." I frowned. "Have I been the world's worst friend?"

He gulped his fruit cocktail. "No, you have not. You might have gotten caught up in painting Johnny as the devil in disguise a couple times."

Johnny's temper in those two instances had been enough to raise my hackles and get my blood pumping. How could that much rage live in him and *not* spill out sometimes? Was it wrong for me to worry about Annika bearing the brunt of it?

Sebastian flipped to the news, and we watched the clips in silence. The lead story was about an NFL football player who'd been shot by his wife. He'd been beating her for years.

"Great timing." He grimaced.

"Do you think someone suspect what was happening?" How could anyone realize and say nothing?

"Maybe. Hard to say." He observed me out of the corner of his eye. "You're going to hate me for saying this, but football organizations protect their own."

"Even when their own are hurting someone else?" I raised my eyebrows. Now I'd wonder whether he was being honest with me about Johnny. "The world's changing, you know."

Sebastian laughed. "The world might be changing, but football isn't. Not yet. This is the same organization that covered up the long-term impact of concussions for years. They understood what those head injuries were doing and did nothing."

"Why do you play?" A sport where players suffered such lasting consequences for money shouldn't be worthy of his love.

"It's in my blood. I couldn't quit, even if I wanted to. I gave up a lot to get here, to be this close to the NFL. Years with my dad in Bermuda, steady girlfriends, tight friendships—all of it for the game. The game comes before everything."

"Worth it?"

He nodded. "So far, yeah. I gotta stay healthy, stay on the right side of the people who matter, and who knows? I could be in the NFL in a couple of years."

"That's the goal?"

"Since the moment I realized the NFL was a thing. Even before I was sure I could play."

"I admire that." And I meant it. "To be so sure of your path is impressive. You were what—thirteen—when you decided to start playing?"

"When I got serious, yeah. My parents' divorce might have had something to do with my initial interest, not that I've ever said that out loud. For them the separation was easy, or at least they made it appear easy. Maybe it wasn't. I've never asked. But for me and Kiara? It was hard. Life as we knew it was gone. I threw myself into football, she threw herself into school."

"School?"

One side of his mouth quirked up. "She's a criminal lawyer."

I laughed. "You're joking. Why didn't you say that before?"

A hint of a smile. "You didn't seem too fond of those types of lawyers."

I gave him a wry look. "I might become one of those lawyers. Who knows?" I patted his thigh. "That's so exciting, Sebastian." I squeezed. "In Bermuda?"

"Yeah, she's starting out. I'm proud of her."

"Well, you should have told me." I searched his face, pleased he gave me a piece of himself. "Do you want another drink?"

"Sure." He handed me his empty glass.

I checked my email on the way to the couch, not that I expected student housing to respond to my inquiry outside office hours.

"Know anyone looking for a roommate?" I passed him his drink and slumped into the cushions beside him.

He tipped his cup up a few times and seemed to be considering his answer. "I know someone who could move in—they're on a semester-by-semester contract at the place they live."

"Who would do that kind of arrangement?" I asked, confused.

"Frat houses." Sebastian took a gulp from his glass.

I stared at him. We were so close, and I wished I'd sat farther away. I'd gotten used to the feel of him against me and sitting far away from him had become more awkward than being side by side. Until now.

"Please tell me you're not suggesting another football player moves in here?"

He chuckled at my panicked expression. "Just me, Nattie."

"You?" I squeaked out.

He smiled, but it wasn't with his usual confidence. "Am I that bad?"

"No, no, it's..." I fumbled for the right words. "Well, how would that work, exactly?"

"I'd pay you rent, fix the little things that crop up, take Annika's room, hang out with you excessively."

Ideas ran through my brain, and they'd make me sound jealous. I wouldn't cope with an endless parade of women heading in and out of his room. We weren't dating, but seeing what he did when he wasn't with me would crush me.

"Uh, well, we're both single and maybe we might want to spend time with other people?" I tried to make the question appear as though I was concerned about myself. My heart thumped a heavy tune in my chest.

Sebastian frowned. "You said you weren't into the one-night stand thing unless you were on vacation? Is that what we're talking about?"

"Uh." I stumbled. Somehow this conversation had turned in the wrong direction. "No, I—I mean..."

He laughed. "Oh, you're worried about me?"

My face was on fire. If there was a mirror in front of me, I'd be able to see that I was, no doubt, ketchup red. He tried to catch my gaze, but I wouldn't let him. "I guess it was going to get awkward at some point. Why not now, right?"

His grin was in his voice. "I'll make you a deal. I won't bring any girls home without telling you first. You want a note? Sock on the door? Code word? Bat-signal meme?"

Nope. None of that. I didn't want him bringing home anyone. "I'm not sure, Sebastian."

"The offer is there. I have to give a month's notice if I'm not coming back. End of November, I'll need to know if I'm moving in here in January or if I'm staying put." He leaned into the couch as though the outcome didn't matter to him.

Meanwhile, my heart raced out of control, and my palms were coated with slick sweat. An image of Sebastian fresh from the shower flashed in my mind. Seeing him first thing in the morning, having him be the last person I saw at night, terrified and amazed me.

He reached out and squeezed my hand. "It'd be okay, Nattie. I promise."

What was he promising? I couldn't bring myself to ask for elaboration. "I'll make a decision by the end of November for sure." Please let student housing respond tomorrow. Someone random sounded wonderfully appealing.

Anyone, anyone but Sebastian.

Chapter Seventeen

Annika put the finishing touches on her makeup, and we locked eyes in the mirror. "Sebastian said he offered to move in here."

"Oh, my God! Are you two BFFs now or what? Why would he tell you?"

"He was trying to figure out how I'd react. I told him having him live here would freak you out."

Pink rose to my cheeks as I examined myself. "Well, you were right."

"Yeah, he said you practically jumped out of your skin."

"I did not." I gave her my best as-if expression. "The thought of him bringing home his parade of conquests made me want to vomit. What he saw was me trying to hold in my vomit."

"Anyway, it's a good idea. He can pay rent. You know him, you like him, he fixes things, and we can hang out together."

"It's a terrible idea. It's an idea for someone who has no other ideas and her rent is due." I pointed at her in the mirror. "You and Johnny have a place picked out, don't you?"

Annika gave me a helpless look. "He fell in love with an apartment not far from here. He might have already put the deposit down?"

I rolled my eyes. "Of course he did. Of course." I pursed my lips in annoyance. "Well, I won't be without a roommate no matter what, I guess." I tilted my head to the side, checking to see if my foundation was even. "You saw the place?"

"Not yet," Annika said. "I didn't want to fall in love with it if you couldn't get someone to split the rent."

"Right." I nodded as though her rationale made complete sense.

But it didn't. Annika and I spent months looking for our townhouse because she loved to search. She enjoyed touring apartments and houses, speculating on layout, where furniture would go, where the TV would look best. Part of the excitement for her was the hunt. He either didn't realize or didn't care. She wanted me to be supportive, despite my reservations. I could do that, but I didn't enjoy it.

"That's great you've managed to find a place so quickly." Pieces of Annika were drifting on the current of Johnny's whims.

"You ready?" She stuffed her products into her bag.

"Are you coming home tonight?" I asked.

"Probably not." Annika smiled. "I can't wait until I don't have to live in two places anymore. I never have the right things at either place."

When I slid into the passenger seat, I was thankful for Annika's cloth seats. Leather was so cold this time of year. I stared out the window while we made the short drive to the stadium.

The team was doing well. Johnny's and Sebastian's names circled campus as whispered prayers. Playoffs, championships, and MVP trophies dogged them. If anyone recognized me as Sebastian's friend, they tried to talk to me about the game or about stats or about something else I knew nothing about. Those experiences were always embarrassing. They probably assumed I was a football bunny—a pretty, but dumb, girl. My embarrassment almost made me want to recommit to learn the rules, follow along closer, understand more about Sebastian's position or what made him so great. *Almost*.

"They're doing well, right?" I asked Annika after we'd parked and started walking to the entrance. Johnny had given her VIP passes, which I didn't even realize happened for regular games.

"Yeah, exceptionally well this season. Johnny and Sebastian make each other better. Best thing to happen to either of them was Sebastian transferring. They read each other on the field beautifully."

"People stop me to talk football." I rubbed my cheeks in embarrassment.

Annika laughed so hard she had to stop walking, and she clutched her middle. "Oh, my God. You must hate that, and the conversation must be so awkward. What do you tell people?"

"I try to go along with whatever they're saying, but then they'll ask me what Sebastian thinks, and..." I made a spiraling motion with my fist and then had it explode, "I can't string together a coherent sentence. I'm a dumb girl, and I *hate* it."

Annika's smile faded. "What are you going to do?"

"Two options." I held up my fingers. "Stop hanging out with any football people." I hesitated. "Or I learn at least the basics." Internally I groaned, but I tried not to let it leave my lips. "Teach me, Obi-Wan."

"Even an incorrect *Star Wars* reference. You must be desperate."

I snorted. "I didn't even get that quote right?"

"Don't worry, I'm not your only hope." She winked. "Sebastian would probably love to teach you a thing or two." She did a shimmy-shake.

"I'm not interested in his thing or two."

"That's not the problem and you know it." She guided us to our seats near the players' bench.

I sighed. "What are we doing after this?"

"A pub, if you're up for it. Johnny wanted low key." She gestured toward the field. "Are you going to commit to learning this time? Or are you going to study your nails and wish you'd remembered to paint them?"

"I'll listen. I might also examine my nails, but I'll listen."

"All right, I'll start with the person I'm most interested in and then move to the person you're most interested in. They work together, so hopefully their interactions will make sense."

I waved her on with a flourish. "I am your humble student."

She snorted. "Humble, sure." She settled into her seat. "Okay, let's do this."

She started talking and pointing to the field. When I invested my brain into the game and listened to Annika's explanations, her connection to Johnny made more and more sense. Speaking about football, she was charismatic. How could he not love someone who worshipped the game as much as him?

At one point, when Sebastian came off the field, our gazes connected, and he grinned. A bunch of girls in front of us turned and rolled their eyes at the sight of me and Annika. I could only imagine what they were thinking. Johnny and Annika were becoming well-known on campus. People who cared about football also realized I'd been spending a lot of time with Sebastian.

When the game ended, I assumed we'd hang outside the locker rooms to wait, but Annika steered us to her car.

"We're not waiting?" I followed a few steps behind her.

"Sebastian's driving them, and he's going to park at our place," Annika said as though I knew. "Making himself comfortable in his new home." She threw the comment over her shoulder.

"If he becomes my roommate, I need to date someone else." I rubbed my hands together while I waited for the car to heat up.

Annika stared at me as though I was being stupid. Her dark hair brushed the steering wheel. "Or you sleep with Sebastian on the regular."

"Or I go insane from watching him sleep with other girls."

She drove out of the parking lot and turned toward the pub. "I haven't said anything because I don't know if Sebastian wants you to realize what's happening. But there haven't been any other girls the last couple of weeks. At least none that I've seen or heard. Zero. Those frat boys are town bikes—every girl wants a ride, but he hasn't accepted any offers."

I shrugged, but my heart broke into a sprint. "Doesn't mean he's not going to their places. He's given me no indication he's not still doing whatever he does."

Annika frowned. "The way he talks about you, Nat..." She sighed. "There's something there."

I pursed my lips. "I wouldn't deny a connection. But it's not enough. It's not enough."

We picked our regular section where people were able to spread out or sit close. Annika ordered Johnny a beer, and I was confident enough in Sebastian's tastes to order him a drink as well.

The players burst through the pub door, and the ruckus drifted to us. As they headed toward our area, there was a mixture of teammates and women. Gabriella, Troy's girlfriend, was with them along with a bunch of others I didn't recognize.

Johnny slid into the booth next to Annika, and his phone rested face down on the table. Sebastian, on the other hand, was busy talking to other people. A girl passed him a drink, and he grinned.

My heart sank, and I stared at the pint beside mine. I spent the night learning football terms I'd never wanted to have cluttering my brain. I went to the game, even though it was cold and damp. I was contemplating having him move in with me—not in that way, but still. And there he was, greeting a chorus of girls, none of them me. I tilted his beer to my lips and chugged it.

Johnny's phone pinged, and he muted it.

"Who's that?" Annika reached for his phone.

He picked it up and angled the display, so it was only clear for him. "Nobody." He slipped it into his pocket rather than putting it on the table.

"Nobody?" Annika's tone was skeptical.

"You know what it's like after a win, babe. Lots of people message to get a word in." He didn't meet her gaze.

Annika seemed satisfied, but I pursed my lips. If the text had been game-related, he'd have let her see it. He liked to share those moments with her. That much was obvious by now.

I slid out of the booth and headed to the bar. I needed a drink, or maybe three hundred. Resting my elbows on the wood, I waited to catch the bartender's attention.

"Buy you a drink?" a deep male voice beside me asked.

I cocked my head, and my chin-length hair swished against the side of my face. He had a football player's build, but I couldn't for the life of me place him or remember his name. Tall, muscular, dark brown hair, pretty-boy-blue eyes. He'd do fine. Sebastian wasn't the only person capable of attracting other people.

I thrust out my hand. "Natalie." I smiled.

He grinned. "I know who you are." He broke eye contact and signaled the bartender with a nod and a finger. "You're the girl who has Sebastian tied in knots."

I turned and leaned my elbows on the polished wood with a heel hooked into the footrest. "You've got the wrong girl." I angled my head in a flirtatious way.

He drew the beers toward him and passed one to me before paying. He glanced over his shoulder and then to me. "Nope."

I refused to follow his gaze. I wasn't giving Sebastian the satisfaction. "If that's what you think, what are you doing buying me a drink?" I raised the glass to my lips.

"Curiosity, I suppose." He drank his beer and swiveled to face me. "I heard you don't even appreciate football."

"That much is true. Though, I did try to learn a couple things tonight." I lifted my chin. "What position do you play?"

"Safety," he said. "You know what that is?"

I scrunched up my nose, trying to remember everything Annika had told me. We'd focused on offense for obvious eye-catching reasons. So, that meant his position was most likely defensive. "Defense?"

He chuckled. "Last line of it."

"Lots of pressure?" I sipped my beer.

"Only if no one else does their job," he said. "I love being a clutch player."

We had settled into a nice rhythm of talking and drinking when I realized I hadn't asked his name.

"Theo," he said, grinning.

"Theo," I repeated, mulling over his name. "I like—" But when I glanced up to meet his gaze, he swooped in, capturing my lips before I finished my sentence. I hesitated for a fraction of a second, thinking of other lips I'd rather have pressed against mine. Stupid. No point in wishing for what I couldn't have. He wrapped his arm around my waist, almost tugging me into his lap.

"Wanna get out of here?" he murmured against my lips.

I chuckled and created space between us. "I'm flattered. I am. But I'm not that kind of girl. Even if I was, I'm not sure getting any sort of involved with another football player is a good idea."

"There is something going on between you and Sebastian?" He arched an eyebrow and downed his pint.

"No, no." I brushed off my slip of the tongue.

"So it wouldn't bother you that he's at the rear of the pub making out with another girl?" He indicated behind me.

Almost against my will, I turned to see a girl who'd tackled him before, draped across his lap. Her waist-length dark hair was a curtain. I couldn't be sure what was happening, but my imagination was more than capable of filling in the blanks.

I focused on Theo with false brightness. "Not even a bit." Inside, pieces of me were splintering into anger and self-righteousness tinged with humiliation.

Annika came up behind me and wrapped her arms around my shoulders. "We're heading out." She gave me a quick squeeze. She must have seen Sebastian's public display of grossness. "Do you want a ride back to the house? I'm staying with Johnny, but we can drop you?" She moved to my side, and her dark, worry-filled eyes searched my face.

I shrugged. "I'm fine." Even though fine was nowhere close to what I was feeling.

"I'll make sure she gets home okay." Theo met Annika's gaze and tipped his chin at Johnny, who stood behind her.

"You heard the man, Anni. Let's go." He scrolled through his phone, not bothering to acknowledge me.

"You sure?" Annika asked again, leaning into Johnny.

"Yeah, I'll be fine."

"Text me when you get home, so I know you're okay." Annika took Johnny's hand.

I nodded and drained the last of my pint.

"You want another?" Theo asked, eyeing me.

"No." I was having a hard time not staring in Sebastian's direction, and that view would lead to madness. "I kinda want to do a couple shots and get the hell out of here."

"Your wish." He signaled the bartender.

We did three shots of tequila each, and when I hopped off the bar stool, I wobbled. Theo grabbed my elbow to steady me.

"Easy there, lightweight." Theo chuckled. "Am I going to have to piggyback you to your place? How far is it?"

"Not far." I glanced up at him. I wasn't a short girl, but he was tall, maybe even taller than Sebastian. The alcohol was doing its job, dulling my senses, and I peeked to where I'd seen him last. He was chatting to another player, his back to me, and the girl was still draped over him, kissing his neck, running her hands over his body. Bile rose to my throat, burning along the way.

"You okay?"

"Peachy." I stumbled toward the door. I'd had more to drink than I realized.

We kept a brisk pace in the cool weather as we walked to my house.

"I—I mean, I'm not going to sleep with you," I blurted out once my street was visible in the distance.

He laughed. "I didn't agree to walk you home so you'd sleep with me." He rubbed the top of his head, messing up his dark hair. "Not that I'd say no if you invited me in."

As we approached my door, I slowed my pace. "Did you want to come in and wait for a cab?" Inviting him in was a bad idea, but it was cold. My stomach rolled with the beer and shots.

"Nah, that's okay. I'll walk."

We stood in my doorway for a moment before he eased his hand around my waist, tugging me close. "One for the road?" He dipped his head to kiss me. Sebastian had said those words to me once. While Theo kissed me, Sebastian was all I could think about. When he drew away, he gave me a quizzical glance.

"Just drunk," I said by way of explanation for what was probably a lackluster kiss.

He gave me another quick peck on the cheek and then disappeared down the path. I struggled to get my key in the lock and then moved around the house, getting ready for bed.

When I was drifting to sleep, loud giggling started up outside and drifted into my room. I threw off the covers and stumbled to the window. I wished I'd fallen asleep quicker.

The dark-haired girl was on the hood of Sebastian's car, and Sebastian was standing between her legs, hands on either side of her. They weren't kissing, but their bodies were intimately positioned, as though they were on the cusp of more.

Whatever point he was trying to prove, he'd made it. We hadn't said a single word to each other all night.

I turned away from the window, disgusted. My noise-canceling headphones were on the dresser, and I stuck them onto my ears. Not comfortable, but whatever. With a yank, the covers came over my head. I was thankful I'd had those last few shots. Otherwise, I'd never be able to sleep.

Chapter Eighteen

♥

Annika paid for my coffee and guided us to a booth. She threw her backpack against the wall and slumped down into the seat. Her makeup barely concealed her dark rings, and her blotchy complexion made her appear as though she'd been crying or under enormous stress.

"How are things going?" I slid in across from her. We were probably mirror images. I hadn't spoken to Sebastian in almost two weeks, and the silence was killing me. The ache in my chest wouldn't subside no matter what I did.

"I don't want to talk about me. What's going on with you and Sebastian? He's a beast at the house. Not even talking to me anymore. Grunts whenever I try to speak to him."

After seeing Sebastian with that girl, I agreed to a date with Theo. It went okay, but nothing about Theo made my heart kick into gear. I didn't want to close my eyes when I was with him and breathe in his scent. I didn't want to snuggle into the crook of his neck and never emerge. Just the thought of Sebastian made my heart jump out of my body and fall to pieces on the floor. Seeing him was ten times worse.

"Nothing is going on with him. I haven't spoken to him in a couple of weeks. I don't have a clue why he's in such a foul mood. Maybe the girl he made out with outside my window has ideas about his attitude? He should probably track her down." My tone was sour, angry. I hated the bitterness, but I couldn't control it.

"Come on, Nat. He saw you kiss someone else in the bar, in front of the team, and they knew how much time he'd been spending with you. Not to mention the fact the guy was Theo. He and Sebastian do not get along." Annika *tsked* and shook her head.

"How would I know any of that?" I sipped my too-hot coffee. "Annika, we've been over this a couple times. Sebastian came into the bar and completely ignored me. I was frustrated. Theo was a perfect outlet for that frustration. Maybe I was wrong? But Sebastian brought a girl to *my* parking lot outside *my* bedroom window. He took it to a whole other level."

"What are you going to go?" Annika leaned into the cozy booth.

This was our favorite off-campus coffee shop, not far from our house. I hadn't come here in weeks because football players sometimes wandered over here from the frat house. I'd done everything possible to avoid Sebastian and his crew.

"Well, after that stunt I can tell you what I'm not doing. I'm not having him as a roommate. Can you imagine?" I clenched my jaw, still so angry with myself and him and football in general. When Annika appeared at our house to get ready for the last game, I'd refused to attend. "I'm showing a couple of people the place after class."

"You haven't locked anyone in yet?" Annika fiddled with her phone.

"No, I haven't." The edge to my voice annoyed me.

She set her phone on the table. "Can I talk to you and you won't freak out and go all Natalie on me?"

Taking a deep breath, I willed my heart rate to settle after discussing Sebastian. I could be the supportive, helpful friend. "Yes."

"I think Johnny is still sleeping around." She took a big gulp of her coffee.

My first instinct was to cringe, and I smothered it. After an extra-long drink, I tilted my head from side to side. "What makes you suspect that?" Questions were good. Maybe I could lead her to a logical conclusion.

"He's been secretive with his phone the last couple of weeks. He's always been protective of it. I never had access to it like he did mine, but he never stopped me from looking at it. But lately, it's always facedown, and as soon as it goes off, he's on it. It's in his pocket, in his bag, anywhere but somewhere I can see it." Annika fiddled with the spoon she'd used to stir her coffee.

Deep breath. "Well, you told me once that you'd be fine with him sleeping around."

"Yeah, well, saying that and doing that are two different things, aren't they?" Annika made eye contact. "I can't sleep. I keep running scenarios around and around in my head. When? Where? With who? How many?"

"Have you asked him?"

"No," Annika admitted. "I think he'd get mad."

"You don't have to move in with him in January if you're not certain about him." I crossed my fingers under the table. I could cancel my roommate interviews. "Give yourself more time to figure out what you want."

Annika sighed. "That's the thing, I *want* to move in with him. I want to be with him. I enjoy feeling like his number-one person. Lately, I just—I'm not sure. Something's not right."

"Trust your gut. If the situation doesn't feel right, there is probably something to that instinct." That was normal, reasonable advice. My real opinion was to run far and fast away from him.

"My request isn't fair, but can you give me a week before you pick a roommate? I'll try to talk to Johnny." Annika tipped up the last of her coffee.

"Yeah, I'll interview people today and tell them I'll be making a decision in a week or so. Seem okay?" I suggested. "You could spend a few nights away from him. See if your absence reminds him not to take you for granted?"

She was quiet for a moment. "What if it makes him realize he can do without me?"

My chest tightened. "Oh, Annika. Any guy who believes that—you don't want to be with them anyway, right?"

"Yeah." She gave a small nod. "Yeah, you're right." Her voice lacked conviction. "If we can get through living in the frat house, things will be better once it's just the two of us."

I nodded, but I didn't agree. His secretive phone behavior and the frat house were two separate issues. On top of that, Annika looked terrible. Johnny couldn't be worth this much stress and anxiety.

"I gotta run," Annika said. "I might come home tomorrow night, if that's okay? You're right. Maybe a little distance will be useful for us."

"You're still paying rent." I smiled. "Probably a good idea to get your money out of it."

She laughed and leaned across the table to half hug me. "I miss you. I'm sorry I'm so scattered and absent lately. Everything will be better once I'm settled in the new place and not trying to live in two places at once."

"You still coaching the developmental football team?" I asked before she left.

"Yeah. Johnny has helped out a few times. The kids love it. He's so great with them." That dreamy look returned to her eyes.

I regretted bringing it up. "That's great." I offered a strained smile.

"Yeah. He'll be a fantastic dad someday." She slouched into the booth, her bag sitting on her lap. "That's the confusing part. One minute he's talking about kids, places to live, marriage, and everything, and the next minute he won't let me see his phone." She shook her head. "You're right. I should ask. Maybe there's a solid explanation." She stood. "I'm outta here. Text me later. I'm definitely coming home tomorrow night."

"Sounds good." I rose to give her a last hug. "I'd do anything for you, Annika. You realize that, right?" I added, in case she needed to hear it.

She grinned. "Oh, Nat. That's why I wanted to talk to you. I can count on you no matter what."

My heart lightened. At least our friendship was on stable ground. "I'll see you tomorrow night. Home manicures and pedicures?"

"Set it up! Oh, and alcohol. Lots of alcohol. I'll be there after I'm done coaching. I won't even bother going to the team practice tomorrow night." She backed away from me and headed for the door.

I gave her a wave and then glanced at my half-full cup. I sighed and slid into my seat and took a sip. On my home screen was a text from Theo. He was persistent and pleasant enough to be around. I replied to his text.

A draft hit me as the door to the coffee shop opened. My heart leapt into my throat at the sight of the guy framed in the doorway.

Sebastian.

He stood for a minute, rubbing his hands and scanning the place. I wasn't positive if he was searching from habit or if he was checking for someone. His jeans and winter jacket made me want to walk over and envelop him. The weather hadn't been cold enough for a winter jacket a couple weeks ago when I'd last seen him. When he perused the coffee shop, his gaze landed on me.

Two weeks ago, he would have broken into a grin, amusement lighting his face. Would he acknowledge me now? Give me a sign we could return to even ground? That what we'd both done wasn't a deal-breaker for either of us? I wasn't even sure that was true.

His gaze shuttered, and he went to the counter to order. With a to-go cup in his hand, he didn't even glance in my direction as he left. My stomach dropped into my shoes. Was that us now? We couldn't manage a hello in a crowded café? He saw me.

I grabbed my backpack off the seat and left my coffee unfinished. I burst out the door, scanning the street to check which direction he'd gone. When I caught sight of his back heading toward campus, I jogged until I got close to him, thankful I'd put on running shoes that morning.

"Sebastian!" I called when his pace didn't slow.

He stopped walking, but he didn't face me. When he did turn, it was slow and deliberate. He waited for me to catch up with him but didn't say a word.

I fumbled at his silence. He wasn't going to give me anything? Not even a hello? "Ah," I said at a loss. "How are you?"

He shook his head. "You haven't talked to me in two weeks and that's all you've got?"

"I wasn't certain I'd ever talk to you again." I twisted the strap of my bag.

A frown creased his brow. "Why *are* you talking to me? You made yourself pretty clear a couple of weeks ago."

I bristled. "*I did*? What about you bringing a girl to my parking lot? The space outside my bedroom, by the way. Such a great show. Thanks for making it obvious what was going to happen next." I crossed my arms, anger coursing through me at the memory. "Seeing you at the bar with her, in the driveway, those images are going to stay with me."

He shrugged. "I guess that goes for both of us, Nattie. Of all the guys on the football team you could have made your point with, you choose the one guy I can't stand. Seemed like a pretty good sign you didn't want me around anymore. Nothing subtle about that either."

I gave him a bewildered look, and my anger deflated in an instant. "I had no idea you didn't like him, Sebastian. How would I know that? We never talk about football or the team or any of that."

"It'd be easy enough to get that information from Annika." Sebastian took a drink of his coffee and stared over my head.

He was this pissed off at me after his display at the bar? I was the one who should have been mad at him. I *was* mad at him, damn it.

"Why would I ask her? What happened wasn't planned. I swear to you, Sebastian." I sighed, frustrated. "He kissed me—I—" Silence hung between us, and I could tell he didn't believe me. "I was mad at you, yeah, but I wouldn't have gone anywhere near Theo if I'd known it would do this to us."

Seeing him with the other girl broke something in me, and I wasn't sure we could be fixed. But those were words I would not say.

"You were mad at *me*?" Sebastian's gaze traveled to mine.

"Yeah, I was mad." I shifted my feet and shoved my hands into my coat pockets. "It was dumb." The distance between us had somehow closed. "I'm mad now, but it's not about something dumb anymore."

"You're mad about that girl?" he asked. His fingertips eased a flyaway strand of my hair behind my ear.

"Of course. Of course I'm mad about that girl. You'd offered to move in with me—not like that, obviously, but still. You'd told me it would be 'okay.' If that's your version of okay, then you and I aren't anywhere close on our definitions."

His hand brushing my hair off my face was warm from holding his coffee. His thumb grazed my cheek, and I wanted to lean into him, press his palm against me.

"I've missed you, Nattie. Can we agree not to do stupid shit to each other anymore?" His eyes were soft with sincerity.

Tears pricked, and I had to break his gaze, afraid I'd burst into tears.

"Come 'ere," Sebastian said, wrapping his coffee-free hand around my back and tugging me to him.

I threw my arms around his neck and rose on my toes. I breathed in his scent and stifled a sigh. Pathetic. Pathetically wonderful.

Sebastian groaned and secured me tighter, burying his face in my neck. "You always smell so amazing," he murmured.

Desire stirred in my stomach at his words, the tone of his voice, his proximity. Anywhere but in the middle of the street, I might have put our friendship at risk by kissing him. Unbidden, the last place I'd seen his lips flashed into my memory, and I drew away, avoiding his gaze.

"Where are you headed?" I asked.

"Campus. I have a meeting with Coach. I played like shit last game." Sebastian kept his arm around my waist. He hesitated and then let me go. "It's none of my business, but are you planning on seeing Theo again?"

"I went on a date with him." Out of the corner of my eye, I caught the tightening of his jaw.

"I know that already." He gazed off into the distance, not meeting my eyes. "I mean beyond that. 'Cause if he's someone you're interested in, we should stop hanging out altogether."

"I'm not interested in Theo." I prayed he didn't ask me any follow-up questions.

He gave a curt nod. "Okay."

"You and the girl on your car?" I stuffed my hands back into my pockets.

He shook his head. "It was nothing. Nothing." He looked me in the eye and then hesitated before plunging on. "It would have been less than nothing if I hadn't seen you with Theo."

What did I say in response? He was interested in me; he'd made his desire clear several times. But the notion that me kissing Theo inspired such a swift, almost vindictive reaction in Sebastian was shocking. Why?

The memory of him with someone else haunted me. Every time I considered caving and trying to see him, one memory reminded me why Sebastian was the wrong choice. There would always be other girls, waiting in the wings, sweeping in. A single misstep from me and, boom, he was gone. Did he take the girl home? Did he sleep with her? The truth might break us forever. He never hid who he was, what he was after.

"Do you have a new roommate yet?" Sebastian asked.

"I'm interviewing people tonight after my class." I shouldn't have left my half-finished coffee on the table. The coffee maker at my house wasn't working.

He took a long sip from his hot drink. He must have noticed my envious glance because once he'd taken a sip, he passed me the cup. "Peace offering?" he suggested.

I accepted the coffee and gave him a half smile. "I guess we have to start somewhere, right?"

He looped his arm around my shoulders and kissed my temple. "I'll walk you to class and then go to my you're-a-shitty-player-this-week meeting."

I looked over at him. "Why weren't you playing well?"

His gaze was thoughtful and tender. "Doesn't matter anymore." He kissed my temple again.

I leaned into him and let him walk me to class, content for the first time in weeks.

Chapter Nineteen

♥

I took my nail polish colors out of my box and set them on the coffee table in front of the couch. Annika riffled through them.

"So, did you talk to him?" I plucked out a pale purple.

"I did." She smiled. "You were right. I should have asked him earlier. He said he'd been organizing a surprise party at our new place and didn't want me to know about it." She shook her head. "I felt like an idiot when he explained it to me."

Weird. I hadn't gotten an invitation to any party. "Oh yeah? When was he planning to have the party?" I hoped Annika would notice I hadn't been told.

"No date yet. He was feeling friends out for weekends and so forth that could work. He didn't want me to catch wind of it. But now it's completely ruined. He was kind of angry," Annika said. "At least I feel better. My gut feeling was nothing." She examined a bottle labeled tangerine and set it down. "So if any of the people you interviewed for the room are good, you can pull the trigger."

She settled on a deep red and shook the container while I mulled over Johnny's explanation for his behavior. I wasn't going to dig, even though I was positive I'd hit on something. His cover was thin at best.

"The potential roommates were duds," I admitted. "I don't want just anyone."

She gave me a sideways look. "Sebastian said you two worked out your misunderstanding."

I sighed and applied the first coat to my nails. "Sure, yeah. Except every time I think about him, I picture that girl perched on his lap, mauling him. Or him standing between her legs with a *fuck me* vibe vibrating off them."

Annika winced. "Ouch."

"Tell me about it." I groaned. "I want to pretend what happened doesn't matter. Nothing has happened between me and Sebastian. Nothing. Not a kiss, a fumble, a drunken tumble. Nothing. And yet, seeing him with that girl was worse than anything I could imagine. Being with him and having him cheat on me? I wouldn't survive."

"You don't know he would cheat," Annika admonished me.

"I also don't know if he even wants a relationship with me. Sex? Yes. A relationship? Not so much." I held my nails out, admiring them. "Besides, you're the person who said professional athletes cheat, right? Wasn't that you?" I eyed her warily. "You can't retract that statement now because you don't want it to be true anymore."

She laughed, but it didn't have its usual fullness. "Maybe I was melodramatic. I'm sure there are athletes who have normal, healthy relationships."

I swallowed my comment. "Right," I said. "Some people get lucky."

"Or they work hard at it. I mean, Gabriella and Troy seem to be able to manage it, right?" She fixed a nail with a Q-tip.

They were a good example, but Troy wasn't a professional. From what I'd heard while hanging around the team, he wasn't likely to get drafted either.

"What would you do if you found out that Johnny was sleeping with other girls?" I asked.

She paused her application and sat back. "Not sure anymore."

I stayed silent and continued to apply my color.

"I love him. Crazy about him. The thought of him with anyone else? I can't." Annika admired her nails. "But the thought of not having him? I think that might actually be worse."

Anger boiled in me under the surface. She was worth so much more than his scraps of affection, and her shortchanging herself made me want to neuter Johnny.

My phone beeped, and I checked my nails before picking it up.

Johnny's been trying to get Annika. Is she there?

I sighed at Sebastian's message. His go-between status sucked.

"Where's your phone, Annika? Apparently, Johnny has been trying to get you?"

She hopped up and reached over the couch. She waggled the blank screen at me. "It's dead. You have a charger?"

"In my room." I waved her away down the hall. "I'll text Sebastian back?"

"No, don't bother," she said from my bedroom. "When my phone is charged, I'll text him or call him myself. He probably wants to find out if I'm going there tonight."

"Okay." I stared at my screen. Sebastian would notice I'd read it. I turned it off, hoping to avoid any other texts or calls while I enjoyed my time with Annika.

A couple hours later, we'd devoured a pizza, painted our fingers and toes, and had a gossip about everyone we knew. We'd also split two bottles of wine. My bed was starting to whisper my name when the door shook. Someone was pounding on it hard enough to make the hinges rattle.

Annika's eyes went wide. "Oh, no. I didn't text or call Johnny. My phone is in your room." She jumped off the couch and headed down the hall to grab her phone.

I checked the peephole. She was right. I swung open the door, a forced smile on my face. "Johnny, what are you doing here?"

"Where's Anni? Is she here? She's not answering her goddamned phone." He shouldered his way past me, fire in his eyes.

"Ah, yeah, she's here. Her phone was dead." I closed the door behind him.

"For hours?" he asked. "What were you two doing tonight?" He searched the townhouse.

"Just girl stuff."

She came up the hall, and Johnny pounced. "What the hell, Anni? I've been calling and texting. I had Sebastian text Natalie. She read it and didn't even bother to respond." He glanced at me, his expression brimming with anger. "How hard was it to tell me what was going on?"

"I'm sorry." She held up her cracked phone. "We got talking and lost track of time."

"Well, grab your shit. Let's go." He ushered her toward the exit with his arm.

"I was going to stay here tonight." Annika hesitated.

"What? Why?" Anger tinged his voice. "Come with me. We can chat about why you have this device if you can't be bothered to answer it."

"Whoa." I held up my hands. He was going too far with the verbal attack. She made a mistake. What the hell was his problem?

"Stay out of this, Natalie," Johnny said. "This is between me and Annika."

"You're being harsh with her." I moved so that I was blocking her from leaving. Now that I was closer, I caught a whiff of alcohol. "I hope you walked here."

"It's none of your business." He kept his attention focused on Annika. "Are you coming home with me or not?"

"I'll grab my stuff." She rushed around the room.

"Annika," I said. "You can stay."

"No, no." She tucked her long hair behind her ears. "It's not worth a fight. I'll go. I should probably go anyway. Johnny's right. I should have called or texted. Of course, he was worried." She rambled as she threw things into her purse. Giving me a quick squeeze, she slipped out the door.

Johnny grabbed her elbow, and she flinched, but he didn't let go. He practically dragged her along the path from our townhouse, close talking in her averted face. The urge to run out and separate them welled up in me. If I did, I'd ruin my friendship with her. She didn't see him the same way I did.

At the end of the path, Sebastian rounded the corner at the same time Johnny and Annika reached the junction. Johnny released her elbow and slid his arm to her waist, as though he hadn't been irate, full of rage. The transformation was so swift and absolute I started to understand why Sebastian had faith in Johnny when I had almost none. His acting was impeccable.

They stood chatting at the end of the path for a moment, Annika massaging her elbow, before Sebastian sidestepped them and came up the walkway with his hands tucked in his jacket pockets. With each step, my heart pitter-pattered and stutter-stopped. The quicksand was dragging me under.

He stopped in front of me, scanning my face. I'm not sure what he saw, but he wasn't smiling. He reached out and rubbed my arm, covered in goosebumps from the cold. I'd been so consumed with watching Johnny and Annika, I'd forgotten a sweater.

"You okay?" he asked. "It's cold out here."

I weighed my options. He wouldn't believe me. Johnny was playing him and maybe all the football guys. But what I'd seen between him and Annika would only get worse.

"Fine." I moved aside to let him in the open door. What was this sensation coursing through me? Lust for Sebastian or rage at Johnny? They were both powerful.

Sebastian stepped past me. "Sorry to show up so late. Johnny was pretty wound up, so I thought I should come check." He took off his coat and hung it up. "But he seemed fine just now."

My heart thumped. "You were worried about Johnny or Annika?" I collapsed into the couch. What I had seen was anything but fine.

"Beer?" He headed for the fridge.

"Why not? I've already had two bottles of wine." I threw a blanket over my legs and plucked at the material. Might as well add a hangover.

He passed me a beer, hesitated at the edge of the couch, and plopped next to me. He picked up the remote. "I was worried about you, not Johnny *or* Annika."

"Me?" I was focused on how he hadn't sat close enough to touch me. So much space between us when there was usually none.

"I know what he's like when he's mad." He glanced at me out of the corner of his eye. "And you don't back down easily."

"I kinda resent that. When we weren't talking, I was the first to speak to you." I gulped my beer.

He relaxed into the couch and nodded. "It's different when you're defending a friend. Sometimes you say or do things you wouldn't do for yourself."

That was certainly true.

Here I was, sitting next to Sebastian, drinking beer, wishing I could figure out a way to be close to him and far away at the same time. If Annika was doing this push-pull with a guy, I'd tell her to knock it off.

"Is Johnny seeing other girls?" Annika's suspicion was fresh in my mind.

Sebastian avoided eye contact. "I don't want to get in the middle."

"You're already in the middle if you're texting me to get Annika to text Johnny. You let yourself be put there." His non-answer was answer enough.

"I'm not giving anyone dirt on anyone else. I'm not blowing up relationships or saying things that might not be one hundred percent true." Sebastian drank his beer, jaw rigid. "That's the middle I'm talking about."

At some point, the middle might be the least of Sebastian's concerns. He'd have to pick an actual side if Johnny's behavior got any worse. I'd be standing with Annika once the dust settled. I was afraid I knew where he'd be too.

"You want to talk about something else?" I plucked the remote from his hand and flipped to a music only station.

He chuckled, the tension leaving. "Yes."

"Do you want to hear how terrible my roommate interviews have been going?" I tucked the blanket around my legs.

Sebastian tugged at the blanket, stretching it over his legs too. He took a long drink of his beer. "Sure, Nattie. Give me your horror stories."

"One of the girls asked about my policy on drugs. She did a little light dealing of cocaine and heroin and wanted to be sure I'd be okay with that. I'm glad she mentioned it, but also—who says that?"

Sebastian shook his head. "A dealer?"

"She wasn't even the worst. Another person was a smoker."

"Oh, no—not a smoker." Sebastian feigned shock.

"Smoking is a disgusting habit and makes everything smell terrible." I held up a finger to stop his laugh.

"Yes, 'cause smoking is worse than drug dealing." Sebastian's lips twitched. "That can't be the end of it."

"One of the guys I interviewed had a snake collection. Real snakes," I said. "The last guy today gave me the creeps. He asked if I had an issue with physical contact between roommates because I was mighty fine. He was gross."

Sebastian went still beside me. He took another drink of his beer and then set it on the table. "Is someone aware you have these guys coming here to check out the place? Should you be interviewing them by yourself?"

I shrugged. "All the interviews are arranged by email, so there's a trail if something happened."

"Why am I more concerned than you are?" Sebastian frowned.

"My dad's a cop. I was taking self-defense classes as soon as I emerged into the world. It's second nature to me." I gave him a steady look. "I can take care of myself."

"Nattie, you're tall, and you do that kickboxing thing, but if a guy is big, and he's determined, he can do a lot of damage."

He was referring to the football field, but his point was clear. I'd watched them run into each other full tilt, and if that was what he was picturing, I could see how he'd have a hard time believing I could look after myself.

"If you're going to interview a guy for the room, can I be here, please?"

"Why?" With each sip of my beer, I was getting farther from tipsy and closer to drunk. I pushed the blanket off me, prepared to get another drink.

"'Cause if anything ever happened to you, I'd hunt the guy down and kill him." He didn't make eye contact, but my heart thump-thumped in my chest. "It would completely ruin my football career." He gave me a wry smile.

"I'd hate to instigate murder. It might make me want to be a criminal lawyer."

"I know a damn good lawyer in Bermuda." Sebastian's lips tilted into a not-quite smile. "Murder could be avoided if you agree to let me be here."

I shrugged. "If it's that important to you, I'll book the interviews around your schedule." I rose to go to the kitchen. "Beer?"

"Nah, I'm good." He settled into the couch.

When I walked away, my phone buzzed. Who would text me at this time of night? Annika? I grabbed the beer, but when I came back, he was putting on his coat.

"You're leaving?" My shoulders slumped in disappointment.

His hazel eyes were hard to read. Was that regret in his depths? "Yeah, practice in the morning." He let out a frustrated sigh and rubbed his head. "Look—Nattie—if you don't want me hanging around, tell me, okay?"

"What?" My drunken brain stalled on this sudden shift. "I agreed to let you come here next week for my roommate interviews. And if I don't pick someone next week, I'm gonna be screwed for rent in January." I rambled, but I was rattled. "Where is this coming from?"

"I gotta go. Text me the times if you want me to come." He opened my front door. The cold breeze swept in, making me shiver. "Just be sure." He shut the door, leaving a chill behind.

For a moment, I stood there, stunned. Then my phone buzzed again, and I hustled to the table, hoping it was Sebastian giving me an explanation for his abrupt exit.

We on for our date this weekend? Looking forward to it.

I stared at my phone in disbelief. Oh shit. I'd agreed to the second date with Theo before Sebastian walked into the coffee shop the other day. He saw my text message.

Chapter Twenty

T he numbers on the clock ticked over to three a.m., and I couldn't sleep. Sebastian hadn't responded to any of my text messages. Alcohol still coursed through my veins, and I didn't have a class until later in the day tomorrow. He had practice in the morning, but worry was eating holes in my stomach.

I threw off the covers and put on my warm clothes. I grabbed my phone and keys. At the threshold of my front door, I zipped my coat up to the top and secured my scarf. Then, I started the cold walk to the frat house.

Sebastian wasn't answering, so I wasn't sure how I'd get someone to let me in. But it bothered me too much to leave things on such a negative note. We wouldn't go another two weeks without talking over a stupid misunderstanding.

I climbed the stairs to the frat's main entrance and hesitated. Music, quiet, but there, snuck out the cracks. Maybe I'd get lucky? I knocked.

Footsteps approached the door, and it swung back to reveal Gabriella, Troy's girlfriend, dressed in her bartending outfit.

"Oh, hey," I said. I'd expected a player.

She grinned. "You the reason Sebastian was in such a foul mood when he got home?"

"Maybe? I don't know what the hell I'm doing, but I'm here and I need to talk to him."

She moved from the door to let me step inside. "Top of the stairs, third door on your right."

I removed my boots and headed up the stairs. At the third door, I bit my lip. This could be a bad idea. I knocked.

"Go away. I have practice in the morning." Sebastian's voice was muffled.

"Sebastian?" I whispered.

Through the thin wood, I heard his feet hit the floor. They padded to the door. He swung it open and pressed his shoulder into the frame. He was clad only in boxer briefs.

Heart meet heart attack. I drank him in like I'd been thirsty for weeks.

"Natalie?" He squinted into the hall light. "You walked here in the middle of the night?"

"I might be drunk." I couldn't force my gaze up from his taut chest. Without clothes he was a masterpiece. God help me. I'd never seen a man in real life so built and muscular.

He chuckled and grabbed my hand, pulling me into his room. I was pleased to see he was tidy beyond my house. Then I became too aware again of his half-naked body. There was only a bed, a desk, and a chair. He switched on his bedside lamp so a soft glow spread across his bedroom.

"What are you doing here? You shouldn't have walked here so late at night alone." He sat on his bed.

"You weren't answering my texts." Sweat was starting to run along my spine. The frat house was hot, or my body was on fire. Either was possible.

He picked up his phone. "I always set the alarm and then turn it off. It turns on when the alarm sounds."

"Oh." I half turned to the door. "Fancy." I stare at the closed door. "I'll go. I shouldn't have come. It was dumb."

"Nattie? What's going on?" Sebastian frowned.

I took a deep breath. "You left so quickly, and then my phone went off. Theo texted me. You saw that, right? But I'm not going on a second date with him. I'm not. I'm canceling it. I wouldn't do that. I forgot. I swear. I forgot. I didn't care enough to remember." To stop myself from reaching for him, I clutched my hands.

"I saw the text. I thought—well, I don't know what I thought." Sebastian stared at the floor before making eye contact. "Half the time I don't know what the hell I'm thinking when I'm around you."

The air grew thick. "So it's not just me?" I asked in a quiet voice.

He rose from the bed and unzipped my coat, pushing it off my shoulders. "You can't walk home by yourself."

"I can—"

"Look after yourself," Sebastian finished for me with a grin. "Please stay with me. It's only a couple hours until I have practice."

"I'm not taking off any more clothes." Fewer layers meant more temptations.

"Not even your scarf?" He teased.

"Okay, the scarf, but no more negotiating." I waggled my finger.

He climbed into his bed and lifted the covers for me to join him. I stood at the edge, staring down at him. Getting into bed with him would be tumbling into a canyon. Would I ever find my way out? With a sigh, I slid in and turned my back to him. He scooted forward, so he was pressed against me and threw his arm around my waist.

Nuzzling my neck, he murmured, "I'm glad you came."

Silence hung between us until I said into the darkness, "What are we doing, Sebastian?"

"I don't know. But I don't want to stop." He held me tighter.

I lay in the pitch black, listening to his breathing even out into sleep.

I didn't want to stop either.

The next morning, I woke up with a raging headache and some-one tapping on my foot. I moaned, rolled over, and realized I was not in my own bed. I sat straight up, pushing my hair out of my face.

"Sebastian?"

He laughed. "Yeah, you seemed pretty drunk last night. I'm glad I woke you up *after* I got back from practice."

He was at the end of his bed, freshly showered. His cologne hung in the room, and I realized I was surrounded by his scent. Would my clothes smell of him? If so, I might be sleeping with various items until his smell wore off. I shook my head, thankful he couldn't read my mind.

"Painkillers?" I placed my palm on my forehead.

He chuckled and went to a box on his desk. "Any prefer-ence?"

"Something legal?" The pounding of my head and my heart were in sync, doubling my agony.

He tossed a bottle to me and left the room. He returned a couple seconds later with a small glass of water. Sebastian passed it to me and watched as I took two pills before giving him the bottle.

After replacing the pills, he leaned against the desk. "You up for breakfast?"

I groaned and flopped onto his bed. "Mornings are the worst," I said. A thought occurred to me and I sat up. "Do people know I'm here? Does this look as though we hooked up?" I checked my clothed body to make sure we had not, in fact, hooked up.

He crossed his arms and stared at the ground. "That would bother you?"

"I—I don't want people gossiping about me." Lame. That was lame. I didn't want people to believe I was a conquest.

He laughed softly. "Sure, Nat. Whatever you say."

I tossed off the covers and stood up quicker than my head liked. When I wobbled, Sebastian steadied me. I glanced up at him, at the hurt etched in his features. I hurt his feelings. Somehow, I needed to fix the expression on his face.

"I wouldn't be embarrassed or ashamed if it was true, Sebastian. But it's not true, so it's wrong for people to assume that's why I came." I hoped that was enough.

"You and me. We know the truth. Whatever anyone else is saying, it doesn't matter." He slid his hand up my arm and around my back, tugging me into an embrace.

With him holding me, I wanted so badly to be his girlfriend. I shouldn't care what other people said about me or about Sebastian, and certainly not about both of us together. The reason I hadn't declared my feelings for him was exactly this situation. I was afraid of the rumors and gossip, but also the truth.

"Breakfast?" I stepped back and gathered up the few items I'd taken off the night before.

"I didn't tell anyone you were here," Sebastian said as I got dressed.

I shrugged. "Gabby knows I'm here, so I would guess Troy knows. How much farther that goes, I have no idea. We won't make a big deal about it and no one else will." I wrapped my scarf around my neck.

"I can ask him not to say anything if it's going to bother you." Sebastian put his own coat on.

"No, leave it. It is what it is." Hurt still tinged the outlines of his face, but I didn't understand how to get rid of it without admitting more than I was willing to say.

When I opened his bedroom door and stepped out, Annika emerged from a room down the hall. She stopped in her tracks, gawking from me to Sebastian and focusing on me. A sly grin crossed her face before she swallowed it.

"Nat." Her eyes flicked between me and Sebastian about a thousand times. "I didn't realize you were here."

She wore a tank top and carried her makeup bag. On the side closest to me, there were marks on her bicep. Bruises? Fingers? I wanted to walk over and examine her. To make her see how him manhandling her out of the house wasn't normal. I swallowed the words. She'd hate me for saying something in front of Sebastian and with Johnny within earshot.

I shrugged at her comment and glanced over my shoulder at Sebastian. "We're going to breakfast."

Her unspoken question floated around the hall.

Sebastian put his hands on my shoulders and gave them a quick squeeze before releasing me. "You and Johnny want to come?"

Inside, I cringed. More time with Johnny wasn't something I needed.

"Ah, I'll check. Just a sec." Annika disappeared into the bedroom. She popped her head out and said, "Give us a second. We're coming."

They both emerged from the room in a few minutes in hoodies and jeans. Johnny wrapped his arm around Annika's waist as we exited the house and headed for the '50s diner Sebastian and I had gone to before.

Sebastian picked the same booth we'd sat in last time we'd come and winked at me as he tugged me into the booth beside him. Our seating choices meant I was opposite Johnny's piercing gaze.

"So from wing-woman to being the one Sebastian beds. Impressive," Johnny said to me as soon as we got our coffees.

Sebastian jumped in before I could respond. "It's not like that, Johnny. Don't be a dick."

"Commenting on how it looks, not what it is." He sat back and gave Annika an amused smirk. "Let the gossip wheel do its thing."

"How's your arm, Annika? Looked as though you might have a bruise." I motioned to where I'd seen it.

Annika flushed and took a sip of her coffee. "I'm fine, Nat. Thanks for asking."

"Yeah, Nat. She's fine." Johnny turned his fierce gaze to me.

I smiled sweetly at Johnny. "Of course she's fine. You do such a great job of looking after her."

He laughed and sipped his coffee. The air was thick with tension, and if Sebastian wasn't regretting his impulsive invite, he had to be sitting at a different table.

"I'm glad you appreciate my ability to satisfy Annika." His double meaning was clear.

Annika's flushed deepened. "You two need to stop talking to each other," she said, motioning between us with her coffee cup. "Johnny, get out of the booth and we'll trade spots. You talk to Sebastian, and I'll talk to Nat."

"What could you two possibly have to say to each other you didn't get a chance to say last night? You were there for hours." Johnny's voice was tinged with humor but laced with something not at all funny. He slid out of the booth and switched with Annika without another word.

He and Sebastian started talking football, and I ducked my head, gathering my composure. "Sorry." My comments to

Johnny made me a good friend and a bad friend at the same time.

"It's fine. You two rub each other the wrong way. I keep hoping the animosity will get better, but it never does." Annika reached in front of Johnny to swap their coffees.

Johnny's gaze connected with mine one last time before sliding away. Sebastian rubbed my back as he continued to talk to Johnny.

Annika nodded at Sebastian's hand and raised her eyebrows.

"I have no idea," I admitted in answer to her question.

She smirked. "I think you do."

"I don't want to talk about this right now." I gulped my coffee.

The four of us fell into a rhythm of talking and eating until we were done. As long as Johnny and I didn't engage, we seemed to do fine. Annika and Sebastian could talk to any of us, but the minute Johnny and I connected on any level, a heaviness fell over the table.

We parted at the restaurant door, with Sebastian offering to walk with me to my place. He grabbed my arm and looped it through his, so I was leaning into him.

"Why were you asking about Annika's arm?"

I stared at the bare trees. "Johnny practically dragged Annika out of the house last night. He was angry. There were finger marks on her bicep this morning in the hallway."

Sebastian let out a deep breath. "I knew he was mad. He needs to figure out how to get himself together before he touches her. But they were fine when I talked to them along the path. She must bruise easily."

"Sebastian," I said. "He practically crushed a cell phone with his bare hand. Her skin isn't the problem."

He couldn't quite meet my gaze when he said, "Maybe not. I wouldn't know."

"If you knew, would you say something?"

"If I knew for sure?"

"Yes. No doubts," I agreed, even though my standard was much lower.

"Yeah, I'd say something to him." Sebastian shrugged his shoulders. "Maybe he didn't realize he was being too rough."

"What if he did or if he couldn't 'get himself together'? What then?"

"It wouldn't come to that," Sebastian said. "Johnny wouldn't risk his football career. He'll be drafted this year. He wouldn't risk his future."

"Because *you* wouldn't, Sebastian, doesn't mean *he* wouldn't."

"I know him, Nat. I know him," he said, glancing over at me. "You don't."

I let the subject drop as we reached my door. They did spend more time together, but Sebastian met Johnny at the start of the pre-season training camp. How well can you know anyone in a few months?

"Do you want to come in and I can give you the interview dates and times I have set?" I suggested. "I can switch any you want to be around for if they don't work."

He rubbed a hand along the small of my back and nodded. "Thanks. That'll make me feel a hell of a lot better."

Chapter Twenty-One

♥

While Annika and I watched the boys' game, she took me through positions, rules and plays, and I was understanding more.

"No luck with the roomie?" she asked when there was a timeout.

"None," I said with a sigh. "Sebastian vetoed the ones he was there to witness, and the others were wrong for other reasons."

"Has Sebastian suggested himself again?" Annika grinned.

"No," I said. "I'm not sure he would since our whole friendship fell apart after he did last time."

"Isn't Monday the 30th of November?"

"Yes, it is. Thanks for reminding me." I frowned. "Going home for Thanksgiving kind of threw a wrench in the roommate search. Then adding Sebastian to the mix was probably a bad idea. There was one guy who I thought would have been fine. He even fanboyed all over Sebastian."

"Sebastian isn't going to let another guy anywhere near you. You're not that dense." Annika raised her hands at a play on the field and turned with an expression of disgust at whatever happened.

"I have no idea what's going on with us. Sometimes I think I should walk away from him. I keep getting sucked deeper and deeper, and I don't even know where the bottom is anymore. We're not in a relationship, but we kind of are," I admitted. "I'm not blind or dumb. But the fact that he hasn't brought up our status, and I haven't mentioned it, must mean that neither one of us wants this connection to solidify, right?"

She shrugged. "I have no idea what any of that means. Sleep with him and see if it sticks."

"That's bad advice, Annika. Terrible advice. I can't get involved with him."

"You basically told me you're involved with him. So, you might as well have sex with him to see whether he's worth your handwringing."

"I haven't kissed him, and you think I should jump into bed with him?"

"All right, then kiss him. But do something already. Please. The suspense is killing me." Annika threw up her hands at another play on the field. "They are playing crappy tonight. Johnny is going to be a beast."

Strange. I also understood what went wrong that time, even though I'd only been half watching.

"What if we do kiss or have sex or whatever and it ruins our friendship? What if we can't ever recover from it? What if all he wants is sex and once he's got it, he stops talking to me?"

"What if the two of you start an amazing relationship?" Annika fired back. "You don't know unless you put yourself out there."

"Well, I also need a roommate, so sleeping with him at this point is a doubly bad idea."

"You're going to ask him to move in?"

"Maybe?" I winced. "I need someone. We get along really well. If I could guarantee he wouldn't be bringing home a string of girls, he'd be perfect."

Annika gave me a look.

"Don't." I recognized the glint in her eyes.

"I'm merely suggesting—hear me out—*you* sleep with him and then he'd have no need to go elsewhere."

"That logic is not sound." My mind went to Johnny. I wasn't convinced he was faithful, and Sebastian's loyalty to him hadn't wavered. "I'm going to think about it more."

"Just what we need—more of the two of you thinking about doing something that's so obvious to everyone else."

"Whatever." I waved her away. "Where are we headed tonight after the game?"

"Gabby's bar. She couldn't get the night off and Troy wants to hang out with her. You're coming?"

I nodded.

"Good. Get super drunk and make a move on Sebastian. Ask him to move in with you or sleep with him. I'm okay with either."

"Thanks, Coach," I said.

"No problem. My wealth of excellent advice is free."

***

At the bar, I did another shot and glanced at Sebastian out of the corner of my eye. He'd made a point of speaking to me first and even tried to convince me to socialize with him. Now, he was talking to anyone and everyone. His outgoing personality was truly awe-inspiring. I should have gone with him. Jealousy was eating at me every time I saw him chatting to any girl.

The game had been the worst of their season, but they'd managed to squeak out a win in the dying seconds. People were fawning over the football players and buying them drinks. The attention wasn't directed solely at Sebastian, but the plethora of women bothered me.

I signaled Gabriella for another drink. She poured a shot into the same glass and leaned over the bar. "Maybe you should slow down?"

I laughed and shook my head. "Nope. I'm just getting started."

The bar was busy, but not crowded. Gabriella was sticking around my section, either through coincidence or by design. I wasn't sure.

"You went out on a date with Theo, didn't you?" She peered over my shoulder.

"Yes." I drank my shot. The glass clattered onto the wood, and I motioned for her to refill it. "Why are you asking?"

Her long dark hair fell in two braids on either side of her face. As she leaned over to pour another drink, they both flipped forward. A twinge of envy went through me. I was going to grow my hair until it touched the floor.

"Theo is headed this way. I wasn't sure how awkward this would be."

"Pretty freaking awkward if Sebastian sees him talking to me." I nudged my shot glass at her again when she didn't fill it.

"You're on a break," Gabriella said. "You might need your brain cells to get you out of this mess in a minute."

Theo's shoulder bumped mine as he took a seat beside me. "Did you cancel on me because you're going to be too hung over tomorrow?" His tone was good-natured as he signaled Gabriella for a beer.

I fiddled with the shot glass in front of me, rocking it from side to side. "Uh, no. But that might also happen." I hoped he didn't dig deeper into why I wasn't interested. Either version of the truth—he didn't set my heart on fire or Sebastian's request to keep my distance—seemed wrong to admit.

"Buy you a drink?" Theo swallowed his beer.

"Better not," I said. "Also, Gabriella has cut me off."

"Oh?" He glanced from me to Gabriella. "You don't seem that drunk."

"She's worried you and Sebastian are going to get into a fight over me," I admitted.

He smiled. "Would you enjoy that?"

I laughed and turned to face him. "No, no, I would not *enjoy* that. I'm not a girl who gets off on overly masculine displays of...well, whatever that would be. Aggression? Possession? Nothing good, anyway."

Theo gave me an appraising look. "But you do what Sebastian asks? I'm guessing he told you not to go on a second date with me."

"Most of the time, I don't do what anyone suggests. But I value my friendship with him. For some reason, he doesn't like you much. I trust him. I trust his judgment." Gabriella must have slipped truth serum into my last shot before she moved on to other customers. She was nowhere in sight.

"Did he tell you why we don't get along?"

"No." I frowned.

"Well, sweetheart, let me fill you in. When he first arrived on campus and was marking his territory everywhere, he slept with my ex-girlfriend—the one I was working on getting back." He chugged his beer and rose from the seat beside me. "Even once he found out, he didn't stay away from her."

"I didn't know." I met his gaze.

"Not surprised. Why would he tell you the truth? Doesn't make him look very good." Theo leaned toward me. "When you're ready for an honest, decent guy, give me a call."

Gabriella was at the opposite end of the bar. I wasn't sure if her abandonment was intentional or a coincidence. I motioned to the bartender closest to me and had three more shots delivered in close succession.

When they were gone, I left my spot to search for Annika. When I couldn't find her, I took my phone out to find a text from her.

Left—gone to the frat house. Johnny is a beast. Talk soon.

I stared at the message for a minute, wobbling on my feet. Go home or go to the bar and get drunk? The polished wood, and my still warm seat, beckoned me. Gabriella glanced up from filling a customer's order and gave me a wink. Enough of a sign. I wandered through the small crowd of people, and I snagged a seat in Gabriella's section. When I looked beside me, Troy was on my right.

"Fancy meeting you here." I grinned.

"You're drunk." Troy took a sip of his own drink before setting it on the wood.

"Nope. But I'm working on it." I wagged a finger at him.

"Who you going home with tonight? Theo or Sebastian? Or are you going to start on another player?" Troy's sly smile took the bite out of his words.

I hadn't seen Gabriella approach, but she slapped his forearm. "That's mean, Troy, not funny."

"I think I might be swearing off players. All of them. That means you, too, Troy." I took the shot Gabriella passed to me.

"Oh really?" Amusement lit up his face. "Why's that?"

"Theo said he and Sebastian were into sharing women," I said. "I'm not good at sharing, so it never would have worked out."

"I don't know anything about that."

"This is about Theo's ex-girlfriend?" Gabriella asked, ignoring Troy's warning glance. "He was never getting her back. Theo pursuing you is petty. She chased Sebastian from the minute he arrived on campus."

"And he had no choice but to give in," I mumbled.

Gabriella laughed. "You've met Sebastian? Turn a girl down? Not likely."

Although her words would normally incite a flinch, I was too drunk to process them. "That's not a helpful comment." I glanced over my shoulder to where he was still holding court with a gaggle of girls. "Why aren't you out there living it up? Soaking up the women and the win and the hoopla?"

He swiveled in his seat to face me. "Have you seen my girl?" He gave Gabriella an appraising glance. "I'd be a fool to screw things up with her. This college fame shit is temporary. She's so far beyond all this, it's not even funny."

I pretended to puke over the bar, and Gabriella laughed.

"Someday, you'll experience what I'm talking about, and you'll realize I'm the smartest man alive," Troy said with a wink.

"Smartest man alive, huh?"

Troy clinked his tumbler with my shot glass. "I'll drink to that." He tossed the last of the liquid into his mouth.

"Hell, at this point, I'll drink to anything." I downed mine.

"Where'd Annika go?" Gabriella scanned the bar after taking a few other orders. The crowd was thinning.

"Went to the house with Johnny-boy. Man, that guy." I observed Troy out of the corner of my eye. "He's probably your ace-boy too or something, but I cannot stand him."

Troy's smile was strained. "I have a lot of respect for Johnny on the field."

Gabriella rolled her eyes. "Johnny is moody. He has a terrible temper. He thinks people are property."

"Sebastian loves him. I don't get it."

Troy shifted in his seat.

Gabriella started tidying the bar for a minute before turning to me. "Johnny is his ticket. Even before Sebastian came here, Johnny was going to get drafted. Now, with how the two of them play off each other on the field, it's a lock, a certainty. Johnny is his ticket to the big leagues. He's not going to say anything against him, whether he likes him or not."

"So he might not like him?" I cocked my head to the side. "'Cause it seems as though he really does like him." God, I was drunk.

Gabriella shrugged. "Maybe he does." She took a rag and wiped the bar. "I'm warning you that if he has to choose between you and Johnny, you're not going to win." She reached behind her and rang a large cowbell, signaling last call.

The sound reverberated around my skull. A shoulder brushed mine on the left, and I turned to see a fuzzy version of Sebastian. I blinked, trying to figure out if it was him or if I was seeing things.

His hazel eyes were tinged with amusement, which morphed into worry. "Gabby! What the hell? How'd she get so drunk?"

Gabriella's grin was wicked. "I think she's got a lot on her mind, Sebastian. Maybe the alcohol will help her get things off her chest." She winked at me.

I rolled my eyes and hopped off the barstool. I stumbled and fell into Sebastian's arms. He sucked in a quick breath as if I'd hurt him. But that was impossible. When I stared up into his open, concerned face, I wanted to sink into him.

"You all right?" He looped an arm around my waist, securing me to him.

"I'm drunk."

"No shit, Nattie." He chuckled. "What's got you so upset? I saw you talking to Theo. Did he say something to you?"

My blurry gaze sought out Gabriella for a second, but then I remembered she hadn't heard the conversation firsthand. "He said lots of things."

He grimaced. "Course he did. He's always running his mouth." Sebastian looked around the bar. "You wanna get outta here?"

I wanted to go home, curl up in my bed, and pretend I didn't care about Sebastian Swan. Standing this close to him, breathing in his cologne and beer mixture made me long to do things that had nothing to do with sleep.

"Take me home."

Which part of me would win tonight? Sleep or desire?

Chapter Twenty-Two

♥

He kept me tucked into his side as we walked to my house. I had trouble walking in a straight line, but he didn't seem to mind. Every once in a while, he laughed when I stumbled.

"Man, Nattie. What'd he say?" he asked. "You got this drunk because of Theo?"

I shook my head. Cotton balls were forming in my mouth. I needed water, aspirin, and a long sleep. "I got this drunk because of you and Annika."

"Me and Annika?" Sebastian's surprise took my comment in a direction I didn't intend.

"Not like that." A drunken laugh escaped, and I whacked him in the chest. "Not like that." I stumbled. I couldn't shake my head, or the wobbles worsened.

"Like what, then?" He squeezed my hip.

I stopped walking so suddenly he carried on without me for a step or two before realizing I wasn't continuing.

"I'm pissed off at Annika for letting Johnny turn her into a girl I don't recognize." My words slurred together, and I took a deep breath. "I'm pissed off at you for sleeping with Theo's ex-girlfriend and not telling me that's why you two don't get along." I pointed my finger at him.

Sebastian ran his hand across the top of his head and squeezed his neck. "I can't do much about the Annika thing. So, I'm gonna ignore that."

"Typical guy."

He chuckled and held up his hands. "All right, feisty Nattie is in the house."

"What about the second part?" Crossing my arms, I swayed and cursed myself. Would I remember this conversation? Didn't matter. We needed to have it.

"You never asked me why we didn't get along. If you asked, I would've told you. I wasn't trying to hide anything."

I raised my eyebrows.

"Okay, maybe I was *lightly* concealing it." He gave me a small smile before his expression turned serious. "I don't want to admit that shit to you, Nattie. It makes me feel like a bad person. Yeah, I did it. She gave me a sob story about how Theo was this terrible cheating asshole. But honestly, I probably would have slept with her, anyway."

I pushed past him and weaved across the pavement, keeping my head down.

"I didn't know you then."

He let me walk away for a few steps, and then I heard his footfalls behind me. I'd memorized the sound of his feet. I was pathetic.

He got in front of me and stood in my path. "I wouldn't do that now," Sebastian said. "Doesn't that count for something?"

"What do you want it to count for?" Anger and curiosity warred within me.

"I want you to see me as more than this jock football player who used to sleep around." He stuffed his hands into his pockets and looked anywhere but at me.

My brain darted between each of his claims. Finally, I settled on the truth that mattered the most in my drunken haze. "*Used to sleep around?*"

He took a step closer. "I've barely looked at another girl, let alone touched anyone since I met you."

I tapped the side of my head. "There are photographic memories that say otherwise."

He brushed my hair off my face, tucking the strands behind my ear. "I was confused and upset. I'll regret that night until the day I die." He gazed down at me, his expression brimming with sincerity.

I met his gaze, but I didn't know what to say. That night fractured something, made me question everything I'd been starting to feel.

"I hurt you." He leaned down so his forehead almost touched mine.

"Yeah, you did."

Silence settled between us while I digested his words. He smoothed my flyaway hair and kissed my forehead.

"Theo is everything you said you didn't want. Watching you kiss him, leave with him. You took a knife to my heart." Sebastian sighed. "I honestly thought you wouldn't care what I did."

"Caring about you has never been the problem." Alcohol had been my solution earlier to my mixed-up feelings, but now I wanted to be sober to be sure I'd remember this conversation.

"Nattie," he whispered.

We were so close the tiniest movement from me would encourage him. I licked my lips, flicking my gaze from his eyes to his full lips. God, I wanted him to kiss me.

He groaned and secured his hand behind my neck, tilting my chin with his thumb, and he swooped down, capturing my mouth. He moved his mouth across mine, and my heart exploded, pounding out an irregular tune, part joy, part panic. I met him hungrily, dragging him deeper. We were lost in each other, each kiss becoming more desperate and uncontrolled. I'd jumped out of the plane, and I was free-falling with no parachute in sight.

I was so engrossed in him I didn't notice when he started to walk backward toward my house. Teasing me with kisses, not leaving enough space for either of us to rethink or reconsider what we were doing.

When we reached my door, I fished out my key. Out of the corner of my eye, the parking lot outside my townhouse came into view. Sebastian and the girl with the long dark hair flashed in front of me.

I unlocked the house, but my heart ached, and I couldn't get any words out. He shut the door behind him and reached for me, but I sidestepped him.

"I'm drunk and tired." I shrugged him off to set my keys and clutch on the table before wandering toward the kitchen. Water, aspirin, and bed. I did not need to have drunken sex with a guy who would ruin me.

"Nattie." His tone was a gentle plea.

"What are we doing, Sebastian?" I shoved my arms out in a wide arc. "I mean, honestly, are we ever going to be a thing? You and me?"

"What makes you think we're not already a thing?" He followed me.

I leaned against the kitchen counter and scanned his familiar face, his broad shoulders, his hands that did amazing things on the field, possibly amazing things elsewhere. When our gazes connected, my cheeks flushed.

"I can't date a womanizing football player, no matter how much I like him." I crossed my arms. "And I want a certain womanizing football player too much to simply sleep with him. I can't."

He moved closer and reached out a tentative hand, as though I was a wild animal he'd caught and was attempting to tame. "What if this womanizing football player wanted to change his womanizing ways?"

A wisp of a smile touched my lips. "Is that even possible?" I gave him a skeptical glance. As I played it cool on the outside, my insides lit on fire at the possibility. I wanted to grab him, drag him to me, and never let go.

"You don't think it's worth trying?" He straddled my feet.

"Just you and me? No one else?" I searched his hazel eyes.

"Just you and me. No one else." His words expanded across the room, filling up what little space separated us. "I'm worried you're not gonna remember this tomorrow." He trailed his palm down my arm.

A shiver of pleasure ran through me. "I might not," I admitted, and I tugged on his shirt. When I drew him closer, I raised my face to his for another kiss.

He leaned into the offer, wrapping his hands around my waist. He lifted me onto the counter and giddiness raced through me. Kissing him made everything in me yearn for more. Making out with him was the best-worst idea I'd ever had while drunk.

Sebastian slid his palms under my ass, and he carried me back to my room. With my legs wrapped around his waist, we hardly broke the kiss. He laid me on the bed and covered my body with his, leaving kisses wherever his lips connected. Every inch of me was burning, and his mouth fanned the flames more. When he caressed and nipped at my neck, a trail of fire sprinted to my core. *God, I wanted him.*

I flicked his belt buckle with my fingers, tugging on the leather. He covered my hand with his, groaning.

"Nattie." My name was a plea. "Nattie," he said when I became more insistent, urging him closer. "Natalie." He gave my ear a gentle nip.

Another shiver ran through me, but his voice penetrated my drunken rush. His face, all the planes and angles so dear to me, were fuzzy. "You don't want to do this? I thought sex was the point?"

He chuckled and shook his head. "Trust me. I want to do this." He swallowed. "God, do I want to do this." He gazed beyond me to the other side of the room. "But if you wake up tomorrow and you don't remember this, it's gonna wreck me. It'd be even worse if you wake up tomorrow and regret being with me."

I released him to crash onto the bed. With my forearm, I covered my eyes. "I think I should be insulted. You sleep with anyone."

Sebastian laughed and collapsed beside me. "I insist my women are sober enough to be sure."

I gave him a sideways glance. "Always?"

He chuckled. "You never take anything at face value." Propping onto his elbow, he stared at me. "It's important to me that you know what you're doing."

"Probably sober Natalie will thank you," I admitted.

"What about drunk Natalie?" He traced me with his gaze.

"Drunk Natalie kind of hates you right now."

He laughed and scooped me up, placing my head on the pillow. "Aspirin, water—anything else?" He crawled out of the bed and headed for the door.

"No, that sounds perfect." I turned onto my side to watch him leave. "Sebastian?" I called just before he disappeared out the door.

"Yeah, Nattie?" He paused in the doorway.

"Are you sure about this? You and me? Sober Natalie is going to be a buzzkill."

He smiled. "What about drunk Natalie?"

"She's fully on board. It's weird."

He grinned and rapped the wooden doorframe with his knuckles. "Sober or drunk, Sebastian's response would always be the same to you. I'm sure. One hundred percent."

I sighed. "That's disappointing. I was hoping for one hundred and ten percent."

He laughed. "I'll keep that in mind. I'll be right back."

With a yawn, I tried to force my eyelids to stay open even as they grew heavy.

Sober Natalie was going to want to murder drunk Natalie in the morning.

Chapter Twenty-Three

♥

Sobbing penetrated my dream, and I snapped awake. In bed, I lay for a minute getting my bearings. The room spun when I propped myself onto my elbows. Was someone crying? Where? I checked the clock. Three-thirty in the morning.

When I turned toward the door, Sebastian's wide shoulders took up most of the mattress. His bed sharing needed work. I sighed and collapsed into the covers, forgetting the noise I heard.

Images from the night before flashed across my eyelids. I'd almost had sex with him. I groaned. What were we thinking?

Dishes clattering in the kitchen drifted toward me, and I sat up again. Had someone broken into the house? I crawled out of bed and eased open my door. My gaze strayed to Sebastian. If it was an intruder, I'd yell, and he'd come running. No need to wake him.

Had we locked the door?

I crept along the hallway, drunken ears on full alert. At the end of the hall where it met the edge of the kitchen, I peered around. Annika sat at the table, collapsed over her arms. Her chest rose and fell in great wracking sobs.

"Annika?" I touched her shoulder. "Hey, hey, what's going on?"

She turned and wrapped her arms around my middle. "Johnny threw me out."

"What?" I asked. "Why?"

"We're done. We're over." Her sobs and my fuzzy brain made it hard to figure out what she meant.

I hauled her out of the kitchen and over to the couch, dragging her into a seat beside me. "What happened?"

She grabbed a wad of tissues off the coffee table. She was crying so hard I was afraid she would hyperventilate.

"It's okay. You don't need to tell me." I wrapped her in a hug.

"I—I couldn't t—take it, Nat. I couldn't take it." Her sobbing subsided enough for me to understand her better.

"What? What was going on?" My heart dipped and then began to race. I checked her for marks or bruises or any evidence he'd gotten rough.

"He's been cheating on me since we started seeing each other." She took a deep, shuddering breath. "I mean, at first I knew, right? I expected it." Annika's big brown eyes met mine. "I thought I was okay with it." She stared at the tissues in her fists, clenching them and releasing them. "Once he told me he didn't want to be with anyone else, I—I started seeing him differently. I didn't want him to be with anyone else either. Just me."

I rubbed her back in slow circles. "Okay," I said. "So how do you know he's been cheating?"

She swallowed, and fresh tears overwhelmed her voice. "A girl turned up at the frat house at two in the morning. Drunk, so drunk." She gulped a sob. "She got into a fight with Johnny in the doorway. I heard the whole thing."

"What did Johnny say?" I pictured the sordid scene.

She sniffed and let out a bitter laugh. "He said the conversation was in my head. He wasn't cheating. The girl was drunk, and I was an idiot if I believed her. She just wanted what I had." A few stray tears slid down her cheeks, but she seemed to be holding herself together better. "I asked to see his phone."

I slouched into the couch. Her request wouldn't have gone over well. "And?"

"He refused. Threw a fit. Packed my things into bags in a rage. He said if I didn't trust him, I could get the fuck out and stop wasting his time." She choked on another sob. "He said there were plenty of girls willing to take my place."

I winced. "Oh, Annika." I enveloped her in a tight hug. "It's his loss. His loss." I smoothed her dark hair and drew away to make eye contact. "You deserve so much better."

Annika nodded, and her gaze slid from mine. The tissues clutched in her hand were in pieces. "He threw my stuff out the window and then he dragged me down the stairs, out the front door, and locked it behind me. I pounded on the entrance to get my coat, but he refused to open it. I left my stuff and walked here." She glanced behind her toward our door. "I didn't have any keys, so I hoped the spare key would be there. But then, it wasn't locked."

Heat crept up my neck and into my face. "I didn't lock it?"

She shook her head. "Probably not very safe. Too drunk?" A hint of a grin flashed across her face.

"Ah, something like that," I said. "I don't want to talk about me. You're going to stay here? We'll get your stuff in the morning, okay? I don't think you should go alone."

A blank expression coated her face. "What am I going to do, Nat? What am I going to do?"

I hugged her tight again. "We'll figure everything out in the morning when we're both sober and full of good ideas."

"We were moving in together." She stood and paced in front of me. "I have nowhere to live."

"I don't have a roommate yet. You can live here. It's okay, honestly. It'll be okay. We'll figure out what to do." I wasn't sober enough to provide any advice. With a gentle hand on her arm, I guided her to her room, and we stood on the threshold.

"I don't want to be alone. Can you come lie with me? Just till I fall asleep?" Annika asked.

I pursed my lips and checked my own door. Sebastian was in my bed. Not returning to him was ludicrous. When I focused on Annika, her anguish was clear. There was no choice.

"Sure." I squeezed her to my side. "Whatever you need."

The coolness of her covers sent a chill through me. I curled onto my side, determined to outlast her so I could go back to my own bed.

My bed wasn't what I missed.

The last thing I remembered before my eyes grew too heavy was Annika saying, "You're such a good friend, Natalie. I'm lucky."

My lids were sticky when I tried to open them. My pounding head elicited a groan that rose from my toes. Alcohol was the devil. When I forced myself awake, I frowned at the ceiling. This wasn't my room.

Easing to my side, Annika's sleeping form lay beside me. All the events from the night before returned in a rush. I moaned and threw an arm over my face.

No, no, no, no, no, no.

The clock on Annika's bedside table said eleven in the morning. Gingerly, I sat up and swung my legs over the edge of the bed. For a moment, I collected myself. I couldn't remember how Sebastian and I had left things the night before. My best recollections were of my conversation with Annika.

Well, that wasn't completely true. With my eyes closed, flashes of Sebastian hovering over me, lighting me on fire, seared my eyelids. I rubbed my face, wishing I had aspirin and water on my bedside table like normal.

Carefully, I rose from the edge of the bed and pressed my palm to the wall as I navigated around the bed. Dread knotted my stomach at the idea of seeing Sebastian. What had I said?

Leaving Annika's room, I peered along the hall, not sure if Sebastian would be up yet or still sleeping. My bedroom was open, so I went there first. At the doorway, I took in the made bed and lack of Sebastian.

With a frown, I turned around and wandered to the kitchen, half expecting to find him making eggs as Johnny had done the one morning. But there was no trace of him. On the kitchen table was a piece of paper, small and insignificant.

I snatched it up, scanning it.

Nattie,

Not sure where you went.

Can't find my phone.

Sorry about last night.

Sebastian

Sorry about last night? Oh, God. What did that mean?

I massaged my fingers into my forehead, wishing I'd woken up less hung over. With the note, I stumbled into my room, relieved to see the water and aspirin beside the table. At least I had enough sense to prepare the hangover essentials.

Crawling into bed, I willed myself to sleep. Just as I drifted into blissful darkness, a faint buzzing noise penetrated my half-asleep brain. I snatched my phone off the nightstand, opening an eye. Weird. Whatever vibrated wasn't mine.

I rolled off the bed and listened for the buzz. Under the bed frame, much farther than I would have thought probable, was a phone. I searched the room for something to prod or sweep it into my grasp. Finally, I located an old wire coat hanger I'd used once to unclog the vacuum, and I swept Sebastian's phone to the end of the bed. I scrambled over on my hands and knees as the voicemail notification lit up the screen.

His phone was flooded with messages.

I clicked the phone closed so the home screen darkened.

With his phone cradled, my morals were at war with my curiosity. Who was I kidding? I pressed the home button and waited another beat for my conscience to kick in. Maybe I was still drunk too. With a deep breath, I scrolled through the notifications.

Annika knocked on my doorframe, announcing her presence. I jumped and then flushed.

She cocked her head, examining me. "Did you get a new phone?" Her gaze landed on my hand.

"Uh—" I was so busted.

She narrowed her eyes and then they widened as she put the pieces together. "Oh, my God. You had someone here last night. Oh, my God! That's why you didn't lock the door. You were too busy."

My cheeks burst into flames so hot that spontaneous combustion felt possible. "Sebastian," I squeaked out, holding up his phone.

"Did you sleep with him? Why do you have that? I have so many questions." Annika dropped to the floor beside me and crossed her legs.

Her face was puffy from crying, but her insatiable curiosity was familiar, almost welcome. Given her blowup with Johnny, a part of me had worried Sebastian might be a no-fly zone.

"We did not have sex." I clarified, staring at the dark screen. So many notifications. "Honestly, I don't remember much else other than we didn't have sex. He turned me down, I think?"

"What?" Annika asked. "Why?"

"I can't remember, exactly." I grabbed his note off my dresser and threw it at her. "Then, he left me this."

Annika scanned the note, frowning. She tapped it against her palm, thoughtful. "I'm sorry? Who writes that?"

"*Why* is he sorry? Sorry he didn't sleep with me? Sorry we made out? Sorry he's a man-whore? Sorry I'm not his type? Bad enough he didn't stay, but to leave that in his place?" The hangover band played a tune in my brain, and I pressed my palm to my temple.

Annika set the note on the end of the bed. "What are you going to do?"

I examined her sweats, streaky makeup, and broken heart. "Today, I'm going to hang out with you and forget about Sebastian. I should return his phone." I bounced it in my palm.

"Did you look at it?" Annika reached for it.

I chuckled. "I was going to, but then you came in."

"Here, I'll look. Then you're not violating his trust. Both of us don't need to get screwed by football players who can't keep their dick in their pants." Her voice brimmed with anger.

I passed her the phone. This was still a violation of his trust, but at least I wasn't the person invading his privacy.

"Do you know his password?" She flicked through the list of notifications.

"No. I couldn't even guess." With a deep breath, I said, "I shouldn't be spying."

"Julia texted him last night for a booty call." Annika didn't bother to sugarcoat the claim. Her voice was flat and unsurprised.

"Julia-Julia? The one we know?" I snatched the device from her. Hard to be sure from the text. Only the name Julia was visible. I rubbed my face and tossed his phone to the floor. It slid farther than I would have expected. Must have been how it ended up under the bed.

"Take it from me, Nat. I thought I could handle it and I couldn't. Him and his player ways will wreck you." Annika stood in a fluid motion.

"How are you feeling this morning?" Her closed-off expression told me she was keeping a tight rein on her emotions. Only the worst feelings needed that sort of control.

"I want to get my shit from his place and forget I ever met him." She stood in the doorway with her back to me. "I have to coach at two. Are you okay to go with me?"

"Whatever you're doing today, I'm doing." My aspirin needed to kick in and quiet the riot in my head.

"My stuff from the frat house, coach the practice, trip to the mall," Annika listed over her shoulder as she headed down the hall. "Ready in thirty, okay?"

"Sure," I called after her, surprised she was functioning so well this morning.

Sebastian's phone taunted me from its spot on the floor. Anything I found on there wouldn't make me feel better. Probably worse, much worse. He hadn't made me any promises. Had never claimed to be a one-woman man. My heart hadn't quite gotten the memo.

Chapter Twenty-Four

♥

I glanced at Annika out of the corner of my eye. We'd walked the perimeter of the house, but hadn't found any of her stuff. Someone had either stolen everything Johnny had thrown out the window or taken it inside.

Sebastian's phone vibrated in my pocket. When we were together, he was never distracted, but the thing had been buzzing nonstop. I stopped checking after the third flirty text from another girl. Each one had made my heart contract so violently I worried it would seize.

"I guess we'll have to knock?" We had thirty minutes to get to Annika's league practice on time.

She nodded, but her chin trembled. Her armor, in place at our house, appeared weakened when faced with the reality of leaving Johnny.

We walked up the stairs, and I knocked. Voices drifted through the heavy wood and both of us took deep steadying breaths. Without looking, I secured Annika's hand in mine and squeezed.

The door swung back, and Troy stood on the threshold. "Ladies!" he exclaimed. "Neither one of you slept here last night? Must be a record."

His happy greeting was met with our stunned silence.

"Come in." He shifted to the side. "Johnny and Sebastian went to the gym, but they should be here soon."

"Oh." I tried for nonchalance when I felt none. "That's okay. I'm returning Sebastian's phone, and Annika needs a few things from Johnny's room."

"Sure, whatever." Troy headed for the kitchen. "Let yourselves out when you're done if you're not waiting around."

We hotfooted it up the stairs to the bedrooms. I hesitated at Sebastian's door while Annika continued to Johnny's room. I removed his phone from my pocket and dropped it face down on his desk. The thud on the surface was final, as though I was slamming a door.

I couldn't dwell on my confused feelings. We needed to get out of here before they both returned and a scene broke out.

In Johnny's room, Annika sat on his bed, holding a frame in her hands. There were no bags. She wasn't packing. Annoyance surged up my throat.

"Are you ready to go?" I asked.

She glanced up from the photo of her and Johnny, tears in her eyes. "He put my stuff back." She rotated the picture so I could see it. "He broke this last night. Smashed it to pieces. It's already in a frame."

"Annika," I said. "We should grab everything and get out of here."

"I want to talk to him."

Defeat made my shoulders slump. This still wasn't enough? "Returning your stuff, putting that photo into a new frame, apologizing, whatever else he does—none of it changes what's been going on." My voice brimmed with frustration, but I couldn't hold it in. "He broke your trust."

At her shoulder, I tugged the arm of her zip-up hoodie, revealing fresh bruises from his rough handling the night before. She shrugged her sweater into place and didn't meet my gaze.

"Annika," I pleaded. "More bruises. This isn't normal."

"Okay, I'll go with you." She stood and replaced the photo. "I'll come for my stuff later."

I grabbed a bag from the floor and tossed her stuff in.

"Nat, I'll be late for practice." She was frozen in the doorway, but she didn't try to stop me.

I glanced up as I shoved more things into the bag. "Since when do you care about being late?"

She crossed her arms. "Let's go. I'll come back later."

"Annika, you're not thinking clearly." The bag dangled from my hand. "If you do that, he'll give you a terrible excuse, and you'll take him back."

She gave me a long look, shrugged her shoulders, and averted her gaze.

A surge of anger rushed through me. I threw the bag on the floor and stomped out of the room. "You're ridiculous. I can't even—" I plowed into Sebastian's chest, and a grunt escaped me at the firm wall of muscle.

His hands gripped my upper arms to steady me, and his gaze met mine. He grinned.

I scowled.

His smile faded to confusion. "You all right?"

"I'll be in the car," I said to Annika. "Your phone is in your room, Sebastian. It's been going off all morning." I brushed past him.

"Nat." He followed me toward the staircase. "Are we gonna talk about last night?"

I whirled on him. "What's there to say? You're sorry. I'm sorry. We're both so Goddamned sorry, right?" I shook my head. "I don't even remember what happened, so let's forget it, okay?" Without giving him a chance to reply, I was down the stairs and out the door.

As I headed for Annika's car, parked on the side of the road near the frat house, Johnny strolled up the sidewalk.

"Anni in there?" he called out.

The anger I hadn't been able to unleash on Annika bubbled in me. I strode over to where he'd stopped. "She deserves so much better than you," I spit out.

He raised his eyebrows and gave me a mild look. "That so?"

"Throwing her stuff out the window? Giving her yet another set of bruises? What'll she do in the summer? Wear sweatshirts everywhere to cover up your damage? Lie about how she got them?"

He thrust his hands in his pockets and rocked on his heels. "She bruises easily. She should probably go to the doctor and get her hormone levels checked. Might help with our fights too." He gave me a cocky grin.

Never in my life had I wanted to punch someone so badly. "My dad's a police officer. I swear to God, if you hurt her again, you'll rot in a jail cell."

He chuckled. "Annika would never press charges. She'd *never* jeopardize my football career." He shook his head. "Besides, what authority does your dad have here? None, Natalie. Don't go throwing weight you don't have." He patted me on the shoulder and stepped around me.

Steam had to be shooting out of the top of my head.

"Anni!" Johnny's voice floated over. She must have left the house.

"I can't talk to you, Johnny," she said.

I turned, surprised. Slung over her shoulder was the bag I'd started packing. Sebastian trailed behind her with a grimace.

She strode toward me, avoiding eye contact with Johnny.

"Annika!" Johnny called, sauntering behind her. "What's in the bag?"

"I think you know! We're"—she choked on the word—"done."

"Come in the house. We can talk it out. We can work this out."

She whirled on him in a burst of confidence. "We cannot work out you being a cheating liar. That reality doesn't work for me—any way you present it." She opened the rear door and tossed her bag onto the seat.

Behind her, Johnny and Sebastian stood. Johnny was tense with anger. With slumped shoulders, Sebastian wasn't watching them; his gaze was glued to me. My heart dove and dipped.

"Johnny, bruh. In the house," Sebastian called when Johnny strode toward us with purpose.

I slid into the passenger seat, and Annika started the car. Johnny banged on Annika's window when she refused to acknowledge him.

"Anni!" he yelled, and his face was red with rage.

Sebastian grabbed his arm from behind, breaking his focus.

"We're not done, Annika!" He pointed at her window. "We're not done until *I* say we're done."

She turned cool eyes to him. "It's a good thing that's what you said last night, isn't it?" Her foot punched the accelerator, and we tore away from the curb.

We sat in silence while she drove until I broke it by saying, "What changed your mind? I thought you were going to take him back." My heart rate was settling in my chest.

"Johnny wasn't the one who picked up my stuff from the lawn." Her voice was hard. "Sebastian did."

Houses and trees rushed by unseen. Sebastian would clean up Johnny's messes on *and* off the field. Yet another reason I needed to steer clear of him.

"He told you that?"

"Yeah. He said Johnny didn't understand he was being an ass. Sebastian said he's *assholeish* sometimes." She rolled her eyes.

I burst into laughter despite myself. That was my word from months ago. "Thank God you're not okay with that behavior. I was getting really worried."

She glanced at me. "I was worrying myself," she said. "Practice and then the mall?"

"Yes. After that, a movie and a lot of ice cream."

She nodded, wiping away a stray tear.

"Oh, Annika." I rubbed her arm, wishing I could hug her.

"I was so close to having exactly what I always wanted. So close. He had to go and blow it all to hell."

"You might still get what you've always wanted. It just won't be with him." I tried to sound upbeat.

In the parking lot of the practice field for her league team, she reached behind her and pulled out her clipboard and a pen.

"You wanna help me?" She raised an eyebrow.

"Me?"

"Yeah, set up and take down mostly for the drills."

"Sure." The drugs had gone to work on my headache, and a distraction sounded good.

With a deep breath, she opened her car door.

Chapter
Twenty-Five

♥

"Nattie!" Sebastian called while he jogged behind me as soon as I exited my classroom building.

I peered over my shoulder, acknowledging his voice but not stopping. The sight of him kicked my heart into gear.

"Are you gonna ignore me forever?" He fell into step beside me.

Forever? That had been the plan. His texts were unanswered. Calls declined. I'd taken different routes to and from my classes. Annika and Johnny were done, so I had no need to be around the football players anymore.

Now, his familiar face made my chest ache with longing. When I thought about him for too long, I hated the flame that flickered to life inside me.

"What do we have to say to each other?" I hitched my satchel higher onto my shoulder.

He placed his hand on my arm, stilling my hasty pace. "Get coffee with me. One hot beverage."

"I have somewhere to be."

"Oh yeah? Where's that?" He shoved his hands into the pockets of his coat.

I sighed. Nowhere, and he knew it. "Fine." I shifted direction toward the school cafeteria.

"No, we're not having this conversation on campus." Sebastian gestured to the parking lot closest to us. "I have my vehicle. We'll go somewhere else."

"You never bring it on campus." There I went showing how much attention I paid to his habits.

"I needed a getaway car. Thought I might have to kidnap you to get you to talk to me." His voice wasn't tinged with his usual humor.

I stole a glance at him out of the corner of my eye but said nothing.

Sebastian sighed. "Football season is almost over. Holidays are coming. I want to be square with you before I go to Bermuda."

"What does that mean?" I asked as we approached his vehicle.

"Get in, Nattie. Okay? Give me this one thing without fighting me on it."

I climbed into his SUV and put my bag on my knee like a shield, but I didn't argue with him.

We drove in silence for a minute before Sebastian said, "What do you remember about the other night?"

Heat climbed into my cheeks, and I focused on the scenery outside instead of meeting his gaze.

"Okay," he said. "So, you remember at least some of it." There was a smile in his voice.

"Yeah, I remember bits and pieces."

"I thought you ran out on me. When I woke up the next morning and I couldn't find you. I thought you were upset with me," Sebastian said quietly.

"What?" I sought his gaze across the distance. "I was in Annika's room. I didn't mean to fall asleep. Is that why you left that note? The 'I'm sorry' crap?"

"Yeah, I wanted us to be okay," he said. "I wanted to avoid *this*." He gestured to the interior.

"Awkwardness?"

"No, this avoidance bullshit. It's bullshit. I told you I wanted to be with you and then you toss me aside like I'm nothin'." His expression was a mixture of frustration and disbelief. "I've been going over it and over it. What'd I do? I did the honorable thing. The *right* thing. And you're punishing me."

"I'm not punishing you," I grumbled, crossing my arms.

I was punishing myself for daring to believe I could ever have something with a womanizing football player. It hadn't occurred to me Sebastian would care enough to feel my absence too. The activity on his phone made it clear he had no trouble filling his time or finding someone to take my place.

"Then what the hell, Nattie? If we should pretend I didn't say it, fine." He seemed to flounder before continuing, "But I want you to stop avoiding me."

The scenery was a blur as I went over what he'd said. He wanted to be with me? His phone, the texts, the messages, the buffet of other women—there was no way.

"I can't be with you," I said.

He sighed. "I shouldn't have talked to you when you were drunk. I knew it, and I did it. So stupid." He shook his head. "Just so you know, drunk Natalie was on board."

"Drunk Natalie is kind of slutty and makes poor decisions. Not an accomplishment to get *her* on board." A hint of a smile threatened.

"I was impressed any part of you was on board."

Unbidden, the image of him hovering over me, scooping up my lips, pressing his body against mine, surfaced. Parts of me were still very much willing, even sober. My idiotic brain couldn't figure out how to make us work without my heart ending up in tatters.

"You only want me because I keep saying no."

"That's not true. There wasn't a lot of 'no' going on the other night." Sebastian gave me a cocky grin.

I took a deep breath and decided to give him the truth. "I'm not sure I'd ever trust you."

Sebastian flexed his hands on the steering wheel, and a muscle in his jaw ticked. "You don't think I'd keep my word?"

I gave him a helpless look. "You have girls all over you all the time. All the time. Every time I see you, someone is hanging off you. I had your phone the other day, and it was man-whore central. Bing. Bing. Bing. What's that? Oh, look. Another flirty notification."

"Have a little faith, Nattie." When he glanced at me, his eyes were earnest. "When I commit to something, I'm all or nothing. I've been that way with football, with friends, with family, with school. When I want something, I work hard at it."

"You persevere the hell out of it?" I raised my eyebrows.

He smiled, but it wasn't tinged with his usual cockiness. "You know it."

"You're serious?"

"Very. I mean it." He turned onto my street. "I want to do this with you." He signaled into my parking lot.

"Aren't we were getting coffee?"

"Your place has coffee." He shrugged. "I want to figure this out with you. If we can be something, I want to be it. And if we can't, if you don't want more, then I want to determine how we can hang out instead of avoiding each other. What we have is important to me. I don't want to lose you. I'll take you in my life any way I have to."

My heart thudded at the sincerity in his voice. My fingers rested on the door handle, and I shifted my bag, willing myself to keep my emotions under control. "Annika might be home, and the coffeemaker is broken again."

"I won't say anything about Johnny, and I'll fix the coffeemaker." Sebastian climbed out of the car and waited behind me while I unlocked my townhouse.

In the kitchen, I gathered everything to make a pot of coffee while he worked his magic on the machine. Some piece of it always ended up getting clogged, but I'd been worried about spending the money to replace it. When he was done, he took up his usual stance of leaning against the counter.

"You gonna talk to me?" he asked.

"I'm thinking." I flicked the coffeemaker on, amazed he understood how to fix everything, always.

He watched me in silence, waiting me out. He was good at knowing when to speak and when to stay quiet around me. It was annoying.

"I can't. I don't." With a deep breath, I said, "How would we even work? You're—we're..." I trailed off, not sure what I was trying to say.

"Do you want to be with me? 'Cause if the answer is no, then the conversation we're having should be focused on how we stay friends." He used his hands to gesture the division between the two options. "If the answer is yes, then the conversation is about what you need from me for you to be comfortable—happy." His gaze bored into me.

"What's the 'I don't know' option, again?" I stared at the coffee streaming into the pot.

He grabbed my hand that had been smoothing out invisible creases in the counter. "Was drunk Natalie a liar?"

Briefly, I met his eyes and half smiled. "Drunk Natalie is many things, but she isn't a liar. I do like you, Sebastian." I sighed. "But you've never been in an exclusive relationship with someone. Ever. If nothing else, that's a steep learning curve."

He laced his fingers with mine. "I'm willing to learn anything you want to teach me."

"See? You made that sound dirty. If you said that to another girl, I'd lose my mind. My head would explode." I held up our linked hands. "This—you being touchy-feely with another girl? Volcanic eruption." I stared at him. "It's not whether I like you, of course I like you. It's whether I want to do this to myself."

"I'm making a list. So far, no flirting, no touching." He held up two fingers. "What else is on your list?"

"No random girls texting you for booty calls."

"New phone number, check." He put up a third finger.

"How many fingers do I get?" I cocked my head. He wasn't balking at anything.

"As many as you need—I'll start listing your rules on my toes if I have to." He wiggled his toes through his socks.

My smile faded around the edges when I dropped the last parameter. "I'm not sleeping with you until I'm sure we can do this."

He gave me a long look and added another finger. "No sex until you're sure about me. Got it."

"Really? All of this is okay? I'm already the jealous, possessive girlfriend."

"All of this is okay if it'll make you more confident about us." He tugged me closer. "You can have the passwords to every social media account. Hire a private investigator to trail me on campus. Get your dad to come stalk me. I'll agree to everything."

I laughed. "That last option would be horrible for everyone." I hugged him around the middle. "You're that sure?" I rested my chin on his chest, staring up.

"I'm a hundred and ten percent sure." His voice held a smile. "I'm going to do everything I can not to let you down."

"What about Johnny and Annika?" That would be all kinds of awkward.

"We'll figure it out." He ran his palm down my back and gripped my waist. "At some point, it'll blow over and they'll either get back together or see other people."

He was right, of course. But the idea of them reconciling sent a chill through me.

"Johnny seemed pretty determined to win her back." Sebastian's breath ruffled the top of my hair.

"It's radio silence here. If he's hoping to win her back, he's doing a shitty job so far."

Sebastian laughed. "Nah, Nattie. You don't know him. This is the calm before the storm."

Chapter Twenty-Six

T onight was the night of the final game of the regular season. If they won, they'd make the playoffs, and Sebastian would have to cut his time in Bermuda short. He hadn't been upset, but he was always giving up something for the sake of the game.

Everything on campus was winding down for the holidays, but Annika was wound up.

"Should I go or not?" She paced around her room.

I'd avoided giving a direct answer for more than an hour while she'd gotten ready as if she was going and then changed her mind. Over and over.

"It's up to you," I said. "I don't care where we sit, but I promised Sebastian I'd be there."

She released her breath in a big gust. "I'm going." Determination was in her voice. "Screw it. I want to see the game. If we sit away from our regular spot, he won't realize where we are."

I'd told Sebastian I'd text him my seat number, so he could look for me. There was a chance Johnny *would* find out, but I didn't want to tell her that. I didn't want to consider the possibility. He'd stayed away so far, and I hoped he'd stay gone.

Sebastian, on the other hand, was turning out to be an impressive boyfriend. Scrolling privileges on his phone were now a thing. Since he had a new phone, there wasn't much on it. For the last two weeks, he hadn't given me a single reason to worry.

"We can sit wherever you want." Another text from Sebastian rolled in.

"What are you two doing after the game?" Annika applied a third coat of mascara.

"Sebastian wants to come here." The rest of the players were going to Gabby's bar, but we'd been avoiding public places. Our relationship was still so new, and I wasn't ready to test it quite so publicly.

"Oh." She paused in her makeup application. "Should I go somewhere else? I'm always around when you two are hanging out—the worst third wheel."

"No." I perched on her bed. "You know it's not like that."

She laughed. "You're right. But I still can't believe you talked him into no sex before marriage."

I grabbed a throw pillow and chucked it at her. "Oh, my God. That is not our agreement! I just..." I pursed my lips. "I need to be sure that he's sure about this relationship thing."

"Well, your level of certainty could change at any moment with the way he's been acting. Any moment he'll do or say something super sweet and, BAM, I'm listening to you two get it on."

"You're ridiculous." But I couldn't help grinning. She wasn't wrong. Being a third wheel wasn't fun, though. "You're always welcome here. I don't ever want you to feel as though you can't be in your own house because of some guy."

"Some guy?" She raised her eyebrows.

"I like him. But he's not more important than our friendship. He just isn't."

She dragged me off the bed into a hug. "How was I ever mad at you? You're the best."

I laughed and squeezed her. "You should remember that. I'm probably always going to give unsolicited advice and opinions. I was raised by a cop."

"Are you looking forward to seeing your dad over the holidays?" Annika leaned against her dresser. She was smart, funny, and freaking gorgeous. Johnny was a fool.

"Ah," I said. "Yes?"

"You haven't told him about Sebastian, have you?"

"I haven't actually told him Clay and I broke up." I covered my face with my hands. "He liked Clay."

"What?" Annika exclaimed, bugging her eyes out. "Nat!"

"I know, I know. But for the longest time, a part of me wondered if Clay and I would get back together." I didn't meet her gaze. "I wasn't exactly expecting Sebastian."

"You never told me that." Annika frowned. "I thought you broke up with him because you couldn't see yourself marrying him, not that you wanted a break from him."

"He was too much too soon. I hoped he might cool off. At some point maybe we'd be in the same headspace."

Annika gave me a side-eyed glance. "Sure." She picked up her mascara tube and tapped it in her hand. "So, what about Sebastian?"

I flopped on her bed, arms out. "I've *never* experienced this gut-deep, soul-deep longing for someone, ever. That's the horrible, terrible truth."

Annika laughed and sat on her bed with her legs crossed. "Why is that horrible and terrible?"

"We're young. He might go to the NFL. One of us could so easily screw this up. I'm already in so deep. How far down can I go?"

She gave me a dark look. "Pretty far, Nat, pretty far."

"Shit." I sat up. "Sorry. I didn't mean to bring him up."

She held up her hand. "It's fine. I'm fine." She stood. "We should get going or we'll have no chance to even get a seat."

We walked to the stadium instead of taking Annika's car. She said the fresh air would help to clear her head. I kept glancing at her as we walked, expecting her to break down or turn around and go home. We'd been so good about avoiding Johnny. Going to the game was playing with fire. Sebastian had warned me Johnny wanted her back. At what point would that no longer be true?

Once we took our seats, in a different section and higher than normal, I texted Sebastian the section and row. When they came running onto the field, he scanned the rows and sections, lasering in on me. I grinned but didn't wave. When I turned to Annika, her expression was stunned. Down on the field, Johnny was staring at her the same way Sebastian had stared at me. After the game, Sebastian and I were going to have a chat about not throwing my friend under the Johnny bus.

I touched Annika's arm, and she turned startled eyes to me. "How'd he see me so quickly? There are thousands of people here."

The text I sent Sebastian was on my home screen, and I showed it to her. "I'm guessing he asked Sebastian where I was sitting or outright asked where *you* were sitting." I shook my head. "Sorry," I mumbled. "I'll talk to Sebastian."

"No, no." Annika's attention was glued to Johnny on the field. "It's okay. It's fine."

If I heard the word "fine" from her one more time, I might scream. A mix of worry and panic stirred in my stomach. Their eye contact had been electric, crackling across the distance. Once I'd seen them together, I never doubted their connection, only Johnny's ability to be a decent human being.

"You're going home after the game, right?" I tried to focus on the action on the field.

She hesitated. "I might go see Kristy or one of the other girls."

I sighed. Sebastian and I would be at Gabby's bar after all. Annika wasn't headed to Kristy's after the game. The lure of Johnny was too great.

We were outside the locker rooms at an exit no one ever used, waiting for Sebastian to emerge. Sebastian had started coming this way to avoid the fans and groupies so I'd feel better. This route also removed any temptation for him. He was a very affectionate person, and the no-touching rule was hard for him.

He and Johnny came out shoulder to shoulder. I scanned Sebastian's face first, trying to figure out if he'd engineered this meeting or Johnny had. Sebastian caught my eye and gave a little shrug. I sighed. Johnny had weaseled his way into following Sebastian out.

Annika hung behind me. "Hey, Sebastian," Annika greeted him. "Good game. Sorry you'll have to cut your holidays at home short."

Sebastian grinned, looping an arm around my waist. "I wish my girl was going to be around since I'm stuck here." He tucked me tight against his side.

His freshly showered scent was one of my favorites. Who was I kidding? He smelled incredible to me all the time.

"Hey, Anni. How are you?" Johnny asked when she didn't acknowledge him.

She shot a quick glance in his direction and then gave me and Sebastian her full attention. "Are you guys going out?" she asked.

"Most of us are going to Gabby's bar." Johnny took a tentative step toward her. "Are you coming?"

When she met his gaze, she was a goner. Love and longing coated her face. I couldn't imagine Johnny didn't see, didn't realize he could lure her to return.

"I've missed you, Anni. Nothing's as good without you," he said.

"Don't." She held up her covered hand. "Just don't, okay? I don't want to hear you lying to me."

Sebastian started to lead me away, but I dug in my heels. "Annika?" I needed to be sure she wanted to be left with him. She could choose whatever she wanted, but I wouldn't abandon her.

Her dark, helpless eyes met mine. "Give us a sec."

I let Sebastian lead me away. A small crowd gathered to greet both guys. Our secret exit was no longer a secret. If Johnny had arranged this too, he would end up neutered.

"We're going to your place?" Sebastian moved into my direct line of sight so I couldn't stare at Johnny and Annika talking.

"I don't like that." With my lips pursed, I gestured to them.

"I get it. But Annika is a grown-ass woman, and if she wants to take him back, that's up to her."

"How'd he find out where she was sitting?" I narrowed my eyes.

Sebastian sighed. "He asked me where *you* were sitting."

"And you didn't wonder why he'd ask? He hates me. Why would he care where I was sitting?"

Sebastian shrugged and stared into the distance. "We were getting ready. Your text rolled in. He asked. I answered. I didn't think anything. I just answered."

Maybe it was that simple.

"If Annika decides to go to the bar, we're going. Okay?" I rubbed his arms, thinking about the things I'd rather be doing with him at my place.

He leaned down, gathering me to him, his lips skimming the place on my neck that made my knees collapse with desire.

"You're playing dirty," I breathed.

"That's the only way I like to play," he murmured, tightening his hold.

"Yo, Casanova!" Troy called. "You coming out tonight or what?" He made a whooshing noise and pretended to crack a whip.

"Whatever, bruh." Sebastian peered at Troy over his shoulder. "We're going to your girlfriend's bar so you can slump into a barstool all night." He made the same noise and motion to Troy.

Troy laughed good-naturedly. "Yeah, yeah. You coming or not?"

Sebastian turned to me with the question unspoken. Johnny and Annika were deep in conversation. With a sigh, I said, "Yeah, we're coming."

Chapter
Twenty-Seven

♥

The bar was packed. Annika had disappeared into a corner with Johnny as soon as we arrived. Whatever lines he was feeding her, she was gobbling them up. Sebastian was working hard to keep me distracted. When he left to get more drinks, Kristy came out of nowhere and bumped my hip.

"Sebastian's so whipped." She sipped her drink and grinned at me. "Are Johnny and Annika back together?" She motioned to where they were deep in conversation against a wall.

"No idea on that one." I scanned the bar for Sebastian. "You were at the game?"

I spotted Sebastian heading toward us with two beers. A girl appeared out of nowhere and tried to hug him. He side-stepped her and shook his head. He grinned to soften the blow and leaned in her direction, yelling something. She turned and stared at me.

Ah, the girlfriend card. Didn't take long to brandish it.

Kristy took another drink. "Yeah, a bunch of us were there. You should have said you and Annika were going. I thought she was avoiding Johnny or I would have texted you guys." She followed my gaze. "I didn't know about you and Sebastian."

"It's new." He passed me a beer and kissed my temple. "Sebastian, do you remember Kristy?" I asked. "We lived on the same floor last year."

"We met at Nattie's one time, right?" He kept his palm pressed to my lower back.

"Yeah." The word was dragged out as she looked between us, grinning. "Okay, I have to say this development is sort of shocking. Nat hated football last year and football players. But seeing you two together—it makes so much sense to me."

I gave her a lopsided grin. "Thanks, Kristy."

I wanted to ask Sebastian about the girl who'd approached him, but I couldn't become obsessed with whatever happened before we became official. Dwelling on the past wouldn't help us build a relationship.

"I'm working on winning her over."

Kristy's smile was sly. "She looks pretty won to me."

Heat raced up my neck, and a self-conscious laugh escaped before I passed Sebastian my drink. "And on that note," I said. "I'm going to the bathroom."

Sebastian's expression morphed from relaxed to panicked. Until people understood his new hands-off approach, these first few nights would require a lot of explanation to everyone who was used to getting a piece of him.

"Kristy will keep you company." I nudged her with my shoulder. "If anyone tries to touch him, knock them out with a death stare or just punch them. I'm okay with either."

"Death stare, death stare," Sebastian said, taking a drink of his beer. "Though girls fighting over me has always seemed kinda hot..." He trailed off, smugness oozing out of him.

I laughed and punched him in the arm.

"Fighting over me, Nattie. Not beating me up." He gave me a quick kiss before I left. "Hurry back."

"I'll protect him," Kristy called as I walked away.

When I approached the bathrooms, I was still grinning. Coming out of the men's door was Johnny. He slowed to a stop when he saw me.

"Natalie," he drawled.

"Johnny," I said, mimicking his tone.

"Annika's coming home with me tonight, so you don't need to wait." He made it sound as though he was doing me a favor.

"Is that so?" I raised my eyebrows. "I'll double-check with her."

"She needed time to miss me, to understand we've got a good thing." He shoved his hands in his pockets. "I knew she'd come around."

Looking at him made my blood boil. I made a noncommittal noise and tried to decide if I could squeeze past him in the hall without touching him. We'd met in a crowded spot, and I was trapped. People eased around us in the tight hallway. The publicness of the encounter was good; the closeness was not. I should have gone to the other bathroom. More crowded, but also more open.

"You don't believe me, but I love her."

I glanced at him. "People don't leave bruises on those they love."

He shrugged. "Sometimes I don't realize my own strength." He searched my face, and I hated the calculation I saw. "You've made it so clear you don't like me, Natalie. No one is ever going to believe anything you say about me." He shook his head in mock regret. "Here's the real kicker. Your interference is often what sets me off—the phone password, planting seeds of doubt in Annika about me—if you'd just stay out of my relationship, Annika and I would be fine."

I met his steady, determined gaze and marveled at his nerve. "I'm the reason you can't keep your temper in check? I'm the reason you sleep with other girls? Man, Johnny. You must spend a lot of time thinking about me."

His jaw clenched, and his hands flexed in and out of fists. "I have no idea what Sebastian sees in you."

"Thank God for that."

He stepped around me, and as he did, he said to me, just loud enough to hit my ears, "Watch yourself. Seb's not always nearby."

A chill raced through me. For a minute, I stood frozen. Sounded an awful lot like a threat. Would Sebastian believe me if I told him? I wasn't sure he would. As close as we were getting, Johnny was the guy he was closest to on campus. He'd tell me Johnny was being intense again. Or maybe I'd misheard him or misunderstood.

Forgetting about the bathroom, I rotated on my heel and pushed through the crowd. Kristy was still with Sebastian, along with about ten other girls, but none of them were touching him. He was laughing with one of them when I came up behind him.

"Have you seen Annika?" I ran my fingers along his back.

He tugged me into a hug. "Man, girls and their bathroom lines." He shifted and examined my face. A frown marred his forehead, and he leaned in to whisper in my ear, "You okay?"

When he passed me my beer, I drained it. "I want to leave. Have you seen Annika? I need to talk to her before we go." My pulse pounded.

Sebastian motioned to a booth off to the side. "She's sitting with Johnny and a couple of the other guys."

In the booth, she was smiling and laughing. When Johnny caught me looking, he grinned and had the nerve to nudge Annika and point to me. She waved me over.

I grabbed Sebastian's hand, mumbled goodbye to Kristy, and headed to their table.

Johnny rubbed Annika's back and spoke to Sebastian. "I ran into Natalie outside the bathrooms."

"Oh yeah?" Sebastian turned to me. "Everything okay?" He drew me into his side and nuzzled my ear.

I couldn't say anything. The words were stuck in my throat.

"We cleared the air," Johnny said. "Yeah, yeah. I wasn't treating Annika right before. But I'll be better this time."

My stomach churned.

"Annika?" I asked.

She hit Johnny's leg. "Let me out. I should talk to Nat quickly."

My heart sank.

She pulled me off to the side and stared at me for a beat. The words might not have left her lips, but I could tell from her helpless, hopeful expression what was coming.

"We're trying again. It was a misunderstanding."

I said nothing. Would she believe me if I told her what Johnny said? Would she understand his words were a threat?

"You're not going to say anything?" Annika asked.

"What do you want me to say? Giving him another chance is a mistake, but it's your life and you get to make your own choices." Part of me wanted to tell her not to come running to me the next time he screwed up, but I'd never want her to feel she couldn't turn to me. Even if it put me in danger too.

She shifted from foot to foot. "He'll be better this time. He really wants this." She bit her lip. "He said you two cleared the air?"

"We both said things." No point in getting into what the words we exchanged were about since it was clear she was determined to believe him. "Are you coming home tonight?"

"Uh." She shrugged. "I'm not sure. I guess we'll see how the rest of the night goes."

With a deep, shaky breath, I hugged her. "If you need anything at all, ever, call me."

She smiled and her shoulders lowered. "I'm good. Our relationship will be better this time. The first step is admitting you have a problem."

Did any of us agree on the problem, though?

Instead of asking, I squeezed her tight one more time and went to Sebastian. I laced my fingers with his. He was laughing with Johnny and turned to brush a kiss on my temple.

"We're outta here. See you at practice tomorrow." He gave a general wave to the footballers gathered. "Have a good night, Annika."

She beamed at Sebastian as she slid into the booth beside Johnny.

The last thing I saw before I left them was Johnny's triumphant smirk.

We'd no sooner exited the bar when Sebastian said, "You two didn't clear the air, did you?"

I laughed, but it held no humor. "No, we did not."

"You don't believe Johnny can be faithful?"

Such a slippery discussion. If I said I didn't, we might steer into a discussion about him. We were building our trust, and I didn't want to ruin that. He and Johnny weren't the same.

The farther we walked from the bar, the more I started to convince myself I couldn't have heard Johnny correctly. Did he threaten me? Why would he bother? Annika was falling into his arms without any protest.

I shook my head. "We don't get along. It's not like it's a secret."

"Is there something you're not telling me?" He stopped in the middle of the sidewalk. Confusion and concern mingled on his face. "Something doesn't feel right to me."

"No." I avoided eye contact. "It's fine. I'm worried. You know me."

He kissed the top of my head. "I do, Nattie. So, I realize there's more to the story. But I'm gonna trust you'll tell me at some point."

I gave him an extra squeeze as we walked to my house, grateful he wasn't going to push the issue.

Chapter
Twenty-Eight

♥

Sebastian was sprawled across my bed while I packed. Soon, I'd be starting the drive home to see my dad and my sister for the holidays.

"When are you coming back?" He tossed a football into the air and caught it over and over.

"You play on the 31st, right? I'll be here on the 30th." I stuffed the last few things into my suitcase. There were clothes of mine at Dad's, so packing was somewhat pointless.

"You tell your family about me?" He sat up with the ball gripped in his hands.

My nail kit was in my hand, and I didn't turn around. Was honesty the best policy when it might hurt your boyfriend's feelings? I was going to tell my dad, but I hadn't yet.

"That's a no." He sighed. "Why not?"

Leaning against my desk, I couldn't meet his gaze. "I wanted to make sure we stuck. When I'm home, I'll tell him."

"You worried your dad's not going to like me?" he asked quietly.

"What? No. Why?" My gaze flew to his.

"We've been spending a lot of time together. Figured you might have mentioned me, that's all." He stared out my bedroom window.

I took a deep breath. "Does your family know about me?"

"My mom does, yeah. She told my sister. She texted me something the other day that made me think she knows. They're gonna be at the game on the 31st. I was hoping—well, it would be nice for them to meet you."

"Oh." I sat on the bed beside him. "You want me to meet your family?"

He let out a frustrated breath. "Yeah, I want them to meet you." He shook his head. "You're really frustrating sometimes."

I scooted closer to him. "I'm frustrating?" I looped my arms around his neck and buried my face in the space just under his ear. My favorite spot.

He tossed the football to the ground and dragged me across his body, so I straddled him. "Yeah, you are." He squeezed me tighter.

His lips found mine in a dance we both knew so well. He flipped us over and lifted me farther up the bed, closer to the headboard. When he pressed into me, my resolve was tested. I'd never wanted anyone the way I wanted him. He rained kisses down on me. My insides were liquefying, and I tugged on the bottom of his shirt. He let me yank it off. My hands roamed over his muscles as he continued kissing me. He was mine. There were moments when I couldn't quite believe this was happening. Me with a football player. Me with Sebastian.

He kissed me deeply one last time and then drew back to stare into my eyes. He searched my face, and there was something in his hazel depths I was afraid to name. The air grew thick with what we weren't saying.

Finally, in a rough voice, he said, "I'm going to miss you like crazy, Nattie."

The words were on the tip of my tongue. Three of them. I'd said the phrase to a few people in my life. But I couldn't let them out. What if he didn't say them in return?

Unexpectedly, I ached for my mother. I longed to sit and chat with her about how she'd known my dad was the one for her. When I scanned Sebastian's face, what I felt for him was so much bigger than such a small word like love.

Instead, I said, "I'm going to miss you too."

"You gotta get going, right?" He was poised over top of me when he glanced at the clock.

Reluctantly, I turned to check. "Yeah, I'm supposed to pick Kristy up in half an hour. I'm dropping her off on my way home."

He shifted and tugged me up off the bed, right into his chest. His hand went into my hair, drawing me to him again. I met his lips hungrily, wishing time would stand still. Maybe I would have to return early to surprise him.

He squeezed me tight. "I don't want you to go." The words were muffled against my neck.

"I don't want to go either." I ran my hands over his coarse, closely cropped hair. "But, I promised Kristy a ride, and I promised my dad I'd be home in time for dinner."

Sebastian released me, put his shirt on, and then he grabbed my suitcase to take it out to the rental car I'd picked up that morning. My dad was paying for it, and Kristy was giving me half the gas money. So much easier than trying to catch a bus.

Annika was at the frat house and was going home later today. She and Johnny were on in a big way. I kept waiting for her to suggest Sebastian move in here so she could resume her previous living arrangement. But so far, she'd been quiet about that situation.

Once I was in the car, I rolled down my window. "You'll lock up and give the key to Annika?"

He grinned. "I'll lock up. No guarantees I'll give the key to Annika. I kinda enjoy being able to come and go as I please."

"Keep the key, then. It'll give me a reason to come straight to you when I get back." We had the spare key, but seeing him right away sounded better to me.

He rested his forearms on the window frame. "You don't need a reason, Nattie." He kissed me. "I want to be your first stop whether I have a key or not."

Gripping his shirt, I dragged him farther into the car one last time, kissing him as though it was the last opportunity I'd have for years instead of a single week. Our separation would be a lifetime given the amount of time we'd been spending together.

I released him and he backed up, crossing his arms over his chest from the chilly winter air. When I drove away, my gaze kept finding him in the rearview mirror until I couldn't see him anymore.

My sister Claudia met me at the front door as I hauled in my bags.

"Uh, you realize you have clothes here? And you're only home for a week?" Claudia tried to take the suitcase from me.

I swung the case away from her and shook my head. "Nope. I got it." I wheeled it farther into the foyer. "Where's Dad?" I peeked into the main living area.

"Not here. Why?"

"No reason." I took off my coat and hung it in the side closet.

"Dad asked me why you weren't bringing Clay home for the holidays," Claudia said, raising her eyebrows. "Was a tad awkward. You haven't told him about Sebastian?"

I gave her a helpless look. "He liked Clay so much."

"Shut up, Nat. That's not it. Are you and Sebastian a thing or not? Because it sounded as though you were completely gaga over him the last time we talked."

In the living room, I flopped onto the couch. "We're definitely a thing, and I'm—almost literally—insane about him." I tucked my hair behind my ears. "He's on my mind constantly. I want to be with him every second of the day. I can't get enough of him."

"Okay." Claudia held up her hand. "We might be getting into overshare territory. We're sisters, but I'm not keen to picture you having sex with him."

"Well then, I have fantastic news for you because we haven't...yet."

"What? Why not?" Claudia sat in the recliner across from me.

"There *was* a reason, but it doesn't feel valid anymore. We're solid. He's a good guy." A sappy grin lit my face.

"Who's a good guy?" Dad came into the open-plan kitchen-living room with a grocery bag.

My dad and my sister were clearly related. They were both fair, whereas I was a brunette, like my mother. Sometimes when they looked at me, they saw her. It made me happy and sad.

"Natalie's new boyfriend," Claudia said before I could get a word out.

"What?" Dad asked in disbelief. "What happened to Clay? I figured I was getting a son-in-law."

"You still might." Claudia's grin was wicked. "It just won't be Clay."

"So, who is this guy?" He stood at the island, putting the groceries away, waiting for me to start talking.

I gathered my arsenal of responses. I wasn't sure how this was going to go. "His name is Sebastian."

"What's he taking?" My dad ripped open the bag of peeled carrots and bit into one thoughtfully. "Huh, I thought Clay was the guy. I'm surprised."

"You're disappointed?" His reaction was definitely part of the reason I hadn't come clean earlier. I slouched deeper into the couch.

My dad shrugged. "He seemed like a good guy. But you've always had impeccable taste. I'm sure this—"

"Sebastian," Claudia said in a singsong voice.

"Right, I heard. Sebastian, is a nice guy." Dad moved around the kitchen putting away the last of the groceries. He turned to me again. "Major?"

"Business." I picked at an invisible spot on my pants.

"How'd you two meet?" Dad faced us with his back resting against the island, and a small stack of carrots was cradled in his hand.

"Uh—"

"He's a football player, Dad. A really *amazing* football player." Claudia was enjoying my discomfort.

We got along well, but over the years, whenever she had a chance to drop me in shit with either of our parents, she never failed to do it.

Dad frowned, chewing on his carrot. "Football player?"

"Yep," I said. "He plays football."

"I didn't think you liked football," Dad said. "Is this one of those moments where I'm the dumb dad?"

I laughed. We'd had a few of those moments. Dad didn't always pay close attention to what was going on with me and Claudia. He tried, but things we said and did baffled him.

"No, Dad. You're not wrong. I don't enjoy football, but I'm learning to appreciate it."

He chuckled. "Ah, that's Nat-speak for you're tolerating it." He smiled and came over to ruffle my hair. He sat next to me, and I knew what was coming next. "Now, football players, honey. They come in all shapes and sizes."

"So do people, Dad." I gave him a sideways glance.

"Yeah, well..." He trailed off. "Some of those football players, if they're looking for an edge, they do things, take things that change them."

"I know, Dad. Sebastian's not like that," I said. "Honestly, he's a good guy. We're just casually seeing each other. It's not a big deal."

Claudia stared at me and rolled her eyes. I glared in response.

"How's Annika?" Dad crunched through another carrot, ignoring the tension between me and Claudia.

"She's doing okay." Another loaded topic. Especially since he'd just finished his speech about football players sometimes being unpredictable.

"She dating anyone?" He went to the kitchen and grabbed dip from the fridge.

I cleared my throat. "The quarterback," I mumbled.

Dad laughed. "Now, that makes sense. That must be how you met Sebastian."

I smiled. "Yep."

"He treats her well? Is he a good guy like Sebastian?" His back was to us while he took vegetables out of the fridge to get dinner ready.

"I haven't spent much time with him." I went to the foyer to get my suitcase. My room was calling me. Discussing Annika and Johnny with my dad was a bad idea. If I overreacted to this kind of thing, my dad was on a whole other level.

He gave me a long look when I returned with my suitcase. "Natalie Ann. That's an evasive answer. Is she in trouble? Am I worried about the wrong person here?"

God, sometimes I hated my dad's cop instincts. They always seemed much better whenever I mentioned my friends too. He could spot trouble in other people a mile away.

I sat and pursed my lips. Claudia's eyes were wide. I hadn't told her this yet either.

"Johnny and I don't get along. Sometimes I wonder whether he's treating Annika very well. They've split up a few times and gotten back together."

Annika was convinced Johnny would never seriously hurt her. To my mind, he wasn't a good boyfriend. But was he truly dangerous? Would he do anything worse than finger bruises? For me, that would be enough, but for Annika, his behavior was acceptable. How did I convince her otherwise? So far, I couldn't, and the mere suggestion she might be making a mistake had almost cost me her friendship.

"Not treating her well as in not a nice guy or as in abusive?"

"I'm not sure," I admitted. I didn't have any proof other than a couple bruises Annika dismissed as accidental.

My dad came over and sat beside me again on the couch and glanced at my sister. "I've said this many times before, but if either of you ever needs me—as your dad or as a police officer—I will drop everything and come. I will believe you. I will believe your friends." He made eye contact with Claudia and then met my gaze.

"I know, Dad," I whispered, sliding away from his intense stare.

He started making dinner, but there was a weight on his shoulders. He was probably thinking about Annika. They'd only met a few times, but they'd gotten along well. Dad admired her spunk and her contagious laugh.

"Nat." Claudia came over to take Dad's spot. "Is Annika in trouble?" Her voice was low.

"I think so, but I'm the only one who believes that." I matched her tone.

"Sebastian doesn't see it?" Claudia frowned.

"He thinks Johnny is 'intense' and sometimes 'doesn't realize his own strength.'"

"Oh." Claudia gave me a worried look. "That's not good."

"Yeah." I examined my hands in my lap. "Another reason I worried about telling Dad. If this blows up, I'm not sure where Sebastian will fall." I laced my fingers together in my lap and released them.

"That would be..." Claudia trailed off.

"Bad, yeah. Bad for me and Sebastian. Bad for Sebastian with Dad. Bad for Sebastian and Annika. Bad, bad, bad."

No matter where my thoughts went, it always led to disaster if Sebastian chose Johnny and the team over my best friend. Maybe she would leave Johnny or I'd been jumping to conclusions about Sebastian's loyalty. His words and actions pointed to football being his top priority, and Johnny was a huge reason Sebastian was getting so much attention this year.

"Any chance you're wrong about Sebastian?" Claudia leaned her shoulder into the couch beside me.

I gave her a small smile. "I guess there's always a chance, right?"

She patted my leg and then went to help Dad in the kitchen. My phone pinged, and when I checked it, I grinned. Sebastian had sent me a Photoshopped picture of him as Superman with the words: *This is me, flying to you. Miss you already.*

An ache sprouted in my chest. I missed him already too. But my conversation with my dad and Claudia was ringing in my ears. If Sebastian had to choose me or Johnny, who would he pick?

Football. Which meant he'd be picking Johnny too.
I had never wanted to be so wrong in my life.

Chapter Twenty-Nine

♥

We stood outside the back doors, which were deserted. Annika was beside me, gripping my hand. The team had won. They'd made it to the National Championship for the first time in years. A huge deal, and an opportunity Sebastian had talked about for weeks.

The biggest thing on my mind, though? I would meet Sebastian's family tonight. After dinner, we'd meet everyone else at Gabby's bar to celebrate.

Annika squeezed my fingers. She was vibrating. "Sebastian and Johnny are going to be over the moon."

"Who needs sex when you can win a massive football game?" I gave her a fake rah-rah cheerleader jump.

I'd come back to campus last night, and Sebastian and I'd spent the night almost having sex, but not quite. If that was the preview, I was ready for the real show. He hadn't once pressured me for more the last few weeks. We went so far and then he backed off.

Annika barked out a laugh and then covered her mouth with her palm. "Yeah, sure, whatever you say, Nat."

"Hey—what's with that?" I removed her hand. "All night when you've gone to laugh, you've covered your mouth. Did you eat a lot of garlic or something?" I leaned in and sniffed.

"No." She gave me a brief smile. "Johnny said my laugh—well, that I use it to draw attention to myself."

"Your laugh is awesome. It's contagious." What I didn't say was that her laugh was the whole reason Johnny was attracted to her in the first place. He was tearing her down, one brick at a time.

"I'm trying to calm it down, you know. It makes Johnny uncomfortable when we're out, and people stare when I laugh. He said the sound seems forced—I'm trying too hard."

Trying too hard? Her beautiful, contagious laugh, one of the things I loved most about spending time with her, wasn't "forced." He was censoring her laugh. What else was he convincing her about when no one else was present?

"Annika, your laugh is great. I would tell you if you were making an ass of yourself. You're not. It's one of my favorite sounds. I love your laugh."

"I'm self-conscious about it now. Johnny's mentioned it a few times." She gave me a small smile. "I can't believe they won. I mean, I *can* believe it because they've been playing awesome ball. But I can't because this win is such a big deal."

Johnny and Sebastian burst through the doors. Sebastian rushed me, sweeping me off my feet into a huge hug and swinging me. I clutched him close and chuckled in his ear. He set me down, cradled my face, and kissed me as though we hadn't just seen each other a few hours ago.

"Lord, did I ever miss you," he said when we broke apart.

"I missed you too." I drew him in for another kiss. "Congratulations on the win. You guys must be so excited."

Sebastian laughed. "Excited doesn't cover it. Even if we don't win, man, getting there is huge."

"We'd better win," Johnny said from beside Annika.

"I think we've got a good shot." Sebastian smoothed my hair and tugged me closer. We couldn't seem to get close enough.

I kissed him beneath his ear. Every time I was this tight to him and our eyes connected, something came alive between us. An electrical current hummed, unnamed, but so strong it felt like its own living, breathing entity.

"You ready to go meet my parents and my sister?" he asked.

"I'm not sure I'm ready, but I'm prepared." I smiled. "I need to get changed at my place. Rolling up to dinner in jeans and a hoodie isn't a good first impression."

"I better not go in the house while you do that."

When I looped my arms around his neck, I pressed myself even closer. "You don't want to come in?" I purred into his ear.

He chuckled and gave me a squeeze. "Nattie, you are gonna kill me." He buried his head in my neck and nipped at my earlobe.

I shivered.

"We'd never leave the damn house if I came in."

He was not wrong.

I waved to Annika and, rather reluctantly, Johnny as we left the exit and headed for Sebastian's SUV in the parking lot. I slid into the passenger seat, and as Sebastian turned on the ignition, I flicked the heated seat button to high.

"You know my parents aren't going to care what you're wearing. They'll be happy they're finally meeting a real-life girl I'm dating." He held my hand with one of his, and he steered with the other.

"Gee, thanks. Now their expectations will be sky high. You've never brought someone to meet them before?"

He laughed. "They were probably starting to wonder if I ever would. My sister is a serial committer like you. We've met a few of her boyfriends."

"Serial committer. Should I be going around killing people with commitment? That's how it sounds."

Sebastian pitched his voice to carry the tune from the movie *Psycho* and made a stabbing motion.

"That's deeply disturbing." But I couldn't hold my laugh.

"It's you, Nattie." Sebastian shrugged and grinned. He grabbed my hand and brought it to his mouth, kissing the back of it. "Man, I love hanging out with you." He laced our fingers together.

"The feeling is mutual." My heart pounded in my chest at the word "love" leaving his lips.

He snagged the parking space closest to my front door. I undid my seat belt and leaned over to kiss his cheek. When I moved back, he wrapped his arm around my middle and tugged me across him. My body landed between him and the steering wheel. The position was awkward, but as soon as my lips met his, I didn't care anymore.

In a gruff voice, Sebastian said, "We're never going to make it to dinner if you don't get out of this vehicle now."

I chuckled and ran my fingertips along the side of his face. When our eyes met, the air hummed. With one last soft kiss, I tried to wriggle myself to my side of the SUV. He watched me for a moment, desire and amusement flickering across his face. Finally, he secured his arms around my waist and helped lift me into my seat.

I ran into the house and yanked off my sweater and jeans. The purple dress was at the rear of the closet, and I tugged it down before I shimmied into it. I hadn't worn it since that first night at the frat house. I also grabbed a light sweater in case the restaurant was cold, and I threw on my heavy winter coat. In my high heels, I teetered out to the vehicle.

When I opened the passenger door, Sebastian whistled. "That dress has made an appearance or two in my dreams."

I glanced at myself and raised an eyebrow at him. "This old thing?" I slid into the seat.

Sebastian stared at me for a few minutes, not making any move to leave the parking lot.

"What?" A half smile played at the edges of my lips.

"They're gonna love you, Nattie. You're smart, funny, and absolutely gorgeous. They'll wonder what the hell you're doing with me." His expression brimmed with sincerity.

I grabbed his shirt and tugged him to me. Before his lips met mine, I said, "In this moment, I couldn't imagine wanting to be with anyone else."

He crushed his lips to mine, deepening the kiss. His seat belt released, and he murmured against my mouth, "They can wait."

I laughed and pushed against his chest when he started to climb over. "No, Sebastian. No. I can't be late the first time I meet your family. We might as well carry a cardboard sign that says we were too busy screwing to be punctual."

"You got markers and cardboard in your house? I'll gladly make that sign." But he eased into his seat, giving me a sideways glance.

"I do have markers and cardboard in my house. But they are for your final game of the season. I have big plans." I threw my hands wide.

He put the SUV in reverse. "Big plans, huh? You mean, Annika has big plans?"

I raised my eyebrows. "Nope, this is me. I have ideas, Sebastian, ideas about football that are my own."

He placed a hand over his heart and looked shocked. "Ideas about football because of me?"

"Yeah." I gave his thigh a squeeze before gazing at him again. "Watching you on the field, now that I understand how it works, well, I'm so proud of you. I see you out there prancing." I glanced at him out of the corner of my eye with a small smile. "And I can't get over how good you are and that you're mine. That I know you, really know you."

The air between us electrified. There was so much more I could say. But I wasn't going to declare my love for him while we were in his SUV driving to dinner.

"I'm proud of you all the time too." Sebastian's gaze rotated between me and the road.

"Oh yeah? Why's that?"

"You're so strong. Man, you're probably one of the strongest women I've ever met. You're solid in your convictions, and you don't back down, even when it would be easier. I admire that. A lot. You got a good head on your shoulders." He cupped the back of my head.

I grabbed his hand as it left my head and sandwiched his between mine. Even though I'd decided I wasn't going to tell him I loved him in the car, the words were bubbling, threatening to boil over.

"That's incredibly sweet," I whispered.

"It's not sweet, Nattie. It's true." He turned into the restaurant parking lot. When the SUV was in park, he focused on me. "Look at me. I'm not even nervous about them meeting you."

"I'm probably nervous enough for both of us." I undid my seat belt.

He came to my side as I was climbing out and secured my hand in his.

"Here goes nothing."

He grinned. "Famous last words."

I smacked him in his firm abs. "That's not helping." Having half of my mind consumed with rated R thoughts of Sebastian didn't help either.

Welcome, Gutter. My brain couldn't wait to slide in.

He opened the door to the restaurant and motioned for me to go in first. I slipped past him, my stomach rolling.

He followed behind me, and we stood at the desk for a minute. The place was full of dark wood, dim lighting, and gas fireplaces. Any other time, the atmosphere might be romantic instead of anxiety inducing.

"I see them." Sebastian guided me through the restaurant.

Chapter Thirty

♥

As we approached the table, two women and a man rose to greet us.

Sebastian's mom drew my eye. Her pale skin, light hair, and sharp blue eyes were in direct contrast to his father, whose complexion was much darker than Sebastian's and even his sister appeared dark skinned compared to his fair mother. His mom's lips quirked up as if she knew what I was thinking. She was as white as me.

"Natalie." She smiled and held out her hand. "It's so nice to meet you. I'm Janice. This is Devonte and Kiara." She pointed to Sebastian's father and sister.

I shook everyone's hand and then took the seat Sebastian pulled out for me.

When the waitress appeared to take our drink orders, I got water. Getting drunk with his family was much farther along the dating road. Sebastian grabbed my hand under the table. I smiled at him and gave him a gentle squeeze.

"So, Natalie. Sebastian told Janice you're hoping to become a lawyer. Kiara specializes in criminal law." Pride was evident in Devonte's voice.

"Yes, sir. I haven't decided what I want to focus on just yet." I turned to address Kiara. "I'm not sure if your brother told you, but my dad's a cop, so I'm not sure I can go the criminal lawyer route."

She took a sip of her fruity cocktail. "It's not for everyone. My clients certainly cut a wide swath across society. Bermuda is so small everyone knows everyone. Might not be so bad in a big city."

"Depending on where you practice, I'm unclear how much money is in prosecution." Janice swirled her wine.

"That's true. That's always the push-pull," I said. "I don't have an interest in corporate or real estate. Maybe family law? I have time to mull over my options."

We sat in silence for a few minutes, looking over the menus. Sebastian released my hand and clutched my leg before using both hands to look through the list. Everything sounded amazing, but the price tags were insane. I scanned for the cheapest thing.

Shopska salad for the win. I closed my menu before I could talk myself into something more expensive.

When we ordered, everyone else chose lobster, fish, or steak, and when the waitress got to me, I picked the salad.

Sebastian frowned at me. "A salad?"

"Yep." I nodded. "It sounds delicious." The description wasn't appealing. But it was cheap.

Without another word, Sebastian passed our menus to the waitress. He took a drink from his beer and gave me a sideways glance. I'd once told him salads were what real food eats. He knew something was up with me.

"We were surprised when Sebastian said he was dating someone." Devonte flicked out his napkin. "Janice and I assumed he'd inherited our roaming genes. We didn't figure he had any desire to settle down."

When he finished speaking, I was in the middle of taking a sip of my water. I sputtered and almost choked.

"Dad." Annoyance laced Sebastian's voice. "I can't believe you said that to my girlfriend."

"Welcome to my world, little brother." Kiara gave her father an amused look. "I've been fielding those shitty comments for years while you laughed away."

He shook his head at her. "So, you should be helpful now, sis."

"No way. I choose to mock." Her smile was too sweet.

His family was close, even if they were unusual. Devonte's comment rang in my ears. If Sebastian and I weren't so solid, it would bother me more.

"Mom?" he asked. "You gonna help me out here?"

"Your father and I have a specific philosophy on monogamy. But I'm happy for you and Kiara if you two seek something else." She spread her hands wide.

He chugged his beer and signaled the waitress for another. I squeezed his leg under the table. He laced his fingers with mine.

"You people are killing me," Sebastian said.

"I wondered when you said you were bringing her to meet us. I guess you forgot the awkward meet and greets I've sat through over the years."

He held up his free hand toward his sister. "I don't need a recap. We're good. Seriously."

"You played a heck of a game tonight," Janice said. "Do you follow football, Natalie?"

I never thought I'd be grateful for a conversation about football. Sebastian chuckled beside me, but I wasn't sure if it was because of the question or my previous attitude toward football.

"I don't follow the sport or any players other than Sebastian and his team." I took a long drink of my water.

"Natalie didn't like football when we first met. It was actually her roommate dating Johnny that put us in the same places." Sebastian's shoulder rubbed against mine.

"That Johnny has a hell of an arm." Devonte whistled.

"It's not just his arm that's amazing." Kiara pretended to fan herself. "Is he still seeing your roommate?"

"Yes." I tried to keep my expression neutral.

"Transferring was an excellent idea." Janice leaned back as her food arrived. "You and Johnny work well together on the field."

"I take it you're into football?" I directed my question at his mom.

Janice grimaced. "No choice. He's been crazy for it since the first game he watched. He's given up a lot of other things over the years to get himself close to the top. His college career has been a carefully orchestrated dance to get him to this school this year and eligible to play."

I rubbed Sebastian's shoulder before the waitress set down his food. The familiar swell of pride rose in me. "He's persistent."

Kiara laughed. "I bet he is." Her gaze slid between us.

When the waitress placed the world's tiniest salad in front of me, I realized cheap was not going to fill my stomach. Good thing I hadn't gone for the alcohol or I'd be drunk by the end of the meal.

Sebastian turned to our server. "Can I get a side plate?"

The waitress passed him the plate, and he cut his steak in half, setting it in front of me.

"Sebastian," I whispered.

"Nattie, you're not eating a damn salad. Certainly not a salad that looks like two pieces of lettuce with random things thrown on top." He gestured to my half-empty plate.

When I glanced up, his family watched with amusement.

"Aww. That's so cute," Kiara said.

"Shut up, Kiara. I was going to invite you to come out with us. I'm starting to reconsider." He shot her a warning glare.

"I've hung out with your friends before." Kiara dug into her lobster and popped a piece into her mouth.

"Yeah, I remember the last time you hung out with my teammates." Sebastian huffed.

She stopped mid-bite. "What's that mean?"

"I think you know that that means." He gave her a pointed look.

She snickered. "Yeah, I do."

Frowning, I nudged Sebastian's shoulder.

"I'll tell you later—or I'm sure she will if she comes out with us." He gestured toward his sister.

While we ate, the conversation turned to football, the draft, and Sebastian's plans for the next season. His parents were coming to the championship game, but Kiara couldn't get more time off work.

When the bill came, I got money out of my purse and tried to pay his parents.

"Nonsense." Devonte waved me off. "You're in college and we have well-paying jobs. Someday, when you're working a suitable job, you pay it forward."

"Thank you." Embarrassment lit my cheeks. "It was nice to meet you."

"Yes, it's been marvelous." Devonte took another big gulp from his beer. He'd gone through several during dinner. "Maybe we'll see you again someday."

"Jeez, Dad." Sebastian shook his head.

"Who knows?" I grinned.

"*I* know." Sebastian met my eyes. "You guys are going to be seeing a lot of Nattie. She's not going anywhere."

My grin stretched wider.

"I can't go out with you two if this is what's happening. I can't properly digest my dinner when Sebastian's this loved up. The world is tilting on its axis." Kiara pushed back her chair.

My insides somersaulted at the use of the word love.

"Come on, Kiara," Sebastian said. "I hardly ever see you. I want you to get to know my girl."

"We're heading out." Janice circled the table to hug Sebastian, and then everyone started exchanging hugs and goodbyes.

When Janice hugged me, she whispered in my ear, "He looks happy. I'm glad."

Devonte kissed both my cheeks and gave me a half hug. He looked at Janice for a beat before putting his arm around her and leading her out of the restaurant. As they exited, Janice threw her head back in a raucous laugh.

Before I could ask Sebastian about their behavior, Kiara intercepted. "It's probably best if you don't ask. They're weird."

I nodded. "Noted."

Kiara put on her coat. "I'm going to be the old one at the bar, aren't I?"

"If you drink enough, you won't care." Sebastian helped me into my coat.

"True," Kiara said. "Is that asshole Theo going to be there? 'Cause if so, less alcohol is probably better than more. He was grabby at the start of the year."

"Theo?" I asked, surprised.

"That was his name, wasn't it, Seb?" Her voice drifted over her shoulder, leading us out of the restaurant. "You two got into it, right?"

"Yeah, that was him," Sebastian admitted, avoiding my gaze.

I nudged him. "You never told me that."

"I told you he wasn't a good guy. It's why I followed you home that night from the bar when he was walking you." He met my gaze before sliding away. "We both know how that turned out."

A brief flash of him leaning into another girl on the hood of his car flashed in my memory. "Yeah."

He secured me tight to his side. "Till the day I die, Nattie."

"Me too." I wrapped my arm around him and squeezed him. "That whole night was so pointless." The image of him with the other girl still hurt my heart every time I thought about it, so I shoved it away. He wasn't that guy anymore.

Kiara opened the rear door of the SUV. "You two are disgustingly cute. Sebastian, I always wanted you to get a girlfriend so you'd understand the pain of Mom and Dad. But I'm not sure I can handle this ooey-gooey stuff you two have going on."

"We're that bad?" I asked.

"We're not that bad." Sebastian chuckled. "Kiara's tolerance level for anyone in a relationship when she's not in one is very low."

She pointed at him. "That is true. Take me to the bar so I can meet my next conquest!" Kiara shouted before climbing into the backseat.

Sebastian rubbed his neck. "I'm kinda glad Johnny and Annika are back on. Not sure how I would've handled my sister trying to sleep with him all night."

I smiled, but it didn't reach my eyes. "Yeah," I agreed before climbing in. "He's all Annika's."

Chapter Thirty-One

K iara took a sip of her fruity drink and smiled at me. "Alone at last." She watched Sebastian head for the bathroom. "My brother never spends this much time around me at a bar."

"He didn't use to spend this much time with *me* at a bar either."

"I find that hard to believe. He's weirdly attentive: getting drinks, making genuine conversation, gazing at you adoringly." She used her free hand to secure a bobby pin a little tighter. Her hair was an intricate mass of braids that culminated in a bun-like structure.

I shrugged. "We get each other, I guess. We have a similar sense of humor. I enjoy hearing his perspective on things. I tend to make up my mind quickly about people. He's more open-minded."

"My brother has always been extroverted. He's never had trouble making friends or finding people who want to spend time with him." Her lips quirked up. "But I'm not sure I've ever seen him spend time with someone the way he's spending it with you."

My cheeks were two flames of color in the dimly lit bar, and warmth filled my heart. "That's nice to hear," I murmured, the ice cubes shifting in my drink. "I had a hard time deciding to go all in with him."

Her smile was wide as she took me in. "I get why he likes you. There's this energy around you that kinda reminds me of him. Of the best parts of him."

My blush deepened, and I shifted.

She laughed. "All right, all right. I'll leave you alone. I don't wanna scare you off. Sebastian would never forgive me," she said. "So have you always wanted to be a lawyer?"

My shoulders collapsed, and I was grateful for the new topic. "No. I came here for Exercise and Sports Science. Took me three weeks to realize I was fooling myself. I wasn't sure I wanted to get into the law. Growing up, given what my dad did, it was hard sometimes. He couldn't always leave work at work."

Sebastian's arm looped around my waist, and he took his beer. "Nattie is going to change the world."

"Can't do that taking Exercise and Sports Science," Kiara agreed.

"Sebastian's exaggerating. But I did tell him I realized right away my initial major wasn't the right choice for me."

"You want to make a difference for people, Nat. I think that's admirable." Sebastian dropped a kiss on my temple.

Kiara stared at us and shook her head, grinning. "I'm going to go anywhere but here, okay, Seb?"

"You're leaving?"

"I got a plane to catch tomorrow, little brother." She slid her drink onto the nearest table.

Sebastian released me and enveloped her in a hug, shaking her up and down. They laughed when she protested he was going to hurt himself.

"Thanks for coming, sis. Really. It means a lot to me that you support me."

"Sorry I can't come for the championship." Kiara shoved her purse higher up on her shoulder.

"That's all right. You have a grown-up job now. Sometimes it has to come first."

Kiara squeezed me close. "I loved meeting you. We'll see a lot more of each other, I'm sure."

"That'd be nice. I'm looking forward to it."

Kiara took out her phone. "Do I need to call a cab or are they around on the street?"

I glanced at Sebastian. "Did you want to stay longer, or should we go wait with Kiara and go home?"

"We can go. I had to show my face, but I'm happy to leave." He downed his beer and set it on the table with Kiara's abandoned drink.

I set my half-full drink there too. I wanted to be sober tonight.

Sebastian called Kiara a cab while we picked up our coats and walked out of the bar. We stood huddled in a small circle, gathered close for warmth.

"I never thought I'd see the day when Sebastian left a football party before it was over." Kiara gave him a teasing smile.

Sebastian laughed. "Times are a-changin'." He squeezed my hip.

The cab arrived, and Kiara gave us both one last hug before ducking into the rear of it.

As soon as the cab sped away, Sebastian turned me toward him. "Alone at last."

"It's funny. You sister said that earlier when you went to the bathroom."

"Oh yeah? And proceeded to tell a bunch of inappropriate and highly embarrassing stories? Do I need to chase that cab?"

The happy, amused light shining out of him as he gestured in the direction of the cab caused my heart to contract. "No." I scanned his features. "She said she liked me."

Sebastian dipped to give me a quick kiss. "No surprise there. I figured you two would get along."

"I'm glad you were right."

"My parents, though." Sebastian took my hand. "I'm sorry about that."

I shrugged. "They didn't say anything I didn't already realize." I gathered my thoughts. "You said before you hadn't committed to anyone because you hadn't found someone worthwhile. And I'm not saying I'm not worthwhile, but do you think that's true?"

We walked for a moment while he considered my question. "Maybe I watched my parents' marriage crumble at an age that left a pretty deep impression. As you probably noticed, they still have a weird relationship." He took a deep breath. "I don't want that. I don't want to be like them. I was just—I was worried I'd pick wrong. Someone fickle like them because it's what I've known."

"So you didn't pick anyone?"

"I think, mostly, I let girls pick me. I mean—I don't know—that sounds bad." He shook his head and chuckled. "But I saw you at the frat party with your flask, obviously cock-blocking Johnny, the star quarterback, and I couldn't help myself. I wanted to know who had that much self-confidence. You *know* yourself, Nattie. You *know* who you are."

My face was on fire, but a stupid smile had bloomed across it. "You think those nice things about me?"

"Hell, yeah. I could fill a book full of Nattie-isms that I love."

We'd reached my door, and I turned to face him, pressing my spine against the cool steel. I grabbed his coat and drew him close, and his hands braced against the door above my head.

Our faces were mere inches apart. Indecision flickered in his hazel depths, and I cocked my head in silent question.

"Carpe diem, eh, Nattie," he said quietly.

"Seize the day?" My lips twitched in amusement.

He scanned my face. One of his hands cupped my cheek before he kissed me, slow and deliberate. When he drew away, he rested his forehead against mine.

"I am so desperately in love with you, Natalie Ann Chapman. I had no idea it was possible to feel this way about someone."

My gaze, which had been focused on his lips, wishing he'd kiss me again, flew to meet his. My heart squeezed in my chest, and fireworks went off in my mind. *He loved me?* I dragged him into a kiss, pushing my body off the door. We needed fewer clothes. I needed to be closer, so much closer. How would we ever be close enough?

I dug out my key, still kissing him, and tried to unlock it without breaking lip contact. He chuckled when the key clattered to the ground.

"Shit," I said. "Not very smooth."

He scooped up the keys. The key slid into the lock, his hand in my hair, and he kissed me again, long and deep. "Not smooth," he said. "Noted for my book."

I laughed against his lips and stumbled in the now open door. Sebastian half caught me before I fell to the floor.

"You, on the other hand," I said, "are incredibly smooth." I was drunk, but it wasn't on alcohol.

Sebastian backed me into the room and kicked the door shut with his heel. I reached around him and snapped the lock into place. No interruptions tonight. He unzipped my coat, and my hands moved around him to do the same.

"Is Annika coming here tonight?" Sebastian asked against my lips.

"No." I tugged his shirt over his head and tossed it toward the couch.

We were walking and kissing. Clothes littered the living room and hallway as we made our way to my room.

The back of my knees hit the bed, and as I fell backward, Sebastian caught me, never breaking the kiss. God, I loved him. The realization hit me at once. I hadn't said those words yet, not out loud.

"Sebastian," I murmured against his lips.

He broke the kiss and backed off, giving me space. He always did. No complaints. No question. Just room to breathe.

"You okay?" He searched my face.

I grinned. "Yes." I placed my hands on his cheeks and met his gaze. For weeks, the words had hovered between us, but I'd been too afraid to say them. "I love you, Sebastian. I totally get what it means to be crazy about someone. 'Cause sometimes the way I feel about you seems crazy. But I do. I love you, so much."

He broke out into the most beautiful grin, wide and full, his eyes sparkling. "I know, Nattie. It's why I didn't make a big deal about you saying it." He nudged a few stray strands of my hair off my face. "I know you love me. I feel it. All the time. It's incredible to me that someone as amazing as you could love me so much."

My body liquefied with longing. There wasn't a single part of me unsure about Sebastian anymore, unsure about us. "I want to be with you tonight. No stopping. I want to be as close to you as I can."

He kissed my forehead. "Nattie, that's not why I told you I love you. I told you 'cause I was tired of not saying it, not because I thought you'd have sex with me if I did."

"Oh, I realize that," I said. "God, if I thought that was why you said it, trust me, we would *not* be having sex tonight."

He chuckled. "And that right there is one of the many reasons why I love you."

"Enough to fill a book," I teased.

"Maybe even several."

He slid his hand along the length of me and up the inside of my leg. His mouth teased my jawline and then my neck, causing a haze of sensations. I was breathless with desire. I wanted to feel him, all of him.

When he skimmed over my panties with his fingertips, I moaned and pushed closer. My mind whispered the word *more* with every sensation.

"You like that, Nattie?"

"Yes," I breathed out when he did it again.

"Do you want more?"

"I want it all." Underneath him, I writhed. "I'll tell you when I get what I want."

He chuckled into my neck while his lips teased the sensitive skin. His amusement reverberated through my chest and to my core, making me long for more. He claimed my mouth again. Our tongues tangled, and he slipped under the band of my panties. His fingers slid along my wetness. *More. Closer.* A moan escaped me, and I arched my hips.

I ran my hands along the edge of his boxers, trying to free him so I could get what I wanted.

"Whoa, Nattie. Slow down," he murmured. "We got all night."

My bra vanished with a flick of his fingers, and he tossed it aside. Above me, he searched my face. "I really do love you, you know? Man, I must. You've greenlit me, and all I wanna do is look at you. I could look at you forever and not get tired of the sight."

My hands framed his face while my heart boomed in my chest. "I love you too." I drew him back and before we kissed again, I said, "I want you so much."

He met my lips with more intensity and then trailed kisses along my body. He eased his fingers into the waistband of my panties and dragged them down slowly. I ached with desire as I watched him toss them aside.

When he spread my legs and buried his face against my core, I gasped in pleasure. His tongue circled my most sensitive parts, and I gripped the sheets.

"Harder," I moaned. Sebastian chuckled against me, and I squeezed the sheets. The vibrations of his laugh inching me toward the edge.

"You giving me pointers, Nat? I like that."

"You enjoy having a coach." I managed to gasp out the words between moans.

He chuckled against my thigh, and a shiver ran through me.

Even as his tongue worked magic on my most sensitive parts, I needed more. "I want you. I want you inside me."

"You got me, Nat." He kissed his way back up my stomach and along my neck. "You got all of me."

He stepped back, and I groaned. "Sebastian." I tried to catch him when he left the bed. There was no stopping tonight.

At the nightstand, he opened the top drawer and took out a foil packet. I'd bought them so we wouldn't be caught short at my place when being together felt right.

"Oh, right." I turned on my side to watch him shed his boxers. Protection hadn't even crossed my mind, which wasn't normal. But I'd never been so swept away by the combination of love and desire. I crawled across the bed and rose onto my knees, drawing him into a kiss as he rolled on the condom.

He deepened the embrace while pressing me back into the mattress. He hovered over me, kissing any part of me that came close to his lips.

"I want this to be good for you, Nat." He gazed at me. "Put me in, Coach." He gave me a wicked grin.

I returned his smile. He tilted his head to kiss me and pushed inside. At the delicious contact, we both groaned. Soon, we were slick with sweat and need. Each time he eased out, I urged him to return, desperate to be connected, to unite every part of us.

"You feel so good," he murmured into my neck. He gripped my ass and secured us even tighter.

The muscles along his back relaxed and contracted with each thrust. We were as close as we could be, and I still ached for more. I slid my hand between us to help bring myself to climax.

Sebastian broke the kiss. "Want me to do that?"

"I got this," I said. "I know what I'm doing."

He grinned and gave me a kiss. "I'm a quick study."

"I can—"

"Take care of myself," he finished with a half smile. The next kiss was tender, brimming with love. Then the kiss intensified, and he pushed deeper into me, giving me the tight connection I craved.

I gasped and let myself get lost in the motion. Each time he pressed snug to me, the movement led me closer to the edge.

"Nat, I'm—" Sebastian broke off, closing his eyes.

"Keep going. I'm close," I moaned.

He buried his face in my neck, wrapping one arm around my back, and the other gripped my ass, locking us together.

"Oh, Sebastian," I breathed as my body prepared to tip over.

"Come with me, Nattie," he murmured.

"I'm—Oh, God. Oh, Sebastian." Then I tumbled over the edge.

He thrust a few more times and groaned, shuddering with his own release. With a lazy smile, he placed a soft kiss on my lips. "That was worth the fucking wait." He rained kisses down over my face and neck.

"You're telling me." I sighed.

He brushed my hair out of my face, and he stared at me. "I'm the luckiest guy in the world right now."

I smirked. "'Cause you had amazing sex?"

"Nah, Nattie. 'Cause I got you. I got to have amazing sex with you." He gave me a quick kiss before moving off me. "I'll be right back," he said from the doorway.

I slid under the covers and sighed.

Wow. Wow. Wow.

When he came back into the room, he left the door ajar. He climbed into bed and wrapped one arm around me, securing me flush against his chest.

"I love you, Natalie Ann Chapman." He sighed into my hair before his breathing evened out with sleep.

Once I was sure he was out, I rotated onto my back. His arm was a solid weight across my middle. I lay there admiring his peaceful expression, tracing every inch of him.

I'd never been so happy.

Chapter Thirty-Two

♥

I opened my eyes on a gasp, and then the sound that had yanked me from sleep came again.

The doorbell.

Bleary-eyed, I took in my surroundings. Sebastian was passed out cold beside me. My bedside clock said it was four in the morning. I threw on a robe and hoped Annika was here without her keys. Of course, that would mean she and Johnny had gotten into another fight.

I padded down the hallway, my heart racing. I glanced over my shoulder toward my open room and then rounded the corner to check the peephole.

Clay.

I stared, dumbfounded. I had no bra or underwear on, just a robe. The idea of inviting him in at four in the morning wasn't an unknown concept, but we hadn't seen each other in quite a while. Not to mention my new boyfriend, who I'd declared my undying love to, was sleeping in my bed.

"Clay?" I called through the closed door.

"Oh, thank God, Natalie. I was worried you wouldn't be home. I need to take Annika to the hospital. But she wouldn't go without you." Clay's panic was evident.

I unbolted the door and threw it open, not caring about my state of undress anymore. "Where is she?"

"She's in the backseat of my car. She's a fucking mess." He ran his hand through his brown hair in that old, familiar way.

"I have to get dressed." I rotated on my heel.

Clay sucked in a deep breath and called out, "Annika—she doesn't want Sebastian to know. Is he here? She was adamant she didn't want him involved."

That didn't sound good, but I wasn't in a position to argue with anyone. "Yeah, okay." I rushed down the hall. Before I walked in my room, I closed my eyes, praying Sebastian was sleeping.

When I opened my bedroom door, he sat on the edge of the bed, a sheet covering his lower half. "What's going on?" His voice was rough from sleep.

"I have to go." I grabbed a shirt and leggings from my drawers, throwing them on.

"Where? It's four in the morning."

I couldn't meet his gaze while I put on socks. "Annika's hurt."

"I'll come." Sebastian reached for his boxers on the floor.

"No." I shook my head. "I'm sorry. I'm so sorry. She doesn't want you to come. I don't understand what's going on."

"Who was at the door?" He tugged on his boxers and sat on the edge of the bed.

"Clay." I ran a brush through my hair in brisk strokes.

"Clay?" Sebastian frowned. "Your ex-boyfriend?"

"Yeah. I don't have many details yet. But I gotta go. If she's hurt, I can't stand here and puzzle it out with you. I love you. I'll text you later." I gave him a quick kiss before grabbing my purse off the floor and heading out.

The door was still open, and I realized Clay would understand what happened last night from our clothes scattered everywhere. I avoided making eye contact as I drew the door closed behind me.

"He's in there, isn't he?" Clay strode toward his car in the parking lot.

"Yeah." I struggled to keep up without jogging.

"What'd you tell him?"

"The truth. Annika's hurt. That's what I've been told. I love Annika, but I'm not lying to Sebastian, especially when I don't understand what's happening."

Clay stopped and turned to me. He swallowed. "You're going to want to call your dad."

"My dad?"

"It's bad. Just—brace yourself." Clay climbed into the driver's seat.

I opened the passenger's side, dread coursing through me. The dome light popped on, and in the backseat, huddled in a ball, was a figure who had Annika's shape and size. But her face was so bruised, bloody, and swollen I didn't recognize her. If Clay hadn't told me who it was, I wouldn't have been sure.

"Annika?" I asked softly.

"Nat?" She tried to lift her head.

I left the front seat and squeezed into the small space left in the rear. She moaned when I rested my hand on her side. Bile rose into my throat at the caked blood.

"Annika," I said, my voice pitched low. "What happened?"

She didn't answer me. Instead, her body twitched before great wracking sobs reverberated through the car. She dragged herself toward me and laid her head on my lap. Her dress was torn. Her tights were missing, and her feet were bare. I met Clay's gaze in the rearview mirror.

His shock and despair must be mirrored in my expression.

"I don't understand," I said. "Why do you have her? What happened to her?"

"I don't know what happened other than how it looks." Clay steered the car along the deserted roads to the hospital. "I was walking home from the bar, and I decided to take a shortcut through an alley. I didn't realize it was her at first. Maybe a homeless person or a drunk sleeping it off? But"—he swallowed—"when I got closer, I could hear her moaning in pain."

"She was in an alley?" My voice was a stunned whisper.

He nodded, and his gaze flicked to mine in the rearview mirror. "When I approached her, she recognized me. I didn't know it was her at first." Clay frowned. "She didn't want an ambulance or the police. She wanted you. I carried her to my house." He mumbled, "I'm not even sure she understands we're going to the hospital."

"We have to take her to the hospital." I searched my pockets for my phone. I closed my eyes. It had to be on my floor. It'd been in my pants' pocket when we returned from the bar. "Did you try to call me?"

He grimaced. "Several times. I was hoping you could meet us at the hospital. When I suggested that, Annika got frantic. So, I did the only thing I could think of."

I nodded. "You did the right thing." Without my phone, I couldn't contact Sebastian. I didn't have his number memorized. My life's details existed in my phone, not in my brain.

My dad.

"Can I borrow your phone?" I asked. "You're right about my dad. Mine is at the house." I grabbed his device when he passed it between the seats.

From memory, I punched in my home number with shaking hands. My dad had enough seniority now to work day shifts. A call at four in the morning would freak him out, but waiting until later would piss him off. If Annika was as bad as I thought she was, I needed someone to help navigate this.

"Hello?" My dad's voice was alert.

"Dad?" I asked, even though I knew it was him. My voice cracked; the sound of his deep timbre enough to snap me into the reality of this situation. "I need you."

"Address?" His frantic scramble for a pen was clear even over the phone.

"Lakeshore Hospital." I caught Clay's eyes in the mirror for confirmation.

"You or someone else?" Dad asked. He'd switched to cop mode.

"Annika. It's Annika, Dad."

"I'll be there as soon as humanly possible." Just before he clicked off, he said, "I love you, Natalie Ann. Whatever it is, we'll figure it out."

"Thanks, Dad." My voice caught on a sob.

I hung up and passed the phone through the seats to Clay.

We drove in silence the rest of the way. Annika didn't say anything about the phone call. I wasn't sure if she was awake. Her even breathing made me think she was sleeping. If her wounds were as painful as they looked, it was for the best.

Clay found a spot outside the emergency entrance. He turned to examine me over the seats. "I'll go inside and find out if I can get a wheelchair. It was a long walk from the alley to my house carrying her. I doubt I could get her in the doors."

"Okay," I agreed, wondering if my dad had already left our house. It would take him a couple hours to get here. He should miss most of the traffic at this time of day.

Clay returned with a wheelchair quicker than I expected. We both worked together to get Annika out of the backseat, shifting our grip every time she moaned in pain.

Once she was in the chair, Clay pushed her into the hospital through the emergency entrance doors while I kept my hand close to her arm. In the bright hospital lights, it was hard to tell where the blood had come from. A head injury. There was some kind of facial injury. The wounds on her arms might be defensive.

Defensive. My stomach rolled.

Nurses came forward, their faces neutral as they steered us to a room, bypassing the line of people waiting.

Outside the door, a nurse touched my arm. "Sexual assault kit?" she asked.

"Yeah," I said. "She should be checked for anything and everything. My friend found her in an alley."

"That would be the crime scene," the nurse said gently. "You should have called the police."

"She didn't want them."

The nurse frowned. "Do you think she knew her attacker?"

I hadn't even gotten that far. I should have. "Yeah," I said. "It's possible."

Clay came out of the room. "Annika doesn't want either of us in there while they check her over. I asked if she was sure she didn't want you. She said she is."

I peered through the small window while they got Annika settled on the bed. Then the curtain was pulled around. The nurse who had been talking to me yanked open the door and disappeared inside.

"Should we call Annika's parents?" Clay asked.

"Oh, God. Why am I the worst? I didn't even consider that." I turned wide eyes to Clay.

"Do you have their number?"

"Annika didn't have her phone?"

"No purse, no keys, no phone," Clay said. "She wouldn't say what happened. A mugging, a sexual assault, or…"

"Johnny." I finished for him.

"He did cross my mind," he admitted. "Why else would she insist she didn't want you to bring Sebastian? She really didn't want him involved."

The nurse popped her head out of the curtain. "We're going to be awhile. If you take a seat in the waiting room, we'll come get you when she's ready to see one or both of you."

We wandered to the waiting room in silence.

After a few minutes, Clay said, "Do you want me to go to your place and get your cell? We should call her parents."

Sebastian was probably still at my house. I passed Clay my house keys, just in case. "You don't mind?"

"No, not really. If Annika wants anyone, it'll be you." He took my keys. "Where's your phone?"

"Might be in my pants from last night, might be somewhere else. If Sebastian is there, you can ask him, or you can call it if he's left." The level of awkwardness was going to be astronomical.

"Right." He ran his hand through his hair.

"I'm sorry. I realize this is beyond awkward."

"Considering how Annika looks, a little awkwardness is the least of our worries."

He was right. Things might never be the same again for any of us.

Chapter Thirty-Three

♥

When my dad entered the emergency room through the sliding doors, I checked the clock on the wall. He'd broken so many speeding laws to get to me.

"Dad," I called, rising from my seat in the waiting area.

He headed toward me, and in that moment, I wasn't sure I'd ever loved him more. His familiar stride, his concerned expression, and his calm presence in the center of a disaster soothed me before he said a word. He was here. We'd figure this out. He enveloped me in a hug, squeezing me tight and rubbing my back.

When he released me, he framed my cheeks with his large hands. "What information do you have?"

"Clay found her in an alley." Surprise flickered across my father's expression. "She's been beaten. Possibly sexually assaulted. She didn't have her tights or shoes. Her phone, keys, and purse are missing."

"Did he call the cops? Are they there now?" He took a small pad of paper and a pen out of his rear pocket. Without looking up, he scribbled notes.

"No." That wasn't going to go over well with Dad. No matter what Annika said at the scene, I would have called. But I would have needed help. I couldn't have carried her like Clay.

"No?" Dad glanced up from his paper.

"Clay carried her to his car, picked me up, and then we came to the hospital together. Clay said Annika insisted on no cops."

My dad frowned and tapped his pen on the sheet of notes. "Is it possible she knew the person that did this?"

"Yes," I admitted.

"The quarterback?" Dad made another scribble. "Name?"

"Johnny McDade," I said. "But I don't understand why she'd be in an alley if it was him."

My dad's blue gaze flicked to me and then to his record. He took a deep breath. "All kinds of reasons she could have been there. We'll start asking questions and see how this shakes out. Annika doesn't want cops, but we need them. This has to be documented whether she wants to move forward or not."

I squeezed my hands together.

"Where's Clay?" He scanned the people in the waiting room.

"I left my phone at my house. He went to get it. We thought we should call Annika's parents."

"Good idea." My dad nodded. "Where's your boyfriend? Sebastian, was it?"

I took a deep breath. "Annika didn't want him to come."

Dad's frown deepened. "Sounds as though the perpetrator might have been this Johnny kid. Would Sebastian have information?"

Heat rose in my cheeks. "No."

I'd gone from being so happy with Sebastian a few hours ago to wondering if our relationship would survive Annika's assault. The football team meant more to him than anything. On the field, Johnny was the sun, the brightest star. His connection to Johnny was his ticket to the NFL.

"I'll see what I can find out. Make calls to the local police. Get things rolling." Dad slipped his pen and paper into his rear pocket. He removed his phone and wandered along the hall.

Just as my dad disappeared, Clay came through the sliding door. He passed me my phone.

"Was Sebastian still there?" I wasn't sure what I wanted the answer to be.

Clay gave a curt nod. "Yeah, he was leaving." He hesitated. "Said he had an emergency team meeting at six."

It was almost six-thirty now according to my home screen. What coach called a team meeting—emergency or not—this early? Had the coach heard what happened? Or was Johnny rallying the team?

Anxiety stirred my stomach, and bile shot into my throat. I held up a hand to Clay and ran to the bathroom. I made it into a stall before my dinner came tumbling out. On my knees, I hovered over the bowl, dry heaving. Tears pricked at my eyelids. When there was nothing left, I wiped my mouth with toilet paper.

At the sink, I braced my hands on the ledge and stared at myself in the mirror. Closing my eyes, I remembered the look on Sebastian's face last night as he'd told me he loved me.

Would love be enough?

I washed my hands, rinsed out my mouth, and opened the door to the waiting room. Clay was there, arms open, and I stepped in. He squeezed me tight.

"You're thinking what I'm thinking?" he asked.

I nodded. "It can't be coincidence for the coach to summon them to an emergency meeting the morning Annika is found badly beaten."

I cradled my phone and it buzzed. A text from Sebastian. The words *I love you* were visible through a blur of tears. When they fell, I brushed them away with my thumb.

"I'm going outside to call her parents. Back in a minute."

Clay took a seat in a row of empty chairs. "I'll be here if you need me."

I clicked on Sebastian's message. A few hours ago, I was so happy.

What did I say in response? I loved him too, but I couldn't make myself type a response. Instead, I scrolled through my contacts until I found Annika's parents. I'd only met them a handful of times.

The phone rang forever before a female voice answered.

"Mrs. Babu?" I asked.

"Yes. It's very early. Whatever you are selling, I don't want it," she said.

"Wait!" I called before she could hang up. "Mrs. Babu, it's Natalie. Annika's roommate."

"Natalie?"

"Annika's been hurt. She's at Lakeshore Hospital," I said in a rush. "She's going to be fine. But it's serious."

"We're coming," she said. "Tell Annika we're coming." Her voice was thick with tears.

The dial tone buzzed in my ear. She hadn't even asked what happened. Was it impressive that it didn't matter or worrying? Had Annika told her mother something she hadn't told me?

The sun lit the horizon, and I opened my message again. I ran my finger across the three words and hit reply.

"Nat?" My dad came out of the sliding doors. "Annika wants to see you." He looped his arm over my shoulders and squeezed.

I clicked my phone closed. "Are the cops here?" There were cruisers parked at the side entrance.

"Yeah. They let me sit in while they questioned her," he said. "She's doing much better than I would have expected given her injuries."

"Did she say what happened? Who did it?" We walked down the hall to her room.

His brow creased. "She says she doesn't remember. It's a blur." He met my gaze, anticipating my question. "It's possible, Nat. It's possible."

Outside Annika's door, I placed my fingers on the handle and took a deep breath.

"Supportive," my dad reminded me.

"I know, Dad. No judgment. I listen. I believe." The words I'd heard from him at the dinner table offered a guiding comfort. "My job isn't to establish truth."

Lines appeared at the edges of his eyes when he smiled. "So you did listen."

"Far too many times." My voice thickened. "But right about now, I'm grateful."

"Keep your phone handy. I'm going to tag along with the officers for as long as they'll let me," my dad said. "Right now, they're fine with me hanging around. That could change at any point."

I gave him a quick hug. "Thanks, Dad."

Before I opened the door to Annika's room, two male police officers appeared in the hallway and passed my dad a coffee. The three of them wandered toward the waiting room, chatting. I suspected they'd be talking to Clay next, maybe heading to the alley where he'd found her to search for any clues.

When I entered the room, the curtain was still pulled tight around the bed.

"Nat?" Annika's voice was distorted.

I drew back the edge of the curtain and stepped into her cocoon. They'd cleaned her. Her black eyes were now apparent, a blast of purple across her brown cheekbones. Her left cheek was swollen and had a gash, as though something sliced it. External scars were the least of her worries, but I hoped her face healed properly. The exterior reminder might make it harder for her interior to heal.

"Did they give you medicine for the pain?"

Annika nodded.

I perched on the edge of her bed, taking her palm in mine. When our gazes connected, tears trickled down her face.

"I don't remember anything." Annika didn't bother to wipe away her tears. "I want to remember."

Words failed me. I couldn't imagine waking up in her situation and having no recollection of what happened.

"Johnny's not here?" Her eyes glittered with hope.

I pursed my lips and shook my head.

"Would someone have told him I was here?" Her voice was a whisper, and more tears ran in rivers along her cheeks.

I hesitated. "Sebastian knows you're here. Not why, but..."

Her forehead creased, and a gut-wrenching sob emerged. I enveloped her, trying not to hit on any of her painful wounds.

"Oh, Annika," I said. "I am so sorry this happened to you. You cry. You cry as much as you need to." I rubbed her shoulder blade with a light touch, and she leaned into me.

"I don't understand." She choked out between sobs. "What did I do? Why would he do this?"

"If it was Johnny," I said, "this wasn't your fault. Nothing, and I mean this, nothing you could ever say or do to someone justifies what's happened to you." I drew back, so we made eye contact. "Whoever did this—they're responsible, not you."

She twisted a tissue. "But if it was Johnny, he wouldn't have done it without a good reason."

Her words were stones dropping into a well. "He's hurt you before?"

She stared out the window. "Sometimes," she whispered. "Only when we fought. Only when he had a reason."

My gut reaction was to pounce, to rage at Johnny, at her for not saying anything. I swallowed it. A bitter pill. Did she tell the police about Johnny's pattern of violence? My father's words rang in my ears. Supportive. I rubbed her back and didn't pry.

"I called your parents," I said. "They're on their way."

Annika pointed to the tissue box, and I snatched a couple to pass them to her. "If my mom will be here, you might as well give me the box," Annika said. "Knowing she'll see me like this..." More tears trickled, an endless flood.

"She said 'we're coming,' so I'm sure your dad'll be here too." I tried to make eye contact. "She didn't even ask what happened."

Her chest rose on another sob, but she swallowed it. "She knew."

I grabbed Annika's hand without the wad of tissues and waited for her to continue. My dad's words kept surfacing. The urge to rage at anyone who knew this was a possibility and didn't do everything to stop it made me livid. But I had to include myself in that group, didn't I? He wormed his way so deep into her head and her heart, she couldn't see straight.

"At Thanksgiving," Annika started and then paused again to collect herself. "We were trying on clothes at a store. She passed me something through the curtain in the change rooms and saw my bruises."

"What did she say?"

"She begged me to leave him." Her eyes brimmed with tears, and her voice was thick with emotion. "She had an abusive boyfriend before my dad, I guess."

I searched her face. "Why didn't you leave? I would have helped you."

She dabbed at her tears. "My dad was so excited at Thanksgiving. Johnny McDade was interested in *me*." She shook her head slowly from side to side as though the motion hurt her. "I just—I liked being special. And then when we *weren't* fighting, we got along really well. So well. We had a lot in common. I kept thinking the rest of it would get better."

They did have a lot in common. I couldn't dispute her claim. He was a terrible person, and we never had a nice thing to say to each other. But I never doubted he enjoyed Annika's company in public. Having experienced that level of attention from Sebastian, I understood the intoxication and the desire to keep that feeling at all costs.

"You think it was Johnny that did this to you?"

Annika crumpled, and the breath she sucked in was deep and unsteady. "The last thing I remember was being at the frat house with him."

"The frat house?" I frowned.

Annika's bottom lip trembled. "How did I end up in that alley, Nat? I have no idea."

Thank God Sebastian spent the night with me. There was no way he was part of this. As for the rest of the football players, I doubted Johnny got Annika to the alley on his own.

I began to wonder whether Sebastian's meeting at such an ungodly hour was called by the coach.

Chapter Thirty-Four

♥

While Annika slept, I slipped out of her room to see if Clay was still waiting. He'd gone with my dad and the officers to the alley where Annika had been dropped. I'd texted my dad to make sure Annika had told someone her last memory was of the frat house. She had. Part of me was surprised, but I was also relieved. Maybe she was done protecting Johnny.

In the waiting room chairs, Clay slept at an awkward angle. I shook his shoulder, and he sat up, rotating his neck. He gazed around bewildered.

"Dreaming?"

"Just—" He rubbed his face. "Forgot I was here."

"You can go." I gave him a small smile. "You've probably got things to do. Dad said they'll likely release Annika when the cops come later today. No life-threatening injuries."

Clay ran a hand through his hair and expelled a deep breath. "How's she doing?" He gestured behind me to her room.

I shrugged. "About what you'd expect. Maybe a little better than you'd expect."

He gave me a sad smile. "Your dad said he suspects Johnny."

"Really?" We all wondered if it was him, even Annika, but I was surprised my dad would voice his suspicion.

"Yeah," he said. "He didn't say anything in front of the officers. He said it to me later, in the alley, when they were looking for Annika's things or some sort of evidence."

"Did they find anything?"

"A lot of blood. However she got to the alley, someone has bloody stuff they're trying to conceal." He sighed. "I don't understand how anyone could do that. Doesn't make sense to me."

"That's a good thing." I shoved my hands into the rear pockets of my jeans. "Do you think it was the coach who called the meeting at six this morning?"

Clay searched my face. "No," he said. "Johnny is rallying the guys. Get the story straight. Keep everyone in line." He gave me a long look. "What kind of guy is Sebastian?"

A good man was my gut instinct. He was someone who'd stand up for what was right. But that's who I wanted him to be, and I didn't know if that's who he was. "In this situation?"

"They'll be at the National Championship in two weeks, Nat. A huge accomplishment for the team. Johnny should be punished if he did it, but I can see how a lot of people will feel differently leading up to such a monumental game. Our school hasn't made it this far in decades." Clay rose out of his chair and stretched.

"If he did it, even if the game was for the Super Bowl, that shouldn't matter."

Clay stuck his hands into his pockets. "I can almost guarantee you it'll matter. It's going to matter a lot. We're a football city. Ravens shit is everywhere. Johnny is the golden boy on the field." He sighed. "I'm worried about the backlash Annika might suffer."

"She didn't do anything wrong!" I said. "She was beaten—she could have died."

"I hope I'm wrong. I do."

My dad came striding back through the doors, frowning. "Clay," he said, coming forward. "I'm glad you're still here. I wanted to say this earlier, but it was chaotic. What you did for Annika last night—stopping to help her, carrying her to your house, getting Natalie, bringing her here—you should be proud of yourself." My dad shook his hand with two of his own.

Color rose in Clay's cheeks, and he gave my dad a sheepish grin, his crooked tooth showing. My heart swelled at the sight.

"I'm just glad she'll be okay eventually," Clay said. "I'm headed home." My dad released Clay's hand, and Clay stared at me for a beat too long. "If you need anything, if there is anything I can do for either you or Annika, just call or text. I'll be there in a heartbeat, okay?"

I couldn't meet his eyes. Ridiculous to worry he might get the wrong idea about us when everything else appeared to be falling apart, but I didn't want to take the chance of leading him on.

"Thanks for everything, Clay. I'll keep you posted on what's happening." I flicked my gaze to his. "My dad's right. What you did last night, I can't even begin to thank you."

He shook his head. "It was the decent thing to do. Never any question."

He left through the emergency room doors, and in the distance, Annika's parents and brother approached. I pointed to them. "That's Annika's family."

"Okay," Dad said, going back into police mode. "I'll take them to her room. They'll have questions, I'm sure."

"What are the officers doing now?" I asked.

Dad grimaced. "We're on the same page about the most likely culprit. Now, it's finding evidence and building a case," he said. "The officers seemed a bit reluctant the more obvious the fallout became. This might hinge on how hard Annika pushes to have someone named responsible."

"Reluctant?" I frowned.

Dad didn't answer. He stepped around me to greet Annika's family. I turned and introduced them and explained Dad's role. They followed Dad to the room with her mother clutching her husband's and son's hands.

Dad had given them the same speech about being supportive that I'd heard a million times. But as I'd watched Annika's family react to Dad's words, I understood why he said it well before they reached the room. Once they saw Annika, reason would fly out the window.

I sat down and took my phone out of my pocket. Sebastian hadn't sent me another message since his "I love you" this morning. His silence, more than anything, told me I wouldn't enjoy the next conversation we had in person.

My index finger ran over his words, and I hit reply. What to say? Things between us were already crumbling. I closed my eyes, and images of Sebastian from the night before played like a movie. Then my mind drifted to the people who warned me football came first for him. I'd never wanted to find out if that was true.

I typed my message and hit send without giving myself time to reconsider.

My dad came striding down the hall, squeezing the back of his neck.

"How'd it go?" I stood to meet him.

"They're trying to be supportive. Her father and brother are furious she didn't say something to one of them sooner about what Johnny'd been doing. At this point, that's not helpful. But I understand their reaction."

"Annika told them it was Johnny?"

"No," my dad said. "She told them the last thing she remembered was being at the frat house with Johnny. A logical leap after that, even if the police here don't want to make it."

"I don't understand." I had almost forgotten his earlier comment.

"National Championship, Nat. If they can drag out the investigation for two weeks, he'll get to play in the final game. Then, *maybe* then, they'll do something more concrete."

"You're kidding me," I said.

"I've taken a leave from work. I'm going to try to apply pressure from here," he said, flipping open his notebook. "Name people who live in the frat house."

"Dad—are you allowed to do this?" He shouldn't put his job at risk.

"I'm going to ask questions, not as a cop, as a parent," he said. "I have no authority here."

Hadn't Johnny said the same thing to me weeks ago? "He threatened me once."

"What?" His voice was an explosion.

I covered my face and eased my fingertips along my forehead. Meeting his gaze was impossible. "At the time, I talked myself out of it. But he did, he threatened me. He said Sebastian wasn't always around and everyone knew I didn't like him. No one would believe me if I accused him of anything."

My father's expression morphed into one of disgust. "Name the football players, Nat. Nobody, and I mean nobody, threatens my daughter."

"It's why I didn't tell you. I was worried you'd go all protective," I admitted.

"Natalie Ann, I am your father. My job, beyond being a police officer, is to protect you and your sister with anything and everything I have in me." He slipped his paper and pen into his pocket and placed his hands on my shoulders. "You're one of the two most important people in the world to me."

I wrapped my arms around my dad's middle. He drew me into a hug and said into my ear, "He'll pay, Natalie. The wheels of justice might be too slow to prevent him from playing in the National Championship, but he can kiss his NFL career goodbye."

"I love you, Dad," I said. Bringing Johnny to justice wouldn't be easy. I was sure the football players would toe the team line, at least until after the final game.

I really needed to talk to Sebastian.

Chapter Thirty-Five

I parked my dad's car in the parking space closest to my townhouse and climbed out. I'd texted Sebastian to tell him I was headed home. My dad had stayed at the hospital in case Annika needed anything or anyone showed up to talk to her. Dad wasn't sure if Johnny would try to influence Annika or if he'd stay away.

I took my phone out of my pocket and checked again. Nothing. Sebastian's history of trying to clean up Johnny's messes made me nervous. Would he help Johnny now, too?

When I got to my door, I found it unlocked. Cautiously, I pushed it open. "Hello?"

"Nattie!" Sebastian jumped off the couch and turned to face me.

"You used the spare key?" I dropped my purse and keys on the little table.

"Yeah, I—how's Annika?" His brow furrowed.

"Beaten pretty badly. Most likely sexually assaulted." I listed her trauma in a flat voice because dwelling on it would send me spiraling. A downward slide would come, but I couldn't let myself sink into it yet. Rounding the couch, I fell into a seat.

He eased down on the other end, not close like he normally would. A lump formed in my throat.

"Do the police know who did it? What happened?" He rubbed his legs.

I swallowed my tears. "What was the emergency meeting about this morning?"

"Coach wanted to talk to me." He kneaded his thighs with his fingers.

"About what?" I slouched deeper into the couch. The tension between us was thick. Something bad festered.

He stood and strode into the kitchen. "You want a beer?"

"No, I don't want a beer. It's ten o'clock in the morning." Anger boiled in me under the surface. Below the anger, disappointment and heartbreak were lodged, waiting to break free.

Sebastian returned with an open bottle in his hand, and he perched on the edge of the couch, rolling the beer between his hands.

"Come out with it." It was obvious where this was headed. Might as well face it head-on.

He set his beer on the table and ran his hands along his face. "I can't come out with it. I don't want to do this."

"Then make a different choice."

"It's not that simple," he said. "Coach called me into his office this morning. Not a team meeting. Just me. He asked me how my season was going, if I enjoyed playing for the Ravens, for him. He asked where I wanted to go in my career."

"Okay." Wouldn't those be normal questions toward the end of a football season? Sebastian still had one more year left to play, and this was his first season here.

"Then he asked about my social life. I mentioned you. He said he'd heard you were Johnny's ex-girlfriend Annika's roommate."

"Ex-girlfriend?" I sat up.

"Yeah, surprised the hell outta me too." For the first time since I got home, a glimmer of the man I loved appeared.

"And?" I rested my elbows on my knees.

"Coach said he was looking at the roster for next year, at the scholarship allocations, at playing time and so forth. He told me he was on the fence about whether he was going to keep me." He snatched up his beer and took a long drink.

"*What?*" I asked. "You've been playing well. Like, really well. Even I can recognize that."

"He's telling me to keep my mouth shut, Nattie. He's threatening me. If he drops me from the team, I can't play anywhere else without him signing off on my transfer. I can't go to another college for football. My football career would be done. No senior year. No draft. Nothing."

"That's ridiculous. He can't have that much power."

Sebastian gave me a long look. "He does. Even if he didn't, alumni, sponsors, football fans, scouts—anyone associated with football will think I'm not a team player."

"So what are you saying?"

He chugged the rest of his beer and set it on the table. He wasn't making eye contact.

Tears pricked my eyes and welled up to blur my vision. With my gaze trained to the ceiling, I willed myself not to cry.

"I'm saying I have to be a team player," Sebastian said quietly. "He's got me cornered."

I closed my eyes, and tears rolled down my face. When I opened them, Sebastian's anguish caused cracks across my heart.

"I don't wanna assume anything. I love you, and I want to be with you. This situation is not what I want. But he's got me pinned. If I go against him, he'll ruin any chance I have of playing football." He focused on his beer bottle.

"What are you asking me, Sebastian?" My voice was thick with tears.

"I'm asking whether you'll still be with me if I stick with the team."

His face, his dear face, overflowed with love and sadness. I wanted to ease his pain, part of me wanted to make this decision easy for him. If I said yes, I didn't understand how our relationship would work. I'd be harboring secrets, information about the case. Maybe he would too. If he didn't come forward with whatever he knew, I would never forgive him.

I'd given him pieces of my heart, and they were strewn around this house: on the couch, at the front door, the kitchen table and counter, my room, even Annika's room. Those pieces would vanish with him when he walked out the door. My heart might never be whole again.

"If you choose the team, we're done." My words were a whisper. I cleared my throat. "This isn't something we can compromise on, Sebastian. This isn't what food to order or where to go on vacation. She's my best friend, and your teammate beat her so badly last night"—my voice caught on a sob—"that I hardly recognize her." I took a deep, shuddering breath and let my anger rise over the pain. "If you're choosing to stand by him, then you're not a man I want to stand beside."

Sebastian had never asked or expected me to be anything but myself, which was one of my favorite things about our relationship. I'd never be someone who could look the other way at injustice. It wasn't in me.

He gave a curt nod and took his empty bottle into the kitchen. I sat on the couch, waiting for him to return, but when he didn't, I went looking for him. I rounded the corner from the kitchen table, and his back was rising and falling as though he was holding in his sobs.

"Sebastian." Each beat of my heart was a painful squeeze in my chest.

He turned and wrapped his arms around me, sobbing into my neck. I drew him tighter and let my own tears fall onto his shirt.

"I love you so much, Nattie," he murmured into my ear. "Tell me we can figure this out." He rested his forehead against mine.

The love and regret reflected in his expression caused fresh tears to slip down my face. "It won't work," I said. "There's no way I can be with someone who supports what Johnny did."

"I don't support it." A burst of anger raised the pitch of his voice. "I don't support what he did. But I've given up so much, *so much* to get to this point in my football career. This has been my dream since I was thirteen. I'm on the cusp of something big."

I stared at him for a long time. Part of me understood. Football took up the bulk of his life. I avoided his gaze when I said, "I guess I'm one more thing you have to sacrifice to get that dream."

Sebastian flinched. "I don't accept that."

"This isn't something you can persevere the hell out of. You're making a choice."

"What about when this situation is resolved?" he asked. "What then?"

I shook my head. "We'll still be the same people who made these choices now."

"So, if I go, I'm going forever?" His voice cracked.

I closed my eyes and wished for the floor to open up, swallowing me whole. I wanted to go to sleep and wake up in bed with Sebastian, have the last eight hours be nothing but a bad dream. If he chose the team, how would I ever look at him the same again?

"I don't know, Sebastian. I don't know."

He drew me into his chest. I went willingly, breathing in the scent of his cologne. Would this smell bring me to my knees years from now when I walked past a stranger in the mall? He had branded my senses.

"I love you," I said. "Part of me understands why you're doing what you're doing. I do. But I'm not sure I'll ever be able to forgive you for it."

"I'm gonna figure something out," he murmured into my hair. "It's happened so fast I haven't had time to think of a solution, but there has to be one. There's always a way for us to be together and for Annika to get justice," he said. "I'm not giving up on us."

Desperation was plain in his voice. My heart was a weight in the middle of my chest, a load I had to carry. It was no longer light and complete like last night. I never realized a heart in pieces could be so heavy.

"If you're going," I said, my hands bunched in his shirt. "You should go. My dad's coming here soon, and if you're choosing the team, I'd rather he didn't meet you."

Sebastian stiffened. My words were another punch, one of many during this conversation.

He kissed my temple, not meeting my gaze when he drew away. This wasn't right. I didn't want him to go. I latched onto his arm, and my hands trailed along until he was almost out of my grasp. The reality of what was about to happen sank into me, filling me up. A sob spilled out.

Sebastian turned without a word and swept me into his arms, and his lips crashed into mine. I met him with equal parts desperation and anger. We shouldn't end like this. We shouldn't end at all.

I wanted to beg him not to go. I wanted to shove him out the door.

"I'm going. But I'm not going forever." He wiped my tears with his thumbs. "I love you. I love you so much. And I'm gonna figure this out."

For what might be the last time, his wide back disappeared out my front door. If things got as heated as I suspected they might, I didn't see how we'd ever find a way back to each other.

Chapter Thirty-Six

♥

Annika had been discharged from the hospital a week ago and went home with her parents to heal, rest, and receive counseling. I didn't expect her to come back to Northern University to spin in the center of this chaos. My dad had taken over the living room until it became clear she'd be gone for a while. Now, he slept in her bedroom, even if all his stuff was scattered everywhere.

My phone pinged. Kristy's text message glowed on my screen. Every time an alert went off, my heart accelerated. At least part of me still expected to hear from Sebastian. But there'd been no communication this last week.

He'd met my dad, but it wasn't the meeting or circumstances I'd hoped for. Dad had interviewed him for his investigation of the frat house. He said Sebastian seemed nice, if misguided.

With a sigh, I texted Kristy back. Going anywhere was the last thing I wanted to do. I hit send, and my dad wandered out of Annika's room. He took in my pajamas and messy hair.

"You should get out of here soon." Dad shuffled papers I wasn't supposed to read but spent a lot of energy gathering into a neat pile.

He thought the investigation was too dangerous. Some football players were hostile or aggressive when Dad spoke to them. Dad's involvement jeopardized their futures.

Whoever helped Johnny put themselves in jeopardy. Every time I remembered what they'd done to Annika, I wanted to hit something. I'd been attending a lot of kickboxing classes since she was beaten and raped. I'd met every guy on the team. Annika knew them well—all of them—and they dumped her in an alley like a piece of trash.

"Who texted you?" Dad took his pen out of his pocket and scribbled a note off his phone.

"Kristy. A bunch of them are getting together tonight."

"You going?"

"I don't want to."

"Natalie." He glanced at me from his papers. "I only met Annika a few times, but she wouldn't want you sitting here, afraid to live your life."

"I'm not afraid, Dad. I'm pissed off. So, so angry." And heartbroken, but I didn't need that discussion.

"You haven't showered in two days. That's not anger."

"Any progress?" I nodded at his notes.

He raised his eyebrows.

"Oh, come on." I threw up my hands. "You can't tell me if you're getting anywhere? I have news for you, Dad. You leave enough stuff lying around I could read it myself."

"You're not a lawyer yet. You wouldn't understand my shorthand." He slouched into the couch.

I stared at him. Did he realize the internet existed, and I could search his shorthand codes? Not a mystery when I've got Google at my fingertips. I'd riffled through those papers a few times, phone clasped in hand, search engine at the ready. If I told him, he might actually be tidy.

"They'll be bringing Johnny in for questioning this week. Truthfully, they have enough evidence to arrest him. But they want to figure out who helped him. I don't disagree with their logic. The football players have closed ranks, and none of them are talking." My dad sighed. "Have you spoken to Annika?"

"She said the night is a blank. Other than Johnny being the last thing she remembers, she's not much of a witness."

"Her documenting the instances of abuse was helpful." He twirled his pen. "You tell her that?"

"I don't remember telling her, but that's something you've mentioned. So, I could have."

"They might come after you to testify."

"Me?" I wasn't completely surprised.

"Establish a pattern for the abuse leading up to this incident."

"Right." I shifted on the couch. There had been a few heated conversations about my suspicions and how I handled them. "I'm going to my room."

"You should text Kristy back. Get out. Do something that doesn't have to do with this." He gestured to his strewn paperwork.

"I'll think about it." I wandered to my bedroom and collapsed on the bed.

The day Sebastian left, I'd torn my sheets off and washed them. When I took them out of the dryer, I regretted my impulsive decision. No faint whiffs of his cologne. Then I burst into tears at the finality of it.

Instead of trying to evade him, I took the same routes to my classes. Testing fate. But I hadn't once run into Sebastian. For the first time, he was avoiding me. Maybe our lack of contact was for the best. What could we say to each other? Even still, when I went to my class with a clear view of the stadium, I searched for him.

Sometimes, I caught a glimpse of a guy who bore a passing resemblance, and my heart kicked. But it was never him.

My phone pinged again. Kristy was certainly persistent. I turned it off and curled up on my bed for a nap. At least when I slept, I wasn't thinking. My general philosophy—anything to avoid turning on my brain and my heart.

I woke to a familiar knock on my bedroom door. Familiar, but out of place.

"Claudia?" I asked, groggy.

She popped into my room, not waiting for an invitation. "Dad said you were in rough shape. You look homeless. Come on. Get up. We'll go out. Buddy system. Text your friend. I brought bar clothes." Claudia held up a bag. "You and I are sharing a bed tonight. Just like old times." She grinned and then charged me, jumping on top of me when she landed on the bed.

"I'm not going out." I tried to tug the covers over my head, but with Claudia sprawled out beside me, it was impossible. My sister's enthusiasm was contagious, and my will to resist was weakening.

"You are. You really are. I'm not taking no for an answer. And neither will Kristy."

I gave her a side-eye. "How do you know her name?"

Claudia laughed. "Dad. I met her last year when I came to visit. We exchanged numbers, but I never thought I'd get to use it. Made it easy-peasy to work out a plan. I'm not sure Dad realizes we'll be going to a bar. He called it a girls' night. He probably thinks we're painting nails and eating cupcakes." She rolled closer, so she was spooning me. "Come on. You secretly want to shower, smell pretty, put on makeup, and wear a kickass outfit. I brought you sexy clothes. For a change."

I gave her a gentle punch to the arm. "I don't want to go out."

"Why not?"

What if there were football players there? Or fans who didn't realize Sebastian and I weren't together and tried to talk to me about him? I was also afraid I wouldn't see the most important player. My heart was in pieces, and I couldn't decide if seeing him would stitch them back together or tatter them more. I shifted so we were facing each other.

"Sebastian?" Claudia asked.

"Yeah. Our breakup has been hard, Claudia." She stared at me with her blue eyes so different from my brown ones. "Every time I think about him, about what's happening, I either want to scream or cry. I tried for so long not to be with him, and now I'd give anything to have this go away so I could have him back."

"Just because Dad wouldn't understand doesn't mean you can't be with him, Nat."

A dark chuckle escaped me before I could stop it. "If it was only Dad I had to worry about, it'd be fine. Dad's worried the other players might be dangerous right now. National Championship is next week. Whoever helped Johnny doesn't have a problem doing whatever they need to do to make sure they play that game."

"Would they do something to you?"

"Dad's the one pushing for Johnny to be investigated, questioned, arrested. None of them would touch me, but intimidate me? Yes, definitely. Make me feel unsafe? For sure. Could be any of them. That's the scariest part. This season is a big deal to so many."

"What would Sebastian do if a teammate came after you?"

"I don't know. He loves me. He loves football. Right now, he can't have both. His coach is in on it. Maybe the college. I have no clue how far the cover-up goes. Dad's not worried about the spider web, only the spider."

"Wow."

"Apparently football is a big deal?" I said.

Claudia cracked a smile. "Who knew?"

"I wish I didn't."

"You regret Sebastian?"

I sighed. No matter how terrible this was right now, I couldn't regret the connection we had. "No. No." I sat up in the bed, the comforter pooling at my waist. "I regret Johnny McDade hearing Annika's laugh the first night. She doesn't even laugh like that anymore."

We sat in silence with Claudia on her side, staring at me while I played with the edges of the covers.

"God, this is so fucking depressing."

"Don't let Dad hear you use that word," I said.

"He left when I showed up. He wanted to give us space." Shoving my shoulder, she hopped out of bed. "Operation make Natalie Ann feel better—well—maybe just different, is in full swing!"

I rolled my eyes, but I turned my phone on and checked the details of Kristy's texts. Frequent football player locations were off-limits, so I was happy to see the all-ages bar she suggested. We'd never gone there with the team. I texted her back.

Reluctantly, I swung my legs over the side of the bed. From where I was sitting, Claudia's bag brimmed with things that sparkled. I sighed.

There was only one thing to be done.

"Claudia, grab the tequila. I need to pre-drink hard or I won't go. I cannot face this sober anymore."

"Done and done." She rushed out of my room.

***

I couldn't remember the last time I'd stood in line to get drunk. It might have been at the frat house, and even then we'd been waved in early. The memory made me shiver. When I'd been going out with the football team, we never paid cover, and we never waited in line. Now, I was back to freezing my ass off to pay ten dollars for the privilege of getting drunker. I was well on the way.

Ah, tequila. My long-lost friend.

"This sucks." Claudia shivered beside me.

"Tell me about it." I took my flask out and passed it to her. It had also been a while since my lovely flask had needed to make an appearance. So far, I hated everything about this night.

Once we entered the bar, I missed the openness of Gabby's. This place was claustrophobic with the strobe lighting, the crush of bodies, and the packed dance floor. Why was it so busy? Was it always this busy? I hadn't been here since my freshman year.

Claudia grabbed my hand and dragged me to the bar. She got us drinks while I texted Kristy to figure out where she was camped out in the crowd.

"Bring me two drinks," I called to Claudia when the bartender came over. I was focused on Kristy's reply.

"Natalie?" The familiar voice was audible over the din of the crowd.

My heart froze. I glanced over my shoulder to Gabby's quizzical expression from behind the cramped bar. I swallowed the dryness in my throat, grabbed the shot of tequila off the counter, and tilted it back.

"You work here now?" I shouted over the noise.

"Yeah. My old boss didn't want the football guys there after everything hit the press. So—new job. I'm here Saturdays and Sundays." She searched my face for a minute. "You doing okay?" She poured another shot and passed it to me.

"Fan-fucking-tastic, Gabby." I threw it back and returned the glass to her. Other people were watching our exchange with interest. Having dated and hung around the football team, I wasn't anonymous amongst this crowd. "Are they coming?"

She bit her lip. "Troy is, but that's it. The coach has them on a firm lockdown with everything happening."

I hated how she reduced Annika's abuse to *everything happening*. Johnny raped and beat Annika. He hadn't done it alone. I wanted her to say the words, to make it clear the football team understood what had happened, the depth of betrayal they committed. For months Annika had been one of them, and they dumped her in an alley.

Claudia tugged on my arm. "Come on. Let's go see Kristy."

Annoyance flickered in me, and I jerked away. "I'm fine. I can get there on my own."

"But I can't," Claudia said. "I don't know where they are."

I weaved through the crowd, pushing people out of the way until we got to Kristy and the group of girls she came with.

"Whoa," she said as soon as she saw me. "You look like you're asking for a fight."

"I'm hoping if I get drunk I won't have any fight left in me." After I sipped more of my mixed drink, I realized I should have told Claudia to order me a beer. According to her, short skirts and sparkly low-cut tops equaled too sweet drinks.

"How are you doing?" Kristy's fingers gripped her straw and guided it to her lips while she raised her eyebrows at me.

"Terrible. You?" I took the straw out of my drink and gulped it back.

Claudia swung her arm around my shoulders. "FYI, Kristy. It's polite to ask. But we're keeping Nat focused on anything but how she's feeling tonight. Oh—and like—no football or any of that shit either. Let's talk about shoes, shopping, whose skirt is shortest."

I looped my arm around her waist. She was a little fuzzy. This was good. This was really good. "Thanks, Claudia," I said, meaning it.

She kissed my temple. "You're my big sis. I gotta look out for you."

I laughed. "It's supposed to be the other way around."

Claudia hip checked me. "You've done that for me more than I've done this for you. I've never seen you so down before."

"I wish I wasn't like this." I drained my second drink. "Anyone need another?" I raised my empty cup. Another bar, one that didn't have Gabby working it, was behind us. Being at the back of the club meant it was less crowded.

Everyone in our group avoided meeting my eyes. Fine. No one else wanted to get as drunk as me. Whatever. I wandered to the bar.

Coming here was a mistake. I was in no shape to be with people.

While I waited in line, my money clutched in my hand, the first wave of nausea hit me. I wobbled and someone steadied me. I glanced at the guy but didn't recognize him.

"Natalie, right?" He smiled.

I nodded.

"You're Sebastian Swan's girlfriend?"

"Was," I mumbled, stepping forward to order.

He slid in beside me. "Was?"

"We broke up," I said, not looking at him as I waited.

"I'm Jake." He held out his hand for me to shake.

I tossed my money on the bar, grabbed both my drinks, and gave him a lopsided smile. "And I'm leaving. Have a good night, Jake."

Pushing through the crowd, I passed Claudia her drink. Tipping up my beer, another wave of nausea hit. I shoved my bottle into Claudia's hand.

"I gotta—oh, God. Alley." I pointed and rushed for the emergency exit.

Claudia followed behind me a moment later. In the alley, with my eyes closed, I hyperventilated, sick from more than the alcohol.

I let Annika down. I saw the signs in Johnny, and I let her down. Somehow, I should have done more.

"You gotta find a better way to deal with this, Nat," Claudia said.

"You have no idea. You can't possibly understand." Sebastian's grin and hazel eyes flashed behind my eyelids. Annika's battered body in the backseat of Clay's car.

"Then tell me," Claudia said.

"Natalie Chapman," a voice drawled from the alley.

My blood ran cold. I glanced over my shoulder to see Theo and Johnny striding toward us.

"We need to go back in." Panic shot through me in a million tiny pinpricks, sobering me in an instant. "Back in. Back in."

She yanked on the door, but it was locked. Her expression turned helpless and scared.

"It's Johnny," I whispered before facing him and Theo.

Chapter Thirty-Seven

♥

"Must be my lucky day." Johnny stopped a few feet from me and Claudia. "Meeting you and your hot friend in a dark alley. What do you think, Theo? Is this a stroke of luck or what?" He smirked. "I haven't had much freedom lately, what with your dad hounding me and my friends day and night."

I shoved Claudia behind me. There was no way I'd let him touch my sister without a fight, even if I was too drunk for this confrontation.

"Remind me again. When was the last time you were in an alley with a woman?" I asked.

Johnny smirked. "I was so sorry to hear about you and Sebastian." His smile was sly. "Though I'm not sure the woman in his room last night shared my sadness." His gaze traveled over my body in a leisurely way. "She reminded me of a prettier more pleasant version of you, actually."

Theo chuckled beside him.

They both deserved to be slapped. Claudia squeezed my shoulder, as if sensing my drunken urge. "Why would I ever believe a word that came out of your mouth?"

His eyes were cold and calculating. "I wonder what it would take to get your dad to back off," he mused.

"That's easy, Johnny. Be innocent. Simple."

"How is Annika?" His voice dipped, mimicking sincerity.

"Someone who actually cared would have gone to see her in the hospital, sent flowers, been a *decent* human being."

"I regret not going to her," he said, looking everywhere but at me.

"I'm sure you do. Made you look extra guilty."

His eyes flashed. "I loved Annika."

"No one wants a love like that." I took a step toward him. Claudia clutched my arm. "No one deserves that kind of love. I hope you rot in jail."

"Careful, Nattie. Sebastian isn't here to protect you." His voice was low, menacing.

Theo stood behind Johnny's shoulder, and I focused on him. "Would you let him hurt me? You told me you were a *good* guy. Do good guys dump injured girls in alleys?"

Theo shook his head and wouldn't meet my gaze. "You're drunk, Natalie. You should go home before things get out of hand."

"Like they did last week at the frat house? That kind of out of hand?" I pressed. Claudia moved closer to me, tense.

"Come on, Nat," she whispered. "Dad would be pissed at you."

"Dad?" Johnny perked up. "Two for the price of one. Both his daughters here—"

From behind us, the exit door popped open. My gaze didn't leave Johnny, but whoever it was, Johnny recognized them.

"What's going on out here?" Warning edged Troy's thunderous voice.

Over my shoulder, I caught Troy's worried expression. I wasn't sure which football players I could trust, but I would bet money on him not being involved.

"A friendly chat." Johnny stepped around me, not making eye contact. Theo trailed behind him. They squeezed past Troy into the bar without a backward glance.

Troy stared at me for a beat. "Besides being very drunk, are you okay?"

I nodded. With both hands, I rubbed my face, and the tension slipped out of me.

"Jesus," Claudia breathed out in a whoosh. "That was scary tense. He's always like that?"

"Around me? Yes. We've never gotten along."

"You coming in or what?" Troy propped the door open wider.

My sister slid past him and moved through the crowd to Kristy and the rest of our group. Troy touched my arm before I could follow her. When I gazed at his hand, I realized I was trembling.

"Seriously, are you okay?"

I opened my mouth to answer, but a set of broad shoulders in the crowd stole my attention. The mirage had happened so many times over the last week, I shook my head to clear it. Maybe I was wrong. When he shifted, and his profile was visible, my breath caught. The thud of each heartbeat echoed in my ears. My blood thickened and slowed. Warmth invaded in a rush.

Sebastian.

Without thinking, I took a step in his direction. Troy's grip on my arm became firmer. "You don't want to go over there."

In a daze, I glanced up at him and cocked my head.

"We're in public," Troy explained slowly. "Johnny is here. I don't want trouble at Gabby's bar. She just got this job. If Sebastian heard Johnny cornered you out there...well, if he ever did that to Gabby, I'd kill him."

"I won't tell him. I didn't last time."

Troy frowned. "Last time?"

"It's not the first time Johnny's threatened me. Only the first time anyone's witnessed it."

As though he sensed me, Sebastian craned in our direction. He spotted Troy first, and then his focus strayed to me. The moment he recognized me, his expression darkened with concern. He took a step in my direction, a reflex, like me.

I shook my head, and he stopped moving. I wanted him to come over, but I was afraid of what I'd say and do if he did. Nothing had changed since I saw him a week ago. The crushing pressure in my chest was almost too much to bear. Maybe Sebastian had been right to avoid me. Maybe not seeing each other was easier than being so close and not being together.

"I gotta go," I said to Troy without looking at him. The nausea I'd felt earlier had returned two-fold. I broke eye contact with Sebastian, but before I did, another woman tried to snag his attention. My stomach heaved. In my heart, I understood Johnny lied. There hadn't been someone else already. But there would be. It was inevitable.

I weaved through the throng until I found my sister. "I want to go."

"You've hardly spent any time with us," Kristy said.

"The football guys are here. It's—I can't." I pressed my fingers to my forehead.

The claustrophobic nature of the club returned, and I dragged Claudia through the crowd to our coats. Everywhere I went, I imagined Sebastian following me. Wishful thinking.

We stepped into the chilly air, and I could breathe again. I hooked my arm with Claudia's, and we walked in quick steps through the night to my house. A thin layer of snow lay on the grass on either side of the sidewalk. The alcohol didn't let the cold penetrate.

"What happened? Was he there?" Claudia asked, the silence too much for her.

"Yeah." The sight of him was burned into my eyelids.

When we made the turn up the path to the house, familiar feet pounded the pavement behind us. I slowed. My heart kicked double in my chest.

"You go ahead," I said to Claudia, looking over my shoulder.

She glanced back and grinned. "Now might not be the time, but man. He's gorgeous."

"Yeah, not helpful." I gave her a small smile. She unlocked the door and disappeared inside.

Sebastian approached cautiously. "I saw you, and I—I couldn't let you go. Are you okay?" He closed the distance between us.

Staring up at him, the pieces of my heart slotted into place and released again. My head and my heart didn't understand what to make of him, here.

"Yeah," I said. "I couldn't stay."

"Because of me?" he asked. "That girl who tried to get my attention. I didn't—I wouldn't—that's not who I am anymore."

Even though I hadn't trusted what Johnny said, the pressure in my chest released at his words. I sighed, and my shoulders dropped.

Sebastian read me with ease. His brow furrowed. "You didn't think that, did you?"

I shook my head. "No, I—" Meeting his gaze, my breath caught in my throat at the look of confusion on his face. I was too drunk for this, again. "I ran into Johnny. He said some things. He said you had a girl over last night."

"That's not true. I didn't and I wouldn't. Lord, you're all I think about. How can I fix my life? Nothing is right anymore. It's all fucked up." Sebastian studied me for a moment. "What else did Johnny say?"

I shrugged. He chose football when he left me. I didn't want to ruin his chances of playing next year. Johnny would pay for what he did. My dad would make sure of that.

"Hey, hey." He stepped forward and brushed tears from my cheeks. "Nattie, talk to me."

"I can't. You're not here anymore." My words were garbled by sadness.

He flinched. Looping one arm around my waist, he drew me closer. "Tell me what's going on, Nat. How can I make things right if I don't understand everything that's wrong?"

I swallowed and rested my cheek on his shoulder. With my eyes closed, I breathed in his scent. "Johnny threatened me."

Sebastian stiffened.

"Tonight, he intimidated me and Claudia in the alley. I thought I was going to throw up, and I went out the side door. Claudia followed. Theo and Johnny showed up. He started saying things about you. He wondered what it would take to get my dad to leave everyone alone."

Sebastian rubbed my back and squeezed me tighter.

"I was scared, but I didn't want him to realize it. I kept thinking I had to keep him away from Claudia." A shuddering breath escaped me.

"He didn't touch you, did he?" Sebastian's voice was gruff.

"No, but—but—I kept picturing Annika. You didn't see her that night, Sebastian. I can't stop thinking about how scared she must have been when they left her in that alley. She doesn't remember, but she still carries the assault. It's in her somewhere.

It'll always be there." Tears kept falling, and a lump formed in my throat. I tried to swallow it. "Part of this is my fault. If I'd told Annika Johnny threatened me, maybe they wouldn't have been together anymore."

Sebastian tensed again. "This has happened before?"

I nodded and took a couple of deep breaths. "The night they got back together. He cornered me outside the bathrooms and warned me that you weren't always around to watch out for me."

"You shoulda told me, Nat." Anger spilled out of him.

"I wasn't sure you'd believe me," I whispered.

He put some space between us. "Whether I believed he meant it as a threat or not, I would *never* be okay with him saying something like that to you. I'm sure as hell not sitting around and letting him intimidate you now, either."

"I don't want you to get in trouble. Don't do anything stupid."

He cupped my face. "No one says that shit to my girl and gets away with it."

"I'm not your girl anymore, Sebastian."

His lips quirked up, and my heart burst with love. "You'll be my girl till the day I die, whether you wanna be or not. I'm always going to celebrate your successes and rage against anyone who hurts you. Always." With a steady look, he searched my face. "I'm gonna take care of this."

"Sebastian," I pleaded. "I don't want you in jail."

"It'll be okay, Nattie. I promise. Someone should have done something already. *I* should have done something already."

If my sister and my dad weren't in my house right now, I'd drag Sebastian in to make sure he didn't do something dumb. But inviting him in wouldn't change anything else. We weren't on the same team.

"Thank you for following me here," I said.

He kissed my forehead, and his thumbs grazed my cheeks. "I miss you. I'm not giving up. I'll figure out a way to save us and get Annika justice."

"My dad's working on the justice thing."

"He's having a hard time getting the guys to talk to him. The coach has threatened everyone. Not that any of us are talking to each other either. A few subtle remarks here and there."

"So he hasn't targeted only you?"

"Nope."

My drunken brain started ticking. "Have you heard who helped Johnny?"

Sebastian's jaw hardened. "No. I have my suspicions." He smoothed my hair. "Nothing for sure yet."

"Does my dad realize the coach has been threatening people?"

Sebastian rubbed the back of his head. "Not sure." Regret flickered across his face. "I should go."

Instinctively, I reached for him, lacing my fingers with his, tugging him toward me again. "Don't go."

"I can't stay, Nat. Your dad's inside, and he's at war with the team. He should be." He stared at me. "He should be. Whoever hurt Annika deserves to be brought down. But I can't stay."

I ran my fingertips across his brow and down to his chin. When our gazes connected, his expression mirrored my anguish. He hesitated before he dipped his head, capturing my lips with his. My drunken brain flicked onto high alert. I wrapped my arms around his neck, dragging him to me. He lifted my legs and walked us backward, my skirt riding up almost to my waist. He braced my back against the side of the house, and we deepened the kiss, pushing ourselves closer together. I snuck my hands under his winter jacket and shirt. His skin was music to my fingers. Desire shot through me like a drug.

"Nat," he said in a hushed voice. "Nat, we can't."

"Please," I murmured against his lips.

"Nattie," he muttered into my neck, and his lips met mine. "Lord, I have missed you." He pushed his hips forward, and I gasped.

"Please. I need to be close to you," I moaned. "I can't take this." I tried to reach between us for the button on his jeans.

"You'll hate me in the morning." His hand was firm over mine, stilling my search, and he kissed me again. "I love you too damned much for that." After leaving a trail of kisses along my face and into my neck, he drew away to make eye contact. He cupped my cheek with his palm. "Not like this, okay?"

Ice settled over me. "If we're not doing this, then you should go." I shoved his chest.

"Nattie," he groaned, and his forehead touched mine.

I shifted in annoyance, and he lowered my legs. He didn't meet my gaze while I straightened my skirt.

My anger was back in full force—at him, at Johnny, at every football player who wouldn't stand up for what was right. "I guess I'll see you around." I headed for my door.

"Natalie." He reached for my hand, but I yanked it away.

"We're torturing ourselves." I kept my back to him at the door. "Next time, don't come after me."

Clasping my anger to me, I disappeared inside without a backward glance.

Chapter Thirty-Eight

♥

I t took me until noon the next day to face the sunlight. Claudia was up and gone long before that. She had homework she needed to finish for Monday. I was glad she came, even if our outing ended as a spectacular failure. Once Sebastian left, I crawled into bed beside her and cried silent tears while she slept.

"How was your night?" Dad asked from the living room while I made myself something to eat.

I loved my dad, but he wasn't getting those details. Claudia must not have told him before she left or else he'd have busted down my door already.

"I talked to Sebastian." I watched him for a reaction while I grabbed a seat at the kitchen table and took a bite of my sandwich.

He raised his eyebrows.

"The coach is threatening all of them."

He sat back into the couch and steepled his fingers. "None of them have told me that personally. You said Sebastian felt threatened."

"Not felt threatened. He *was* threatened, Dad. Sebastian said the coach has talked to the team. They're being kept in line by the threat of no longer playing for Northern University. There must be something you can do with that information."

"We need proof. One of the players has to file a complaint against the coach or we need a record of the threat."

"Like a video or audio?"

He shook his head. "Not admissible in court if he doesn't realize he's being recorded."

I smiled. "But Dad, he's a football coach at a top-notch school. The court of public opinion is equally important."

"Natalie, blackmail isn't a good idea. You want to be a lawyer. If this got out, you'd ruin any future career."

"I'll figure out a way to keep myself out of it. It's not as though I can book an appointment and he'll confess. This isn't *Law and Order*."

"Would Sebastian do it?"

I frowned and didn't meet my dad's eyes. I couldn't ask him to, even though he might. If my plan didn't work, the stakes were too great. Any of the other players who wanted to make a living off football one day wouldn't be persuaded. For them, the risk wasn't this season or even next season, it was the rest of their lives.

"Not him," I said. "I have someone else in mind."

"Care to share?" It was a mom-ism. Her memory made me smile.

"Not right now, no. But if it works, you'll be the first to hear. At least a few of those guys must be as angry as we are about what Johnny did to Annika." I'd be betting a lot on that claim.

"Just be careful, Natalie. The National Championship is this coming weekend. They are headed out of the state starting on Thursday. Johnny is being brought in for questioning on Wednesday before he leaves."

"What happens if they charge him?"

"If they did that, he wouldn't be able to cross state lines. No championship for him. But they won't. Even if they have the evidence, they'll delay arresting him."

"Makes me furious." I shoved my empty plate into the middle of the table.

Dad sighed. "I don't agree with their reasoning, but I understand it. There are players on the team who are counting on this exposure to be noticed by the NFL. Regardless of who Johnny is off the field, by any account he's a hell of a ball player. That shouldn't matter more than Annika's assault. That's not always the world we live in."

"Sebastian's counting on that exposure."

My dad's pale eyes softened. "I understand, sweetheart. Caring about him, wanting what's best for him, doesn't make you a bad friend to Annika." He stared at his files and crossed his arms. "I'm not sure what I would have done in his place at his age."

"I was convinced you were going to hate him." My throat tightened and a thin sheen of tears coated my vision.

He came to the kitchen table and sat in the chair beside me, so our knees almost touched. He took my hands and held them in his own. "Do you hate him?"

I shook my head. "No, but sometimes hating him would be easier."

"Hate, like love, is complicated." He dropped my hands and leaned into the chair. "I didn't tell you this because I was annoyed with how you handled Annika's downward slide into this kind of violence. I also wasn't certain you'd want to hear it."

"Are you going to tell me now?"

He gave a half smile. "When I spoke to Sebastian and your name came up, he thanked me for raising such a strong, independent woman. He said he'd never met anyone like you before, and he admired how you were standing by your friend."

Tears pooled in my eyes and slid down my face before I even realized they were coming.

"There's no chance I could ever hate a man who loves my daughter that way. A man who sees the things I value in her and is grateful for them."

"Dad." My voice caught.

He wrapped his arms around me, and I sobbed into his chest.

"It's so hard," I cried into his shirt. "I keep seeing her so battered. Someone she loved did that. She loved him." I took a heaving, shaky breath. "I feel so bad for her and so guilty I didn't do more. The signs were there, but I couldn't make her believe me." I pressed my forehead into my dad's chest. "But I also miss Sebastian so much."

"We're going to get Johnny. We'll get him. We'll get whoever helped him too," my dad said into my hair.

I nodded and drew away, wiping my face self-consciously. Tears didn't come easily to me, but I'd been doing a lot of crying lately. "I have a couple things to do and then I'm going out for a while," I said.

"I force you out of the house once and now you're going to leave me sitting here twiddling my thumbs every night?"

Between sniffs, I laughed. "No. Operation Nail Johnny to the Wall needs to get into swing. If they won't arrest him before this weekend, I want to make sure he's getting his ass handed to him when he gets home."

My dad smiled and ruffled my hair. "There's my strong, tough girl."

The club opened at six, and I wanted to be there when the doors were unlocked. I wasn't positive what time Gabby's shift started, but the football schedule meant that if Troy was going to be there, he'd arrive early and leave early.

Clay had agreed to come with me. Despite Sebastian's vow to handle Johnny, I wasn't sure he'd back down.

"I went to see Annika." Clay stuffed his hands in the pockets of his coat while we waited in the cold for the doors to open.

"She texted me and said you stopped by. That was nice of you." The drive to Annika's house took three hours. Why he'd gone hung between us.

"You're probably wondering why I went."

I smiled. "You went because you're a nice guy."

He shook his head. "I went because I couldn't get the image of her in the alley out of my head. I needed to see her getting better." He glanced at me, and a ghost of a smile played on his lips. "She was always so full of life. She had this great laugh and this passion for things. To see her so..."

That's how I felt, and I hadn't found her. I was about to respond when the lock on the door flicked open.

"You think this will work?" Clay pulled on the handle.

"No idea. But it's worth a shot. I completely misread Troy when I first met him. I'm hoping I'm reading him right this time."

We were the only ones there. Surreal to be in the bar without the crush of bodies, the loud music, and the strobe lights. Music blared out of the speakers, but it wasn't techno blasting from them.

We slid onto stools, and Gabby emerged from the rear room carrying a case of beer. She paused mid-stride when she saw us.

"Back for round two?" Her voice was light, but her expression wasn't friendly.

"Not quite." I shifted in my seat.

"Tequila?" Gabby put the case of beer beside the fridge.

"Is Troy coming by?" I asked.

"Is this your new boyfriend?" Gabby smiled at Clay.

Clay thrust out his hand with a grin. "Old boyfriend. Turned concerned friend. I'm Clay."

Sometimes his ability to gloss over awkward situations amazed me. He didn't always sail through, but when he did, he was a sight to behold.

She gave him an assessing look and then accepted his handshake. "I'm Gabriella. Troy's girlfriend."

"Natalie says Troy's a good guy," Clay said, still smiling.

Gabby scanned his face and then shifted her focus to me, wary. "What are you after, Nat?"

"I want to chat with Troy."

"He's not going to roll on Johnny. Trust me, we've talked about it several times."

"So, he knows something?" I asked.

Gabby shrugged. She took a deep breath and sighed. "The only one who knows absolutely nothing is Sebastian, if that makes you feel any better. Since it's your dad sniffing around, he's pretty much persona non grata on the team. He's moved out of the frat house too."

I tried to hide my surprise, but I was a terrible poker player.

"You didn't hear that, huh? Yeah, when he returned to the house last night, he went a few rounds with Johnny. Told Johnny, and I quote, 'Stay the fuck away from Natalie or I'll kill you.' *Really* messy. We thought we were going to have to call the cops. Then Sebastian packed his shit and left."

I swallowed. "Last night?"

Clay's worried gaze bored into me. "What happened last night?"

"Johnny threatened me. That's why I wanted backup today."

Clay stiffened beside me. "You told Sebastian?"

"We ran into each other. I was upset. I probably shouldn't have told him."

Gabby waved my comment away. "Johnny needed someone to take him to task. I'm confident he's the one who hurt Annika, or at least played a big part in it. I'd put money on Jeff and Theo being involved too. But I can't prove anything."

I rubbed my face. "Troy won't flip?"

Gabby shook her head. "I liked Annika." She couldn't quite meet my gaze when she said, "I realized something bad was happening with Johnny. He never treated her like shit or hit her or anything around us. But sometimes, the way she moved, she looked sore. She always blamed it on the gym, but I wondered. I wondered, and I never asked." Gabby met my gaze, her eyes sad. "I should have asked."

"Gabby, I did ask. Said he was bad news. Tried to get her to stop seeing him. Nothing worked." Even as I comforted her, my own guilt ate at me. I could have done more—should have done more. The signs were there. So, now I'd do everything to get her justice.

"I'll try talking to Troy again, but the coach is keeping them on a tight leash."

"That's actually what I wanted to discuss with Troy. I'm not going after Johnny directly. The coach threatened Sebastian. Sebastian is certain he's threatened other people. To get anyone to talk, we have to reduce the coach's power."

"How are you going to do that?" Gabby asked.

"By getting him on tape threatening the players."

"You want Troy to record him?" She sighed. "Oh, Natalie. He won't do that."

"Clay can wire him." Before now, Clay's IT degree was only helpful in removing viruses from my computer. "The device wouldn't be obvious, but the recording gives us leverage to bring Johnny to justice."

At the entrance, the door swung open, and Troy wandered in. The first time I saw him, I'd given him the nickname *Steroids*. He was still huge, but now that I knew him, I doubted he was using drugs. When Troy recognized us, he stopped in his tracks.

"What are you doing here, Natalie?" He kept his distance.

"I came to talk to you."

"Shit blew up last night in the frat house. So much for not telling Sebastian," Troy said. "We play in the National Championship this weekend and half the team isn't even on speaking terms."

All my muscles tensed at the accusation. Keeping Johnny's threats and behavior secret is what got everyone into this mess. Only the truth would absolve us and give Annika the justice she deserved. "That's not my fault. Your teammates beat and raped my friend and then dumped her in an alley. You want to blame someone, blame them."

Clay sucked in a breath beside me. I'd always been too direct for him.

"Gabby, I'll see you later." Troy turned on his heel.

"Wait." Clay jumped off his stool and rushed after Troy.

"You're not going to win him over like that," Gabby said to me.

I huffed out a breath. "I'm tired of everyone pretending what Johnny and whoever else did isn't godawful. Johnny caused this situation, and the team is enabling him because he can throw a football kinda far." Was I playing down his role on the team? Yes. But he wasn't a god, and he shouldn't be able to do terrible things and suffer no consequences. "He did this. He did it. Other people are paying for it. Annika could have paid with her life."

Gabby's steady gaze met mine. "Troy's not heartless."

I sighed. "I'm not trying to be a jerk. But he's not going to the NFL. You've said that. He's said that. Other people say that. The risks aren't the same for him."

"They're his friends."

"Well." I stared at her. "Whoever hurt Annika isn't a friend I'd want. Whoever is covering up what happened isn't a friend I'd want. But maybe that's just me."

Troy returned with Clay at his side. When he made eye contact with me, I was struck by the change in his expression. Whatever Clay said to him, Troy was different.

"I'll do it." Troy's gaze traveled from me to Gabby. "I'll wear the wire." He covered his face, and his arms bulged. "I'll ask the coach for a meeting, and I'll tell him I'm having second thoughts about keeping quiet." He splayed his arms wide in a helpless gesture. "But I've got nothing, Nat. I swear. I'm not convinced telling the coach I'm going to flip will be enough."

"It's worth a try, Troy. Thank you." When I glanced at Clay, his expression was haunted.

"You've got my cell?" Clay asked Troy.

"Yeah, I'll text you so we can meet up." Troy's focus never left Gabby.

Something about the way he was looking at her saddened me.

"Come on, Nat," Clay said to me. "We have to get organized."

I hopped off the stool and stood in front of Troy. "Thank you."

He tore his gaze from Gabby and gave me his attention for a beat longer than normal. "Whoever dropped her in the alley should be shot. I had no idea, Natalie. No idea they left her in that condition."

Once we were outside, I turned to Clay. "What did you show him?"

"Pictures of Annika from that night."

"What?" My heart dropped into my feet. "You have photos?"

Clay nodded and kept walking. "She asked me to take them at the hospital. It's not as weird as it sounds." He stopped short and thrust his hands in his jacket pockets. He took a deep breath but wouldn't make eye contact. "She was worried that it wouldn't be enough."

I frowned. "I don't get it."

"Once the bruises healed, if charges weren't pressed, if he came around again..." Clay trailed off.

"Oh, my God." I covered my mouth. His words sank into me, each one a stone. "You're not kidding?"

Clay shook his head. "She wanted someone to have the photos in case she was ever tempted. Or in case she ever picked the wrong guy again."

Tears pricked at the back of my eyelids. I had to look at the dark sky to collect myself. "I don't understand that mindset."

Clay shrugged. "I don't either. But it's why I have them. I'm glad she's getting counseling. Troy wouldn't listen to me. So, I showed him the photos."

"And then he listened?"

"He was shocked, but the pictures weren't quite the turning point. Gabby is still around those guys. Not that much different from Annika. If they could do it to her, they could do it to Gabby too. They might have a taste for it now."

A chill coursed through me, and I shivered. He was right. Annika's assault wasn't necessarily an isolated incident. We had no idea what set Johnny off in the first place, and we hadn't yet pinpointed who helped him either.

Chapter Thirty-Nine

♥

Tuesday, Clay heard from Troy. I'd texted Sebastian to see where he was staying, but he hadn't responded. His fist-fight with Johnny wouldn't have gone over well with his coach this close to their championship game.

Clay's living room was sparsely furnished and surprisingly tidy. Normally there were dishes in the sink, clothes strewn about, and an odd scent had made me wonder if he had rotting food under the couch. I couldn't imagine he tidied up for Troy. That meant the cleaning was for me.

I checked my watch again. "What time did Troy say he'd be here?"

Clay popped his head out of his room off the kitchen. "Soon."

I perched on one of the lawn chairs he used as furniture. He had a couch, but I didn't want to end up sitting next to him. He wandered out and plopped onto the couch.

I twisted my hands in my lap and took out my phone to check for messages. Tomorrow, Johnny was being questioned. Thursday, the football team left for the National Championship.

"Looks as though no matter what Troy comes up with today, Johnny will get to play in the game." Clay scrolled through notifications.

"Yep." I settled deeper into the chair. "I don't understand how the coach can protect him."

"I'm not sure what to tell you, Natalie." He placed his phone on the couch beside him and turned tired eyes to me. "The coach and the players have been working years to get to this spot. The college hasn't been in this championship game in decades. You realize the hours they put in for practices, games, external workouts, and so forth. If Johnny doesn't play, those people suffer."

"Not nearly as badly as Annika."

"Yeah, you're right. You're completely right. Johnny is a disgusting piece of shit. If I could put him in jail, I would. Some of those guys have enabled him. If I can go to a party and hear Johnny is abusive, then they heard it too."

My mind drifted to Sebastian. He'd never given any indication he believed Johnny was violent. Had he heard things? Did he ignore incidents at the frat house? The idea made me ill. Maybe he hadn't seen anything. He'd been in the house and on the team for the shortest amount of time, and over the last few months, he'd spent any free time with me.

The doorbell rang, and I jumped, startled. Clay stood and walked to the apartment door, swinging it open.

Troy was on the other side, shoulders hunched. He moved past Clay and into the apartment. He was so tall, broad, and muscular he made the room feel small.

"Well?" Clay said, and I stood to face Troy.

I squeezed my hands together, giving him a hopeful expression. If our plan didn't work, I wasn't sure what to do next.

Taking a deep breath, he examined both of us. "The coach isn't keeping the team under lockdown because of what Johnny did to Annika. He's trying to hide something else."

I frowned and reared back. "Something else? Worse than Johnny abusing Annika?"

"Just listen to the recording. Then we can figure out what it means. I don't have a clue what to do with what he said. It's not what I expected."

I closed my eyes, and my tension rushed out. Frustration swept in to take its place. Another complication wasn't what I anticipated.

Clay held out his hand for the small device he'd given Troy earlier. At his laptop on the kitchen island, he plugged the unit into the side. He cranked up the volume.

Troy sat on the couch and put his head in his hands, listening without looking. I took a stool at the island, and Clay slid onto another beside me.

The three of us listened in silence, and I started to wonder if Troy was exaggerating about the importance of the conversation. He took forever to get to the point of the meeting.

"I saw photos of what happened to Annika. Johnny's girlfriend. I don't feel right about staying quiet anymore." Troy was more confident than I expected.

There was a heavy pause and what sounded like the creak of a desk chair. *"Photos?"*

"Yes."

The chair creaked again as though the coach was rocking it. *"Do you remember freshman year when Johnny got that shoulder injury?"*

I pictured Troy frowning. *"Yes."* His voice when he responded was laced with confusion.

"It was important to me and to him that he got better. We were sure he was going to go places. Hell of a talent, that kid. So, I gave him supplements, vitamins, and such, to aid his recovery."

"Okay," Troy said slowly.

"One of the side effects of those supplements can be aggression. Not always, but sometimes."

"Are you telling me you gave him a drug that caused him to beat his girlfriend?"

"No, no. Not at all." The coach's voice became louder, as though he was leaning into Troy. *"What I'm telling you is that sometimes a situation isn't what it appears. Sometimes, more people are at risk than you might realize."*

I'd seen the coach many times. I could picture his steely gaze in my mind.

"Have I brought the best out in you, Troy? Have you fulfilled your potential?"

"Yes sir, you've been a great coach."

"That's what I do. I bring out the potential in my players. Sometimes that's through drills, watching game tape, a conversation…and sometimes that's through other means."

"What happened to Annika, sir—"

"Was unfortunate. It was. And if Johnny had anything to do with it, the police are capable of figuring it out without any help from the team." The chair squeaked again, and when the coach spoke, his voice was louder. *"Loyalty and gratitude are such important qualities for a person to possess, don't you think?"*

There was a heavy silence. *"So are honesty and integrity, sir."*

The coach laughed, a deep guttural sound. *"Yes, that's true. That's true. Of course, my two will get you more in your last year at this school. Only a few credits shy of graduation, aren't you?"*

"Jesus." I drew out the word.

Troy glanced at me as the recording cut out. "Coach and the dean are tight. Hell, Coach and everyone at this school are tight.

Especially since we've done so well this year." He ran his hands through his hair in frustration. "I can't afford to retake courses, to not graduate."

"He threatened you and admitted to giving Johnny an unknown drug. Side effect—violence. I mean, that's a jackpot." I started to pace.

Clay transferred the file onto his laptop and unplugged the device. "If the coach was giving Johnny a drug or multiple drugs and they made him act violently, could Johnny get off for what happened to Annika?"

I stopped pacing and whirled. "I don't know." The last thing I wanted was for Johnny to have a glimmer of hope.

"He was a dick freshman year, even before he hurt his shoulder," Troy said. "Looking back, I'm pretty sure he beat his girlfriend, Dawnesha Taylor. She ended up filing a restraining order or something. Hush-hush then, but it makes sense now."

I stared at Troy before I focused on Clay. "Why are you just telling me this now? Why didn't anyone say a word when I was worried about Johnny hurting Annika?"

"Seb wouldn't have known—if that's what you mean. I didn't remember either. Gabby reminded me the other night after you guys left. Gabby and I started hanging out around the time Dawnesha disappeared."

"Not really disappeared, though, right?" Clay said from his stool, alarm in his voice.

"No. Stopped coming around. After her, there wasn't a regular girl until Annika. An endless parade of women."

The parade didn't stop with Annika, either. "Is Dawnesha at our school?"

"No idea. I haven't seen her. She probably avoids football."

"So, those IT skills." I turned to Clay. "Any chance you can dig for a Dawnesha Taylor on campus?"

"Yeah, I can poke around. Why, though?"

"Establish a pattern of violence."

"Are you going after Coach?" Troy asked.

I shifted from foot to foot and rubbed my hands together. "Don't know." I took a deep breath. Did I want an answer to my next question? Everything would become even more complicated. "Did Johnny understand the side effects of whatever the coach gave him?"

Troy stood up to face me and Clay. "He's militant about what he puts in his body. The only thing he's relaxed about is alcohol, and even then I'm not sure I've ever seen him drunk."

"So he'd have asked?" I pressed.

Troy's headshake was almost imperceptible. "He was a freshman. Coach is God. If he was told to take it, he might not have asked questions. Now, yeah, probably. But when he started? I don't know. That's the truth, Natalie. *I don't know.*"

I sighed and backed up to sit on the high stool again.

"You want me to tell you Coach told him, but I can't. Makes the situation and fallout cleaner if he realized he'd get violent, and he took them anyway."

"Yeah."

Troy checked his phone. "I gotta go. I have shit to do. Look, if you're going to use the recording and drag me into it, give me a warning, okay?"

Clay nodded beside me. "Of course, man. We appreciate this."

I stood up and followed Troy to the door. There was just one last thing I needed. "Troy?"

He sighed and turned. Raising his eyebrows, he looked at me.

"Where has Sebastian gone if he's not at the frat house anymore?"

"He's sleeping in his SUV. I talked to him at practice this morning."

"What?" I asked. "No one on the team offered to take him in?"

"And risk pissing off Johnny? No. A lot of us might think Johnny is an asshole. We might even wonder if he hurt Annika. But he's our team captain. He's still the best damn player on the field. The coach's golden boy." He gave me a long look. "And honestly, Nat. If your dad or the cops or whoever can't nail him down for this, he's going to the NFL. He'll have money, power, influence... No one wants to mess with that." He shrugged. "Sebastian wouldn't either if it wasn't for you."

I flushed. "I shouldn't have told him."

Troy gave me a sideways glance. "You should have told your dad. Whether you want to believe this about yourself, Nat, you told Sebastian because he'd do what no one else had been willing or able to do. And he did. He went after him."

I pressed my hands to my cheeks to block the heat. "That's what you think?"

"Yeah." He scrunched up his face. "I don't blame you. Those pictures of Annika. When I was sitting across from Coach today, all I could think about was how terribly she's been treated. When you love someone, you do whatever you can to protect them. To keep them safe."

"Or to get them justice," I said quietly.

"Yeah," Troy said. "That too."

"Thank you. I mean that, Troy. I'm not sure where we go from here, but I'm grateful to you for getting the information today."

"Annika didn't deserve what happened to her. She was a lot of fun around the frat house. I don't understand how—that night doesn't make sense."

"You weren't there?"

"No, I stayed at the bar late because Gabby was closing, and then I went to her place. We never go to hers, but her roommate was out of town. I wonder sometimes—would it have happened if we'd been there?"

I patted his arm. "We all have things we question. Ultimately, though, none of us did it. Johnny, maybe Johnny and others, made those choices."

Troy nodded and examined me for a beat. "I get what Sebastian sees in you. I hope, when the dust settles, you two figure things out."

The urge to hug him surged in me, but he didn't seem like much of a hugger. Instead, I smiled and said, "Me too."

Troy disappeared out the door, and I turned to Clay.

"Well," Clay said. "What now, Sherlock?"

"I go to my dad with this. You find out if Dawnesha Taylor goes to college here." I grabbed my purse from the door handle.

"Will we ever have the full picture of what happened that night?" Clay asked as I dug through my purse for my bus pass.

"Does it matter? Nothing can justify what Johnny did. If he's taking these supplements or rage pills or whatever you want to call them, those might explain a little of it. But there's no justification. Nothing will ever justify what happened to Annika." My fingertips brushed against my pass, and I took it out. "Call me if you find Dawnesha Taylor. I'll text you what my dad says about the rest of this."

I grabbed my coat from the couch and slid it on.

Before I closed the door, Clay called after me, "You're going to be a great lawyer someday."

Was law school what I wanted? I'd started to enjoy being on the front lines.

Chapter Forty

♥

After I exited Clay's building, I scanned the parking lot while I headed to the bus stop. Clay would have given me a ride home, but I needed time to myself. What was the best path to take with the coach? If Johnny didn't realize the pills would make him violent, was he less culpable for what happened to Annika?

There'd been a pattern of violence, and he didn't get help. Maybe he didn't understand his rage would go that far, get that bad. His comments about Annika's laugh, the weird diet he'd gotten her to go on, or the obvious escalation of the violence couldn't be explained by the drugs. He wasn't a good guy, pills or no pills.

My phone buzzed. My heart sped up at the image on the screen of Sebastian and I—one of my favorite pictures—which meant he was calling me.

"Sebastian?" I checked both lanes for traffic before crossing the road.

"Want a ride?"

"What?" I got to the bus stop and scanned the road. "Where are you?"

"In the commuter parking lot. Do you want a ride?"

"Are you following me?" My eyes narrowed even as my heart beat triple time.

He sighed. "Maybe. Do you want a ride or not?"

I searched the lot behind the bus stop and spotted his SUV. He was tucked into the far corner, obscured by abandoned transport trailers.

I hung up and stuck my phone into my jacket pocket. I rubbed my hands together from the cold while I walked to his vehicle. The bus wasn't appealing in this weather, but accepting a ride from him was a bad idea. Our last few conversations hadn't gone anywhere productive.

He rolled down the driver's side window. There was a heaviness in his eyes, like he hadn't been sleeping. He'd lost his razor or forgotten how to use it. The urge to run my fingers along his face was almost overpowering. I pushed my hands deeper into my pockets.

"You look exhausted. Troy said you're living out of your car."

"I told Johnny to stay away from you, but I doubt he'll listen." He glanced at me and gave me a crooked smile. "Can you get in? It's freezing out there."

I went to the passenger side and slid in. The warmth of the car enveloped me. I sighed. Winter was my least favorite season. I should have picked a college in a more southern state. I twisted to see Sebastian better, and my eye caught on his things in the rear.

"You're living out of your car? That's ridiculous. Have you told your parents?"

Sebastian's jaw tightened. "No."

"Why not? They'd help you."

He stared out the front window and didn't meet my gaze. "'Cause then I'd have to tell them everything." He clenched his hands on the steering wheel.

Silence settled in the vehicle. I breathed in his familiar scent and resisted the urge to sink back into us. God, it was hard. Being so close to him and not being with him was the worst kind of torture.

"Did you ever see anything at the frat house? Any indication Johnny was abusing Annika?" I kept my voice quiet, free of accusation.

His hands flexed and released on the steering wheel. Skin was missing from his knuckles. Unable to resist, I took his closest hand and cradled it in mine.

He glanced at me and squeezed. "I never saw him do anything I would've considered abusive. I've been thinking about it a lot. Was I that dumb? But he was good at hiding his behavior. I guess she was too. You recognized it, but I didn't. I just didn't."

"You never heard any rumors?"

"I never went anywhere without him. He was the team captain, my roommate. He was my ace boy. Feels wrong to say that, but it's true." He grimaced. "I'm not convinced anyone woulda told me with him standing beside me. They sure as hell aren't telling me now."

My phone vibrated in my pocket, and I took it out. Clay had found an address for Dawnesha Taylor. He offered to be my backup. I glanced at Sebastian, letting the silence between us deepen.

"So, if you're out of their loop, do you want to be in mine?" I asked.

Sebastian's face filled with surprise. "What do you mean?"

"I need a ride to Johnny's ex-girlfriend's place. I'm making a house call to see what I can dig up."

"Your dad know about this?"

"Nope."

"Is this a good idea?"

"Maybe not." I ran my hands through my hair, gathering it up. It was almost long enough for a tiny ponytail. I sighed and made another calculated choice. "Has the coach ever offered you any supplements? Anything to improve your performance?"

He reared backward. "You think I'm doping?"

"No, not you. Well—are you? You didn't answer the question."

Sebastian rolled his eyes and shook his head. "No, Natalie, I am not taking any performance-enhancing drugs. They test for that shit."

"Must not test too well. Johnny's on something the coach has been giving him. Side effect? Rage."

"Oh, shit," he said, breathing out the words like a prayer. "Oh, shit, Nattie. How the hell did you discover that?" He took a deep breath and puffed out his cheeks. "Are you positive you don't want to be a detective?"

I grinned. "Impressive, right?"

He swiveled in his seat, and his brow furrowed. "I knew he was taking something. I didn't realize it was illegal. He mentioned he had special supplements from China."

"China?"

"I don't know if that part is true. If the coach is dealing black-market or off-the-market drugs, they could be coming from anywhere." He appeared lost in thought for a moment. "How'd you find this out?"

I pursed my lips and turned away from his scrutiny.

"Had to be Troy."

I shrugged. "What makes you think that?"

Sebastian laughed, the deep sound filling the car. "If you're going to be a detective, you need to take notes from your dad. I guessed, but now it's written all over you."

I smacked his arm and faced him, annoyed.

He laughed harder. "Lord, I've missed you." His chuckle faded, and he reached for me across the seat. His palm rested on the back of my head and then moved to cup my chin.

"It was Troy," I admitted. "He got your coach on a recording."

Sebastian's grin vanished. "What are you going to do with that?"

"I planned to threaten the coach with impeding an ongoing investigation. But the pills complicate things. With an excellent lawyer, Johnny could get off."

"Nat, you're not a cop, and you're not a lawyer. I don't want people coming after you. Christ, I'm not sleeping as it is, and it's just Johnny I'm worried about. If you go after the coach given the season we've had? You'll have to switch schools."

"Or he'll get fired." I jutted out my chin.

Sebastian shook his head. "Maybe he will. Not gonna change how Ravens's fans will feel about you."

"I'll be fine. I can take care of myself." With a huff, I turned to stare out the window again.

"Can you? Have you ever experienced that level of attention? 'Cause I have. That kinda negativity grinds on you, Nat. It wears you down." Sebastian took a deep breath. "If you decide to go after Coach, I'll do it. I don't want you to have any part of it."

"No," I said in a burst. "No. Absolutely not. You haven't worked for the last ten years to get to the cusp of the NFL to throw it away on a gamble. You said whether he gets fired for this is only a 'maybe' so unless it's a touchdown, you're not running the ball."

He let out a frustrated noise. "Maybe I don't care so much about football anymore."

"That's bullshit."

"If it's you or the game, I pick you. I'm stalking you because I'm worried about what Johnny might do. I can't sleep. All I think about is how I can make this right. The answer is simple. I'm on the wrong team, Nattie."

"The coach—"

"Is already pissed at me because I beat up Johnny. That dickhead didn't even defend himself very well. Pissed me off even more."

I frowned. "Why not?"

Sebastian held up his hands. "He needs these to be in good shape to throw the ball."

I rolled my eyes. "He didn't seem too worried about them when he beat Annika."

"Whatever happened that night, Johnny snapped. He's a dick, but he's also a massive control freak."

Silence settled in the car again while I pondered his words.

"Are you sure about switching sides? Helping us? Really sure? Ten years from now, are you going to hate me? Are you going to resent your choice?"

Sebastian's shoulders relaxed. "Doing the right thing is better than doing what's best for me. I lost sight of who I am for a while. I just..." He seemed at a loss for words. "It's always been football first. I wanna help you. I don't want you doing this alone." He swallowed. "Or with Clay."

"This is because you're jealous?" I narrowed my eyes.

"No, yes. Okay, maybe a little jealous, but it's also the right thing to do." He scanned my face, taking me in. "I'm in love with you. Seeing you spending so much time with another guy—it kills me. Knowing that other guy has seen you naked before, that you once thought you loved him, that you're bonding over this whole thing." He laced our fingers together. "I never got what the big deal was, this feeling, until I met you. I can't lose you. So far, I haven't made the right choices. But I'll do better starting now."

I squeezed his hand. My heart expanded in my chest, flooding my body with warmth. "You're completely certain?" Was I going to get him back?

"Yeah, Nat. One hundred and ten percent."

I launched myself across the divide, wrapping my arms around his neck. He chuckled as his lips met mine. In a few quick movements, he had his seat moved, and he'd settled me on his lap. Commuter parking just got a lot more exciting.

Once we came up for air, I brushed the back of my hand over Sebastian's face. "No razor?"

"You don't like it? I was hoping to earn sympathy points." Sebastian ran his fingers across his chin.

"You can't keep sleeping in your car."

"I know." He sighed and kissed me again. "Now that I've got you and I'm part of Team Nattie, I'll talk to my parents."

"I don't understand why you didn't tell them before."

"They're proud of me. They raised someone who does the right thing. I wasn't doing the right thing. I was letting fear and intimidation rule me. That's not who I am."

"I'm glad you changed your mind." I brushed my lips against his. The week and a half we'd been apart could have been measured in years.

"So, Coach," he said with an exaggerated wink to make me laugh. "What's our first play?"

I wrapped my arms around him and huddled close, breathing him in. "A few more minutes of me doing this." I kissed his neck, up to his ear. He hugged me tighter, and he groaned. "Then," I said into his ear, "we track down Dawnesha Taylor to find out what happened between her and Johnny freshman year."

"I love it when you talk dirty to me," Sebastian said, laughter evident in his voice.

"Talking is the last thing I want to do." I pressed myself closer, rocking against him.

"You want to take this into the bedroom?" He jerked his head toward the rear of the SUV.

"Definitely." Despite what we still had to do, I was giddy with happiness. We were back on the same team, and now anything was possible.

Chapter Forty-One

♥

Sebastian drove with one hand while the other kept a firm grasp on my leg. I rested mine on top of his. At the address Clay had given me, he turned into the parking lot. I'd told Clay I could handle Dawnesha on my own. Small white lie. Telling him the truth in a text was awkward. Even more awkward in person.

"You want me to come in?"

"No. What happened between her and Johnny might have soured her on football players."

"She might not recognize me."

I rolled my eyes and patted his arm. "You're Sebastian Swan. That name has been whispered across campus by legions of women and adoring fans."

"Ah, you're busting out the legions of women? That's a pretty firm *no* to me coming in."

"I'll call or text you if I need you."

"Well, I'm not leaving this parking lot until you come out."

"Bed in the rear is comfortable." I jerked my thumb over my shoulder. Seeing him looking so tired made my heart hurt.

"Better suited to things other than sleeping." Sebastian drew me toward him for another kiss.

Part of me wished we were some place more private when I pressed myself closer. Not that a lack of privacy stopped us in the commuter lot. Reluctantly, I broke the kiss and opened my door. The semi-detached house was in the older section of the city. The pale blue siding had seen better days, but the rest of the property was in good shape. A white door off the driveway was newly painted. I double-checked the unit number on my phone and knocked.

It didn't take long for someone to approach the door. When it swung open, an attractive black woman stared at me with an inquisitive expression. She was dressed in sweats, but her hair and makeup were immaculate.

I smiled. "I'm looking for Dawnesha Taylor?"

She frowned and then narrowed her eyes. "Why's that?"

"Are you Dawnesha?"

"Depends. Are you trying to sell me something?"

I laughed. "No, I'm not selling anything." My smile faded. "I'm actually here about Johnny McDade."

"Ah." A partial smile tilted her lips. "You looked familiar." She examined me from head to toe. "Sebastian Swan's girlfriend. You're friends with that girl Johnny beat."

I sucked in a breath.

"So, whose side are you on?" she asked.

Bewildered, I stared at her for a moment. My brain faltered at the implication I'd be on any side but Annika's. I hadn't expected her to be so upfront.

"Oh, yeah. I heard all about that. I'm surprised no one came here earlier."

"You could have come forward." I tried to keep the annoyance out of my voice.

Dawnesha shrugged, and then a shiver raced through her. "You wanna come in? It's cold out here."

I followed her through the narrow hallway and into a more open living room. The house was broken up into several small rooms, like older houses tended to be. Considering I'd turned up unexpectedly, the place was tidy.

"You want a drink or something?" Dawnesha asked when we passed the galley kitchen.

"No, thanks." I scanned her photos on the walls and tables.

She sat on the couch in the cozy living room and reached for her water, which was sitting beside a gossip magazine. I took the recliner, resting my hands on my knees. I wasn't sure if I should just jump in or try to do this with some subtlety.

She cradled the glass between her hands and cocked her head. "So, why are you here?"

I cleared my throat. "Johnny beat my friend. Really badly. I'm trying to figure out whether people should have seen this coming."

She raised her eyebrows and set her water on the coffee table. "You want to know if he beat me?"

My hands clenched in my lap, but I forced myself to meet her gaze. "Yes."

"Twice. He hit me twice." She crossed her arms. "But I had other injuries sometimes. The first time he left a mark, I believed it was an accident. We were out with friends and another guy got grabby. Then, Johnny got grabby with me on the way home. He bruised my wrists and upper arms. We got into a terrible fight. Our first one. Not our last." She took a deep breath. "Forever ago and just yesterday."

"I'm sorry," I said. "Reliving this must be hard." I rubbed my thighs. "Had he hurt himself at that point? Was he taking any medication?"

"No." She shook her head. "But I see what you're getting at. He tried to get me to sign a nondisclosure about those pills when we broke up."

I sat forward. "So, he understood what he was taking was bad?"

Dawnesha laughed and rolled her eyes. "Nothing went in that man's body without his knowledge. He and his parents tried to offer me a shit-ton of money to sign the agreement. But it also said I couldn't ever talk about the abuse. I come from a good family. I wasn't having that shit on my conscience."

"You realized there would be others?"

Her jaw hardened, and she nodded. "How could there not? He had a temper, and those drugs just made it worse."

"But you got out."

She grabbed her water off the table and took a long drink before answering. "No, I didn't get out. I was removed. My older brother saw my bruises and told my parents. They stopped paying my tuition. They yanked me out of school and into a counseling program for battered women." She flicked her hair over her shoulders. "I've always considered them assholes for doing that." She set her glass back down. "Then I heard about your friend."

I laced my hands together, twisting my fingers in intricate patterns, and willed my brain to keep the images of Annika at bay. "Whoever did it left her in an alley."

"I've been devouring anything I could find. Is she—will she be okay?"

I nodded. "As okay as anyone ever is after something like that."

Dawnesha sank deeper into the couch and put her head back. "It coulda been me."

"Why didn't you press charges or lay a complaint?"

Sitting forward, she said, "I did. Well, neither of *those things*. But I have an active restraining order against him."

"You do?" Troy and Gabby hinted at something similar, but I didn't realize it was still *active*.

"Yeah. Once I said no to the NDA, he started stalking me. He'd show up at my house, outside my classes, at my job. Without the nondisclosure, he worried I'd screw him over." She laughed. "Turns out he might be right about that."

"The police are investigating Johnny. My father is helping them. Would you be willing to speak to him or the cops? Both?"

Pursing her lips, she stared at me for a beat. "Have you thought this through? I mean, the drugs make the coach look terrible, but they provide an attorney with an excuse, if you get what I'm saying."

"But you just said he was violent with you *before* he ever injured himself. He wasn't taking the pills then, right?"

"That's true. He wasn't taking them when we first started dating, the first few times he *accidentally* hurt me." She took a deep breath. "But the two times he hit me—I mean laid into me—it was right after he took a double dose of those pills."

I sucked in a deep breath. Worry created tiny pinpricks across my skin. "A lawyer would argue—"

"Exactly," she said. "It's why I didn't come forward. Without the pills, he's a violent asshole. With the pills, he's a violent asshole with a reason."

My brain ticked so quickly I wasn't sure I was conscious of the thoughts flicking through it. I needed to talk this through with someone. My dad made the most sense, but Sebastian was also outside waiting.

"He would have abused Annika, regardless."

"Yeah, probably," Dawnesha said. "Would she have ended up beaten in an alley without those pills? I'm not so sure about that."

Frustration whistled through me like a boiling kettle. I wanted to scream FUCK at the top of my lungs. I covered my face with my hands. If there was a good chance Johnny would get off, I didn't want Sebastian picking me. He was going to throw away his football career on a principle.

"There are other girls," Dawnesha said quietly.

Raising my head, I frowned. "Other girls?"

She held up her hands. "Nothing I can prove and no names. But when I came back to campus after being in counseling, I had a girl show up on my doorstep. She said Johnny raped her at a frat party. She asked if that's why I left campus. If he'd raped me too."

"Oh, my God." I breathed out the words. My heart pounded in my chest. "He never—"

"No, he never raped me. He was violent, aggressive, possessive, but he never forced himself on me. But, Natalie, when he was in a rage...I only saw it twice, but it was terrifying. He broke my rib."

I rubbed my hands down my face. A cold sweat sprouted under my armpits. "He knows what those pills do to him. He must realize they turn him into this terrible person."

Dawnesha nodded. "He once told me fucking up someone else's life was better than screwing up his own."

"So he was fine with any collateral damage as long as he could still play football." I pinched the bridge of my nose. "Would you testify to this?"

"Yeah, of course." She sighed. "Look, I'm no legal expert. But if I can believe anything I see on TV, a good lawyer can pin this on the coach."

"The coach values loyalty. Guess we'll see how loyal Johnny is. I'll talk to my dad." I rose from my seat and put my hands in my coat pockets. "I don't know what will happen. But I trust his judgment. I'm sure he'll be around to speak to you himself." I passed her a piece of paper. "Here's my cell in case you think of anything else or change your mind about my dad."

She walked me to her door. "I'm fine to chat with your dad. Just make sure you understand what you're doing. It'd be a shame if he got off for this. He's aware of what he becomes on those pills. He doesn't care—it's football first."

As I strode over to the SUV, Dawnesha watched me from the door. I climbed in, taking in Sebastian's sleeping form. He looked so peaceful. Every part of me wanted to keep him, but if Johnny wouldn't suffer the consequences of his rage, it was unfair to make Sebastian stay, to risk his dream, to let Johnny take one more thing from someone I loved.

Out the window, Dawnesha gave me a brief wave before closing her door. I sat for another minute, contemplating what I'd say to Sebastian. I shook him awake.

"Nattie?" He looked confused. He rubbed his eyes and put his seat into an upright position. "How'd it go?"

Taking a deep breath, I said, "You picked the wrong team."

Chapter Forty-Two

We argued on the way to my house. Around in circles we went about what was best for him versus what was best for us as a couple.

"If the pills come out, he'll get off," I said again to emphasize my point. "Even if they have enough to charge him, none of this will be as bad for him as it should be."

We were in my parking lot now, and Sebastian let out a frustrated huff. "My choice is made. I wouldn't have left you in the first place if you hadn't told me we couldn't have a relationship. I never wanted to go, but you said if I was siding with the team, I was siding against you. That's what you said."

"That's how I felt. I thought you'd find out things about the case. You'd overhear, or they'd tell you."

"And I'd have to keep quiet."

"Yes," I said. "If you were keeping your career intact, that's what you'd have to do. I understood it. I didn't like it, but I understood." We sat in silence for a beat. "Sebastian, if Johnny goes to the NFL, if the coach doesn't get fired—you might *never* play football again. Even if *you* think you're okay with that, *I'm* not."

"It's not gonna come to that." His voice was firm. "You have the audio of Coach. For Johnny to get off, assuming he's arrested, he'll have to roll on Coach. Right?"

I scanned Sebastian's profile, trying to read him. "Yeah, I think so."

"We can work this out. One of them will go down. We'll have to see how everything falls together or falls apart. But I'm not leaving you, Nat. I'm not. I'm done with that."

"You're going to persevere the hell out of it?"

"Yeah, I am. There are angles I can work. I'm sure of it." His intense gaze met mine.

"You should call your parents and talk to them. They understand how hard you've worked. You need an objective person."

He laughed. "My parents aren't objective. They want what's best for me, always."

"Well, then maybe they'll be able to help you figure out what that is."

"What's best for me is you. I know this. No one needs to tell me. I don't care what they say. I don't care what you argue. You're not pushing me away." He took a deep breath and grabbed my hand. "Unless this is just a way for you to get rid of me."

"Oh, God. Sebastian. No. I love you. I love you so much. But this could be a life-changing decision. You didn't do anything wrong, but you might end up paying the biggest price."

He stared at our two hands, the dark and the light mixing. Linked together, I'd always felt so safe.

"I'll call them," he said. "You going in to talk to your dad?"

"Yeah, his car's in the lot here." I pointed to where it sat. "You'll come in after you're done talking to them?"

For a minute, he didn't say anything. "I'm serious about this. You need to hear me. I'm not calling them to see whether I should be with you. This is what I'm doing, and that's what

I'm telling them. I'm with you. They can help me sort out my options if things go badly."

Tears welled up in my eyes, and I stared at the roof of the car, willing them not to fall. "I don't want you to be hurt by this too." My voice was thick with unshed tears.

"Come here." Sebastian used our linked fingers to drag me across him. He pushed my hair back. "It's you and me, Nattie. We're doing this. I love you, okay?"

I curled on his lap and buried my face into him, breathing in his scent. My heart raced in my chest, but it wasn't from anxiety. Being this close brought my body to life. Lights switched on in a dark house. One after another, I became distinctly aware of each part of me responding to his proximity.

When I drew away, he kissed me, long and deep. His hands burrowed into my hair, locking me into place. There was nowhere else I wanted to be except with him, always with him.

Sitting across from my dad, I stared at the papers strewn on the coffee table. When I glanced up, having told him almost everything, his thoughtfulness startled me. Anger or resignation would have been his normal reactions.

"He'll get off, right?" I sighed.

"Not sure. You can't be certain either." He steepled his fingers. "Look, Natalie. If you want to be in the justice system, then part of that is doing what you've done. You dig. Sometimes, what you turn up isn't what you'd want for your case. This one is personal, so it's different for us. Normally, I remind myself, when I find something which goes against my case, that my job isn't to determine guilt or innocence. My role is to get to the truth. I seek the truth."

"The truth is that he knew those pills would make him violent, and he took them anyway."

"Unless Johnny comes out and says those words, it'll be his word against Dawnesha and anyone else who might have known."

"What about the other girls Dawnesha mentioned?" I asked. "Clay said there were rumors, Dad, about Johnny abusing other women. There must be something there too."

"Usually smoke means fire, but not always." He tapped his pen on the table. It was a habit I often found annoying.

A knock sounded on the door. I glanced at my dad, gauging his reaction. "That'll be Sebastian."

Dad pursed his lips. "You trust him? He'll understand a lot about this case if he's around here now."

"I trust him. Completely."

My dad nodded and went to answer the door before I could rise. When the door opened, Sebastian's startled expression was clear from my position on the couch. He must have expected me.

"Sir—"

"I hear you're playing for our side now." My dad offered a small smile.

"I am." Sebastian nodded.

Dad moved aside to let Sebastian in. The corners of Sebastian's lips tipped up when he glanced at me. Despite his nap in the SUV earlier, he looked tired.

"What did your parents say?" I asked as he took a seat beside me. I resisted the urge to snuggle into him once he plopped down. Instead, he rested his palm on my leg, and I covered it with mine.

"A lot." A dark laugh escaped. "We'll chat about it later, okay?" He sucked in a deep breath. "I called my sister too."

Scanning his face, I wished my dad wasn't there. But my dad was in detective mode since he had a cooperative player. Even if he was one who didn't possess important details.

"What's your gut instinct on what happened that night?" Dad asked Sebastian without any preamble.

Sebastian raised his eyebrows and shifted. Though he'd told me he was on board, I wondered if his conversation with his family might have changed things a bit.

"I have no proof." Sebastian met my dad's gaze.

"I realize that. I'm looking for direction. None of the players are talking. The fact Natalie got Troy to record the coach is a step down the right path."

Sebastian gave a curt nod. "I've got no love for either of these guys. If you say this came from me, that'll be their defense. But Theo and Jeff were involved. I don't know how."

"Why do you think that?" Dad asked.

"Before this, before Annika was beaten, Johnny and I spent a lot of time together. A lot. If I wasn't with your daughter, sir, I was with him. But ever since that night, he's been spending his time with Theo and Jeff. The three of them huddle up on the field, in other places, having intense conversations. They're never joking around."

My dad would be angry with me, but I had to mention it now. "I saw Theo and Johnny together at the bar the other night."

Dad froze. "What?" I knew that tone.

I swallowed and glanced at Sebastian. He squeezed my hand in response but didn't look at me. "Johnny and Theo spoke to me and Claudia at the bar."

With raised eyebrows, my father said nothing.

"When I brought up what happened to Annika, Theo didn't answer me." Wasn't that what happened? I needed to stop drinking so much.

"Anything else I should be told?" Dad's voice was steely.

"Um, he might have mentioned I should be careful, and he was angry you wouldn't leave him alone."

With a face of thunder, my father rose from his seat. "I'm going to the station."

"Dad." I stood with him.

"Don't *Dad* me. I'm going to give the police everything we've got. I'll see about executing a search warrant on Theo and Jeff's places. We're still missing some of Annika's things. If one of them isn't too bright, we might find it." Grabbing his coat, he paused before opening the front door. "You know, Natalie. You're an adult. But if someone threatens you, you need to learn to take that seriously. Johnny, whether he goes down for this or not, is dangerous." With that, he slammed the door behind him.

Sebastian whistled. "I gotta agree with your dad."

"Don't." I held up a hand. "I get it, okay?"

"It's serious. I'm glad you told me, but I can't believe you didn't tell your dad."

I sighed and closed my eyes, sinking into the couch. "You didn't grow up with Mr. Overprotective." Claudia and I hadn't told him we were going to a bar, and I'm sure I'd get an earful on that later. Then I remembered the conversation Sebastian and I didn't finish. "Speaking of parents. What happened when you talked to yours and your sister?"

"My sister said she's seen cases like Johnny's go either way. Depends on how the pieces slot together, how good the defense attorney is, how prepared the prosecutor is." He shrugged. "Not overly helpful. My parents..."

"Want you to ditch me and stick with football."

"Not exactly, no. But they're worried I'm not being smart, given how uncertain everything is with Johnny's case and Coach's involvement."

"What do you want to do?" Even though I'd been pressing him to reconsider, it wasn't what I wanted. Being without him for two weeks had torn me apart.

Tipping my chin, he forced me to meet his gaze. "I'm doing it. I'm here."

For a moment, I stared at him. I didn't want to push him away anymore. "You should stay here until you leave for the championship game. Your sleep is important. You can't be well rested living in your car."

"Your dad—"

"Will understand. I'm an adult."

"He'll be fine with me sleeping in your room?"

I laughed. "Uh, no. Probably one of us will have to pretend to sleep on the couch."

"Ah." Sebastian kissed my neck and laid me into the couch. "Pretending to sleep sounds like a plan."

"Don't you have practice soon," I said, breathless. Who needed a cardio workout when you had a Sebastian? My phone buzzed in my pocket. "Just a sec." I pressed on his chest.

Backing off, he sighed. "You're right, I got practice."

Taking my phone out of my pocket, I had a text from an unknown number. I punched in my passcode and clicked on the message.

Johnny's agent was just here. Tried to get me to sign the NDA again. Offered more money this time. Seemed as though they were going after the women he's screwed. There was a stack of NDAs in his bag.

I stared into space for a moment and then typed. *Did you sign it?* My heart started racing for a different reason.

Dawnesha's response was immediate. *No. But lots of other people did.*

"What's going on?" Sebastian asked.

"Johnny's locking down his loose ends."

Chapter Forty-Three

♥

Dad had come back from the police station in a foul mood. He'd given me pepper spray and a Taser, taking me through how to use both half a dozen times before he was satisfied. Technically, I needed a license to use the stun gun, but Dad said that if I was using it, the last thing he'd be concerned about would be the license.

Johnny had been hauled in for questioning as promised on the Wednesday before leaving for the championship game. They hadn't arrested him.

Annika had asked me to watch the National Championship with her on TV. Part of me couldn't believe she even wanted to dwell on anything football related, let alone view the game. But I figured since I was going to be watching it anyway, I might as well make the trek to her house to gauge how she was healing and dealing with everything that had happened.

I knocked on the door of her parents' modest bungaloft. Fidgeting with my phone, I texted Sebastian one more good luck. My heart lodged in my throat every time I thought about what tonight's game could mean for him.

When the door opened, her brother was dressed in the opposition's football jersey. "Hey, Natalie," Arjun said, stepping back to let me in. "Annika's in her room. She's not watching the game with the rest of us."

"Oh." I was glad Sebastian's jersey was concealed by my jacket. A frisson of fear raced through me. I had to see his game. This might be the biggest of Sebastian's career. Trying to catch it on YouTube postgame would suck, especially if he called me later to chat.

"Can I take your coat?" Arjun held out his hand.

"Uh, no. That's okay. I'm still cold." I slipped off my boots and shot him an apologetic smile.

"You remember where you're going?"

"Just up the stairs, right?" I pointed to the staircase on the left.

He nodded and padded back down the hall to the living room. The TV blared the pregame from the entrance. My heart sank. I climbed the stairs, part of me hoping Arjun was wrong but another part of me hoping he was right. Why would Annika want to view the championship? Wouldn't it be reliving a piece of her trauma?

I knocked on her door.

"Come in," she called, her voice stronger than the last time I heard it.

Opening the door, I took in her appearance. Her bruises had faded but weren't gone. The gash on her cheek I'd been worried would scar looked much better than I expected.

When I met her gaze, her eyes were clear. "My face isn't too bad now. The rest of my body is a multicolored mess." She patted her bed. "Wanna get in?"

"Do I?" I smiled. "Has someone washed your sheets for you?"

She laughed. Our running joke had been her distaste for doing laundry. Half the time, I ended up washing hers for her.

"They're clean-ish." She grinned. "Come on. Why do you have your coat on?"

Sheepishly, I unzipped it. Annika squealed.

"Sorry," I said. "I thought we were watching the game."

Annika laughed and dragged her laptop out from underneath her covers. "I can't believe he got you to wear his jersey. I might faint from the cuteness." She started up her computer while I slid into bed beside her. "We *are* watching the game." She typed away on the keyboard. With a few clicks, the game was streaming live.

My breath lodged in my throat as I caught sight of Sebastian. I glanced at Annika. "Are you sure about this?"

"Yeah," Annika said. "I just didn't want my family judging me or checking for a reaction every time his face came on the screen." Color rose in her cheeks. "I'm getting better, but I'm not better yet."

I wrapped my arm around her shoulders and gave her a squeeze. Tears pricked at the back of my eyes, and I leaned over to kiss her temple.

"No judging from me. You wanna cheer them on, fine. You want to sit here and scream *asshole* at the screen, I'm cool with that too. You want to bawl your eyes out? I'll hold you while you cry."

Annika nodded, and tears filled her eyes. "Sometimes I think it would be easier if I remembered, if it felt like it really happened. That whole night is a surreal blur. I can see the bruises, but I don't remember getting them. None of them."

"What does your counselor say?"

She laughed. "You mean my psychologist?"

Rubbing her back, I shrugged. "I didn't want to pry too hard."

"Yeah, well, apparently I'm clinically depressed. Didn't ask anyone if I could watch the game. I'm just doing it. What happened is a blank space—a void. It feels like it happened to someone else. I understand what I should feel. But I don't feel anything."

"Okay." I spotted Sebastian on the screen out of the corner of my eye.

Annika gave me a small smile and leaned her shoulder into mine. "It's weird seeing you like this."

"Like what?" My attention was split between her and the laptop resting between us.

"So loved up."

I grinned. "That obvious, huh?"

"It's nice to see you so happy." Her features softened. "Kristy told me Sebastian went after Johnny."

I sucked in a breath. "God, Kristy is such a gossip."

Annika laughed, and there were hints of her old laugh in the undertones. I glanced at her.

"She is." Playing with the comforter, Annika avoided the screen. "Sebastian texted me too."

I straightened and swiveled to make eye contact. "He did?"

"Yeah. When you two were broken up. He said he was sorry about what happened to me." Annika didn't meet my gaze. "Johnny threatened you?"

My breath left me in a whoosh. "Kristy again?"

Shaking her head, Annika's dark eyes met mine. "No. That's the only reason Sebastian would go after Johnny." She searched my face. "He didn't hurt you, did he?"

"No, he didn't. He cornered me and Claudia, threatened us. Troy intervened before the situation got out of hand."

She closed her eyes. "I wish I'd listened to you. I kept thinking if I could wade through the shit with him, we'd be good." Her expression brimmed with anguish. "But the shit never ended, it just got deeper. It would have kept getting deeper."

"I met his ex."

Annika raised her eyebrows. "Johnny said Dawnesha was psychotic."

"Did he?" I let the comment sit between us.

She sighed. "I suppose that wasn't true either." Swallowing, she adjusted her pillow. "What'd she say?"

"I shouldn't say. I'm not sure if you'll have to testify. My dad would lose it if I screwed things up by talking to you about this."

She huffed out a breath. "Tell me. I'll deny I knew if I have to."

That was enough for me. "Did you ever see Johnny taking supplements or pills?"

"Like vitamins?"

"No."

Annika flushed. "Yes." She rolled her shoulders as though she was loosening up for something. "He didn't take them all the time. Mostly if he hurt himself."

"Did you ever notice any changes in him when he was taking them?"

Annika's gaze shifted to me, but she didn't speak right away. Wheels turned behind her dark eyes. "The pills made him violent?"

I maintained eye contact.

"He was moody whether he was on them or not. I never knew what would set him off. That's part of the problem with trying to piece things together. I could have said anything. Anything."

Johnny's face appeared on the screen. I avoided looking at Annika, but out of the corner of my eye I saw her turn away from the screen.

"We don't have to watch this." I only partially meant it. Seeing Sebastian play was important.

"No, I'll be fine when the game starts. Once it starts, I can focus on how they're playing, not who they are."

"If you change your mind—"

"I won't."

I checked the countdown to kickoff on the laptop. "Your family is watching this game downstairs?"

She shook her head. "My dad and brother think Johnny should rot in hell. They're probably down there cheering for the opposition."

Thank God I had enough sense to keep my coat on. Otherwise, they'd have thought I was an insensitive asshole. Annika hadn't been expecting me to wear a jersey. Why would she?

"It would have been fun to go there with you," she said.

"To the game?"

"Yeah. Remember how you bought those markers and bristol board? We were going to make ridiculous signs to wave. The girlfriends of the two star players. We were sure we'd get on camera."

She rattled off the details as though it wasn't heartbreaking to realize how we'd changed. That had been our plan. We'd giggled our way through the dollar store together, joking about the inappropriate things we could write. I'd told Sebastian I had big plans. Just one more thing Johnny ruined.

When the commercial break was over, the teams were on the field, and the ref blew the whistle. Annika leaned forward.

"Here we go." A touch of excitement entered her voice.

We exchanged thoughts on plays but avoided comments about specific players. At one point after a particularly brutal play, Annika said Sebastian was playing like a man possessed. He knew he had to make an impression. He might need this game as evidence of his talent if things with his coach went sour.

The game was dying down. It was close—so close. Annika was biting her nails, a habit she'd worked hard to crack in freshman year. If something had to give, her nails were the least of her worries.

"They need a touchdown," she mumbled.

"I hate this part of the game. So little time left, but still so much time to make a play. It's too easy to win or lose a game in the dying minutes of this sport."

Annika laughed. "That's what makes it exciting."

"Yeah, but why play the rest of it? Let's just play a five-minute game instead. It would save a lot of time. It's arbitrary, anyway."

Annika laughed. "Have you had this conversation with Sebastian?"

My laughter burst out of me. "Oh, yeah. He thinks my theories are crazy. Sports and their rules aren't the problems. I'm the problem."

"Exercise and Sports Science was the worst major for you."

"I was so dumb in freshman year."

"Oh, shit." Annika's eyes were glued back to the screen.

"What?" I searched for what she'd seen.

"They're going to have to go long. I mean, pretty freaking long. They're falling apart a bit."

Watching the game had been a constant push-pull for me. Sebastian needed to look good and the one person who could help him do that was also the one person I wanted to play poorly. Every time Johnny had the ball, which was a lot as the quarterback, I cringed. When he'd been sacked, I considered jumping on the bed. I'd held it together. Barely.

"What's the rule again?"

"The ball has to have left his hand before the clock runs down. Then the play goes until it's done."

I checked the score. This either worked or they'd lose. Taking a deep breath, I released it. No part of me wanted Johnny to have this moment. Victory in any sense shouldn't be his. But

Sebastian had played his heart out today. For him to lose felt wrong too.

I wished I could grab the camera and focus it on Sebastian. Gluing my eyes to him, I blocked out everything else on the field. They zoomed in on Johnny as he released the ball. I hopped off Annika's bed and started pacing.

"Where's it going?" I couldn't watch.

"Sebastian, I think. It's still in the air."

"God, that's a long throw."

"I told you." She sat up straighter, the laptop bouncing on the bed. "He caught it. Sebastian caught it. Oh, shit. Nat, you need to watch this."

I leaned across the bed, my eyes glued on Sebastian as he danced his way around the last player and into the end zone. Relief flooded me. He'd done it. Sebastian was swarmed on the field, and I pushed off the bed to jump around the room. Taking a deep breath, I stopped jumping and snapped Annika's laptop closed.

"Hey! They'll interview Sebastian." She started to open it again.

I put my hand on hers to still it. "They'll interview lots of people. We don't need that. I'll catch Sebastian's on YouTube later. He'll understand."

Annika gave a curt nod and put her laptop on the floor beside the bed. "Are you driving back tonight?"

"I have class in the morning."

"I haven't left the house in weeks. Can we go get a coffee somewhere before you leave?"

"You bet." My heart was light. I couldn't wait to talk to Sebastian. Nothing could ruin my good mood.

Chapter Forty-Four

♥

I woke with a sigh. I'd had the best dream. I stretched and hugged my pillow, savoring the good start to my morning. Today was going to be an excellent day, I could feel it.

Sebastian had been so happy when I'd talked to him on the phone. He kept saying how much he wished I was there. My heart ached each time he said it, as though he was a phantom body part.

Climbing out of bed, I grabbed my phone off the dresser. With my thumb, I scanned my notifications and paused when I came to a text from Annika at three in the morning.

Tell your dad, I remember. I remember it all.

Blood rushed to my head when my heartbeat picked up. Instead of texting her, I hit the call button.

"Annika?" I said when she answered. "Did I read that text right?"

Her sigh was deep, wavering, soul shattering. "Yeah, you did. I don't know why now. My therapist said it might happen like this. I had a dream. I woke up screaming. My parents came rushing in, and when I calmed down, I realized why I'd been screaming." Her voice hitched. Muffled sobs traveled across the miles into my ear. "It was him. Johnny. Theo and Jeff were there, in the frat house."

"Okay," I said. "Okay, I'll tell my dad to come see you."

"I thought," Annika started, then stopped. "I thought I wanted to remember. But it's so much worse. I had no idea. I just—" Her voice broke, and I wished I was there to give her a hug.

"I'll come with my dad and ditch my class."

"No." Her voice was a little stronger. "I don't want to be responsible for you missing more class."

"I don't care about my class. If you need me, I'm there."

She took a deep, shuddering breath. "It might be easier to get through retelling it if I'm stating the facts to your dad. If you come, I think I'll—I'll fall apart."

My heart sank, but I understood. "Okay. But if you want to talk later…"

"I need your dad to tell me what I do now." Her voice took on an unnaturally high pitch as though on the cusp of panic.

"I'll go talk to him, okay? We'll figure it out, Annika. It'll be okay."

"I gotta go." Her voice was strangled, and she hung up.

I threw on my robe and rushed out to find my dad drinking his coffee at the table.

"Annika remembers," I said. "She said she remembers it all. She wants to talk to you."

The cup clattered onto the table, and my dad got to his feet, grabbing his notepad and pen off the table. "I'll have to take the police with me. Does she have a lawyer?"

I shook my head. "Not sure."

"I'll call her parents on the way." He grabbed his keys off the side table by the door and then stopped short. "I didn't see you last night when you got home. But Sebastian played a hell of a game."

My heart swelled at my dad watching Sebastian play, cheering him on.

"Oh, Dad," I said. "I can't believe you watched."

He gave me a slight smile from the door. "They're back today. Pepper spray and Taser with you. If Annika remembers everything, and Johnny finds out, he might think he's got nothing to lose."

I sunk onto one of the kitchen chairs. My phone pinged, and I snatched it off the table to find a text from Kristy.

Are you and Sebastian on or off?

Frowning, I texted her back: *We're on*. My brain kicked into overdrive. When there was silence on her end, I texted her again to discover what was going on.

Shit on Instagram. Probably nothing.

Sebastian never posted anything, ever. He called social media a time suck. I opened the app, searching for whatever Kristy had seen. There was nothing on his page or my home feed. I searched the hashtag for the National Championship. Then I saw it. A GIF of Sebastian making out with another girl.

Nausea rushed over me like a tsunami, wiping out sanity. I went to my text messages to check whether Sebastian sent me anything. Nothing. What did that mean? I checked my missed calls, but there was nothing there either.

Sebastian didn't post the GIF, another player did, but they'd tagged him. Such a tiny moment to capture. I watched it again, a knife stabbing me over and over.

He wouldn't.

Would he?

I'd watched Sebastian pack his bag. Had that shirt been in the pile? I tried to be rational while my stomach threatened to revolt. Standing up, I went to my room. Tossing gym clothes into a bag, I snatched the Taser and pepper spray off the counter on the way out the door. I couldn't sit around here wondering.

When I asked him about it, the truth would be written on his face. Lying over text or the phone was too easy. They were flying home tonight. I could wait.

Maybe the GIF was nothing.

Maybe he got drunk and made a mistake.

My conversation with Annika months ago returned in a rush. There were always girls around him, circling. Temptation was everywhere.

I should have gone to the game. Why didn't I go to the game?

While I walked to the gym, my head and heart fought a bitter battle. Every possible scenario played out. If Sebastian did get to the NFL, this could happen. Would I always be wondering what to believe, who to believe? My stomach rolled, and I pressed a hand to my gut.

I worked out at the gym until the lightheaded feeling got the best of me. My phone was off because I was unable to face whatever else might appear. Was it one girl? A single post?

What would I do if it was true? Could I overlook one mistake?

If he didn't sleep around while we were broken up, he wouldn't do it now. He was Team Nattie. He wouldn't.

My brain kept circling. One minute I was convinced there was no way he was making out with a random girl last night. My next ideas encompassed the ways it might have happened.

Class was a bust. I couldn't concentrate on the lecture and ended up having to ask someone else for their notes. Walking home, my brain kept ticking off the possible scenarios, every reason the video might have been posted.

I cleaned the house from top to bottom while I waited for Sebastian to return. My dad and I exchanged a few texts, but I couldn't ask him whether Sebastian might have cheated on me. The one person I wanted to talk to already had too much on her shoulders. My drama was so trivial in comparison.

When the door handle rattled and a set of keys jangled around midnight, I froze in the middle of washing the baseboards. All the furniture was pulled out from the wall, a bucket beside me, a rag in my hand. I dropped the rag in the bucket and yanked my phone out of my rear pocket. Still nothing from Sebastian. He was supposed to be back hours ago. I sighed, sitting on my haunches. My dad would take one look at me and know something was wrong.

Braced for an interrogation, I watched the door swing open. My heart stutter-stopped when Sebastian poked his head in.

"Nattie? You still awake?"

"Yeah." I sat on the floor, frozen. "You scared me."

"Shit, sorry." He stepped in and dropped his things with a thud. Exhaustion coated his features like a thin layer of paint. When we made eye contact, he grinned. "We won!"

I smiled, not moving off the floor. "It was a great game. You guys must have had a lot of fun last night." The words came out of my mouth, wooden.

"It was all right. I kept wishing you were there. Then I lost my phone somewhere. Did you try to text me?" Shaking his head, he rounded the couch and plopped down. "I haven't seen you in days. I hoped I might get a bit more of a greeting." He took in the chaos of furniture and cleaning supplies. "What are you doing?"

"Cleaning."

"Okay," Sebastian said slowly.

Silence hung between us.

"All right, what's going on? You're freaking me out. Did something happen while I was gone?"

I grabbed my phone off the ground beside me. Scrolling through the hashtag on Instagram, I found the post and gave Sebastian my phone.

His brows pulled together, and he frowned as he watched it. "What the hell is this?"

"Took the words right out of my mouth."

"You're wondering if this is from last night?"

"It was posted last night by one of the guys on the team. Malcolm, I think."

"Did you look at it?" He peered at me, not defensive but curious.

I rolled my eyes. "A few times."

"So you realize it's from the frat house, right?"

"What?" I sat beside him and peered over his shoulder.

Using his finger, he pointed out everything in the background of the GIF. "I don't understand why Malcolm posted this last night, but this is old. Like, when I first got to campus, old."

I pressed a hand to my forehead while relief cascaded through me.

"Nat, you gotta stop thinking the worst of me." He put his arm around my waist and kissed my temple. "I swear there isn't a woman alive who compares to you. There just isn't." He held my phone between us.

"I'm sorry."

Taking a deep breath, he tugged me until I straddled him. "Look at me."

Reluctantly, I raised my eyes.

"What do you need to hear?"

Shaking my head, I broke eye contact. "What if you get super famous and this happens?"

His eyebrows pulled in. "What if what happens?"

"If it looks like you're cheating on me."

He smoothed my hair with both his hands and then leaned forward to kiss my forehead. "I realize what I've got with you. There will be no cheating. I promise."

"There's always going to be other girls after you."

"Not always. Someday I'll be old and fat."

I laughed and shoved his chest. "You know what I mean."

"I do."

When I looked at him again, my favorite half smile was on his face.

"You think I don't worry about the same thing?" he asked.

"I don't have guys hanging off me everywhere I go."

"You're smart. You're gorgeous. I worry you'll wake up one day and realize you can do so much better than some football player with an okay GPA."

"That won't happen." I cupped his cheek before kissing him.

"If you ever wonder where we're at, how I'm feeling, ask. Honesty, always, okay?"

I nodded, playing with the bottom of his shirt. "Honesty, always."

"Where's your dad?" Sebastian looked around. "Sleeping?"

I scrolled through my messages. "Looks like he's not coming home tonight."

"Why? What's going on?"

Meeting his worried gaze, I said, "Annika remembered. She remembered it all."

Chapter Forty-Five

M y dad stuffed the last of his papers in his bag and then wandered around the living room, checking for anything he'd left behind.

"They're arresting Johnny today?" I asked again from the couch.

"Yes." My father's voice was laced with deliberate patience. "They're picking up Johnny, Jeff, and Theo."

"They found Annika's tights, phone, and purse in the wheel well of Jeff's car, right?"

Dad stopped gathering the last of his things and stood staring at me. "What's wrong?"

"I don't know. It feels weird to have you leaving. Are you sure you don't want to stay longer?"

He smiled and came over to give me a hug. "I'll return once the trial starts. But I need to get back to work. I'm out of personal days and holidays. The police have a good case. The pills complicate things, but it's a strong case. Annika remembers. If they can convince Jeff or Theo or both to roll on Johnny, they've got an excellent shot at a conviction."

I'd spent the last four weeks lamenting my dad's lack of tidiness and his general presence, but I was going to miss seeing him, bouncing ideas off him, knowing I wasn't alone.

"Annika still planning to return to school in a couple weeks?"

"Yeah, I think so."

He grabbed his bags and placed them by the door. "Sebastian's here soon?"

"He went to the gym and to class." I checked the clock. "Should be here any minute."

"Pepper spray and Taser with you at all times, okay? They're arresting him, but he'll probably be given bail. He could still get off these charges, so he'd be dumb to come after you. But hotheads like him can be unpredictable."

"I got it, Dad."

He enveloped me into a hug. "I love you, Natalie Ann. I'm proud of the work you did on this case."

My grin was going to split my face. "Really?"

He placed one hand on each of my shoulders. "Really. You're remarkable. Your mother would have been so proud of how you've handled yourself. I know I am."

At the mention of my mom, my throat tightened. "Thanks, Dad. Thanks for everything."

"I'm just a phone call away. You need me for anything, you call."

"It'll be okay."

With one final hug, he picked up his bags and headed to his car. From the door, I watched him drive out of the parking lot. Anxiety fluttered in my chest, and I locked the door.

When I took my phone off the side table, there was a text from Clay. He'd been keeping his distance since Sebastian returned, but he and Annika were in regular contact.

Taking immense pleasure in Johnny and his boys at the station.

How are you seeing that?

Local news. Watch it. It's amazing.

Going around the couch, I snatched the remote off the coffee table and flipped to the news station. Sure enough, Johnny, Theo, and Jeff were walking through a crowd of reporters flanked by lawyers and police officers.

Every time Johnny put up his hand to shield his face from prying questions and camera flashes, the sunlight caught his championship ring. Seeing it sent a jolt of anger through me. So unjust for his success and Sebastian's to be linked.

Keys jingled outside, and Sebastian came in the door. His gaze strayed to the TV, and he grimaced. Rounding the couch, he sank into a seat, elbows on knees.

"I hope it's enough," he said as Theo, Jeff, and Johnny were walked into the station.

"Me too." I scanned his face. "Nothing from the coach?"

"Not yet. He's probably waiting to see where this heads with the guys."

"You're not worried?"

"Not worried at all." He leaned into the couch. "I caught the damn ball and did a hell of a run during a nationally televised game. Yeah, Johnny threw it, but I caught it. He's not going to kick me off the team because of Johnny's arrest. He either goes down with him for the drugs or he coaches next year."

Johnny's lawyer took up the whole screen. We both stared at the TV, only half listening as he made a statement declaring Johnny's innocence.

"What'd your dad say before he left?"

"It's a solid case. Who knows?" My summary was close.

Sebastian grabbed my free hand and drew me across the couch beside him. He grabbed the remote and switched off the TV.

In one swift movement, he flipped me so that my back was pressed into the material and he was lying on top of me. Sometimes his strength and speed were breathtaking off the field too.

I grinned at him. "Alone at last."

"I should start looking for a place to live," Sebastian murmured.

"Why?"

"Isn't Annika coming back in a few weeks?"

"She says she is. I'm not so sure." I sighed as he nibbled on my earlobe. "You could live here for now?"

"Nattie, are you asking me to move in?" His hazel eyes danced with merriment.

"Maybe." I drew out the word. "Could you can handle it?"

"I like the idea of going to bed with you, waking up with you every day."

"There's also dishes, laundry, cooking..." I rattled off the other things we'd have to negotiate.

"I'll do everything." He gave me a quick kiss.

"I have standards." I kept my voice light, but I wasn't joking. My own father didn't meet them.

Sebastian chuckled. "I can take it, Nattie. I wanna do this with you." His face clouded. "If Annika does return..."

"I'll talk to her. She might enjoy having you here."

"If she doesn't, I'll move out, okay? It's not a big deal. Maybe when the lease is up here?"

"Definitely."

"Really?" he asked. "You'd do that?"

"As long as Annika is doing okay by then, yeah, I'd live with you."

He scooped me up, and I wrapped my legs around his waist as he carried me to the bedroom. "We're gonna need to seal the deal."

"The roommate deal?" I laughed. "Seal it with what?"

"A little close contact."

"Just a little?" I teased.

He tossed me on the bed, and as I bounced, I giggled. He followed me down, scooping up my lips.

"Maybe a lot."

"I'm so glad Johnny's been arrested." Even as the words left my lips, I remembered his bail and my dad's warning. Until Johnny was locked up for good, he was a danger to me, to Annika, maybe to Sebastian too.

"Hey," he said. Something in my face must have given me away. "We got this, Nattie. He's going down. I'm sure of it. Okay?"

Stroking his face, I kissed him, and I wished I could be as confident. At the edges of my happiness was a deep unease. Johnny didn't seem like the type to go down without a fight.

Chapter Forty-Six

♥

I grabbed the last bag out of Annika's car and held it until
Sebastian came around to my side and took it from me.

"I'll take it in." He gave a small smile and brushed a kiss across
my lips.

Annika reached into her vehicle and grabbed her final things.

"I realize you're here, but are you sure this is a good idea?"
How many times had I asked her this question? A million,
maybe more.

The college had been supportive of her grades and classes.
She'd completed work from home already. Annika didn't want
to lose a year. Part of me thought she should be transferring
schools, even if leaving was unfair. She hadn't done anything
wrong.

Johnny was out on bail, and with Annika back in the city, I
was worried.

"I'll be fine. I promise. The nightmares are mostly gone. I'm
not numb anymore about what happened. Remembering has
been hard, but it's helped me." The words came out like a speech
she'd rehearsed.

"And you're sure you're okay with Sebastian being here?"

She slammed her car door and shoved more garbage into a McDonald's bag. "Yeah, it's fine. Honestly. You said it was until the end of the year, right? It's March, so it's not that long."

I nodded. I hadn't told her we were moving in together the next year. He came out of the townhouse and down the small pathway. Watching him walk toward me made my heart too big for my chest. The confidence oozing out of him spoke to me on a deeper level.

He caught me staring and grinned. Once he reached me, he looped an arm around my waist and tipped his head at Annika. "You got everything?"

She sighed and peered into the car. "Yep." Stepping past us, she headed up the path to the townhouse.

I watched her retreating figure for a moment with anxiety bubbling in my stomach, and Sebastian squeezed my hip.

"I'm not sure about this," he said.

"Me either." I took his hand and followed Annika.

Once we were inside, she disappeared into her room without a word. Sebastian grabbed his keys off the side table and gave me a quick kiss.

"I'm gonna go out. Go to the gym. Give you two some space."

"Thank you." I dragged him to me for a second goodbye kiss before he could disappear out the door.

"I got a bad feeling about this." He jerked his head in the direction of Annika's room. "She doesn't seem okay."

I sighed. "She's not. But it's not my place to tell her she can't be here."

"I get that. I just... I don't know." He squeezed my hand, leaned in for another kiss, and then closed the door behind him.

When I turned around, Annika was in the entry to the hallway with her bag slung over her shoulder. "I have to be on campus. I'm meeting with an academic advisor to look over my courses to figure out how I stay on track to graduate."

"Before you go." I pointed to the pepper spray and Taser on the side table. "Can I show you how these work? Maybe you should take one with you?"

Annika stared at me in silence and then dropped her bag. "He's not going to come after me. He'd be dumb to do that."

I picked up both items, letting their weight settle in the palm of my hand. "If there's one thing I can say about Johnny, his only concern is him. If he thinks he can convince you to change your statement..."

"Show me." She stepped forward.

I took her through what my dad had shown me and then let her get the feel for both herself. "Which one do you want to take with you?"

"Taser," she said. "If he approaches me, I'll get immense satisfaction in watching him writhe on the floor."

"You can do that?" I didn't make eye contact.

"Yeah." She shoved the Taser in the front pocket of her bag. "You weren't there. You don't understand."

"Do you want to talk about it?"

She snorted. "All I've done is talk about it." Shaking her head, she put her bag on her shoulder. "You know what discussing it has taught me?"

I stared at her, not saying anything.

"None of what happened was my fault. Whenever I remember any of the episodes of abuse—any of them—I can't figure out what I did wrong that other people wouldn't have done." She shrugs. "There's only so much talking you can do when the answer is stupidly simple. I had too much faith in someone. That was my problem. I was too trusting, convinced he wasn't the person he was showing me."

"I wish—" But I wasn't sure how to finish.

"Me too. So many things." Annika gave me a small smile. "But I don't want this event to ruin me. I said that to Clay the other night when we were talking. What happened with Johnny can't set the tone for the rest of my life."

"I'm glad," I said. "I'm glad you're figuring this out."

"You know what was different that night? You know what I've realized made his rage worse?"

I shook my head.

"I fought back. He didn't understand I was just starting. I'm going to keep fighting, forever." Tears pooled in her dark eyes, and she turned away from me.

I hugged her from behind. "I love you, Annika, and I'm proud of you. You'll get there."

She squeezed my hands and sniffed before releasing me. "I'll be home later. I have the Taser."

"Hopefully you don't need it." I walked with her to the door.

"Thanks." She gave me a half hug before heading out. She walked down the path to her car in the parking lot, and then I closed the door, flipping the lock.

After consulting the clock on the wall, I realized I had a while before Sebastian returned. He'd been spending hours in the gym as off-season conditioning for football. I grabbed my laptop out of my bag and set it up at the kitchen table, my back to the front door.

Unable to resist, I searched for any recent articles on Johnny's arrest. The headlines bothered me. Almost every single one led with "Star Football Player" or "Quarterback Prodigy" and then followed with his crimes. I'd never understand why his ability to throw a football trumped his incapacity to be a decent human being.

When the front door rattled, I checked the time. Annika had been gone an hour, and Sebastian would be at the gym for at least two hours. Frowning, I twisted toward the entrance. Annika's meeting was quick.

The door popped open, and when I saw who was there, I stood so quickly my chair clattered to the ground. "You shouldn't be here."

In the doorway, with the spare key in his hand, was Johnny. "I'm looking for Annika."

Panic gripped my chest. How did we forget about the spare key outside? *So stupid.* The pepper spray sat on the side table, closer to him than to me.

Oh, God.

"Most people knock, call ahead, or, when they're accused of raping and beating someone, don't show up at all." The words tumbled out of my mouth. Being calm and quiet was a skill I hadn't mastered.

He closed the door behind him. "I want to talk to her. Where is she? I heard she was coming back today."

"Why would you need to talk to her?" My brain searched for a way to grab the pepper spray or run to my phone in my room. Why had I left it so far away?

"Her memory of that night is... Well, it's wrong. She can't torpedo my life like this."

"She's not the one doing that." I slid a pen off the table beside me. How hard would I have to stab him for it to be useful?

"You're right about that." Johnny came closer. "I don't blame Annika. I blame you. If you hadn't kept pushing, she'd have been fine with our arrangement."

"The one where you did whatever you wanted to her or with others and she took it without complaint?" I gripped the pen harder.

He grinned, his dimple on full display. His face had been on the front of countless newspapers. Touted to be a first-round draft pick, strong GPA, a wealthy family, and looks to kill—his arrest baffled people. He was candy for the tabloids.

"Our relationship worked fine. Your snide comments, and Sebastian giving in to your irrational demands were the problem. I mean, why?" He examined me. "It's not your personality or your appearance. So, you must be awfully skilled in other areas."

Bile rose in my throat. "You'll never find out." I stared him down.

Casually, he swiped the pepper spray off the side table and moved forward. "Is that so?"

He wouldn't touch me without a hell of a fight on his hands. My grip on the pen was so tight my sweat would cause it to slip when I needed it the most. I forced myself to relax and focus, pretend like this was a kickboxing match. I could do this. I scanned our townhouse layout, trying to figure out where to go, what to do.

"Your dad give you this?" Johnny waggled it in his hand. "Where is he now? Or Sebastian? Or Clay? Or Troy?" He smirked. "It's just you and me, *Nattie*."

Chapter
Forty-Seven

I stepped to the side of the kitchen table. He could pin me against it or on it. There was still hope he was too dumb to use the pepper spray. Maybe he'd stay too far away for it to work well.

"You don't want to touch me. Any of them will come after you, laws or no laws." If I could get past him and dash along the hall, I might be able to reach my room and lock the door before he got there. Or I could race to the kitchen and grab a knife from the block on the counter.

"I'm going to lose everything anyway," he said. "Might as well go out swinging."

"You don't know that." I tried to keep the edge of desperation out of my voice. I needed to make a decision soon—kitchen or bedroom. "You could get off. If you hurt me, you'll have no chance."

When he glanced at me, his blue eyes were hollow. "She remembers. Who in their right mind won't believe her?"

"You could get help. Take a plea. A shorter sentence." I threw out ideas.

Johnny shook his head. "There's no plea for me. Jail kills my career. There's football or there's nothing."

When he stepped forward again, I sprinted to the hallway, running to my bedroom. Behind me, Johnny chuckled.

"The thrill of the chase," he called out, laughing. "At least you'll make this interesting."

My heart raced, painful in my chest. I hit the door with my shoulder to get in faster. As it sprung open, Johnny grabbed me, yanking me back.

Closing my eyes, I let my self-defense and kickboxing classes take over. I brought my heel down on the top of his foot hard, twisted and elbowed him in the side at the same time.

His grip slackened, and I surged forward into my room. Throwing my weight against the door, I didn't have a chance to get it locked. He pushed back, his shoulder against the wood. He'd had far more practice at this than I had. While he put pressure on the door, his arm came around, spraying. I ducked my head, and the pepper shot across the room, missing me.

I was glad for my bare feet, which were gripping well on the hardwood floor, but I wasn't sure how long I could sustain the pressure. My phone mocked me on the nightstand. Letting go would mean I wouldn't get to it, but if I kept up this losing game, I was a goner anyway. Either way, I was screwed.

"You don't want to do this." I leaned harder, digging my feet into the floorboards.

"I've wanted to do this for months." His voice was hard. "Now, I have no reason not to." He eased the pressure on his side, throwing me off balance. I stumbled. He slammed the door with a blast of power, knocking me off my feet, and sending me sprawling across the floor.

He stalked toward me, and I crab crawled backward, searching for some distance so I could stand up, scanning for anything I could use as a weapon. Somewhere, I'd dropped the pen.

In the corner, one of Sebastian's helmets sat. I lunged for it, and Johnny snagged my foot. Using my momentum, I swung around, trying to smash the helmet into Johnny's head. I hit him, but only in the shoulder.

He chuckled and sprayed me square in the face. My eyes lit up, and everything went black. Through a haze of pain, I was aware of him tugging at my clothes. I tried to keep moving, squirming, kicking, anything I could do while my eyes burned. Touching my eyes would make the burning worse, but I wanted to press the heels of my hands into them.

Twisting and grunting, I scratched at him. Any part of his body near my face, I tried to snap, bite, wound.

"Nat!" Annika called from the front door. "I'm back!"

Johnny stilled over me.

"Annika!" I screamed while squirming underneath him. "Get out of here! Johnny's here!"

He rose off me, and his footsteps retreated. I prayed he didn't take the pepper spray with him.

Crawling on my hands and knees, I tried to make my way to the door. My eyes hurt so much. They wouldn't open.

"Anni," Johnny said, his voice calm. "I was hoping we could chat."

"Where's Natalie?" Her voice was full of tension.

"In her room, I think. I'm not sure. I was waiting for you."

"Annika, he has the pepper spray," I called. Hopefully, he wasn't close enough to use it. If we were lucky, he left it in here somewhere.

"I don't have the pepper spray." I pictured him holding up his hands.

"Good," Annika said.

The sharp staccato of the Taser as it made contact with Johnny filled the silence. His body thumped to the ground, and his deep groans reached my ears as I stumbled toward the doorway.

"Call 911," I said to Annika. "I can't see. My eyes..." I trailed off.

The sharp staccato sounded again.

"Annika, are you okay?"

"You bet," she said. "Johnny's body parts might be burnt. I want to do it again and again."

His groans filled the hallway, and Annika's footsteps approached me. The beep-beep-beep of her phone hit my ears before she crouched beside me.

Thank God, she's calling 911.

"Hi, yes, we have an intruder, an armed break-in in progress." Annika helped me stand while rattling off our address.

"Grab the pepper spray," I said, bracing myself against the door. "The Taser might not keep him down."

She raced into the room, footsteps brisk across the floor, while talking to the 911 operator. "Got it." She took my arm and led us down the hall.

"We need to get out of here." I groped for her in the darkness.

She latched onto me and guided us around Johnny, who was groaning and banging his heels. I understood his pain but had no sympathy.

I stumbled a few times on the way out the door, and I was glad for Annika's tight grip, even if her guidance was terrible.

In the distance, sirens blared.

"Are you okay?" Her voice was unsteady.

"Other than wanting to rip my eyes out of my head, I'm okay." I clutched her arm. Judging by the route we'd walked, we should be standing in the parking lot. "I'm not sure I would have been if you hadn't come home when you did."

She squeezed me tighter. "I know it's not my fault. But I'm so sorry. I'm sorry I brought him into our lives."

"His choices aren't yours to apologize for. I mean that. He can't stand losing on or off the field."

She hugged me and nodded against my shoulder as a police car pulled up, sirens blaring, followed by another set of sirens, identical to the first.

"Ms. Babu?"

"Officer Bradley," Annika said, relief in her voice. "Johnny. Johnny's in the house. He—he attacked Natalie." Her hands gripping my arm shook.

"He's armed?" The snap of his gun being released was loud to my ears.

"Maybe a Taser or pepper spray." Annika turned away from me.

His footsteps raced up the path, along with another set from an officer who hadn't spoken. I missed being able to see. With some hesitation, I tried to open them. The sun was too bright, and I had to close them again.

"Nattie?"

Sebastian's voice caused me to whip my head in his direction. "Sebastian?" His name caught on a sob.

"Oh, Lord, Nattie. What happened?"

In a heartbeat, his arms came around me. He prodded my face.

"I don't know if you should touch it. It's pepper spray." My voice wavered with unshed tears.

"How'd that happen?"

"Johnny," I whispered.

With that, the officers pounded along the path. Chancing a look, I squinted in their direction and could make out the three forms. Sebastian blocked me from Johnny with his body.

"I told you to stay the hell away from her." His rage was palpable.

Johnny scoffed. "She ruined my life. I wasn't going to let her get away with it."

"Nah, man. You ruined your life. My girl smelled your rotten soul before the rest of us." Sebastian held me tight against his side. "You're not worth anyone's time anymore. You're done."

We watched them stuff Johnny into the rear of the police car.

I squeezed Sebastian tight. "I have to call my dad. My eyes hurt so much."

"I'll call your dad to tell him what happened," Annika said. "I searched pepper spray treatment. Soapy water. Maybe use the dish soap? Isn't it supposed to clean oil spills off animals?"

"Are you okay?" With my head pressed to Sebastian's shoulder, I couldn't see her face in enough detail to be sure.

"I want this to be over. I'm so tired." Annika tucked her phone against her ear.

"Can someone tell me how the hell this happened?" Sebastian swept me up into his arms.

"I can walk," I protested.

"You were attacked and pepper sprayed. I'm gonna take care of you. If I'd gotten here before the cops, I would've killed him."

I wanted to press my face into the hollow of his neck, but I didn't want pepper spray on him. "Annika saved me," I said. "She saved us."

Epilogue

I took the photo from Sebastian and placed it on the mantle. "I think it should go there." We'd moved into our apartment two weeks ago, and we were still unpacking boxes. Sebastian's stuff might fit into the rear of an SUV, but mine had taken a couple of trucks. Finding a place for each of my things was starting to make me feel guilty.

"I don't need my family picture on the mantle." He shook his head and snatched it back. "A spare room or back in the box...or anywhere but there."

"But my stuff is everywhere. You'll make me seem like a space hog."

"I'm glad your stuff is everywhere. It makes me happy every time I realize we're doing this."

I grabbed his shirt and yanked him closer. "So, roomie, when is practice?"

"You haven't memorized my schedule?" He feigned hurt and kissed me.

"Well, the new coach set up a different routine. I learned the last one under protest." I wrapped my arms around his neck and kissed him again, deeper.

When we broke apart, he said, "I'm glad Annika has Kristy. I would've felt bad moving in together otherwise."

"It all worked out."

Sebastian frowned. "Johnny's sentence still pisses me off."

I shrugged and grimaced. At the closest box, I grabbed more things for our shelves. "He got lucky with his judge. A good old boy who still believes sports figures are gods. Someone who figures a coach can make a player do something he doesn't want to do."

"We've talked about it before, but anyone who heard Annika's testimony and didn't crucify him—"

"I know." I shook my head. "Trust me, I know."

"Out in six months," Sebastian said.

We'd gone to the courtroom every day in solidarity for Annika. He'd pleaded down his assault on me to a misdemeanor. He'd had a spare key, and I hadn't been seriously injured. Mentioning the plea only sent Sebastian into a ranting tailspin. I hoped the two of them never met in a dark alley.

After watching the trial, I realized becoming a lawyer and a judge would be the best route for me to make a difference in the world. The judge's treatment of Annika, Johnny, and the case, in general, had been enough to send me to kickboxing classes twice a day for the duration. Another person on the bench instead of that man would have led to a better outcome.

The ruling made me so angry.

The one great shining light in this was Sebastian. I wasn't sure how we managed to make it here, but I was pretty damn glad we had.

"The guys on the team are treating you okay, now?" I was almost afraid to broach the subject again.

Theo and Jeff's involvement had fractured the team. A lot of the players who were loyal to Johnny graduated, taking their rage at Sebastian and Troy with them. But there were still a few, like Malcolm who'd posted that video of Sebastian, who enjoyed pushing his buttons. I wasn't sure how smooth this year would be for him on the field. He'd told me more than once that the best teams in history often had decent camaraderie on and off the field. The new coach had his work cut out for him.

"We'll be cool, Nattie. It's gonna take time."

I abandoned my sorting. "You'll persevere the hell out of them?"

He laughed, linking our hands together and tugging me into his chest. "I've got mad perseverance skills."

"Where else have you got skills?" I raised my eyebrows.

His grin spread wider and then disappeared in favor of my favorite half smile. "Oh, a few places."

"I may need to perform quality control. An inspection." I walked backward toward the bedroom, holding his hand. With my free hand, I gripped the bottom of his shirt.

"You'll have to tell me if my skills are first-down worthy." He slid my shirt over my head.

"You might even score a touchdown." I laughed while I dragged him onto the bed with me.

"Look at you with the football terms."

"What can I say?" I murmured against his lips. "I love a guy who prances around in tight pants."

"Just one?"

"Just you."

Want more of Natalie and Sebastian? They appear in Fake Crown by W. Million. Get Fake Crown here: mybook.to/No rthernUniversity

Enjoyed the story? Sign up for my newsletter to receive bonus chapters at:

www.wendymillion.com

What else have I written?

Bellerive Royals Series

Fake Crown (Brent & Posey)

Scarred Crown (Nick & Jules)

Heavy Crown (Alex & Rory)

Fallen Crown (Brice & Maren)

Tucker Billionaires

Temporary Love (Gage & Ember)

Fierce Love (Nathaniel & Hollyn)
Colliding Love (Sawyer & Logan)

Reckless Love (Ava & Stephen)

New Adult Sports

Saving Us (Natalie & Sebastian)

Fake Crown (Brent & Posey)

Donaghey Brothers Mafia Series

Retribution

Resurrection

Redemption

Little Falls Series

Rival Hearts (Grady & Maggie)

Mending Hearts (Tyler & Mia)

Healing Hearts (Trent & Emily)

Guarded Hearts (Pasha & Alyssa)

First Date Challenge (Makenna & Kai)

Adult Contemporary Romance

When Stars Fall (Wyatt & Ellie)

Miss Matched (Simon & Tayla)
The Nanny Pact – coming soon (Paige and Ash)

Acknowledgments

As always I am deeply grateful to my supportive family who are always buying my books and cheering me on. I'm grateful to my first readers on Wattpad who keep me motivated. A special thanks to my writing bestie, Cole Lepley, who is always willing to share her experiences or commiserate with me when something doesn't go right.

About Wendy Million/W. Million

Wendy Million is a high school teacher whose award winning contemporary romances about strong women and troubled men have captivated her loyal readers.

Writing as Wendy Million, she is the author of the romantic suspense series *The Donaghey Brothers,* as well as the contemporary second chance romances, *When Stars Fall*, and *Miss Matched*.

Writing as W. Million, she's the author of the *Bellerive Royals* series, the *Little Falls* series, and the *Tucker Billionaires* series.

When not writing, Wendy enjoys spending time in or around the water. She lives in Ontario, Canada with two beautiful daughters, two cute pooches, and one handsome husband (who is grateful she doesn't need two of those).